Dirty Crazy Bad

BOOK TWO

USA TODAY & WSJ BESTSELLING AUTHOR

SIOBHAN DAVIS

ISBN-13: 978-1-959194-29-3

Edited by Kelly Hartigan (XterraWeb) editing.xterraweb.com

Proofread by Aundi Marie, Nicki SG, Carolyne Belso, and Amanda Rash (Draft House Editorial Services.)

Cover design and luminary symbol design by Shannon Passmore of Shanoff Designs

Licensed interior imagery – © depositphotos.com

Licensed cover imagery - background © adobe.com and © bigstockphoto.com

Licensed cover imagery - skull image © shutterstock.com

Formatted by Ciara Turley using Vellum

In the secret society of The Luminaries, no sin will go unpunished...

The Greed & Gluttony Luminary has trapped us into executing his evil plans, and it seems we have little option but to agree. Carter has orchestrated Chad's kidnapping, and he holds my mom's life in his hands.

Then he drops a game-changer

We must play our parts—or at least look like we are—because the fate of our loved ones, and the world at large, depends upon it. There is no choice.

It's a delicate balancing act, with many obstacles and no guarantee of success. Carter has spent years planning his takeover and knowing who to trust is impossible.

Teamwork is the only way we can defeat him. But that is challenging when relationships are fractured, the guys are sworn enemies, and loyalties have been pushed to their limits.

It's up to me to make this work, so I will push my grief aside to be there for Ares, Jase, and Chad.

Rhett Carter cannot become Lord of the Luminaries and we're the only ones that can stop him.

LUMINARY

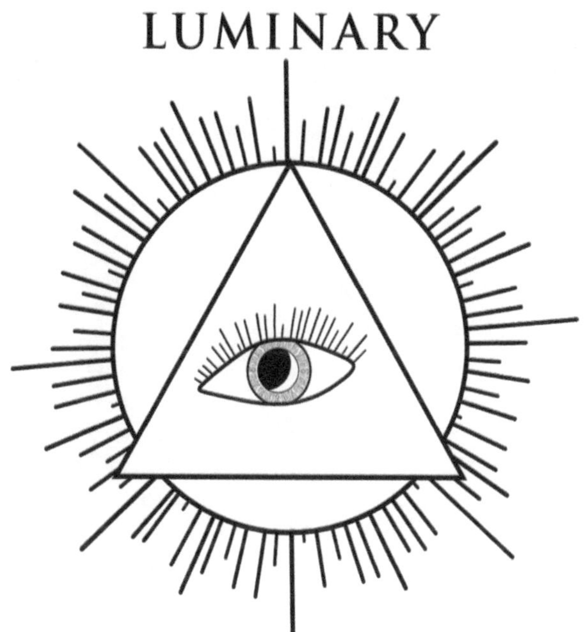

LUMINARY FAMILY

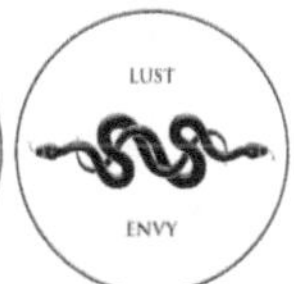

The Luminaries

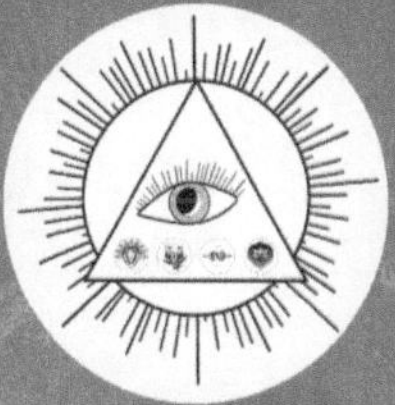

CARTER	MANFORD	SALINGER	STEWART
GREED & GLUTTONY	SLOTH	PRIDE & WRATH	LUST / ENVY
RHETT CARTER LUMINARY	JAMES MANFORD LUMINARY	WALTER SALINGER LUMINARY	ERIC STEWART LUMINARY
KNIGHT CARTER HEIR	JULIA MANFORD HEIR	TOBIAS SALINGER HEIR	BALTHAZAR STEWART HEIR

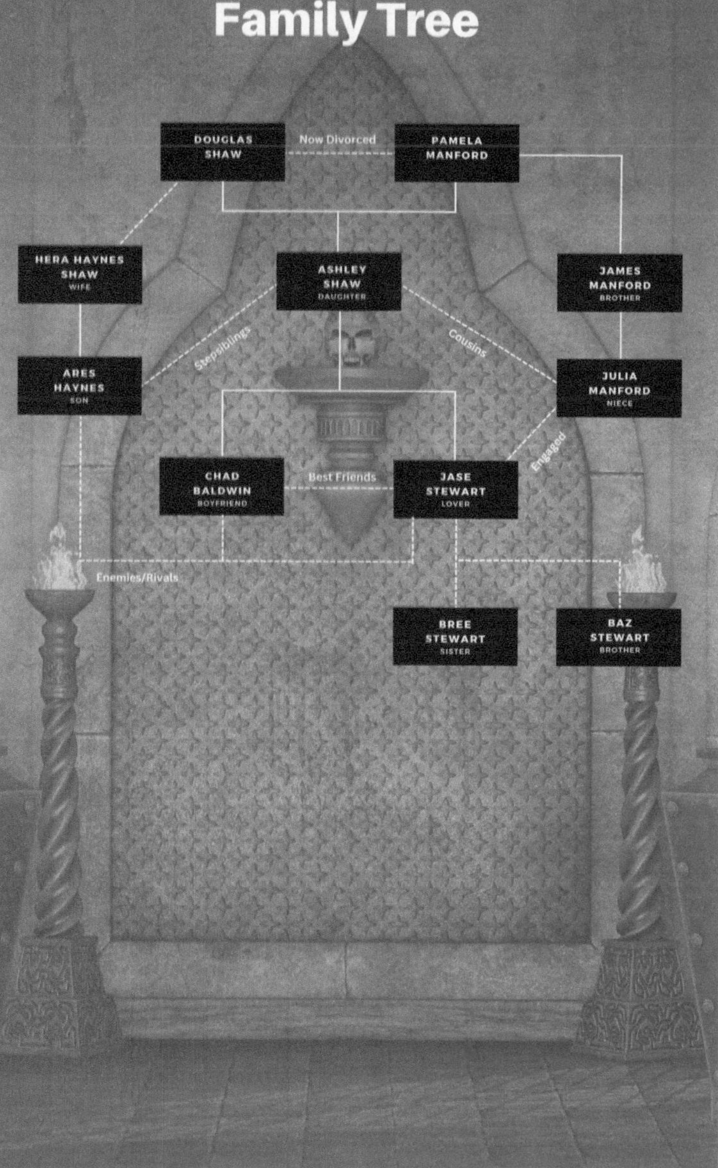

Family Tree
DOUGLAS SHAW
Now Divorced
PAMELA MANFORD
HERA HAYNES SHAW
WIFE
ASHLEY SHAW
DAUGHTER
JAMES MANFORD
BROTHER
Stepsiblings
Cousins
ARES HAYNES
SON
JULIA MANFORD
NIECE
Engaged
CHAD BALDWIN
BOYFRIEND
Best Friends
JASE STEWART
LOVER
Enemies/Rivals
BREE STEWART
SISTER
BAZ STEWART
BROTHER

Dirty Crazy Bad

BOOK TWO

Chapter One

Ashley

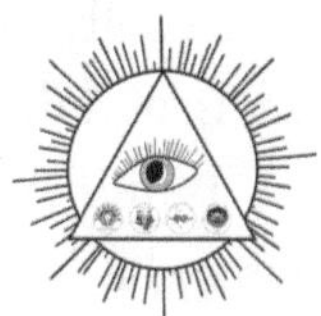

"The vision our founding fathers had has gotten lost somewhere along the way," Rhett—my despicable newly revealed bio dad—says, waving his hands around in an animated fashion as he explains his plan for world domination. His eyes are alight as he talks, and he reminds me of a cartoon character. The stereotypical villain with the menacing eyes and exaggerated dark chuckle. Except the man standing before me is no fictional creature. His grandiose plans are not the figment of some writer's imagination. He truly believes the rhetoric, and he's hell-bent on ruling the world.

A shudder ripples over my body as I contemplate how dangerous this man is and how precarious our situation is.

He is a bona fide psychopath with the resources, wealth, and contacts to make his dastardly plan come to fruition.

I don't know how we are going to stop him, but we must try. He cannot be allowed to become Lord of The Luminaries.

I'm scoffing in my head, but the danger is very real.

"I am going to modernize our society and the world we live in. I will take the necessary action to eradicate those who drag our world down and hold us back from realizing our potential," he says. His eyes continue to burn with enthusiasm and conviction. He most definitely buys into the bullshit he's peddling. "Our founding fathers wanted to create egalitarian control, and that may have worked for a time, but it no longer serves our society well."

"And will installing yourself as Lord of The Luminaries serve our society better?" Jase coolly asks, arching a subtle brow as he expertly hides his disdain and disbelief.

The Greed & Gluttony Luminary removed the tape from Bree's and Jase's mouths when he began explaining, so at least he's giving them the opportunity to contribute to the conversation. We all know we're pawns in this twisted game, and our contributions won't make a difference, but at least we can question him about his intentions and leave here more informed than when we came in.

"I know it will." Rhett puffs out his chest, stepping over the bullet-ridden body of his young lover on the ground.

Am I a bad person for feeling relieved Julia is dead? I feel a tinge of remorse for my thought, but I can't summon much more than that. She tried to kill me. The throbbing pain in my skull and my aching body are testament to that fact. I have no doubt if Rhett had let her walk out of this crypt today she would have attempted to murder me again.

So, no, I don't feel guilty for my thoughts.

Julia brought this on herself.

Rhett drags a chair over and places it in front of Jase. Flipping it front to back, he sits with his legs spread on either side of the chair as he eyeballs my ex-lover. "Spreading the power evenly across The Luminary families was a lofty ambition, but it's been clear for some time that it's not working. If it was, we wouldn't have so much sin in the world. Increasingly, we disagree on how to run things, and our lack of cohesion is causing costly delays. My peers are too weak. They aren't prepared to make the type of decisions our society needs to restore it to greatness. In our new world, I will have the controlling vote as president and Lord of the Luminaries. The four other Luminary positions will still yield considerable power, but they will work under my control and to my agenda. My word will be law, and no one will challenge me."

He is legit insane, and he must be stopped.

"Four?" Bree interrupts, a frown marring her pretty face. "Don't you mean three?"

Rhett shakes his head. "There was once an eighth sin. In the Middle Ages, it was referred to as 'acedia.' Today, it is what we know as despondency. This sin is an outlook of gloom and despair, a sense of utter hopelessness that one cannot come back from. This is the one sin that cannot be forgiven. The sense that one is damned eternally goes against Christian beliefs, and it challenges our God's infinite capacity for forgiveness. It could be argued despond is the most heinous sin. The rising global suicide rates point to the seriousness of this sin. It requires sole focus. Despond and Sloth will be the ultimate ruination of our world, and it's our responsibility as Luminaries to eradicate it before it destroys humanity. That is why I have been pushing for a fifth Luminary family."

"It was you who started the separatist movement." A muscle pops in Bree's jaw.

"I did. I had no choice when the other Luminaries persistently refused to seriously discuss the creation of a new Luminary family who would have responsibility for Despond."

"You cannot just create a Luminary family," Mom says. Her voice is thick with exhaustion, and she's struggling to keep her unswollen eye from shutting. "History says it is four, not five."

Rhett reaches across Jase to grab Mom's chin, tilting her

face up and forcing her gaze on his. "You lack vision, Pamela. You always have. You would have made a terrible wife. I suppose I should thank you for being a manipulative cunt. I shudder at the thought of being tied to you for a lifetime."

"News flash, asshole," I hiss, spewing the words from my mouth before I stop to question the wisdom of them. "You *are* tied to her for life through me."

An icy chill pervades the air as he drops Mom's face and swivels around to face me. His brown eyes blaze with anger, and I hate seeing my eyes on his face. Why couldn't I have inherited Mom's blue ones? I don't want to share anything with this psycho. I am sick of the thought of his blood swirling through my veins. I project defiance as I stare at him, even knowing it's not smart to poke the beast. But this asshole raped and beat my mom. He killed my dad. He kidnapped Chad and handed him over to his sicko wife.

Pain presses down on my chest, and I work hard to swat it away.

I hate him, and I don't care in this moment if he reads it on my face.

His fingers curl around my chin with more tenderness than I was expecting. The angry lines on his face and the poison in his eyes fade as he pins me with a soft look. "You have so much spirit, and you are loyal. Qualities I admire, so I will overlook your words and your tone. This time." His fingers tighten on my chin, and he tips my head back.

The throbbing in my skull spikes. An involuntary whimper flees between my lips as I am reminded I have a concussion and a bruised body.

"You're hurting her," Jase snaps, sending daggers at Rhett with his eyes. "Let her go."

Rhett releases me, turning to face Jase again. "Your loyalty to my daughter is commendable, Jason. It's one of the reasons I approve of you for her. But that does not give you the right to make demands of me. Watch who you are speaking to."

"Can we just get on with this?" Bree drills him with a bored expression. "Pamela and Ashley need medical attention, and if we don't get out of here soon, our father will start asking questions."

Rhett slaps her hard, and her cheek instantly pinks. "Impudence won't be tolerated, and impatience is a sin, young lady."

"So is kidnapping and torturing people," I hiss, glaring at him. "If you truly want to form a relationship with me, you will stop hurting the people I love."

"Careful, Ashley." His tone is like ice dripping down my spine.

"Just tell us what you want." I hold his dark stare with one of my own. "We understand you want to create a new Board of Luminaries with a new family who will control Despond, and you will be Lord of The Luminaries. What do we have to do with it?"

"You will vote to approve my plan when it is presented to the board."

"How?" Jase asks. "None of us sit on the board."

"Yet." Rhett grins, waggling his brows and smirking at Jase.

"You intend to install Ashley as the Manford heir," Mom surmises.

It's where my mind has gone too. Julia was an only child, and Pamela is James's only sibling. While I am sure there are plenty of potential male heirs within the extended Manford line, I am the next in the hot seat. A match was already approved between Jase and the Manford heir, so I simply replace Julia in that arrangement. Rhett already alluded to as much when he stated earlier that I would get to marry Jase.

"Ashley *is* the rightful Manford heir, and she will claim the role she was always destined to fulfill." He takes my hand in his, and it requires colossal willpower not to yank it back or shiver from the feel of his cold skin against mine.

I want to get out of here sooner rather than later, so I need to stop antagonizing him and at least look like I'm game to play along.

His gaze bounces between me and Jase. "You two will marry this week, and when we appear before the board to explain the treachery of Julia and James, I will table a motion to have Jase immediately installed as the Sloth Luminary."

"And if we don't agree, you'll kill Chad? But if we do agree, you'll keep him locked up to force us to toe the line? Neither scenario is enticing me to go along with your plan." Jase levels Rhett with a lethal look.

"I thought you loved my daughter and wanted to marry her?"

"I do, but that's not what I asked."

"As long as you cooperate, I will keep my wife on a leash when it comes to Chad. When you have proven your loyalty to me, I will release him into your care." Rhett stands and walks around the chair, staring me straight in the face. "Chad's future depends on you." He glances at Mom. "Your mother's too. I can hang James out to dry, or I can implicate Pamela as well. The choice is yours."

"There is no choice. You've made sure of that," I reply.

"I don't see what the problem is. You love each other, and this way you get to be together. Jase will become the Sloth Luminary. You will both have untold power and the kind of lifestyle others would kill to have." He leans down, putting his face up in mine. "You will want for nothing. You will be loved and protected your whole life. You can take Chad as your lover knowing your husband approves. You get to have everything your heart desires." He straightens up. "So, yes, there is no choice. But this works perfectly for everyone."

Except he will dangle shit over us our entire lives to force our loyalty, because he knows he hasn't earned it the right way and he never will. We will be prisoners in a luxurious cage, forced to bow to the demands of a madman.

It's not going to happen, but he needs to believe it will.

"You give me your word you won't throw Mom to the wolves, and you'll see to it that Chad isn't harmed?"

He nods.

"I want him taken out of that cage. I want him moved to a room with a bed and for him to be given three meals a day. I want your wife to keep her sleazy hands away from him." I grind my teeth to my molars, trying not to think about the things Chad might be enduring at this very moment.

A grin tugs up the corners of Rhett's mouth. "Marry Jase and support me at the meeting, and I will see what I can do about it."

"Not good enough," I snap, gripping the armrests on my chair and digging my nails into the leather.

"It will have to be," Rhett coolly replies.

I feel Jase's eyes on me, and I turn my head so we are face-to-face. He nods, the look in his gorgeous green eyes conveying he's on the same page as me. Humor the monster, and we'll work to extract Chad from the mess we put him in some way.

"Fine," I say, turning away from Jase and refocusing on my sperm donor.

"Pamela." Rhett eyeballs her. "Do I have your agreement?"

"Yes." Her cold unfeeling tone is one I'm familiar with. "I will do whatever is necessary to protect my daughter and keep her safe."

Rhett chuckles. "Oh, how it would pain James to hear you say that." His tongue darts out, wetting his lips. "He has always had an unnatural obsession with you. Tell me, how many times did you let him fuck you when you were both horny teens growing up in the same house?"

"He's my brother, you sick prick," Mom retorts. Her expression doesn't waver from that dispassionate look she has perfected, but there is a hint of fire behind her words, and I wonder why.

"Takes one to know one, bitch."

"Where do I fit in?" Bree asks. I appreciate her attempt to keep the asshole focused so we can get the hell out of here.

"You will marry the Pride & Wrath heir after I have Walter removed from the position for his treachery. And you will vote my plan in when it's presented to the board. Your father will concur. He won't go against me when I have the majority vote and with two of his children in positions of power in other Luminary families. He would be crazy to."

That seems like a risky strategy to me. Unless Rhett is confident in his ability to force us to do his bidding.

Bree cocks her head to one side, looking cool calm and collected as she eyeballs him. "You said earlier I would get to kill the prick. I assumed you meant Toby. If that's not the case, and I'm still expected to marry Toby, why the fuck should I agree to anything you want of me?"

Rhett smiles, and it's creepy as fuck. "If you don't play ball, I'll hand over the evidence from South America and let the board dole out the necessary punishment."

Jase and I whip our heads in Bree's direction. She is staring at Rhett Carter with panicked eyes and pale skin. Jase turns to look at me, and I shake my head. I am as clueless as he is over what could have happened in South America to put that look on his sister's face.

"Okay." Bree composes herself. "I'll do it. I'll marry Toby and vote your plan in."

"That is excellent news, Breanna. I knew you would see it

my way." He tips his head to the side, staring at the far door—the one that leads to the ancestors' room. For the first time, I spot the man standing guard outside the door. He is unfamiliar to me. Obviously one of Carter's lackeys. Rhett nods in some form of silent command, and the man raps on the door.

"There is just one minor amendment." Rhett straightens up, and he lets his grin loose. "You won't be marrying Toby. He's not the true Pride & Wrath heir."

Shock splays across all of our faces.

"Let me introduce you to your intended," Rhett adds, glee evident on his face when the door to the ancestors' room creeks noisily as it opens.

Chapter Two

Ares

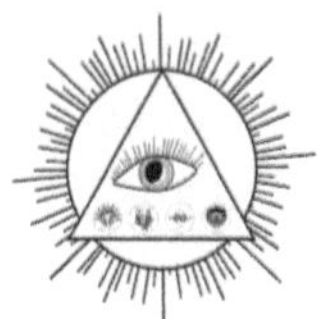

I wake on a cold stone floor in a darkened room with the motherfucking headache of the century. "What the fuck?" I mumble as I pull myself upright, staring at the creepy shit surrounding me. Every wall is full of shelves of skulls. Row upon row of them. Crammed full of skulls, some with small lights behind their eyes. I look up, my jaw slacking as I spot the circular tower-like structure that extends skyward, farther than my line of sight. The skulls go all the way up to the top. It reminds me of the catacombs I visited in Paris with Mom and Lilianna, a few short months before they moved back to the US and I relocated to the UK.

Staggering to my feet, I clutch the wall behind me when my limbs threaten to go out from under me. I don't know what shit the cloaked assholes on the road injected me with or how long I've been out, but I still feel the drug lingering in my veins.

"Sit down and shut up," a man with a gruff voice says. Narrowing my eyes in the semi-dark room, I squint at the armed man standing guard inside the room, just by the door.

"Make me." I silently curse my uncooperative limbs as I

stumble forward, unable to walk in a straight line. Guess there goes my plan to beat the shit out of this asshole, grab his gun, and shoot my way out of this mess.

Ashley!

The rest of the events of this evening come back to me in a flash, and I grab the side of the long table residing on an elevated platform before I tumble to the ground.

"I'd be happy to," the asshole says, stalking toward me. "But my instructions are to ensure you come to no harm."

"Where is Ashley?" I demand, summoning hidden strength as I grab a fistful of his shirt.

The man grinds his teeth as he forcibly removes my fingers from his shirt. "What part of shut up don't you understand?"

Before I have the chance to retaliate, a succession of sharp raps hammers on the door. The asshole removes his rifle, prodding it into my ribs as he grabs my arm and shoves me toward the door.

"What's going on?" I ask. "Why am I here and what is this place?"

If it wasn't for the fact Ashley, her mom, Jase, Bree, and Chad were taken too, I might have thought this was gang-related or somehow related to my investigation into Lilianna's kidnapping. But it can't be.

This is bigger than me.

The dick drags me toward the door, remaining silent, letting my questions go unanswered.

Another memory resurfaces in my mind. Oh fuck.

Doug is dead.

I watched some fuckface in a black cloak kill him on the road right after they ambushed the ambulance carrying my pretty little dollface.

His death will devastate Mom and Ashley.

I have no more time to think those thoughts because the

door is opened, and I'm dragged out into a large wide rectangular room.

Jase, Bree, and Pamela are all tied to chairs, the latter looking like she's taken a savage beating. Shock is etched upon all their faces, but I only feel relief when my eyes lock on my stepsister. Ashley appears unharmed with no new injuries to report. She is unrestrained and lying on a comfy recliner chair as she stares at me with her mouth hanging open.

Loud clapping rings out in the large room as the guard manhandles me across the space. I want to shove the dick away, but I honestly don't think my legs will carry me unsupported. My limbs are weak and floppy thanks to whatever drugs are still in my system. I eyeball the weirdo clapping. I don't know who he is, but there is a look of familiarity about him.

He's tall and broad with dirty-blond hair slicked back off his face. The custom-fit designer suit he's wearing looks out of place in this room. The high-ceilinged windowless room is made entirely of stone. Several banners hang off the walls, and lit candles illuminate the space, casting eerie shadows every place they touch. An icy draft and a musky scent waft through the air.

"Welcome." The unfamiliar man grabs my upper arms, yanking me from the guard. He slides one arm around my shoulder, squeezing it and grinning at me as if we're long-lost friends. He turns me to face the others. "I'd like you to meet Blade Salinger. The true and rightful heir to the Pride & Wrath Luminary."

Shocked silence rings out around the room until Pamela breaks it.

"No way." Her assessing eyes rake over me from head to foot. "It can't be."

The prick stuck to my side scoffs. "Come now, Pamela. You're not blind. Look behind the vile piercings and body ink, and you'll see he's the spitting image of his father. It's like looking at Clint Salinger reincarnated."

I muster the strength to push the prick off me, grabbing the top of a nearby chair to steady myself. My eyes land on the lifeless body on the floor, and I grip the chair tighter.

Fucking hell.

Julia is riddled with bullets and lying in a pool of her own blood. I don't know who this prick is, but he's clearly dangerous and not to be underestimated. Lifting my head, I stare straight at the dude. "I don't know who you are, but you're either crazy or misinformed. My name is Ares Haynes. My father was Andrew Haynes, and he died serving his country when I was a baby."

He stares at me, and I get the sense he's looking for the lies behind my words. I don't know why he thinks I'm this Blade dude or that Clint Salinger is my father when neither of those things are true.

The prick chuckles. "Wow. Your mother's deviousness knows no bounds. I'm quite impressed."

"Are you saying you think Hera is Daphne Salinger?" Disbelief oozes from Pamela Stewart's face as the words leave her lips. "Rhett, she can't be. They look nothing alike."

"It's amazing what cosmetic surgery can do," Rhett replies. "Drop twenty pounds, add in some hair dye and colored contacts, and you can literally recreate yourself."

"You're delusional," I snap, lunging for the guy.

The guard yanks me back before I make contact, wrapping a meaty arm around my neck and constricting my air supply. Slamming my head back, I crack my skull against his, yelping as pain rattles around my brain.

"Stop." Ashley's voice sounds stronger than she looks. "Fighting is pointless. Just listen to what he has to say." She looks up at Rhett. "What did you do to him? He looks dead on his feet. Please let him sit."

"He'll be fine." The man dismisses her concern, turning the chair at his side around. "Strap him down."

It's not in my nature to go down without a fight, but Ashley's pleading eyes are the only thing that could make me willingly sit still while the man binds my arms and legs to the chair with rope. "Are you okay?" I rasp, drilling a look at Ashley. "Did they hurt you?"

"I'm okay. They didn't hurt me."

"Ashley is my daughter," the prick in the suit says. "She's a Carter, and she has Manford blood from Pamela's side."

My eyes startle wide as I stare at my dollface. She subtly nods, and I'm gobsmacked. What the actual fuck is happening here? What is this place, who is this man, and what the fuck does it have to do with me? *Is* this connected to my father? Is that why Mom always told me to lie if I was asked about him?

"It is not my intention to hurt her or anyone in this room," he adds, pulling me out of my head.

"How do you explain that then?" I ask, biting back a wince as I jerk my head in Pamela's direction. "I doubt she just fell onto your fist."

The man doesn't reply, but I don't know what expression is on his face as I'm too busy staring at Ash to ensure she's okay to bother looking at him. Pain rages behind her eyes, but she's doing her best to disguise it. She stares back at me, silently begging me to go along with this. I'm not going to fight. I'm in no fit state. I'm late to the party, and I have no clue what is going on. I have no choice but to trust my stepsister.

And the truth is...I do.

I don't know when it happened, but I trust Ashley.

I have fallen so far from my original agenda it's laughable.

What is this girl doing to me?

"If you don't believe me, maybe this will convince you." Rhett thrusts a photo in my face.

It's an image of a man and a woman on their wedding day. The man has the woman pressed possessively against his side as he stares at her like she is the goddess Aphrodite brought back to life. His eyes flare with adoration as he looks at his bride, and a lump wedges in my throat. He gazes at her like she is his everything. As if he would burn the world down to have her and hold her. He's tall and broad, and he fills out the fitted gray suit he's wearing well. The woman has neck-length wavy blonde hair, and her simple white dress drapes seductively over her ample curves. The look of love in her eyes is unmistakable. The rapture she's feeling is showcased in the blinding-white smile on her face.

I suck in a shocked gasp as I focus on her smile.

It's Mom's smile.

I see nothing else, besides her height, that gives her away.

But the smile does it.

My chest clenches as I examine the man's face.

"The resemblance is stronger in this one." Rhett shoves a second photo in my face.

This photo is of the same man standing alongside three other men. They hold themselves almost regally in the shot. They are similarly dressed in expensive suits. Haughty expressions paint all of their faces except for the man from the wedding photo. His expression conveys fear and pride and anxiety.

Staring at his face is like staring at a mirror. We have the same dark hair, broad nose and hazel eyes and the same shaped face. Even his stature is similar to mine.

I am so confused, and I guess it must show on my face.

"This picture was taken the day your father was initiated as the Pride & Wrath Luminary."

My brow puckers in more confusion. "What does that even mean?"

"He was the youngest to ever hold the position," he replies, ignoring my question.

A growl slips from my lips. I wonder if this jerk is in politics because he deflects questions with the skill of a politician.

"Your grandfather died unexpectedly," he continues. "Sudden heart attack. Your father wasn't prepared to assume power so young, but he rose to the challenge. Your father was the same generation as me, Eric Stewart, and James Manford."

He says that like I know all this. I know Eric is Jase and Bree's dad and James is Julia's father. He mentioned a few minutes ago that Pamela is a Manford too. Actually, now I think about it, there was mention of Julia being Ash's cousin back at the hospital, so they are definitely related. I recall the photo Rocky took of Jase and Baz outside a bar. Toby Salinger and Knight Carter were the other two guys in that pic. I am guessing Toby and Clinton are related, and going on looks, I think Knight Carter must be Rhett Carter's son. They share the same surname and dark-blond looks.

I still don't know how any of it is connected though. And what did he mean when he said Pride & Wrath Luminary? I need fucking answers, and I need them now.

Before I can form a question, he continues. Dude sure loves the sound of his own voice. Rhett points out the other three men in the pic, one at a time. "Your father was the same generation as myself, Eric Stewart, and James Manford, but he assumed control way earlier than the rest of us. He worked mainly with our fathers. They are the other men in this photo."

"I know nothing about any of this," I truthfully say. "I don't understand."

He clamps a hand on my shoulder. "I did wonder if you knew and were just adept at concealing it, but it's clear to me now you are completely in the dark." His grip on my shoulder tightens, and my fingers twitch with the craving to punch him in his smug face. "Don't worry, son. There is much you need to learn, but we'll get you caught up."

He thinks he can mold me to his will, but fuck that shit. And how does he think he is calling me *son*? I grew up without a father, and I sure as fuck don't want one now.

"Your mother has lied to you your entire life." He pushes a birth certificate under my nose. The words are all blurring together, thanks to the confusion racing through my veins, but I see enough to spot the name Blade Salinger alongside my actual date of birth and the listed names of my parents—Daphne Helen Salinger and Clinton Andrew Salinger.

"It's not real. She wouldn't do that to me." Mom told me stuff about Dad as I got older. Explaining why we had to leave the US. So why would she lie about his name? None of this is making any sense.

"Let me see that," Pamela says.

Rhett walks over to Ash's mother and shows her the pictures and the birth cert. I share a look with Ash and then one with Jase. It's clear this is news to them too. Bree stares at me strangely, and I wonder what that's all about.

"I knew Clint," Pamela says, effectively claiming my attention. "He was a couple of years older than me, and all the girls in our circle were madly in love with him. He was one of the good guys. There are so few of them in our world," she adds, side-eying Rhett with unconcealed venom, "that he stood out." Her eyes soften as she looks at me. "I don't know why I didn't see it before, but you are so like him."

"That doesn't prove anything," Ash says. "Why would Hera lie about this to her own son? It makes no sense."

"It makes perfect sense," Pamela replies.

Rhett bobs his head, urging her to continue. Maybe he

thinks I'll accept it easier from Pamela, but the woman means nothing to me, and I trust her about as much as I trust him.

"Clinton Salinger was murdered by zealots from a religious organization who had discovered part of the truth about The Luminaries. Daphne and Blade disappeared the next day. My brother told me they deployed considerable efforts for years trying to find them, but when no trace could be found, they assumed they'd been killed too."

"Daphne had help." Rhett rubs a hand along his smooth chin. "It's the only explanation that makes sense. There's no way she could've concealed herself and her children without help."

"I don't know what the truth is anymore." Pamela squirms a little in her chair as she looks at me. A grimace flashes across her face, and it's obvious she's in pain. "But I believe you are Clint's son. The resemblance is too strong for it not to be so. And I know that Hera is a good woman. I didn't know her well back then, but I spoke with Daphne a few times at official events. Her goodness shone like a beacon. Her and your father were so in love, and they gave all of us hope."

Her comments are cryptic, and I plan to interrogate her when we get out of here. *If* we get out of here, because I still don't know what this dickhole wants with all of us.

"If your mother went to great lengths to conceal your identity, even from you, she had a damn good reason for doing it. She was protecting you, Ares. I would stake my life on it."

"I agree," Rhett says as his phone vibrates in his pocket.

"I don't understand why she would come back though," Pamela muses.

At least that one I know the answer to.

"We need to make a move." Rhett scowls at whatever he sees on his phone. He lifts his head and stares at me. "I need to give you a Luminary crash course and explain our history.

Ashley, Jase, and Bree can fill you in on some of it. I will need you at the meeting with the board, and we must organize your initiation."

Out of the corner of my eye, I see Ash jerk at his words.

I have no idea what any of it means, but I'd rather we are released, and I can ask Ash at home.

"How do you plan to remove Walter and instate Ares in his place?" Bree asks.

"You don't need to worry about the minor details. I have it covered. For now, just focus on planning your wedding."

Bree's eyes fly over my head to Ash, and I frown, hating to be so in the dark.

I'm not expecting Jase to take pity on me, but he does. "I'll give you the CliffsNotes version," he says, staring at me. "Rhett here is staging a hostile takeover, and he needs all of us to achieve his nefarious plan. You're to marry my sister and take control of the Pride & Wrath Luminary. Then you will vote him and his new structure into place."

I bark out a laugh. I know crazy, but this is some super weird crazy shit. I half expect to wake up and discover it's some creepy dream. I smirk at the delusional jerk. "I don't know what shit you're smoking, asshole, but I'm not marrying anyone or taking control of anything."

He returns my smirk and then some. "You are going to do exactly what I say, and you won't argue with anything."

"Oh, yeah?" I ask, humoring him. "And why is that?"

"I know where Lilianna is."

All the blood drains from my face.

"If you want to see your little sister again, you will obey me, or I'll see to it that she dies."

Chapter Three

Jase

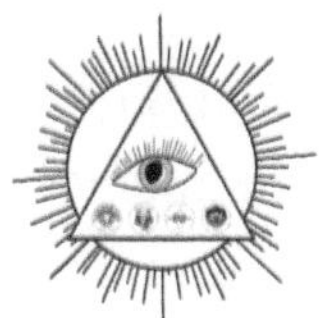

Ares lunges at Rhett, the chair breaking underneath him, and the motion sends wooden shards scattering across the room. Carter's henchman grabs him before he can reach the Greed & Gluttony Luminary. Pity. I would pay good money to watch Ares go nuclear on his ass.

I have never liked Rhett Carter. Often wondered how Knight turned out so decent when his parents are total assholes. But it's obvious we have all underestimated his father. The shit that's gone down today is clearly years in the making. He's been playing nice with the other Luminaries on the surface while plotting to stab them in the back behind the scenes.

When you think about it, we should have expected it.

He is greed personified.

Of course, Rhett Carter would want it all.

Salinger didn't see it coming because the Pride & Wrath Luminary is too arrogant and full of himself to even think anyone would dare to cross him. He loves causing conflict and inciting wars, but he never considered anyone would dare to bring the war to him. Manford and my father are ambitious but only so far as it pertains to their responsibilities. They have been so focused on their families and familial responsibility they didn't spot the snake hiding in plain sight.

The other Luminaries have been blind while Carter has been building his own empire in the shadows. Now he is poised to execute his plans, and I fucking hate he is using us to make it happen.

"If you touch one hair on my sister's head, I will fucking kill you!" Ares yells, snarling and bucking as two of Carter's men attempt to restrain him. "If I find out you'd anything to do with her kidnapping I will end you, motherfucker!"

Rhett grabs Ares around the neck, digging his fingers into his flesh. "You should be thanking me, you ungrateful little prick."

Ares continues to thrash around, but he's losing strength, and his face is turning an unnatural shade of gray.

"You're killing him!" Ashley yells, almost falling as she scrambles out of her chair. She is weak and unsteady on her legs. It doesn't seem like mere hours ago she was shot when so much has happened in between.

"Let him go, Rhett!" Pamela screams, fixing her daughter with concerned eyes. "Ashley is going to injure herself, and it will all be your fault."

Those are probably the only words that could get through to that arrogant crazy fucker. Rhett retracts his hand from Ares's neck, and the guy sucks in greedy lungsful of air as he glares at Ash's bio dad like he can't wait to rip him limb from limb. I will happily side with my rival to make that happen. I want to gut the motherfucker as badly as Ares does.

"You said you'd let us go, so let us go," Ash says, collapsing onto my lap. I wish I could wrap my arms around her, but they are still tied to the chair.

"I will let you go as long as Blade understands the deal."

"My name is Ares, fuckface."

"Ares, please." Ashley implores Ares to get with the program using her words and those puppy-dog eyes that suck me in every time she uses them on me.

"I'm not marrying Bree," he huffs out before darting his gaze in my sister's direction. "No offense intended."

"None taken. I don't want to marry you either." Bree's gaze drifts toward Ashley, and I fully understand her hesitation. I think, if the circumstances were different, Bree would marry anyone if it meant getting out of a life tied to Toby Salinger.

"They *will* marry." Ash rests her head against my chest as her fingers begin unraveling the rope at my wrists. "We will do what you want us to do. I'll make sure of it." She casts a glance at Rhett as the rope falls away from my left wrist. Flexing my numb fingers, to bring feeling back into them, I reach out and softly stroke my Temptress's cheek. Ash is very warm to the touch despite the chill in the air.

"Don't fucking speak for—"

"Shut your mouth, Ares." Ash shuts him down, maneuvering on my lap as she releases the rope from my other wrist. I wrap my arms around her, holding her close as she repositions herself so she is facing her bio dad. "Tell him what he needs to know about his sister."

I expect Rhett to throw another hissy fit, but he must want out of here as badly as we do. "I had nothing to do with her kidnapping, but when you and your mother showed up, I started investigating. I discovered what'd happened to her, and I went to see her."

All the fight leaves Ares instantly. The tortured look on his face is one I never thought I'd ever see. "She's alive? Lilianna is really alive?" he croaks, his emotions wafting into the air. Rhett nods, and Ares attempts to compose himself. Not an easy feat when he looks emotionally slaughtered. "I need proof."

Rhett calmly scrolls through his phone before showing it to Ares.

Ares's face crumples. A thousand different emotions wash over his features as a strangled sound rips from his throat. His eyes turn glassy, and I watch my love watching him with fresh appreciation.

I inwardly groan. The situation with them is way worse than I thought. He kissed her without reserve at the hospital, and I wonder exactly how close they are now.

I don't blame Ashley.

Chad and I let her down in the worst ways.

But I don't trust Ares.

He's a manipulative dick.

We knew he had an agenda. I still don't know what it is, but it evidently involves his sister.

Doesn't change the fact he has lied to everyone.

Ashley doesn't deserve this.

She deserves better than all of us.

A group of armed men enters the space from the main stairs, instantly splitting up and aiming for us. They work on freeing us under the astute eye of their colleagues.

"Okay." Ares looks like a shadow of himself as he stares at Rhett Carter. "I'll do whatever you want, but nothing happens to my sister, and you get her out of there ASAP."

"Nothing will happen to her, but her freedom comes at a price. When you have delivered what I expect of you, and I am assured of your loyalty, I will have her released into your care."

"No deal," Ares spits out. "You get her out now, and I'll burn the fucking world down for you if you want."

"This will go down my way or not at all." Rhett shoves his phone back under Ares's nose.

Ares growls, snapping his teeth, looking like he could bite Carter's head off if his goons weren't currently restraining him.

"What is it?" Ash asks, wrapping her slim fingers around my arms. I hold her closer as one of Carter's guys works to remove the rope at my ankles.

"He has my mom."

Bree and I trade looks. Rhett has this all planned to a T. How the fuck did he get away with this without any of the other Luminaries spotting something? What a bunch of idiots.

"Really?" Ash's anger bursts to the surface again as she sits up straighter, pointing her finger at Carter. "It's not enough you're holding Pamela and Chad over my head. Now, Hera too?"

"I didn't think you cared." Rhett flicks a piece of lint off the arm of his jacket. "Hera is necessary. She is Ares's additional incentive to play the game." He tips his head to one side. "Besides, I need to have a little talk with her. I want to know who has been helping her."

"This is such bullshit!" Ash rises slowly to her feet. "You can't just do this!" Her voice elevates along with her anger. "You can't claim you care about me and then hurt and use everyone I love against me!"

I stand the second the goon at my feet frees me, only narrowly avoiding the urge to kick him in the face. Pulling Ash back against my body, I press my lips to her ear. "Calm down, Temptress. He will get what's coming to him. Right now, we need to get out of here."

She sags against me, gripping my arms, and I know she's seconds away from collapsing. "Ash has a concussion and possibly a fever now. She needs medical attention." I glower at Rhett Carter. He claims to care about her, but these are not the actions of a loving father. Only those of an egomaniacal psychopath.

"A medical team is already waiting for you at the townhome." Rhett approaches Ashley, and she flinches against me, but it's barely discernible. I know my girl is trying her best to play the game, but it's hard when faced with such evil. Especially knowing he has already killed the only father she's ever known, and he's threatening everyone else she loves. "I'm sorry the truth had to come out like this. But I only have your best interests at heart."

Bree coughs, mumbling under her breath. It sounds suspiciously like "bullshit."

"If you hurt anyone else I love, I will murder you myself." Ash faces off with her sperm donor.

"As long as everyone does as I say, I give you my word no harm will come to any of your loved ones."

None of us believe it.

Not for a single second.

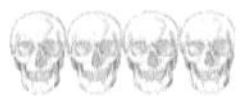

The journey back to the house is fraught with tension and silence. We dare not speak a word while we're in the back of a van with a ton of Carter's armed goons. The Greed & Gluttony Luminary left us much to think about. We are under strict orders not to mention a word of what went down today. He wants to time the reveal about Julia, so he's putting plans in place to hide the fact she's dead. The same with Doug. He is arranging a meeting of the Board of Luminaries for later this week, and we are all to attend. There, he plans to reveal everything in one killer blow. To make the first key move on the chessboard. Ash and I have been told to prepare for a quick wedding. Something I have no issue with because I desire her as my wife, but I'm not sure how Ash feels about it.

She is currently sleeping, stretched out across Ares and me. Ares looks hugely troubled, and he's deep in thought. My sister has been biting her nails the entire trip as Pamela dozes against her side. Carter took off in a separate vehicle the minute we got outside the crypt. Several of his lackeys are on guard duty, acting as a permanent reminder we are under his control and totally fucked.

It's almost two a.m. when we are finally dropped off in front of Ash's townhome. Ares cradles Ash against his chest as he carries her up the steps. I wanted to be the one to do it, but there's a time and place to pick a battle, and this isn't it. We have bigger things to worry about. Pamela is awake as I carry her into the house. Bree heads to our place to freshen up while the medical team waiting in Ash's living room tends to Ash and Pamela.

I wander into the kitchen to make coffee, leaving Ares to preside over things in the living room. Bree appears as I'm loading a tray with cups, cookies, and the coffee pot. "I'll take that," she says, thrusting a backpack at me. "You should change. I grabbed some of your things."

I head upstairs to Ash's room, swallowing painfully as I walk past Chad's room. I never wanted him to get mixed up in our shit, and now he's in the thick of it. After grabbing a quick shower, I get changed in the clean white T-shirt and gray sweats Bree brought me. Then I pad downstairs in my bare feet, feeling a little more human, at least on the outside.

Ash is awake when I enter the living room, and I make my way toward her. She is sitting on one end of one of the couches with everyone else sitting apart. Tension is thick in the air as we all mull over today's revelations. Dropping down beside her, I slide my arm around her shoulders and pull her in tight against my body. She curls into me, and I press a kiss to the top of her head, ignoring the scathing vibes Ares is throwing in my direction.

"This is so fucked up," Bree says, breaking the silence.

"He's a monster." Pamela pulls the fluffy pink blanket up

higher on her body. She looks terrible, and I wonder how she plans to hide this from her new husband, our uncle Richard.

"He's worse than a monster," Ash says in a calm voice that surely belies the turmoil she feels inside. "He planned this all out for God knows how long, and he has trapped us all. We need to stop him. To make him pay. But how the hell do we do that when he is clearly a hundred steps ahead of everyone?"

"I don't know, but we'll find a way." I trace my fingers up and down her arm. "Chad's life depends on it."

"My sister's life depends on it," Ares grits out.

Ash lifts her head and stares at her stepbrother. "You lied to me. You, Hera and...Dad." Her voice cracks the same time Pamela emits an anguished whimper.

I wrap my arms fully around her, wishing I could absorb her pain. "We'll make him pay. I promise," I whisper, hoping it's a promise I can keep.

"It was necessary." Ares stares off into space. "And Doug didn't know." His eyes bore into Ashley. "He bought the lie too."

Chapter Four

Chad

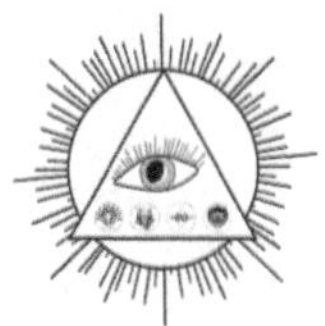

When I come to, I'm lying on my side in the cage, still butt naked, staring across the way at the dull gray-blue eyes of the man in the cage next to me. Tucking my knees up into my chest, I fight the almost-painful urge to stretch my cramped form. My belly rumbles, and my mouth is dry. I haven't eaten or drunk a thing since the protein bar and bottle of water I consumed before training.

I move a fraction, my body unused to being huddled in such a small space, instantly wishing I hadn't when pain throbs between the cheeks of my ass. Rage and shame pummel me from the inside as I recall the things that woman did to me. I squeeze my eyes shut to ward off the horrific images, but it doesn't help.

"It gets worse."

I blink my eyes open at the words, staring into the emotionless eyes of the man across from me.

"It gets so much worse," he adds when I don't reply.

I'm not sure I want to know.

"Shut your face," another man hisses in a low tone. It's

come from farther down on this side of the room, and I don't have the strength to move my body to look. "You know there are cameras in here."

"I don't care," the man across from me says. "I want that depraved bitch to kill me. I'd rather that than spend another year caged like a dog."

"A year?" My eyes pop wide. "You've been here a year?"

"At least. Could be longer. It's not like we have any way of telling the time."

There are no windows in this place, and we don't have a TV or a clock on the wall to tell the time. Panic bubbles in my veins. This can't be happening. I can't be chained up. I have a life. A woman I love I need to make things up to. A mom and little sister who are relying on me. I have friends and college and my whole life ahead of me.

Fuck football.

I've been depressed for weeks at losing my scholarship and my place on the team, but who gives a shit?

It pales into insignificance when faced with the prospect of losing my freedom and possibly my life.

"Who is she?" I blurt, understanding this line of questioning will probably end in some punishment. But I don't care. Not when this guy seems in a talkative mood, and I might get some answers.

"Rhett Carter's wife."

"Shut the fuck up, man. You're going to get us all killed!" the other man says.

"Should I know who that is?" I ask before adding, "Is she related to Knight Carter?" He's the only Carter I know and barely at that. He's one of our neighbors, and we've shot the shit a couple times at parties.

"He's her son."

Well, shit. Did she target me through him? But then why

was Ash's ambulance ambushed? Why did they take Ares too, and where is he? I already know he's not in here with me. It was the first thing I checked the first time I woke after the bitch felt me up and made me come. I had a vision of Ash's horrified eyes, but I can't tell if that was reality or my imagination.

The other guy lets loose a string of expletives.

"Wake the fuck up, man!" the guy across from me yells. "None of us are getting out of here. No one ever does. Death is the only freedom now. If this conversation accelerates the process, then good!"

"I don't want to die," I truthfully admit. "I need to get out of here to make sure my girl is okay and to beg her for forgiveness. I have family who relies on me. I need to escape."

"There is no escaping this place," the guy replies, all ire gone from his tone. "Even if we could get out of this basement, there are cameras and doors that require codes everywhere. She feeds us so we have the strength to fuck her the way she wants, but she drugs us so we're too out of it to even attempt to escape. She makes it so we feel like we want it, want her, but it's all the psychedelics. She literally blows your mind so you blow hers, and we're the ones left dealing with the agony of the reality when the high goes away." A wrangled sound travels up his throat. "I can't do it anymore. I want to be free of her. I'm ready to die."

I stare at the clearly traumatized man wondering if that is my fate.

Fuck no. I won't let that happen. She can abuse my body and trick my mind, but she'll never claim my heart or my soul. As long as I cling to my memories of Ash and my resolve to get back to her, Mom, and Tessa, I won't give up. I know Ash and Jase won't either. Jase's family is well connected, and he can get his hands on intel not even the cops could uncover.

If I can't find a way to escape this hellhole, I know my friends will come for me.

Ash and I are broken up. Things are totally shit between us. But she won't let me down. I saw her looking out the car window. She knows Ares and I were taken. She will try to find us. I know she won't give up on us even if we don't deserve it.

I need to get out of here because I need to tell Ash how sorry I am for all the ways I have hurt her and failed her.

Ares manipulated Ash into sleeping with him, and I know he did it to get back at me. My animosity with her stepbrother placed a target on her back. He used her to destroy me, and I'm the idiot who let him. Instead of forgiving her, I broke up with her and tried to punish her by messing around with her cousin. It doesn't matter I didn't sleep with Julia. What matters is I did it deliberately to hurt the one woman who means everything to me. I was so consumed with my own pride and hurt, and in so much inner pain, I lost sight of the only thing that matters.

I was a dumb bastard, and it would probably serve me right if I died here at the hands of this sick bitch.

But I owe it to Ash, Mom, and Tessa to not give up. "What else can you tell me?" I ask the man across from me.

"She throws parties for her friends once a month. She lets them do whatever they want, and they love humiliating us while taking from our bodies." A flicker of emotion ghosts over his face before the dead look reappears in his eyes. "Other times, she makes us fuck each other. She gets us amped up on X, GHB, or meth, and we can't control our urge to fuck." His eyes close momentarily, and I want to tell him to stop talking, but knowledge is power, and I need to keep my wits about me if I'm to survive this.

"What else?"

"She films us," someone who hasn't spoken yet says. "Sometimes it's live recordings."

Jesus Christ. An involuntary shudder cascades over my bare skin at the thought of something like that being out on the dark web or the internet.

"She ties us up and beats us too," my buddy across the ways says. "She gets off on causing pain and humiliation."

My eyes protest as blinding light envelopes the room unexpectedly. "Guess what, V," a woman whose voice I am unfortunately familiar with says. I pull myself up a little straighter in the cage, leaning against the side in the most upright position I can attain. I keep my legs closed and my knees raised, shielding my cock, though there's nothing I can do to hide if she decides she wants to play with me again.

The bitch stalks across the room, wearing a glamorous gold evening gown that is more suitable for a ballroom than her basement den of iniquity. Earlier, when she was here, she was wearing full dominatrix gear. It's obvious my cellmate's bait worked, and she's been called in from whatever event she was attending. The look of displeasure on her face is crystal clear. "It's your lucky day. I'm about to fulfill your dying wish." She flashes him a set of dazzling white teeth as she instructs the three men with her to unlock his cage.

The men drag him out of the cage, dumping him at her feet. He makes no effort to avoid his fate. I guess he really does want to die.

We are forced to watch as her men beat the shit out of him with their fists and a baseball bat while she drinks champagne from a small bottle. Her eyes flare with heat whenever he cries out in pain. She truly is a sick bitch. Panic blooms in my chest when she raises her eyes to meet mine, but I plant a defiant look on my face, unwilling to show any fear in front of her.

"Lucky for you I had an unexpected new toy delivery," she says, kicking at the man's chest until he rolls over onto his back. Her goons have stopped beating him as they stand back and let their boss have her fun. She digs the heel of her stiletto into his ball sac, and there's a collective sharp intake of breath as we feel the phantom pain between our legs. Pulling my knees up closer, I barely even feel the soreness in my ass. "So I'll let you go before your time is up. Pity," she says, leaning down over him. When she stands, she has put cuffs on both of his wrists, pushed his knees back to his chest, and placed a spreader bar behind his thighs, locking it securely to his wrists so he's all trussed up.

I gulp over the rising bile in my throat. His puckered hole is on display, the edges red-rimmed and the skin around it already shredded from whatever she last did to him. I suspect it was his breaking point. I want to look away as she moves down between his legs, but I don't want to show any weakness in front of her. So, I force myself to look as she pushes the champagne bottle into his ass. She leaves the end jutting out. One of her men helps her to stand while another places the baseball bat in her hand.

V's agonized screams bounce off the walls as she hits the bottle with the bat until it smashes, tearing him up from the inside. Some broken pieces of glass litter the floor around him. Putting on black gloves, she picks up the largest piece and kneels at his side. Leaning down, she kisses him on the lips as he writhes in pain with tears rolling down his face. "I will miss you, V. You were my favorite pup." She pets his body all over before she starts slicing at his flesh with the glass. Her cuts become more vicious and deeper the harder he cries out. Her crazed eyes are alight as he lies in a broadening pool of blood, his cries dying out as his life force slowly bleeds from his body.

When there is nothing but silence in the room, she stands, hovering over her victim's dead body, looking triumphant and proud as she surveys the gore at her feet. She is dripping in blood. Patches cling to the exposed skin at her chest, over both arms, and up one side of her neck. Her makeup is no longer immaculate, her face sprinkled with a myriad of bright red dots. Her glorious golden gown is covered with bloodstains. Almost like someone took a paintbrush and flicked red paint all over the dress.

I feel sick, and I want to look away, but I won't give her the satisfaction.

"That worked up an appetite." She hands the bloody piece of glass to her sidekick. Her dark eyes find me in a nanosecond, and I brace myself. "Prepare the red suite," she says to no one in particular because her eyes are locked on mine. "Let's try GHB this time. And set up a tripod. I have it on good authority my new little toy fancies himself as a porn star."

Stepping over the dead body, she walks up to my cage and laughs as she approaches. "It seems tonight I'm all about making dreams come true."

I don't move a muscle. I'm still in the same position, leaning against the side of the cage with my knees pulled into my chest.

Humiliation churns in my gut as she parts the cheeks of my ass. "Pity you're still bleeding. I wanted more playtime with this hole." I force my body not to flinch as her finger intrudes, pushing deep inside. "But it can wait." My relief when she removes her finger is short-lived. She cups my balls in her palms before forcing my thighs apart. She grips my dick in a firm hand as she slowly starts stroking me while grinning.

I don't know if it's smarter to fight my body's natural reaction to a hand around my dick or to give in and get it over and done with sooner. Licking her lips, she moans as my dick hardens in her palm, and the devilish glint in her eyes tells me what she has planned is going to be way worse than her earlier violation.

Being drugged doesn't sound so bad now.

Chapter Five

Ashley

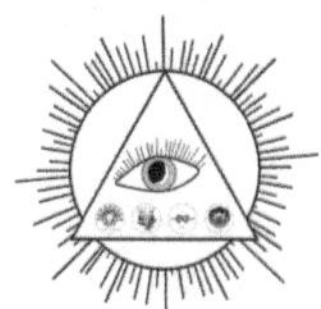

Exhaustion wraps around me, and I struggle to keep my eyes open as I snuggle against Jase's side. I want to know about Lilianna and all the things Hera and Ares were keeping from me. From Dad. But I know now isn't the time. As I look around the living room, every face wears the same weary expression.

"I think we should head to bed and talk in the morning." Jase plucks the words out of my head before I can articulate them.

"I agree," Mom says, fighting her own battle to keep her eyelids open. "There is nothing to gain from having this conversation at two a.m. We all need to sleep on it."

"I think you should stay here," I say to Jase and Bree. "I don't like the idea of any of us being separated right now." I know what Rhett said, but I don't trust a word out of his treacherous mouth. I don't trust he won't try to hurt more of my loved ones if he thought he could get away with it. It seems like he needs Jase and Bree, but I won't take any chances. "In fact, I think you should both move in here."

Out of the corner of my eye, I spot the scowl forming on Ares's face. Which is something else I need to deal with tomorrow.

Jase nods before pressing a kiss to the top of my head.

"That's cool with me. I'll move my stuff into one of the guest rooms tomorrow," Bree adds. Her eyes move fleetingly in Ares's direction, and knots twist in my gut. I do not have the energy or the desire to consider my best friend marrying my... whatever Ares is to me now.

It's all so fucked up.

No one says anything else as we switch off the lights, set the alarm, and head upstairs. Bree gives me a quick hug as she escapes into one of the guest bedrooms on this level.

I tug on Jase's arm as he starts to walk up the stairs to the next level. "Wait."

He stalls on the step above me as Mom and Ares continue to the upper level where Ares's, Chad's, and my bedrooms are. "What's wrong?" he asks, turning to face me.

"You need to sleep down here," I say, leaning against the banisters as I try not to let the crestfallen look on his face get to me.

"I don't expect anything, Ash, but I want to stay with you. To make sure you're okay."

"I'll be fine. I have already taken pain meds, and I'll just set my alarm to wake me every few hours."

He folds his arms across his broad chest as his emerald eyes peer into mine. "I know I hurt you and I need to make it up to you. I know it's not as easy as me saying I'm sorry or that I was trying to protect you. But please don't shut me out. You are injured, and someone should stay with you."

"I'll stay with her." Ares's gruff voice echoes from above.

I look up, spotting him hanging back on the top step.

I expect Jase to argue. There is little love lost between those two. But he surprises me.

He fixes his gaze on Ares. "Make sure you wake her every four hours. And come get me if there are any issues during the night."

Ares equally surprises me when he nods agreeably.

Jase pulls me into a tender hug. Pressing his warm lips to my ear, he whispers, "I love you, Temptress. Whatever you need, I will give you."

Tears stab my eyes at his words. I know what this must be costing him. "I love you too," I whisper, stretching up to kiss his cheek. "But that doesn't magically solve all our issues."

"I know." The look of adoration on his face as he tucks stray strands of pink hair behind my ears is almost enough to change my mind. "We need to talk about a lot of things."

I bob my head as I extract myself from his embrace and move around him. "Yeah, we do. Night, Jase. Sleep well."

"Night, baby."

I don't look back as I make my way upstairs, wishing I could snap my fingers and be in my bed already. Ares doesn't say anything as I brush past him, heading toward my master suite. Light trickles out from under Chad's room as Mom gets settled for the night, and pain pierces me through the heart. I can't bear to think about what Chad might be enduring now. If I go there, I will never be able to shut my mind off to sleep.

Ares and I get ready for bed in silence, but it's comfortable. Maybe I should be mad at him too, but the truth is, I have always known he was keeping secrets. He hated me upon sight. That pointed to an agenda from the outset. Discovering it's something to do with his sister makes me understand him a little better. I don't have the facts yet, but I don't need them to know whatever he was doing was for her.

Plus, Ares was lied to as well. There is no denying he had

no clue who he really was. He isn't that good of an actor to have faked such a genuine reaction. We have both been lied to and then thrust into this world without any preparation. I need him as much as I hope he needs me.

Ares turns off the light as I crawl under the covers. He climbs in beside me, in just his boxers, instantly pulling me back against his warm, hard body. "Sleep, Ash." His arms band around my waist.

I want to ask him how he's doing with all of the revelations, but his comforting arms and body heat instantly lull me into a deep sleep.

Ares wakes me after a few hours, insisting I take some more pain pills, and I fall back asleep in seconds. When I wake the next time, the space beside me is empty. The sheets are still warm, so it must not have been long since Ares got up.

"Hey." A warm hand lands on my arm as Jase claims my attention. Turning my head, I find him seated in a chair by my bed. "How are you feeling?"

"Okay," I say over a yawn, pulling myself upright against the headboard. One strap of my silk sleep top falls down my arm, and Jase's eyes are like heat-seeking missiles as they follow the trajectory. I fix my top as he clears his throat. "What time is it?" I ask. "And where is Ares?"

"It's just after nine, and he went to his room to call in sick to work."

"Did you sleep?" I ask, noting the bruising shadows under his eyes.

He scrubs a hand along his prickly jawline. "Not much. I couldn't switch my brain off."

I'm sure I only slept because of my injuries and the medication. "I'm terrified for Chad."

"Yeah, me too." Resting his elbows on his knees, he buries his head in his hands for a few seconds. When he looks up, pain is written all over his face. "I am aware of Cleo Carter's BDSM kinks, and I knew she was a domme, but I had no idea she was abusing men and keeping them prisoner. I haven't even heard any rumors. She has gone to great lengths to hide this."

"Which means she must kill them," I surmise. My lips tremble. "We need to get him out of there, Jase." I whip the covers back, exposing my small sleep shorts and my bare legs. "We need to get him out of there now."

"I have a few ideas," he says, offering me his hand.

"Where's my mom?" I ask, taking his hand and letting him help me to my feet.

"In the kitchen with Bree."

"She can't be a part of this. I don't trust her." It pains me to say that about my own mother, but she has proven over and over she can't be trusted. "She told me there'd be no more secrets, but she concealed his identity from me. How could she do that? She had to know he had figured it out when he was the one pushing for my initiation, but she still said nothing. I can't forgive her for that."

"I don't blame you, and I don't trust her either. She has a lot to answer for."

Darts of pain shoot across my chest, tightening it to the point where I can scarcely breathe. A strangled sob rips from my lips. "My dad is dead," I whisper as tears automatically stream down my face.

Jase reels me into his arms, wrapping his muscular arms around me. "I'm so sorry, Ash. Doug didn't deserve that."

Sobs burst from my mouth as I let myself feel. "He sacrificed his life for me. He married a woman he didn't love to protect her and her unborn baby, and he loved me as if I was his own." I know Dad felt guilty for the years they left me to largely fend for myself, and he was trying to make it up to me. I wish I had known the truth. I would not have been so flippant or fought him so much when he tried to make amends. I wish I had told him I loved him more often. I wish I had spent more time with him. Now all of that is lost to me.

I fall apart, giving in to everything I am feeling. Pining the loss of a man who gave everything to me. I cling to Jase as I sob against his neck. He holds me close, smoothing a hand up and down my back and pressing kisses into my hair, as I expunge my grief.

The door opens, and I look over as Ares slips into my room. His hair is damp, and little beads of water cling to his brow, confirming he's not long out of the shower.

Without a word, Jase passes me over to Ares, and I sink into his arms, inhaling his masculine scent and the warmth of his strong body as it envelops me. His arms wrap around me as he bundles me into his body.

Eventually, my tears die out. Sniffling, I pull out of his arms, scrubbing at my swollen eyes. Jase hands me a tissue as his arm slides around my shoulders. "We're going to get justice for Doug, Ash."

"And we're going to make that motherfucking asshole pay," Ares adds in a growly tone. "This will devastate my mom. She was alone for years, grieving my father, until she met Doug. He brought her back to life. Reminded her what it was like to love. I will always be grateful to him for that."

"Was it real, Ares? Does she really love him?" I couldn't bear it if Dad died with memories of a love that was fake because I know it was real for him.

"It's real, Ash. She loves him. He made her so happy. This is going to destroy her."

"It was the first time I saw him in love," I softly admit. "The first time he was really truly happy. I hate that bastard robbed him of a lifetime of love with Hera."

"He will regret it," Jase promises, gently cupping one

cheek. "Go freshen up. Then let's get rid of Pamela and start making plans."

The guys are talking in hushed tones when I emerge from my bathroom ten minutes later, feeling more human after a shower. Wrangling my wet hair into a loose ponytail, I pad into my walk-in closet and pull on a pair of yoga pants and one of Chad's old football T-shirts. I slide my feet into my fluffy slippers and head back out.

"I hope this means you two are going to put aside your differences," I say when I find the guys still deep in conversation.

"We can't defeat that bastard unless we're united," Ares says.

I breathe a sigh of relief I don't have to have that conversation with them.

"And it means we need to put everything on the table." Jase side-eyes him. "No more holding back."

"I already told you I'll explain everything," Ares snarls as he rises to his feet. "Just because we're working together to defeat our mutual enemy doesn't mean I answer to you or anyone."

I work hard to stop from rolling my eyes. I guess Ares wouldn't be Ares if he didn't still try to exert control. "We will make decisions as a team and execute them as a team. Unless we want to fail, there is no other way," I say.

"Agreed." Jase stands and threads his fingers in mine. "I was just filling Ares in on some of the Luminary background."

Ares opens the door. "I doubt I would've believed it if I hadn't seen that creepy shit for myself."

"You haven't heard the half of it," Jase replies, steering me out of the bedroom.

"I still can't wrap my head around it, and I only know the basics," I admit.

"I can't believe Mom lied to me about this. I get she was trying to protect me, but she should have told me the second I landed back on US soil." Ares's jaw clenches tight as we walk the hallway. "As soon as I get her away from that bastard Carter, she has a lot of explaining to do."

Chapter Six
Ashley

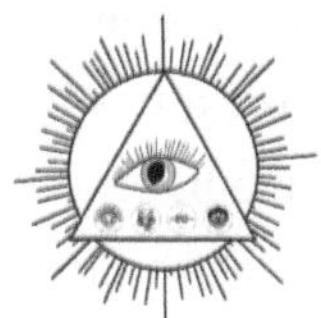

"I mean it, Ashley." Mom turns around in the doorway to pin me with one of her looks. "Just focus on finding Chad and leave the rest up to me."

Not fucking likely. She has done such a stellar job of handling things thus far. How many more must die for her to wake up and smell the coffee?

But I let her believe she still holds the power. That I don't hold her life in my hands. Or we're incapable of coming up with a plan to defeat Carter by ourselves. If she wants to pretend otherwise, let her knock herself out.

She has always brushed me aside and underestimated me.

Right now, I just need her to get out of our way so we can get on with things. "Okay, Mom. I hear you."

I'm just not going to listen.

"What are you going to tell Richard?" I inquire.

"I'm telling him the truth. I don't keep secrets from my husband."

That's fucking rich. Pity she didn't adopt that motto with me. Maybe Dad would still be alive if I'd been made aware of all the facts. Anger sparks to life inside me, but I tamp it down. "What about James?"

She winces, and her mouth pulls into a grimace. "I hate lying to my brother, but I have no choice. I have Julia's phone. I'll keep up the charade she's alive, tell him you didn't need treatment at HQ after all, and keep him away from here."

"He might never forgive you when he finds out."

She wraps her arms around herself. "That's a risk I have to take." There's a strange look on her face as she stares into space. "Julia was way too much like her mother. James knew it too. It's why he was pushing marriage to Jase." She returns her focus to me. "He knew Julia was too self-obsessed and selfish. He needed someone strong to mold into his successor, and Jase fit the bill." She shakes her head. "James was too lenient on Julia after Lucille's death. He tried to overcompensate for the loss of her mother, and his inability to love her properly, by giving her everything she asked for, but he should've taken a firmer hand with her." A harsh laugh bursts from her lips. "She was such a fool believing a man like Rhett Carter would ever be interested in someone like her. Honestly, I'm embarrassed for the child."

I really couldn't care less at this point. I have had my fill of Julia conversation. "Enough, Mom. Excuse me if I don't want to stand around talking about that bitch. She tried to kill me. I have little feeling about how she ended up. She brought it on herself. And you can't blame her failings on her father or the lack of a mother. I had to grow up without one too, and you didn't see me plotting to murder her out of spiteful jealousy."

Mom at least has the decency to look ashamed, but I don't know if it's sincere.

"You should go. Give Emilie a kiss from me." I attempt to close the door, but she jams her foot in it before I can shut it.

"You're angry with me, and I deserve it." Her throat bobs as she gulps. "I have failed you and Doug." Tears spring to her eyes, reminding me she is human somewhere underneath all of that cold exterior. "But I'm going to fix it." Her eyes drill a hole in my face as she stares at me. "Don't take this upon yourself. You need to heal and focus on rescuing Chad before that awful woman ruins him for life. Just do what the monster wants for now until I figure a way out of this mess."

"We're not idiots, Mother. We know we need to do what he says."

She slowly nods. "Don't do anything rash, Ashley. I can't lose you too."

Her words irritate me. I wish I could believe them, but it's hard with everything that has transpired. "Go home, Mom. I'll talk to you later."

She walks off without another word, and I shut the door. Leaning against it, I huff out a tired sigh.

"Is she gone?" Bree asks, appearing at the end of the hallway.

I nod as I push off the door, making my way toward my friend. Bree is dressed similarly to me, in yoga pants and an oversized hoodie, with her glasses on and her blue hair in a messy, damp topknot.

"Are we okay?" she asks, biting down on her lip.

"I don't know," I truthfully reply. It's clear Bree knew Jase's betrayal wasn't all it seemed. She swore she wouldn't keep things from me again, and it hurts she did. But I understand it came from a good place, and honestly? With everything else we have going on, does it even really matter? "But we can work it out later." I loop my arm in hers. "We have more pressing problems."

"I won't marry him if it'll cause further issues between us," she blurts, pulling me back before I can walk into the kitchen where the guys are waiting for us.

"You don't have a choice," I remind her, rubbing a tense spot between my brows. "You need to do it."

"It won't be real." Her eyes probe mine. "I know you think the worst of me now, and with good reason, but I could never come between you and him. I doubt anyone could. I know you're falling for one another. He only has eyes for you. Everyone can see it. Whatever we need to do, it will all be for show. I promise you nothing else will happen. I wouldn't do that to you, and I don't think Ares would either. You can trust him with me."

"I know, Bree. That isn't the issue between us."

"Okay, good." Her shoulders visibly relax. "I am so sorry about everything, Ash. I hate this for you."

"This is bigger than me. Bigger than us," I say as we step into the kitchen together. "We need to set aside our differences and issues and work to stop that crazy lunatic before he destroys the world."

"He might be crazy, but he's fucking smart too." Ares looks over his shoulder from his position at the stove.

Jase pulls out a stool for me and his sister, helping me to sit up. His fussing over me is endearing. I need his comfort at a time when it feels like I've lost all the parental figures in my life.

"Ares is right, and we cannot underestimate Rhett Carter or the power he has amassed," Jase says.

"The separatists have been gaining momentum steadily for the last ten years," Bree explains, jerking her head in thanks at Ares when he slides two steaming mugs of coffee in our direction. "If Rhett is behind it, he has a lot of minions ready to do his bidding."

"So, how do we take him down?" I blow gently on the steam rising from my mug.

"We turn the tables and give him a taste of his own medicine. We need something to blackmail him with," Jase says.

"It shouldn't be hard," Bree says in between sips of her drink. "He has got to be bending rules all over the place. We just need to find evidence of that and use it against him."

"My gut tells me he's involved in what happened to my sister," Ares says in a low pained voice as he sets heaping plates of eggs, bacon, and toast down in front of us. "From what Jase has said, that's not something that would be permitted of a man in his position."

"Can we park that for a second," I say as Ares hops up onto a stool across from me. "I want to know about Lilianna and about South America," I add, sending a pointed look in Bree's direction. Her face pales, but she nods. "But I think we need to discuss Carter first. What if we're overcomplicating things?" I have been mulling it over as the others spoke.

"In what way, babe?" Jase asks. He shovels a mouthful of creamy scrambled eggs into his mouth.

Ares and Bree pin me with intense gazes as they eat, waiting for me to elaborate. "So, Carter wants to be Lord of the World, blah, blah, blah. The only way he can achieve that is by taking control of the board and having the majority vote. What if we give that to him? We go along with his plan." I eyeball Jase. "We'll get married. He'll get James removed from the throne, and you take his place." I turn my stare to Ares. "You'll be initiated and then marry Bree. He'll get rid of Walter, and you'll be in charge of Pride & Wrath." My tongue darts out, wetting my lips. "The only vote left is the Stewart one."

"Would your father side with us?" Ares queries, instantly understanding where I'm going with this.

"I don't have the best relationship with him. We clash over a lot of things including how he sees no wrong with our lifestyle and the things our Luminary responsibility forces us to do. He won't ever give it up," Jase supplies. "But he also won't bow at Rhett Carter's feet. I believe he'll side with us."

"I think so too. If he needs any convincing, Baz can help," Bree says with confidence I'm not sure her younger brother shares. "But what about the fifth vote? Remember he said he is going to elevate a family to Luminary status." She bites off a chunk of crispy bacon. "That throws a wrench in the works."

"That can only happen after the current board votes for Carter's plan in the first place. We would obviously need to act before that part of the plan is executed," I say. "So, if we agree to his madness, we will automatically control two of the four votes." My gaze jumps between Bree and Jase. "Your father controls the third, and Carter, the fourth."

A sly smile graces Jase's mouth. "I see where you're going with this."

"Assuming your father sides with us, we then control the majority vote, but it really doesn't matter. What matters is that we will be united in standing against Carter's plan." I pop a piece of bacon in my mouth and chew while I let my words sink in. "Who will hold us accountable if we just kill him? We can frame it in such a way that the public doesn't know. Only we would. It's not like we're going to punish ourselves for breaking the rules, right?"

"I'm down to kill him." Ares cracks his knuckles. "I volunteer as tribute." He flashes me a wicked grin as he licks his lips in anticipation.

It shouldn't turn me on, but it does.

"It doesn't necessarily mean his plan will die with him." Jase pushes his empty plate away as he attempts to refocus the conversation.

"Of course not. He's amassed loyal followers. Many who will continue his plans in his absence, but this way, we buy ourselves some time," I explain. "We will gather evidence of his abuse of power, and maybe we stage his murder as a suicide?" I shrug, thinking off-the-cuff.

Suicide is a big sin in the Luminary world because these people lack basic empathy. They fail to see how the things they do through their manipulation drives despair and despondency and exacerbates the situation. From what I've seen, Luminary policy and behavior causes a lot of the problems society faces. The world would be better off without them and their antiquated ideals.

Carter dying by reason of suicide would be irony at its finest and the ultimate humiliation to Carter's legacy. I'm liking it even more as it plays out in my mind. "We go public with that, and it will stall even his staunchest supporters, at least temporarily. Then we weed out those supporters and clean the ranks."

"We can even implement changes," Bree says, her eyes lighting up.

I admire my friend's optimism and philanthropic goals, but I'd rather just eradicate the entire structure. However, it's not an achievable goal. I'm not naïve enough to believe it is, so perhaps Bree's way is the way to go. Work to change the organization for the better from the inside out.

"We can show we are progressive and fair while still adhering to our core values and traditions," Bree continues, her voice and face getting more animated. "We can show there is a new, better way and transfer some of that allegiance to us."

"The zealots will never be swayed," Jase says. "But it's time they were tackled anyway. The board has been remiss letting that go unchecked."

"We're forgetting something," Ares says, finishing the last of his breakfast. "What about his heir? It's Knight, right? What if he's in on this with his father? What if we chop off one head only for another one to immediately grow? He could continue his father's plans and then we're back to square one."

I shake my head. "Not fully. We won't approve Rhett's plan, so Knight will have no authority to put his father's plan in motion."

"He could still plot to overthrow us all, but it wouldn't happen overnight." Bree hops down off her stool to grab the coffee pot. "It would give us time to clean house."

"I'm not so sure Knight would side with his father anyway," Jase adds, holding out his mug for a refill.

"How do we test that theory without risking ourselves?" I ask.

Jase purses his lips as he thinks about it. "I'm not sure. Let's add it to our list."

"We can't take him out until I know what he knows about my sister," Ares says, jerking his head at my plate and urging me to eat.

I scoop up a forkful of semi-warm eggs and shove them in my mouth.

"I have spent over two years trying to find out what happened to her. He knows where she is." His voice cracks as he looks down at his lap for a few seconds. The torment in his eyes guts me when he lifts his chin and stares at me. "He had a video of her on his phone." Emotion glistens in his eyes. "I never let myself believe she was dead, but it was hard to cling to hope when I kept meeting dead ends. Even Mom had given up."

The air is charged with tension, and his pain is palpable. Yet I see the hope lingering at the back of his eyes, and I hear it in his desperate tone.

"We can't kill him until I get Lilianna back."

"Of course," Jase says with sincerity. "Rescuing Chad and Lilianna takes priority, but timing is of the essence. We can't let too much time pass, because if Carter elevates a fifth family and the new structure is made public, it means we are accountable if we take him out, and we might not have the support we hope for."

"If we have to die for the greater good, I'm okay with that," Bree says, way too calmly.

"I'm not." Ares glares at her.

"Neither am I. I'll be no martyr, thank you very much." I agree with my stepbrother.

"No way am I fucking sacrificing myself because a bunch of deranged lunatics think they are gods," Ares adds in a scathing tone. "I'll kill every fucking one of them before I'll let that happen."

"We're not going down at the hands of that bastard," Jase agrees as the front doorbell chimes. He arches a brow. "Expecting company?" he asks as Ares grabs his tablet from the counter behind him.

I slide off the stool to go answer it.

"Wait a sec," Ares says. "Let me check the outside camera."

All the fine hairs stand to attention on the back of my neck. "We have cameras?" I narrow my eyes at my stepbrother as he taps away on his tablet. When he lifts his head a couple of seconds later, I spot the grin he's trying to fight. Oh, hell to the no. If this means what I think it means, I am going to kick his ass from one end of Lowell to the other.

"Do you know either of these men?" Ares turns the tablet around, showing us the image of the two tall dark-haired men standing at our door.

"That's Vincent Fox. He's my trainer," I say, pointing at the man on the left the same time Jase says, "That's Victor Fox," pointing at the man on the right.

"They are brothers and well-respected masters attached to the Salinger family," Bree explains.

"They are friends of our father and good guys," Jase confirms.

Ares brow puckers. "What are they doing here?"

"Only one way to find out," I say, stalking toward the front door with Bree hot on my tail.

Chapter Seven

Ares

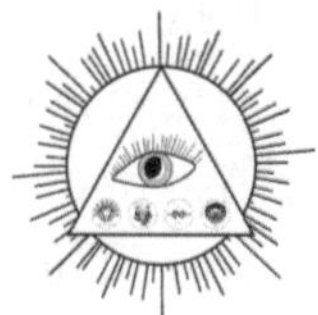

A shrill scream rings out, and Jase and I jump up as one, racing out into the hallway. The second I round the bend, something whizzes through the air at me, and a sharp sting pinches the side of my neck. The effect is immediate. I slump to my knees as I reach a hand to the small object embedded in the side of my neck. Losing all feeling in my fingers, I can't pull it out. The last things I see as darkness encroaches on my vision are Jase collapsing beside me, both girls lying comatose on the floor, and a swarm of men in black military-style fatigues piling through the front door.

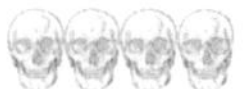

"Ares." My eyes flicker as the whisper of her voice floats through my ears. "Ares, wake up!" The darkness calls to me, not wanting to let go, and my eyes go still as sleep returns to claim me. "Hey, asshole." Ash's voice is louder this time, and my shoulders vibrate as she shakes me. "Wake the fuck up. Right now."

"Always so bossy," I murmur, my voice thick with sleep as I force my eyes to open. It all comes back to me in a flash, and I jerk upright, smashing her against my chest as I take stock of our surroundings.

"Can't breathe," she mumbles, struggling to get free.

I narrow my eyes at the two assholes standing in front of the open fireplace directly beside the leather couch where Jase and Bree are sitting, across from the couch we are on. Bree is trying to rouse Jase, and he's groaning as he slowly comes to. "What the fuck is going on?" I hiss, tucking Ash under my arm and warning her with a glare not to fucking move. This is clearly more Luminary bullshit. I still haven't wrapped my head around the shit Stewart told me earlier. It sounds like something from a horror movie.

"We'll explain everything as soon as Jase is awake," the taller, slightly older-looking man says.

"They won't hurt us," Ash says, attempting to straighten up. "I know Vincent and—"

I interject before she can continue. "News flash, dollface. They already did hurt us." I tighten my arm around her as I bare my teeth at the older dudes. An ache in my neck has me reaching toward the tiny hole in my flesh. I growl. "What the fuck did you do?" I ask as Jase comes to.

"I apologize, Blade," the slightly shorter, younger man says. "It was only a mild tranquilizer. It won't cause any lasting damage."

Jase's eyes scan over Ash before he jumps to his feet, swaying a little. He turns around, facing the two men. "She has a fucking concussion, you morons." Leaning across the couch, he grabs the older man by the shirt, putting his face all up in his. "You better have a good reason for this, Victor," he growls. "If you don't, I'll have your ass for this."

"We didn't have a choice, Mr. Stewart. Rhett Carter has

cameras all over the townhome, and we couldn't risk talking to you there."

What the fuck? How is that even possible, and did Doug know? Or is this something Carter had done while he had us locked up in the creepy crypt?

"I have checked Ashley out, and she's fine. You'll all likely be a little bit drowsy. Maybe get a headache," Vincent says in a voice that is way too calm and casual for my liking.

"I don't care who you are." I pull Ash to her feet as I stand. "You hurt her again, you touch her again, and it'll be the last move you ever make."

The older man smiles in my direction. "You remind me so much of your father. He was passionate and possessive with your mom in the same way."

Yeah, I'm so not touching that right now.

"You have two minutes to explain yourselves before we're calling this in," Bree says, standing beside her brother. "We outrank you and could have you killed for the stunt you just pulled."

"We need to talk to Blade, to all of you," Victor says, "but the townhome is compromised. We didn't want to put you at risk, any more than you already are, by talking to you there."

"If you had asked, I would've told you I knew about the cameras. I could've switched them off," I say, assuming Carter had just piggybacked off the existing cameras and not implanted new ones.

Ash thumps me in the ribs, attempting to wriggle out from my embrace. I tighten my arm around her, keeping her trapped as I stare at the two men. "Doug asked me to install them. He was worried about Ash though he refused to explain why." It all makes sense now.

"I doubt her father requested cameras to be installed in her bedroom and bathroom," Vincent says. His tone and expression reek of distrust.

"Oops. My bad." I smirk at the self-righteous asshole. I'm focused on him, so I don't see Ash reaching down to grab my junk the same time she bites down hard on my arm.

I yell as pain throbs between my legs, and I see stars. My arm drops from around her as I hunch over, cupping my balls and cursing under my breath.

"You were spying on me in my bedroom and in the shower?" Her screech stabs my eardrums and pierces through the fog in my head. "How the hell did you do it? We found the fucking camera the first day, and I checked for devices again after you broke into my room."

"Those phone apps don't work with more sophisticated devices," I admit because there's no point in concealing the truth any longer. "I planted the first camera on purpose so you'd find it and think you were safe." I straighten up in time to see her clenched fist come at my face.

Her first punch lands squarely on my nose; the second glances the side of my jaw. "Ouch." That actually fucking hurt. Where did my little minx learn to punch like that? I rub my sore jaw as my hand darts out, grabbing the side of the couch to stop myself from falling. Jase would never let me live that one down.

"Nice one, sweetheart," Vincent says.

"I was taught by the best." She waggles her brows at him, and I can't stop the growl racing up my throat.

"That was an asshole move," Bree says, shaking her head at me.

I shrug as I adjust my sore dick behind my jeans. "Never claimed I was a saint, and don't look to me for remorse because you won't find any."

"Guilt is for the weak," Ash snarls, folding her arms over

her gorgeous rack and staring at me like I'm the Antichrist. "I remember."

I look down at her, unable to resist winding her up further. "I haven't shown the footage to anyone. It all just went into my personal stepsister porn collection."

This time, it's Stewart who punches me in the face. "You're a prick," he says.

"And you're a hypocrite." I shove him away from me. "You both film her all the time."

"We have her permission, and it's fully transparent," he roars, lunging for me again.

I can't resist pushing his buttons some more. "I suppose I shouldn't mention that I only messed around with Julia so I could get access to your house to plant a camera in your bedroom?"

"Motherfucker!" Jase roars, slamming his body into mine and taking us both to the ground.

"I knew this truce wouldn't last," Ash mutters as Jase and I roll around the floor and throw punches.

The Fox brothers pull us apart a few seconds later, yanking us to our feet and separating us. "Grow up, both of you." Victor chastises us while jabbing his finger in my face. "I don't care what your motives were. No one deserves to have their privacy breached in their own home. You owe Ashley, Chad, and Jase an apology, but this isn't the time or the place." His gaze dances around the room. "Aren't we all dealing with much bigger problems? Like how Carter has hacked into the feeds and he's been spying on all of you too?"

Well, fuck. That's the confirmation I was after. I wonder how long he's been spying on us and how come Doug didn't spot it. Carter is too smart, and we need to get ahead of the game ASAP.

I shove Vincent off me from behind. "Fuck off," I snap, turning to glare at him.

"Sit your ass down, Blade."

I swing my gaze on Victor. "My name is Ares. I don't answer to Blade."

Victor's expression softens a little. "I'm aware of your new identity. I was the one who came up with it after all."

"You can't take all the credit," a woman says from behind. I whip around, startled to find Mom standing in the doorway. "I do believe I was the one who chose the name Ares."

"Hera!" Ashley sprints across the room, throwing herself into my mom's arms. "We thought Rhett had you!"

Mom hugs her close, running a hand up and down Ash's back.

"He did have you," I say, walking toward her. "He showed me."

"Victor and Vincent got me out." She draws me into their hug.

"Our guy would have gotten you out too, but he was vastly outnumbered at the ambush. If he had tried something, it wouldn't have ended well, and it would have tipped Carter off," Victor says, staring me straight in the face.

"Your guy?" I arch a brow.

"We have had a protective detail on your family since you returned to the US."

"Fat lot of help that was when my sister was taken," I snap.

"Ares. Stop. Victor lost three men the night your sister was kidnapped. They tried to prevent it and died attempting to save her."

"It would've been nice to know that." I glare at my mother. I'm glad she's safe and not in that bastard's clutches, but I'm super pissed at her. She concealed so much from me. Things I should have known.

"I'm sorry." Remorse floods her face, and it seems sincere.

I heave out a sigh. I don't know what to think anymore.

Mom presses kisses to both our brows in turn. "Are you both okay?" She examines our faces before sweeping her fingers gently over Ash's face. "Are you feeling all right, honey?"

"I'm fine." Ash looks up at me. "We're physically fine."

"I'm sure it's been a lot to take in."

"It has, and we still don't know everything," Ash replies.

"Is anyone going to explain what the fuck is going on?" Bree asks, exasperation clear in her tone.

"We were trying, then you all had to start with the unnecessary teenage bullshit," Vincent says.

"Not a teenager," I snarl.

"Then quit acting like one," he retorts.

"Drop it," Ash snaps, rubbing at her head and wincing as if she's in pain, and I instantly feel remorseful.

What. The. Actual. Fuck?

I wish I could reach into my head and scrub that last thought from my mind.

"There is much we need to discuss," Mom says, exchanging looks with Victor. "I wanted to do this with Doug here, but he's tied up with Luminary business."

Ash and I share shocked expressions as Victor subtly shakes his head.

"Let's talk in the sunroom," Vincent suggests, jerking his head toward the double doors in the center of the large, bright living room. He moves over to Mom and begins steering her out of the room. Jase and Bree follow.

"I know she needs to know," Victor says as he approaches us. Sympathy splays across his face. "I know what losing Clinton did to her. Losing Doug in the same way is going to devastate her. I didn't want to lie to her, but this is a life-or-death scenario, Ares. You need to hear what we have to tell you. Then we can sit down and tell her together."

"I am sick of all the goddamn lies!" Ash says, purposely keeping her voice low. "It stops here."

"I'm sorry about the cameras," I say, curling my hand around hers. I don't apologize often, but it's warranted on this occasion. It was a shitty thing to do even if I had to do it. I needed intel, and there isn't anything I wouldn't do to get it. Rescuing Lili is my only priority, and I will do whatever is necessary to get her back.

Ash yanks her hand back. "Not now. We'll talk about that later." She stomps out of the room, sucking all the oxygen with her.

"She's got fire, that one," Victor says, joining me in staring after her.

"She's too good for me," I blurt without thinking.

"Your father used to say that too." Sadness ghosts over his face. "You are like him in so many ways, but you have Daphne's wild passion and reckless streak."

"You act like you know me, but you don't know me at all." Who the fuck does this guy think he is?

He eyeballs me. "I have watched over you your entire life, Ares. It feels like I know you, but perhaps I don't. I hope we get the chance to rectify that now."

Chapter Eight

Jase

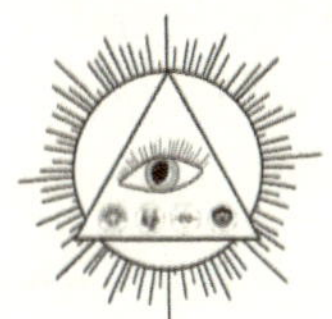

"Wow. The view is stunning here," Bree says as we settle onto the comfy couches in the sunroom. She's not mistaken. The large windows offer a front-row seat to the magnificent landscape outside. The house sits on an elevated site, overlooking a large lake, surrounded by dense forest on all sides and mountains in the background. A light coating of snow covers the ground, glistening off the branches of trees, while a glimpse of winter sunshine highlights the dappled surface of the lake. There are several lakes in northern Cali, but I'd bet my life this is Tahoe. It's the most popular lake in Cali, and though I can't see any houses in the vicinity, I wonder how private it is.

"Are we safe here?" I ask, pulling Ash down onto my lap when she comes bounding into the room with a fierce look on her face.

"Completely," Vincent replies. "This is one of our safe houses. It's on private grounds spanning ten acres in a secluded part of Tahoe. It's bordered by tall walls around the perimeter, solid iron gates, and a high-level security system with cameras all over the exterior of the property."

"There's a secure panic room and a helipad," Victor adds, entering the room alongside Ares.

I glare at the prick. I'm livid he has been watching Ash and me in my room. Enough that I'd fucking kill the jerk if he wasn't a Luminary and we didn't need him to defeat Carter and save the world from his brand of cruel insanity. Chad is going to bust a nut when he discovers Ares was spying on them and using their private moments to get his rocks off. I'm not going to think about how similar their voyeuristic tendencies are or the fact they may be more alike than they realize. It's not cool to breach our privacy like that. I don't care how hypocritical that may sound. It's the fucking truth.

Just as I was starting to find some common ground with the jerk, he has to go and remind me why I don't like him.

There will be fun times ahead. Not.

"You are safe here. No one knows this place exists, and no one followed us." Victor reaches into the back pocket of his pants, removing an envelope. He hands it to Ares. "This is the keys, alarm code, and coordinates to here, along with the pilot's contact details should you need to fly in." He looks around the room. "If you need someplace safe to escape to, at any time, this place is yours."

Ares nods as he pockets the envelope before moving over to sit beside his mom. He knows not to attempt to come close to Ash or me.

"Tell us why we are here." Bree crosses her legs at the ankles. "It's about time we got some answers."

"After Victor rescued me and he told me about the ambush, I asked him to set this meeting up." Hera turns to her son. "I should've been honest with you from the start, but I thought I was doing the right thing hiding who you were and keeping you sheltered from the truth. I never wanted you involved in this world." Her eyes well up. "I wanted to keep you safe. You and Lilianna, and I failed to do both."

"Tell me now," Ares says through gritted teeth. "And don't hold anything back, Ma. That time has passed. We need to know what we're dealing with."

Hera clasps her hands in her lap, dragging her lower lip between her teeth. Ash repositions herself across my lap, and I circle my arms around her waist, urging her head down to my chest. I'm glad she's letting me comfort her. That she hasn't completely written me off. I run my hand up and down her arm as Hera begins explaining.

"I met Clinton, your father, when I was nineteen, and it was love at first sight. I had never known anyone like him. He had this magnetism that oozed from his pores, and it sucked me right in. He was so confident for twenty-one, and I was in awe of him. He treated me like a queen." She averts her eyes, looking absently out the window, and I'm guessing she is lost in her memories. "He was everything I had never dared to dream of, and I couldn't believe he was mine."

"He felt the same way about you too, Daphne. I watched it happen firsthand," Victor says. "I never saw a man fall in love so quickly and so deeply. You were his whole world."

"As he was mine." Hera glances at Ares, tentatively cupping his cheek. "You look so much like him. If I didn't have you, I'm not sure I would have survived his loss. Every day when I saw your handsome little face, I thanked God for giving you to me. For leaving this little piece of my Clint with me. You brought me so much joy, Ares, at a time when joy was hard won."

"Is Lilianna Clint's daughter?" Ashley asks.

Hera shakes her head. "No."

"Lilianna is nine years younger than me," Ares supplies.

"Her father was a man I met in Italy during the time we briefly lived there," Hera explains. "His name was, coincidentally, Liam Haynes. I had randomly chosen that surname for our new identities, and then I met a man with the same name. I thought it might have been a sign." She smiles and pauses momentarily. "Liam was a tourist from England passing through the village we were living in. I hadn't been with any man since Clint, and I met him when I was vulnerable and lonely and desperate to not feel so alone. It was a short-lived affair, and I didn't even realize I was pregnant when he left. We didn't exchange details. We both knew what it was. After I had Lili, I thought of finding him. I knew I could ask Victor and he'd locate him for me, but I couldn't do it. I couldn't drag him into this world. We were running for our lives, and it seemed selfish to bring someone else into it."

"My mom said Clint was murdered by a religious group, and you disappeared after. She said The Luminaries searched for you but concluded you were dead when they couldn't find any trace of you." Ash places her palm on my chest as she speaks. Warmth from her hand seeps underneath my sweater into my skin, and I tighten my arm around her.

"I have Victor to thank for that." Hera smiles at the man. "He protected us when I had no one else and nowhere to turn."

"Who were you to Clinton?" I ask him. I'm sure my father would know, as it was his generation, even if he didn't serve on the Board of Luminaries the same time as Ares's father. Rhett said Clinton gained control when he was young. I know James Manford did too, and I wonder if they sat on the board at the same time.

"Clint was my best friend. We grew up together," Victor

explains. "My family is masters, as you know, and there is a long tradition linking the Foxes with the Salingers. Our fathers were best friends and their fathers before them."

The Foxes are at the top of the masters' chain within the Salinger Luminary. That is something I do know, but I wasn't aware of the strong personal connection between the two families. I probably should have paid more attention in my Luminary History classes at HQ.

Victor fixes Ares with a solemn look. "I made your father a promise on his wedding day and again when you were born. I vowed that should anything happen to him I would look after his family." He leans forward, knotting his hands on his knees. "I keep my promises, and I have done my best to safeguard your family and hide your existence from the board."

"You were responsible for wiping their backgrounds," Bree says. "That's why I couldn't find anything going back more than two and a half years when I ran a search."

Victor nods. "I had to create records when Hera met Doug. I knew there was a slim possibility someone might do a background search."

"You didn't do a very good job," Bree says. "I immediately smelled a rat."

"It happened quickly, and I did the best I could. Doug was only an expert by marriage, and since that marriage had ended, I honestly didn't feel it was a huge risk. That was clearly an oversight on my part."

"I won't let you blame yourself," Hera says. "I knew marrying Doug was a risk, but I was fed up with hiding, and I love him. He's a good man, and I know he will keep me safe." She glances over at Ashley. "I can only imagine what you must think of me now. I'm sorry for concealing so much from you, but it was done out of love and a need to protect you too.

However, I need you to know I love your father very deeply. I never expected to find love a second time, and I had no clue Doug was part of the Luminary world until Victor told me who he was. I tried to walk away, but I couldn't. I was already too invested. I love you and your father, Ashley. Whatever you believe or don't believe, please know that is the truth."

Chapter Nine

Jase

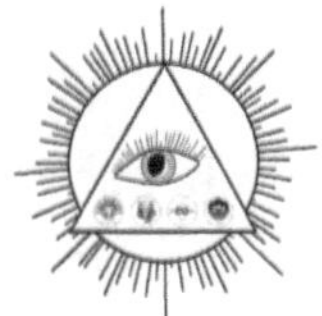

"Does he know who you are?" Ashley asks. Her voice is choked with emotion. From what Hera said in the other room, it's clear she doesn't know Doug is dead. I don't envy Ares the task of telling her.

"No," she quietly admits, shaking her head. "I believed it was better he didn't know, but I will have to tell him now." Her brow puckers as she chews on the corner of her lips. "He's going to be so disappointed in me."

Ash buries her face in my shoulder, fighting tears. I hold her even closer, whispering how much I love her as I cradle her against me.

"You don't shoulder the responsibility alone, Daphne." Victor subtly redirects the conversation. "I should have taken more precautions. If I had, they might not have discovered Blade." His voice is laced with pain. I know he's a good man, and he feels like he failed his dead friend. But he has nothing to feel bad about. He did the almost impossible. He hid Ares for seventeen years. He helped keep him and Hera alive and protected from those who would surely have killed them. We still don't know what happened to the little girl, but I already know it wasn't Victor's fault.

Victor jerks his chin up, looking at Ares. "I'm sorry, son."

"I think that fucker Carter would have found me anyway." Ares rubs a hand along the back of his neck.

"Carter has been planning shit for a long time," I add. "I wouldn't be surprised if he knew where Hera and Ares were all along."

Hera sucks in a sharp breath as her eyes meet Victor's. "I should never have come back here."

"If you hadn't, we may still have lost Lili," Ares says. His body is locked tight, rigid with tension. I saw how Ash struggled—how she's still struggling—with all the Luminary revelations, and it's clear Ares is undergoing the same struggle. It's a lot to take in. I will try to remember that. To cut him some slack.

"Why did you return?" Ash asks what we are all thinking.

"My daughter had a rare form of cancer, and none of the traditional treatments were working for her in Europe. There was a new radical treatment available in the US, and Victor got us into the program. I knew it was a risk coming back, which is why I insisted Ares remain overseas. He went to England, and we came back here four years ago. Lili fully recovered, and no one was after us, so I got complacent. I thought we were okay, hiding in plain sight. That my changed appearance and our new IDs meant we had gotten away with it. Lili loved her school and her friends, and I wanted to give her permanence. We were all tired of life on the run."

Veins strain in Ares's neck as he glowers at his mother. "You lied to me about her kidnapping! You let me believe my father was in a gang and they had taken her! You let me waste over two years barking up the wrong tree! How could you do that to me! It's fucking obvious The Luminaries took her, and you sent me on a wild goose chase!" He thumps his hand on the coffee table, slamming it repeatedly in a fit of rage. "Do you even care about finding her?!"

"Of course, I care!" A sob escapes her mouth. "I have regretted my choices every single second of every day since she has been gone! I have second-guessed myself all the time. I never wanted you to come here, Ares! I tried to get you to stay away so they wouldn't find out about you."

"You should've been honest with me," Ares shouts at his mother as the rest of us watch without interrupting.

"I know." Tears roll down Hera's face. "I just couldn't face the thought of losing you too. If you knew what I had done, the lengths I had gone to, the lies I had told, I was afraid you would never speak to me again."

"Why don't I remember anything from the first five years of my life, Mother?" Ares hisses, narrowing his eyes at Hera. "Why was I told my father was killed by rival gangsters? Why have I been infiltrating local gangs trying to track Lili if the whole thing was complete and utter bullshit!?" He roars, thumping the table again, before he buries his head in his hands. "Was anything you told me the truth?" he asks in a quieter tone, his voice trembling a little.

Ash climbs off my lap and walks over to Ares. She sits beside him and snakes her arm around his back, leaning her head on his shoulder.

Ares inhales and exhales heavily before gradually picking his head up and threading his fingers in Ash's. They share a look, and I know what I'm seeing.

They are in love with one another.

I don't think either of them realizes it.

But I see it.

There has been a connection between them from the

second Ares entered our lives. It might have been fueled by hatred at the start, but it's come full circle.

Hera stares at Ares and Ashley with a look of shock on her face. I'm guessing she didn't know about them. Shaking herself out of it, she wets her lips and stares at her son with a pleading look. "You were there when your father was murdered. You saw it all go down." Tears stream down her face. "He died protecting you because you were his world. You were traumatized for months after it. You had nightmares, and you regularly woke up screaming. I didn't know what to do. I was grieving myself and ill-equipped to help you. I couldn't tell you about The Luminaries, but I had to give you some explanation for the nightmares, so I bent the truth. Told you the bad men were gangsters, rivals of your fathers." She looks away. "It wasn't my finest moment. When I realized I had only made things worse, I took you to a child psychologist, and she suggested hypnotherapy."

She reaches out, taking Ares's free hand in hers. He immediately yanks it back, pinning her with hurt-filled eyes. Ares is not usually emotional, but he is incapable of hiding his feelings in the face of such betrayal.

"It worked," Hera quietly says. "The nightmares stopped, and you became happy again. The memories are hidden in the deepest corners of your mind, along with any other memories you had of your early part of life. It was your mind's way of coping."

Ares stares at her in shock, and for once, he is speechless. I don't blame him.

"Your father was not murdered by a religious group," Hera continues. "He was murdered by The Luminaries because he broke their sacred rules when he married me."

"But they pardoned him for that. I remember my father explaining it to us," I blurt.

"Officially, he was pardoned, but they resented him for forcing their hand."

"I don't understand," Ash says, peering around Ares. "What do you mean?"

Ares clings to Ash as they wait for Hera to elaborate. "I was a plebeian. A normal non-Luminary person," she adds when she spots the confusion on Ares's face.

I keep forgetting he knows fuck all about our world.

"It was forbidden for an heir to marry anyone but their intended. I didn't know anything about The Luminaries at first. Clinton didn't tell me until his father died unexpectedly and he found himself thrust in the spotlight. He came to me that night, told me everything, and asked me to marry him immediately. I knew the risks. He didn't hold back in explaining. He told me we could all die for going against their traditions unless he could convince the board to make an exception based on my condition."

Her eyes glisten as she stares at Ares. "I had discovered I was pregnant ten days previously. Clint seemed happy but worried, and I didn't understand until that night when he told me it all." Her eyes fill with unshed tears. "He loved us enough to offer us options though I could see it was killing him to consider letting us go. He gave me a way out. He told me he would protect and provide for us forever even if I couldn't give up my life to marry him. He told me he understood and he would never hold it against me."

Hera breaks down, sobbing, and it's hard to bear witness to. Victor clearly agrees as he gets up, perching on the arm of the couch and holding Hera as he consoles her. She wipes at her damp eyes a few minutes later, accepting a handkerchief from Victor. "Perhaps I am a terrible mother because I couldn't give Clint up. I took the risk. I married him that same night, knowing we all could die."

Tension bleeds into the air, but no one says anything.

Hera blows her nose into the hankie before composing herself. "Your father smoothed it all over. He was given special dispensation, and the board agreed to let it pass. Clint never got complacent though. He knew some of the heirs weren't happy about it. He suspected they were biding their time to retaliate. He just never expected his younger brother to betray him."

I sit up straighter. "Are you saying Walter killed Clinton?"

"We have never been able to prove it, but we believe so," Victor replies. "Walter was always envious of Clinton growing up. He was an arrogant son-of-a-bitch even as a kid. He had a heightened sense of his own importance, and he hated how lenient Clint was." Victor leans back in his seat, blowing air out of his mouth. "Clint was a great Luminary, and he would have achieved so many amazing things if he hadn't been taken out in his prime."

"How did the others let him get away with it?" Bree says. "Surely, they must have known what happened? You can't kill a Luminary. It's one of our most sacred rules."

"They may have given Clint special dispensation," Hera says, "but it sat uneasy with them. They hadn't really had a choice at the time. Clint had made sure of it."

"The board was split down the middle, and if Stewart and Manford had forced the issue, if they had demanded retribution for the killing, it would have meant all-out war." Victor looks at me. "You should talk to your father. He can tell you more, but ultimately, James and Eric chose to believe the bullshit Carter and Salinger were peddling for the greater good."

Ash perks up. "Carter was involved too?"

Victor nods. "Don't ever underestimate a scorned woman."

"What the fuck does that mean?" Ares demands to know.

"Cleo Carter was supposed to have married Clinton," Hera

says. "She was only paired with Rhett, a few years later, after his arranged marriage to Pamela fell asunder."

"Rhett doesn't need much incentive to break the rules and usurp his peers," Victor continues, "but avenging his new bride gave him the credibility to feel justified in plotting with Walter Salinger to kill his brother and take his crown."

A muscle clenches in Hera's jaw. "And Manford and Stewart let them get away with it."

Chapter Ten

Ares

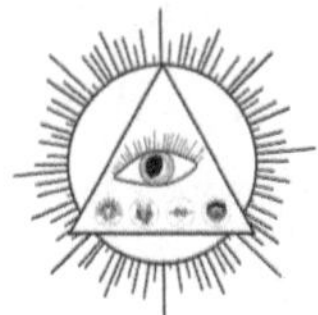

My head is about to explode with all this new knowledge, and I'm itching to gut a few motherfuckers. Every muscle in my body is stretched tight with rage and a deep sense of futility. Right now, my priority is getting my sister back. Everything else can wait.

"If you knew The Luminaries had taken Lili, why did you have me chasing the wrong leads?" I ask Mom, working hard to keep calm. It's challenging because those bastards have had my innocent little sister for almost three years, and I'm ready to slaughter the world to get her back. I don't know if I can ever forgive my mother for lying to me about it. If I'd known the truth, we might have found Lili already.

"You're not chasing the wrong leads," Victor replies. "If The Luminaries are behind this, they have covered their tracks well."

"What do you mean *if*?" I lean forward, clenching and unclenching my fists. Ash sits pressed up against me with her hand on my thigh. Mom is staring at it but trying not to make it obvious.

"We have found nothing to link her abduction to them," Mom says, stifling a yawn. Daylight has set outside, and night is steadily creeping in. It's been another long-ass day, and I can tell everyone wants to get out of here.

"So what? She was just a random victim?" Disbelief drips from my tone. "I don't believe in coincidences."

"I don't either, but it seemed unlikely they were involved." Victor scrubs his hands down his face. "Discovering Carter is aware of your identities changes things," he admits.

"How old was your sister when she was taken?" Bree asks.

"Ten." I squeeze my eyelids shut for a few seconds. It pains me to remember her beautiful smiling face, knowing I may never see that version of my sister ever again. I cannot even consider the kinds of things she has endured since we last saw her.

"I don't mean to be insensitive, but if you suspect she was trafficked, our father might be able to help," Bree says.

"How?" I snap, blinking my eyes open.

Ash slides her arm around my shoulders and presses a kiss to my cheek. It's surprisingly comforting, and I can't decide whether I like it or loathe it. A part of me wants to shove her away from me while another part wants to cling to her and never let go.

I am not used to this.

We are used to fending for ourselves.

Attachments were never formed in any of the places we lived because we were never there long enough. Getting close to people invited too many questions, so we stayed in our own little bubble.

I know I don't people well, and I don't play nice because I've never had to.

I lived by myself from the time I was seventeen. Xavier is the only friend I made during my time in Boston. There were women. Girls I fucked and tossed aside, forgetting their names by the next morning. But I was still my own island. I was there to find leads to where my sister had disappeared to, and I didn't have the time to form connections.

I never wanted to either.

I don't get close to people, yet Ashley Shaw has wormed her way under my skin and into my heart.

It terrifies me as much as it pisses me off and excites me.

"Ares." Ashley's seductive tone wafts around my body like a security blanket. "Did you hear what Bree said?"

"Repeat it," I command, staring at the woman I'm supposed to be saying "I do" to.

Bree purses her lips at my tone but doesn't call me out on my shit. "Our family responsibility is Lust & Envy. Sex trafficking is something our family works to shut down, not to encourage."

"We lure predators out using bait," Jase explains. "And then we take them down and free the victims. If Carter or any of the other Luminaries were thwarting the rules and running their own rings, my father would know about it. It wouldn't be tolerated."

"Which is what he said when I spoke to him, just after Lili was taken," Victor says. "Your father did some digging, and he found nothing. It was why I was so sure it wasn't Luminary connected. Children are revered in our society, and though some rules are bent, I have never seen any evidence that this one has."

"Please." I scoff. "From what I've heard so far, those rules are made to be broken. The only ones who seem to be held accountable to them are the people below the Luminary rank."

"Ares has a point," Ash agrees. "And we know Carter is the biggest rule breaker of all." She looks over at Jase. "Plus, he seems to have done tons of stuff the other Luminaries don't know about. There is no guarantee your father would know. Not if Carter was able to cover his tracks." Jase frowns as he considers her words. I turn sideways to look at her, watching her mind churning as she taps her finger idly on her chin. Her eyes lift to mine. "If Carter has known who you are for a long time, it's not inconceivable he is behind Lilianna's kidnapping."

"Except my daughter isn't a Luminary. She's a plebeian," Hera says.

"Maybe he took her as a warning," Jase muses.

"Or to use as bait to draw you out," Bree adds. Her eyes quickly meet mine before darting away.

"If he took her as some kind of leverage, why hasn't he played his hand?" Vincent—Ash's trainer—asks.

"He was biding his time," Ash says. "Getting all his ducks in a row."

"If that's the case, then he'll show that hand soon," Jase says.

"I'm not sitting around waiting for it to happen." I crack my knuckles as I growl under my breath. "We need to get my sister out now."

"Ares needs to get into the prison to meet with Ruben. He could be the link we need to move forward quickly." Mom looks up at Victor. "Can you make that happen now?"

"Why the fuck didn't he make it happen before?" I bark, enraged all over again. I stand and glare at Mom and Victor. "I have spent the past year ingratiating myself to Shoulders and Rocky so I could get an in with The Bulls. I spent months sucking up to that prick Marwan, trying to get a meeting with their old prez, and you could've gotten me in to see him without any of that bullshit?" I start pacing, trying to expend some of this reckless, restless energy coursing through my veins.

"It would have raised red flags and brought too much heat,"

Victor says. "We had to tread carefully to avoid arousing suspicion."

"I don't give a flying fuck!" I shout. "My little sister has been held by monsters for almost three years! You had resources available to find her, and you did nothing." I shove at his shoulders, ready to knock him the fuck into next week, only Stewart hops up and pulls me back.

"Do you really want to waste more time talking about all the ways things should have gone or get the right people on the case now so we can find out where she is?" Jase tries to reason with me.

"This is bullshit, and you know it." I shove him away from me.

"We have done our best!" Mom stands. "The trail led to Boston, and we found Jasper Baldwin through that investigation. Jasper led us to The Bulls, and it was The Bulls who took her. They are the key here. Someone in that gang must know where she was sent."

"Pity most of them are now dead!" I roar, losing the tenuous hold on my control.

"We tried that angle and got nowhere. I had someone on the inside meet with Ruben, and he refused to say a single word." Victor rises and walks up to me. "We could have threatened them, ended them, or done any manner of other things to get The Bulls to talk, but they wouldn't have. Gang members are loyal to the bitter end. The Bulls had recently been shafted by The Sainthood, and they trusted no one. My hands were largely tied. It's a balancing act because I can't draw attention to myself. If I do, questions will be asked that could lead back to your mom and you. I have tried to avoid that."

"You should have exhausted every possible option." Folding my arms across my chest, I stare him down.

"The trail would've gone stone-cold if we'd driven The

Bulls into extinction. Having you infiltrate them from the inside was deemed to be the best route to source the information we needed. I still stand by that."

"Fuck you." I shove him. "Fuck you, you prick. I don't care if my father trusted you. You left my sister with monsters and kept me in the dark when we could have been doing so much more."

Eerie silence trickles into the fraught air.

"We'll talk to Baz," Jase says. "We'll go see him tomorrow. He'll get you into the prison on the down-low. It won't look suspicious if it's set up by Lust & Envy."

Ash looks deep in thought, but whatever it is, she's not sharing it with us.

"It's late," Vincent says. "We should make tracks. Our men have cleaned your house and set the cameras up to run old footage on a loop. We took footage from both houses, and our tech team edited them so they are fit for purpose. Carter won't realize it's not live feeds he's watching, so you're safe now. No one will know you were here with us. If anyone looks, it will look like you were all at home today, because I don't trust him not to check up on you. We have a guy stationed at the house, and he says the coast is clear so far, but I don't want to tempt fate."

"We can take a few more minutes," Victor says. "There is more we need to handle." His face shines with sympathy as he looks at Mom, and I'm not relishing the thought of the chat I need to have with her.

I'm seriously pissed at her. In a way I have never been before. But she's still my mom. She has endured hardships to keep us safe all these years, and we were all each other had. I'm fuming she kept so many secrets, but I know her heart was in the right place even if she made some terrible decisions. I can't turn my back on her. Not after everything she has done for me.

Some of my anger flitters away, but forgiveness is still a long way away.

"What did Carter say when he took you?" Victor asks. "What exactly does he want?"

You could hear a pin drop in the room until Ash says, "To tell me I'm his biological daughter and he has plans to install Ares as the rightful heir so he can have more control over the board or something." Ash shrugs, deliberately downplaying it.

And I get it. We can't trust any of these people. Mom included, because she seems far too reliant on the Fox brothers.

"You're Carter's blood?" Vincent's eyes pop wide. He shares a look with his brother. "I wonder if that's why Eric asked me to train her?"

"Hold on." Jase frowns. "My dad set that up?"

Vincent nods. "He asked me for a favor, and I didn't question it too much. He told me Ashley was a late initiate and she needed to be trained."

"Do you think your father knows?" Ash's gaze bounces between Bree and Jase.

"Fuck if I know anything." Jase throws up his hands in exasperation, and I'm feeling it too.

"Watch out for Walter and Toby," Victor cautions. His Adam's apple bobs in his throat. "You can't trust anything Carter says even if it seems like the current Pride & Wrath Luminary and his heir don't appear to know you're Clint's son. Stay off their radar, and avoid them for now. I would put a couple of men shadowing you, but I suspect Carter has eyes on you, and I don't want to arouse suspicion."

"You can't." Ash clamps a hand over her mouth as she yawns. "He warned us not to say anything to anyone, and we think it's best we at least appear to play the game his way."

"Agreed." Victor reaches a hand down to help her to her feet. "Give your concussion a few days to settle, and then resume your sessions with Vincent." He looks around at all of us. "It wouldn't hurt for all of you to attend too. We should be prepared for anything."

The sound of a chopper approaching draws everyone's attention to the window.

"Our ride back to the city is here." Vincent taps on his earpiece, disappearing outside through a door at the back of the sunroom, talking in low tones.

"I won't be coming with you." Mom takes my hands in hers. "It's too dangerous for me now. Victor is taking me to one of his safe houses until we know more about the threat." She pulls Ash over beside us. "I know you love your dad, but I can't do this without him. I need him to come with me. I promise I won't keep him away from you forever, and Ares will look after you." A knowing look crosses over her face. "I can see you two have grown close. It pleases me that you have put aside your differences, but we probably need to have a conversation at some point."

"We need to have a conversation now, Ma," I say, purposely lowering my voice. Jase reaches for Ash, but she shakes her head, sticking close to my side. He clamps a hand down on my shoulder as he walks past with Bree, heading out the door Vincent disappeared through.

"Do you want me to stay?" Victor asks, looking between Ash and me.

"We've got this," I say with more confidence than I feel.

We wait for Victor to exit the room before ushering Mom to the couch. We sit on either side of her, and I'm glad Ash is here for this. I don't know if I could do this alone.

"What's wrong?" Mom's face has turned ashen. "You're scaring me." Her panicked gaze flickers between both of us. "What is it?"

Silent tears pour down Ashley's cheeks as she looks to me to say the words.

"I'm so sorry, Ma. There's no easy way to tell you this. Doug is gone. He was gunned down in the ambush on the road at Rhett Carter's instructions."

Chapter Eleven
Ashley

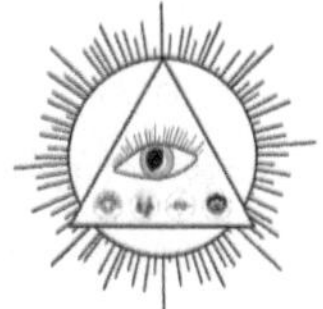

I cling to Jase in the helicopter as the pilot takes us back to Lowell, sobbing my heart out as the pain of Dad's passing flays me on all sides. Witnessing Hera's soul crack apart right in front of us irreparably altered me. She self-destructed before our eyes. As long as I live, I will never forget the harrowing sound of her tortured cries as she fell to her knees and screamed.

Victor and Vincent stayed behind to transport her to her new lodgings, so it's only the four of us heading back home.

Ares is in a trance. I don't know if it's his usual coping mechanism or if his mind has just shut down from such a massive overload. I tried holding on to him, needing to comfort him, but he swatted me away. He hasn't moved a muscle since we took to the air, leaning against the window and staring at the blackened night sky outside.

I won't push him.

He knows I am here if he needs me.

I understand needing space to work through your feelings, and he's grieving too.

For his real dad.

For mine.

And for the loss of his sister.

Now his mom has to leave for her safety, and he can't be the one to console her. I know that must be killing him because those two are close.

When we land, a black SUV is waiting at the private airfield to drive us the rest of the way home. We climb in without a word. I sit in between Ares and Jase, holding each of their hands. Bree is tapping away on her cell phone, and the air is heavy with anxiety and everything we still need to say.

"I ordered takeout," Bree says when the SUV deposits us at the front door of the townhome we all now share. "It'll be here in fifteen minutes if anyone wants to freshen up."

"We should grab our stuff from next door," Jase says as I turn my key in the lock and open the front door.

"There's no need," I say, entering the hallway. "Your stuff is already here." I gesture toward the bags and boxes stacked neatly against the wall.

Ares yanks his shirt over his head, stomping off up the stairs without uttering a word.

"Poor guy," Bree says. "He's had a ton of shit dumped on his lap, and he's clearly heartbroken over his little sister."

"I wanted to ask about Jasper," Jase says, closing and locking the door. "But I didn't want to say too much in front of the others, and I honestly don't think he can take much more of the heavy today."

"It's been a lot for all of us but especially Ares," I say. "Perhaps we should pay Chad's mom a visit? We need to check in on them anyway."

"We'll drop by tomorrow," Jase agrees.

"Ares is going to need you in the weeks ahead," Bree says, walking toward the kitchen.

"He needs all of us." I snuggle into Jase's side, fighting a yawn as we enter the kitchen. My head is pounding, my belly is rumbling, and my limbs are twitchy with a host of unspent emotions. I had a good cry on the chopper, but there's still a maelstrom churning inside me, looking for an outlet.

Grabbing a bottle of water from the refrigerator, I turn to face the Stewart siblings. "We need to be united. We can't defeat Carter or rescue Chad and Lilianna if we are not a solid team. I don't care what issues we have. They are either in the past or we will resolve them in the future. Nothing else matters but focusing on our agenda." I drill Jase with a look. "That shit with Ares today can't happen again. I know I was mad too, but honestly, in the grand scheme of things, it's barely a blip."

"It's not a blip, Temptress." Jase reaches over my head, removing the medical box from the cupboard. "It was an asshole move, but I hear what you're saying, and I agree. Not sure Chad will when we get him back, but we can cross that bridge then." He hands me two pain pills. "Take them, my love, and go grab a shower." He kisses the tip of my nose. "Bree and I will set the table."

"We need to do something about Chad," I say before popping the pills and swallowing a mouthful of water. The longer that sick bitch has him, the more I worry. I don't know what state he'll be in when we get him back. We need to get him out before he is traumatized for life.

"I'm already on it," Jase confirms. "Bree and I pooled our resources, and we have a team of guys discreetly delving into Cleo Carter, trying to locate where she's keeping him. Once we know that and the lay of the land, we can plan his escape." He bundles me into a warm hug. "Don't worry. He'll be home with us before Christmas. I promise."

Placing my hands on his chest, I tip my chin up and peer

into his gorgeous green eyes. "That's only six days away, Jase. Don't make promises you can't keep."

"I fully intend to keep that promise, babe. He can't be far. We'll get him out."

"This isn't our first rodeo," Bree adds, pulling silverware out of the drawer. "Keep the faith."

"We'll have to stash him in a safe house too because Carter can't know we have him. I don't want to rescue him for Chad to be taken again—or worse."

"We'll keep him safe." Jase pats me on the ass. "Now shoo. You look beat. Grab a shower and get changed, and we'll have dinner on the table when you come back."

I'm battling sleep the entire way up the stairs. I'm a little surprised to find my door open and steam wafting from the en suite bathroom when I reach my master bedroom. I'm even more surprised to find the tub filled to the brim, scented oil skimming the surface of the water and swirling around the giant of a man filling the space.

Ares stares at me as I shed my clothes, and his heated stare is a sensual caress against my skin. His gaze is glued to the healing brands over my chest and my upper arm. We lock eyes, and I see the question there. But he doesn't want to ask it now. He can't handle it, and neither can I. Not today. Not when we have already dealt with so much of the heavy stuff. A shiver works its way through me at the thought of his initiation, and bile swims up my throat.

"Come here," he says in a deep, commanding tone while he rests his muscular tattooed arms on the side of the tub and sits up straighter, making room for me.

Water sloshes over the edge as I get into the bath, gingerly lowering myself down in between his legs. A moan slips from my lips as the warm water soothes my aches and pains. I lean back against him, drawing comfort and warmth from the strength of his hard body behind me. His dick is erect, nudging against my ass, inviting my libido to come out to play.

"Ares?" I tilt my head back and up so I'm looking at him. "I'm not going to ask if you're okay, because that's a stupid question, but what can I do?"

His jaw clenches as his eyes darken with unspoken need. His eyes are more brown than green today with those little amber flecks I'm so fascinated with. We move as one, and our lips collide in a feverish kiss as his hands roam my naked body. His tongue prods the seam of my lips, and I open for him, our tongues immediately tangling as his fingers skate over my belly to cup my mound.

"This," he murmurs, briefly breaking our lip-lock. "This is what you can do."

I whimper into his mouth when he parts my folds with one hand while a finger glides up and down my slit. He bites down on my lip before covering my mouth and swallowing my gasps as he roughly shoves three fingers inside me, pumping them in and out with urgency.

Yes! This is what I need. What we both need, and Ares's magical fingers are the perfect remedy.

We devour one another with lips, teeth, and tongues, and I arch my head back, stretching my neck as he bites, licks, and sucks his way up and down my neck while his fingers plunder my pussy with expert precision. My orgasm is building fast. My body is strung tight like a bow, ready to snap in record-breaking time.

"Come for me, slutty little sis," he rasps over my lips as he thrusts his hips forward, grinding his hard-on against my lower back. "Come all over my hand." Curling his fingers inside me, he hits the perfect spot, and I'm moaning and writhing as he works my body like a pro. Stars burst behind my retinas, and I'm cresting higher and higher, bucking my hips, ignoring the throbbing ache on one side, as I focus solely on my impending climax.

I cry out as I tumble over the ledge, my back arching, legs quivering, and chest heaving as the most glorious release ghosts over me. Water leaks over the edge of the tub onto the tile floor. Ares's skillful fingers continue milking my inner walls until every drop of my orgasm is wrenched from my overwrought body.

Wordlessly, he lifts me out of the tub in his arms. He grabs a couple of towels as he brings me into the bedroom. Setting my feet on the carpeted floor, he takes his time drying me before dragging the towel quickly across his wet body. "On your knees, dollface," he demands, wrapping his hand around his hard dick and slowly stroking his erection. "I need to come down your throat."

I sink to my knees without hesitation, guiding his pierced shaft toward my mouth. His hand goes to the back of my head, but his urgent touch is tender, and his concern brings different tears to my eyes. Opening my mouth wide to accommodate his thick girth, I swallow him down, taking as much of him in as I can. My fingers wind around the base of his cock as I suck up and down his length, my tongue tracing around the ladder on the underside of his shaft. I look up, and a burst of pride warms my chest when I see the look of absolute joy on his face as he pivots his hips, driving his cock into my mouth, with his eyes closed, savoring every second of the pleasure I'm giving him.

I know some girls hate giving head, and I would never judge anyone for that, to each their own, etcetera, but there is nothing more enjoyable or more powerful than blowing a guy knowing you are giving him the ultimate pleasure ride and rocking his world. It's a heady sensation. One I'm addicted to.

I'd eat cock for breakfast, lunch, and dinner times three if given the chance.

The thought should surprise me, but it doesn't.

Deep down, I have wanted this.

I want all three of them.

It might be a tall order, considering all the lies, secrets, and betrayals that hang between us, but I have never been the kind of girl to back down from a challenge.

Ares's thrusting becomes more vicious and my jaw aches as I work to toss him over the edge. My hand pumps the base of his dick while he fucks my mouth. His eyes pop open, filling with pride and raw hunger, as he watches me swallow his erection with tears leaking from my eyes and saliva dribbling down my chin and the sides of my mouth. The sound of skin slapping against skin and my muffled moans as I slurp up and down his dick sends liquid lust pooling in my lower belly and my groin, and I know I'm going to need another fix after dinner.

"Fuck, you look so good with my dick shoved down your throat." Ares leans down, pinching one hard nipple. "Get ready." I cup his balls and run one finger back and forth along his taint, feeling him tense up as the moment arrives. A couple of seconds later, he shouts out as he spills his hot seed down my throat. His grip on the back of my head is tighter, and pain rattles through my skull, but I don't mind. Enduring some pain to give him pleasure is a small price to pay.

When he's done, he lifts me up under the arms, reels me into his chest, and slams his lips down on mine.

"Knock, knock," Jase says, tapping lightly on the wood. "Sorry to interrupt, but the takeout is here, and dinner is served."

I turn around, spotting my soon-to-be husband standing in the doorway watching us. His eyes flare with desire, and he is doing nothing to conceal the noticeable bulge tenting his sweatpants. Jase smirks. "That was hot."

Ares growls and flips him the bird. "That wasn't for your eyes."

"You're a funny guy." Jase's grin widens as he cocks a brow. "Close the door if you don't want an observer," he suggests, winking at me before heading back downstairs. I expected him to call Ares out on his hypocrisy, but the fact he didn't pleases me. Jase is making an effort, and it hasn't gone unnoticed.

I know, of the three men, he will be the one least concerned with sharing me. Ares and Chad, however, are a different matter entirely. Assuming Ares actually wants any kind of a relationship and Chad and I can find a way to put the sins of our past behind us to move forward.

The situation is precarious with all three of the guys, for different reasons, so nothing is set in stone.

"I don't share." Ares is grumpy as fuck as he gathers up his clothes from where he dumped them on the floor.

"Not yet you don't." My grin is smug as I walk past him naked, heading into my closet.

"Dream on, slutster."

I bark out a laugh, turning to face him in the entryway to my closet. "It's not a dream. It's going to be a reality, and I'll have you eating your words before you know it."

He mutters under his breath, sending me a glare as he stalks out of my room with my laughter following him.

Chapter Twelve

Chad

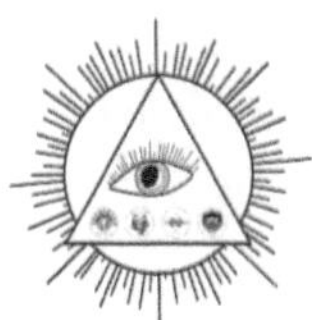

The dick with the bald head, beady eyes, and protruding stomach opens my cage and slides a bowl of slop inside along with a second bowl of water. The taller, stockier man cracks his knuckles as he pins me with a gloating expression, daring me to try something. But I'm not an idiot. There is no point attempting to fight when I'm naked, cold, and weak. All that would do is guarantee me a beating.

If I stand any chance of escaping, and that's a big if because security is tight, I need to keep my strength and my wits about me.

Disappointed I'm not starting something, the two goons slam the cage door shut, smirking as they rake their eyes over me. I'm not worried they will do anything. The boss bitch has her dogs well trained. Although I have no way of telling the time, I'd guess I have only been here a couple of days. In that time, the guard shift has rotated twice. Two men per shift, and they alternate between day and night.

I haven't seen that fucking bitch since she took me into the red room and did shit to me I will take to my grave. Bile travels up my throat at the memory, but I swat it aside. No good will come from reliving it, so I have been doing my best to forget it ever happened. Repositioning my cramped limbs—as much as I can within the confines of this square cage—I kneel in front of the two bowls, trying to convince myself the beige lumpy mess is not something you'd only feed to a dog. Scooping it up with my fingers, I shovel it in my mouth and force myself to swallow it.

It tastes even worse than it looks, but I force it down until every morsel is gone.

Then I drink from the bowl of water, downing it in one go, attempting to wash the gritty, dry taste from my mouth.

I lean back, rubbing my belly, not even close to full, watching the two goons distributing the rest of dinner to my fellow prisoners. No one mounts any protest or attempts to rebel. If anyone had been so inclined, the way the man who was in the cage beside me had been butchered has dealt with it. No one speaks because everyone is afraid it will be them next.

I think the solitude and boredom might kill me before starvation or that depraved bitch. Closing my eyes, I visualize Ash in my mind's eye because her face and our memories are the only things keeping me sane.

Remembering nights spent snuggled together on the couch watching a movie.

Candlelit dinners at our favorite Italian restaurant.

Dancing drunk with her at parties, grinding up against her as she laughed and threw her arms around my neck.

Cooking side by side as we talked about our day.

The way her face would pull into a proud smile when she cheered for me from the bleachers during games.

Going to sleep beside her and waking up with her in my arms.

Her puffy cheeks and exaggerated breaths when she would attempt to keep pace with me while we jogged.

Kissing for hours on end. Only breaking apart when we needed oxygen or we were at risk of lockjaw.

Holding her when she cried because her parents weren't there for some milestone.

Sneaking sly looks at her while we were both meant to be studying, in awe of her intense focus and admiring how stunning she was.

Driving all over the state, scouting ideal locations for her photography.

Taking bubble baths together, daydreaming about our future and all the things we were going to do.

Swimming in Tahoe and Clear Lake during summer break, when we would spend hours in the water, with Ash using my shoulders as her own personal diving board.

Long summer nights spent at the beach, huddled around firepits, sipping beers with our friends and shooting the shit.

Posing for copious pics and letting her use me as her guinea pig while she was learning about lighting and positions.

Walking hand in hand around school, beaming at one another like lovesick fools because I was her everything in the same way she was mine.

I was constantly pinching myself because I couldn't believe she loved me. I couldn't believe I was the one she chose. That this gorgeous girl smiling up at me was my forever, because it often felt too good to be true.

Pain spears me through the chest, and my heart throbs behind my rib cage. Since Dad died, I've been sleepwalking through my life. Barely conscious of all the bad decisions I was making. Pushing the only girl who matters away. I haven't been a good boyfriend to Ash for a while now. I was so wrapped up in my own shit I neglected her and let her down. Allowing pride and hurt to dictate my actions when I discovered what had happened with Ares.

Honestly, it's no wonder he was able to get to her. I haven't loved my girl the way she deserves. All that shit with Jase didn't help either. We left her vulnerable and alone and susceptible to that prick.

I hate he's the one comforting her now. I have no one to blame but myself. If I get the chance, I am going to make it up to her. I am going to be the man she needs me to be, and I'm not losing her again.

I don't even know if she's okay. She was injured, and then assholes ambushed her on the road.

Has Ash been taken too?

Are they all here someplace?

What about my mom and Tessa? Who will look after them if I never return home.

Although it's hard, I shove those thoughts aside. I can't afford to sink into a black hole. I can't lose hope. I've got to believe I'll get out of here because I need to take care of my family and I need to win back the heart of the only girl who exists for me.

The creaking of my cage door drags me out of my head.

"It's showtime, pretty boy." The short, bald dude grabs me out of the cage by my feet while the other guy looms over me with his hand at the holster attached to his side. My hips, one arm, and the side of my head slam against the cage as he pulls me out, causing tremors of pain to shoot through my body, but I don't cry out, biting down on my lips to trap my painful groans. I'm yanked unceremoniously to my feet, and my aching muscles protest the movement. I grab the wall to stop myself from falling as I straighten up, attempting to loosen the kinks from my sore limbs.

The taller dude grabs my arm and thrusts me forward, and

I almost face-plant the ground. The men chuckle, and how I wish I had Jase and my baseball bat with me. We'd turn these fuckers into a bloody pile on the floor. I make a silent promise that, when I get out, I'm coming back to teach these pricks a lesson.

Working hard to ignore my aching body, I straighten my spine and focus on my surroundings as they lead me out of the room. The fact they don't restrain me is telling. They have the utmost confidence no one can better them or escape. I'm praying their arrogance is just that and not the truth.

This time, we turn left down the dimly lit hallway. The previous time, we had turned right. I catalog everything as we walk, counting the doors we pass and noting the position of cameras mounted high on the walls.

I'm yanked to a halt outside a black-painted door, and the first goon raps hard on it.

"You can come in." Her voice is like nails scraping down my back, and acid crawls up my throat at the thought of what she has lined up for me today.

The shorter guy pulls me into the softly lit room. Madame X, as she instructed me to call her, is sitting on a black velvet couch, dressed in another black PVC outfit with a multitude of straps crisscrossing over and around her hideous fake tits, leaving little to the imagination. Fishnet tights and high-heeled ankle boots complete her look. Her face is plastered in makeup, and her painted red lips look cartoonish. Dark hair combed back into a tight, high ponytail pulls her face taut, highlighting the extensive work she's had done. It's a miracle she can even move her face.

Bile collects at the back of my throat, and my eyes narrow at the tub resting in the middle of the space. To one side is a table with toys, chains, whips, clamps, and a variety of collars.

"Close the door," she commands, looking at me as she

instructs her two minions. The men take a few steps back, and I hear the bolt engaging as the door is locked.

I am rooted to the spot, unable to move, and my hands twitch with the need to cover my dick as her hungry eyes rake over me from head to toe. But I refuse to cower in front of this bitch. I won't let her see how every look, every forbidden touch, every intrusive action, has the power to kill me inside.

She hasn't forced me to touch her yet, but I'm guessing that must be coming soon.

Standing, she sashays toward me, holding a soft leather whip in her hand. "My pretty new toy," she purrs, planting her hand on my chest as she leans in to lick a path up and down my neck. "It's playtime," she adds before pressing her lips to mine. I keep my mouth sealed shut as she kisses me, attempting to pry my lips apart. "Kiss me," she growls, her displeasure evident in her tone and the way her hand immediately moves around to my ass. Her finger breaches my hole, and I tense all over. "Submit to me, or this will not be pleasant for you."

I bark out a laugh. "None of it is pleasant. You make me sick. Is this how you get your rocks off, you fucked-up bitch? Kidnapping and forcing younger men to be with you? Is this how you try to tell yourself you're not old and past your prime?" I spotted the band on her ring finger the first time she assaulted me, and later my cell buddy confirmed she was Rhett Carter's wife. "Is this how you try to rationalize it in your head because your husband has no interest in you anymore?" I have no clue what their marriage is like, so I'm projecting, but no happily married woman would resort to these measures unless her husband was as sick as her, and I haven't seen him around.

Based on the high-level security, it's clear she's gone to a lot of trouble to hide this part of her life. From the look of pure rage on her face, I'm guessing I struck gold. Time to really stick the knife in. "It's no wonder he doesn't want you anymore.

Face-lifts, strict diets, and tacky PVC clothes can't disguise the fact you're undesirable. Ugly and old. Washed up and unwanted. Desperate and pathetic."

A stinging pain rattles across my face and through my skull as she slaps me full force. Repeatedly. While she screams and hurls obscenities at me.

Wow, I have really hit a nerve.

Good to know.

I derive enormous satisfaction knowing I have ruffled her feathers and caused her to lose control. I smirk as she continues to slap me, her face showcasing her pain and her anger as she uses me like a personal punching bag.

I don't mind. I'd take this over her grabby hands on me any day.

"Get him in the tub," she commands her goons at the door when she finally calms down.

I spew more vitriol at her as they attempt to get me into the water. I make it as difficult as possible for them, lashing out with my arms and my legs. I know I didn't retaliate back in the main room, but I'm not going to just stand here and let her assault me. One of the dicks tases me, and it fucking hurts like a bitch. Spasms rock my body as I lose control of my limbs.

Water drips all over the floor by the time they get me in the tub, chaining my ankles and wrists so I can't move.

"You displease me." She brings her whip down across one arm in a vicious blow.

Pain darts all over my flesh, but I bite on the inside of my cheek to trap my cries.

"This will hurt a lot more if you don't comply." Removing a washcloth and some bodywash from the table, she kneels beside the tub as her minions' hover in the background. "I will give you one final chance to submit. Do what I say, and you'll enjoy this, I promise."

"Eat shit and die, bitch."

She shoves my head under the water, pushing me down when I attempt to come up, my arms and legs fighting against the restraints to no avail. I'm panicking and gasping for air when she finally lets me up. Grabbing my head, she dries me off before gagging me. The two goons grin at me anytime she isn't looking, and I hate they get to witness my humiliation.

As she starts washing me, I plot creative ways in my head to kill all three of them. Rubbing the soapy cloth all over me, she washes me carefully in a way that is wholly intimate and makes me hugely uncomfortable. Her touch has been rough and painful so far, but I think I prefer that to this soft caressing.

I can handle her hurting me, but this is intolerable.

She's touching me as she would touch a lover, and I hate it.

If Knight Carter *is* related to Rhett, that means this cunt is his mother. I am only a year older than her son, and that makes her the sickest bitch on the planet.

I shout against the gag, my eyes piercing her with every ounce of hatred swirling in my veins. Her lips tuck up at the corners as she continues her sensual assault, slowly lowering the cloth down my body, lingering when she reaches my cock, cleaning it more thoroughly than the rest of me.

Her eyes glow with wicked intent as she drags the cloth over my inner thighs and down my legs before traveling back up. Leaning across me, she pulls the cloth tight, seesawing it back and forth, across, and around my cock, licking her lips as she watches my dick come to life.

I try to think of mundane and gross things to halt my natural reaction, but I'm losing the fight when she wraps her hand around my semi-erect dick, stroking it to full mast. Tears stab me behind the eyes, and I'm screaming inside. Roaring at my body to stop reacting to her touch.

I fight again as her minions remove me from the water, but

they keep the restraints on my ankles and my wrists, so it's futile.

They strap me to some tall vertical contraption with levers and bars until I'm standing before her with my legs spread-eagled and my arms secured to a hook overhead. Other straps secure my upper body to the device, so I can't move at all.

She glances at the men. "Bow before me and then leave us." Like well-trained puppies, they drop to their knees and kiss her boots. She dismisses them with a wave of her hands, and they exit the room.

The bitch trails a whip all over my body, forcing me into a heightened state of arousal as she drags the soft leather across my flesh, and her other hand strokes my dick until it's fully hard. Pain obliterates me on the inside as she parts the cheeks of my ass and takes her time rubbing lube all over my hole. Her fingers are cold as she pushes two inside me, and I squeeze my eyes shut, trying to ignore the invasion. A low hum starts up from behind, and panic replaces the blood flowing through my veins as I feel something vibrating at my ass.

I cry out behind my gag as a foreign object is slowly forced into my hole, latching on to the indescribable pain so I don't think about her dropping to her knees in front of me and taking my dick into her mouth.

Chapter Thirteen
Ashley

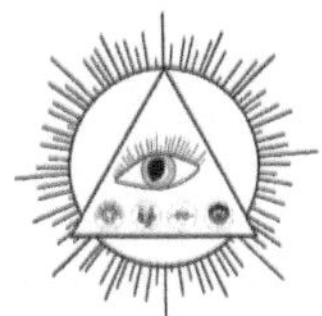

We are eating takeout in silence in the kitchen when armed men burst through the front and back doors of the house. For fuck's sake. What now? We barely have time to scramble off our stools before twenty guns are pointed at all our heads. Adrenaline courses through my veins, and butterflies run amok in my chest as I trade panicked expressions with Jase. Four men grab Ares and manhandle him to his knees as Rhett Carter saunters into the kitchen, looking like he hasn't just scared the living daylights out of all of us.

"What the hell?" I scream at my father. "Was this really necessary?"

Ignoring me, he strides over to Ares, grabbing his chin and tipping his head up. Ares is thrashing against the arms holding him on the ground, trying to break free, uncaring there are five guns trained on him. "Where is your mother, and who helped her to escape?" Carter asks, gripping his chin tight.

"How the fuck would I know?" Ares hisses.

"I was very clear in my instructions," he calmly replies,

pulling a gun out and pointing it at Ares's forehead. "I told you we play by my rules and my rules only. Now, I won't ask again. Where is your mother?"

"Are you for real right now?" I ask, driving my elbow back into the stomach of the guy standing behind me. I have guns trained on me too, but no one is going to shoot me. Or any of us, for that matter.

This is all for show.

Carter needs us alive.

At least for now.

Pushing past the armed men, I make my way around the island and put myself in front of my father. "Let him go. This is ridiculous. If Hera has escaped, good for her, but we had nothing to do with it." I plant my hands on my hips. "Unless you've forgotten how you ambushed us and held us prisoners for hours in the crypt? You brought us back here, and we've been hanging around the house all day." I jut my lip out and challenge him with a stare. "Go check the cameras if you don't believe us. My dad put them all over the place for my protection." I glare at him, visualizing riddling his body with bullets and stabbing him all over.

It helps, a little.

The sperm donor stares me down, and I dish it back at him and then some. "You saw Ares's reaction at the crypt. He knew none of this. Whatever you think he's done, you're wrong. Now let him go, or you'll have an even bigger problem." I fold my arms across my chest, I drill him with a look as I place my hand on Ares's shoulder.

Carter repockets his gun and clears his throat a few seconds later. "Very well." He looks up at his men. "Ransom, go check the cameras. The rest of you, fall back and wait for me outside."

The house clears out quickly, and I will my frantically beating heart to slow down. That was a close call.

Ares rotates his neck as he stands, shooting daggers at dear old dad, and I would bet my inheritance he is imagining various ways to murder the motherfucker.

We can exchange ideas later.

"We might as well go over some arrangements while we wait for my man to verify the situation," Carter says, moving over to the island unit and peering into the Chinese takeout cartons. "That stuff will rot your insides," he says, looking over at me with a grimace. "Your body is a temple, Ashley. You should treat it as such."

"It's a bit late to be acting all parental." I snatch the carton out from under his nose. "And I leave the body worshiping to my men." I waggle my brows and grin as my gaze dances between Ares and Jase.

Jase flashes me a dazzling smile as I slide onto the stool beside him, leaning into his hot body. He presses his warm mouth to my ear. "I'm down for some worshiping after dinner." He peers deep into my eyes in a way that almost hypnotizes me, and my heart beats faster as a throbbing ache takes up residence between my thighs. Jase has smoldering good looks that suck me in and mesmerize me. One heated look often has me melting at his feet.

"You can thank me any day now," Carter says, snapping me out of my daze.

We all stare at him like he's grown horns.

His dry chuckle rings out in the silent kitchen as he waggles his fingers between Jase and me. "You two lovebirds get to spend the rest of your lives together. You're welcome."

"I was never marrying Julia," Jase says. "I would have found a way to marry Ash without your interference."

"Don't be ungrateful. It will only put me in a bad mood."

Bree snorts before cracking up laughing. It's infectious, and a few titters escape my lips. Bree's grin widens when Carter narrows his eyes in her direction. He does not like to be made fun of, but his hands are tied. He needs us alive to do his dirty work, so he'll have to suck it up.

I make a silent vow to rile him up any chance I get.

But I should probably tread carefully until we get Chad back. I don't want him taking it out on him.

That thought sobers me up. "Was there a reason for your visit besides your ridiculous accusation?" Scooping up a large forkful of chicken fried rice, I stuff it in my mouth, knowing it will piss him off.

"I have arranged a special sitting of the Board of Luminaries for Christmas Eve." That's only five days away. "You will get married at city hall on Thursday. Arrange the essentials in the next few days. I'll send a car to pick you up that morning." He eyeballs me. "We can arrange a proper wedding with a reception in the new year. My wife and I will host it at our home. She'll make all the arrangements, so you don't need to worry."

"Over my dead fucking body will I let that sick bitch plan or host my wedding. We'll pick the venue, and I'll organize it with Bree."

"Your insolence is wearing thin on my nerves." He stands.

"Your presence is wearing thin on mine."

Jase puts his hand on my thigh, squeezing me in warning. I quickly count to ten in my head, remembering the endgame. "I apologize." I almost choke on the words. "That was unfair and unnecessary, but this is hard for me." I lower my tone and fix him with sad eyes. "Everything that's happened is a lot to take in, and I'm grieving."

He walks to my side, placing his hand on my shoulder. "I know, honey. But I'm not your enemy. I'm your father, and I'm only trying to help."

I want to retort that kidnapping my ex and using him and

my mother to blackmail me is the exact opposite, but I bite my tongue. We agreed we would placate him, not rile him up any chance we get. It's clear it's going to be easier said than done.

"What about our wedding and Ares's initiation?" Bree asks, getting me out of replying. I shoot her a grateful smile.

"Ares must be initiated before you can marry. Unfortunately, I can't organize that until after the holidays. As soon as a date is set, for both events, I will let you know."

Footsteps approach, and his guy, Ransom, appears in the doorway. "The cameras check out," he says. "They weren't involved."

"Good, good." He squeezes my shoulder, and I want to tell him to get his dirty, scheming paws off me. "I know school is out until January, but it's important you all go about your routine as normal so no one suspects anything out of the ordinary." He points at Ares. "That means work for you." He swings his gaze at the Stewart siblings. "Attending to your responsibilities for you." A sour taste fills my mouth at his words, and if we weren't putting on a show, I would be pushing Jase away at the reminder. His features soften a little when he looks at me. "Your medical condition gives you an excuse to rest up for a couple of days, but go do normal stuff after that, and don't neglect your responsibilities either. The last thing we need is Manford sniffing around here."

"Understood," I say, speaking for everyone.

"Okay. See you Thursday," he says before walking off.

No one speaks for ages. Not even when we hear their cars departing. We wait for Ares to check the security system and the camera feed for interference.

"We're good," he confirms a few seconds later. "They didn't mess with it."

"I don't know about anyone else," Bree says. "But my

appetite vanished the second that prick walked through the door like he owns us."

"I'll eat yours." Swiping the shrimp noodle cartoon from in front of her, I instantly dive in. "I'll take any little rebellion where I can."

"He's such a dick," Jase says.

"I'll end up killing him accidentally if this shit continues," Ares says, finishing his meal. "I'm heading out to the gym," he adds, grabbing his wallet, phone, and keys and leaving the kitchen. Ares never uses the home gym, preferring the equipment at the local gym he's a member of.

"Baz has sent details of an event he wants us to attend," Bree says as she clears the plates away.

"You go." Jase dips his fork into my fried rice. "Ash and I need to talk."

"I can't keep covering for you." Bree dumps the dirty dishes in the sink. "Dad and Baz are going to figure it out soon."

Jase shrugs. "It won't matter for much longer. I'm going to be the Sloth Luminary soon, and my responsibilities to our family will cease."

"They will?" Hope blooms in my chest. I would be lying if I said I hadn't been thinking about the hideous duties Jase has to perform for his family. There is no way I'm permitting my husband to fuck around with other women, no matter how they frame it.

He tweaks my nose. "Yes. Yours will too."

"You mean no more partying and spying?"

He nods. "We'll have advisers to help us transition to our new positions. I imagine the focus for you will be on training and learning everything there is to know about The Luminaries."

"What about school? I'm not dropping out."

"You can probably continue," Bree says, "but I doubt Jase will be able to. Running a Luminary family is a full-time job."

"What'll happen to Manford Media?" I ask.

Jase shrugs again. "I'm sure James has contingencies in place, and the board of directors will continue to run it."

"No doubt Psycho Carter has a plan for it." Bree rinses plates before stacking them in the dishwasher. She straightens up. "I'll talk to Baz about Ares's little sister and Ruben. See what he can find out and if he can set up a meet."

"Be careful what you say," Jase warns. "We can't have anything getting back to Dad."

"I'll ensure Baz is discreet," she says.

Jase wears the usual uncertain expression he always has when it comes to his older brother. It must say something he trusts him to do this though. I wonder if deep down Jase knows he can be trusted and just doesn't want to admit he might have been wrong about Baz all these years.

Shaking the look off his face, he kisses my cheek as he gets up and walks to the refrigerator. He pulls out a beer for him and a water for me. I hate being on pain pills. I could kill for a vodka. Snatching some snacks, he jerks his head in the direction of the basement room. "Grab your takeout, and let's talk downstairs."

"Try to go easy on him," Bree says when her brother has disappeared. "He has taken crazy risks to remain faithful to you, and he loves you so much."

"I'll try," I agree, sliding off the stool. I grab two cartons and follow Jase downstairs.

It's a little chilly down here, but Jase has ramped the temp up on the thermostat, and he's put music on low in the background. I dump one carton on the coffee table before curling into a corner of the oversized couch with the other one.

"Want this?" Jase grabs a blanket from behind, holding it

out to me, and I nod. He places it over my legs, tucking me in, and I get a whiff of his spicy cologne as he leans over me. It's mixed with the citrusy smell of his bodywash, and I'm instantly nostalgic.

Jase smells like home.

The same way Chad does and Ares is starting to.

I'm probably overemotional today, but I need his arms around me stat.

"Jase? Can you hold me?"

"Absolutely." He sits beside me as I set my carton down on the table. Lifting me up, he settles me on his lap, keeping the blanket wrapped around us. Burying my face in his neck, I inhale his comforting scent and wrap my arms around his strong body. His arms go around my back, and he presses his lips into my hair, dotting kisses all over my head. "I love you," he whispers. "I love you forever, Ash."

I still get a thrill hearing him say that because he only said it recently, and it's still such a novelty. "I love you too." I sit up a little so I can face him. "But you betrayed me, Jase, and it hurts so much."

"Baby." He cups my face tenderly. "I know I have kept stuff from you, and that's not cool, but I haven't cheated on you."

I'm instantly pissed off. "I saw you!" My voice rachets up a few decibels. "I saw you in bed with her. *Meredith.*" I spit out her name over the messy ball of emotion clogging my throat.

"Ashley." His face is serious as he stares at me. "I swear to you that I didn't have sex with her. Think back. We were under the covers on purpose. We had our underwear on. I made it *look* like I was fucking her, but I wasn't. If you don't believe me, I'll set up a meeting with her. You can ask her yourself."

I don't need to ask her. I see the truth written all over his face, and it slices a huge chunk off my anger and my hurt. "You kissed her."

His face contorts. "It was only a peck."

"I have seen you kissing other girls at parties."

"More pecks, and that was necessary because Baz had to believe I was taking them upstairs to fuck them."

I arch a brow. "You mean you didn't fuck those thirteen girls you mentioned or anyone else?"

"I needed you to hate me, Ash. I needed you to stay away from me. Nix and Creed had already been hurt, and Chad could have died at that warehouse, and—"

I talk over him, cutting him short. "Wait up. What have Nix and Creed got to do with this?"

"My father told me if I didn't stay away from you he would start hurting the people I love." He brushes his fingers across my cheek. "I did mention all this in the ambulance, but you were heavily medicated, so I'm not surprised you don't remember."

A string of expletives leaves my mouth. "What the hell is wrong with these people? We're all fucking doomed with these pricks in charge."

Lifting my wrist, he plants his lips against my delicate skin. "They won't be in charge for much longer, and we're going to change things for the better. I hate Carter with every bone in my body, but if he gets us in a position where the next generation is in charge sooner and we can make positive changes, at least something good will have come out of it."

"Bree will be happy," I mutter, remembering her passion when speaking about the things she hopes to influence in a more modern Luminary world.

"She will." He holds my gaze as he sweeps his fingers back and forth against my wrist. "I have been faithful to you, Ash. I'm sorry you had to see me kissing some girls, but I did the bare minimum. Enough to make it look like I was fulfilling my duty. Bree helped me to fake it, but she is right. I wouldn't have been able to do that forever. I was prepared to die rather than betray you. The only woman I ever want to be intimate with is you." His earnest eyes plead for me to understand, and I can't stay mad at him anymore.

"I forgive you." I dust kisses all over his handsome face. "I love you." I press my lips to the corner of his mouth, pulling back before he can kiss me. Repositioning myself, I straddle his thighs, pivoting my hips in a slow roll as I let the blanket fall away. "I'll love you a lot more if you give me what I want right now."

"I like where this is going, Temptress." He jerks his hips, pushing his hard length against me. "Tell me what you want, baby." He nips at my earlobe as one hand slaps my ass.

"Fuck me, Jase. Reclaim me and make me yours forever."

Chapter Fourteen

Jase

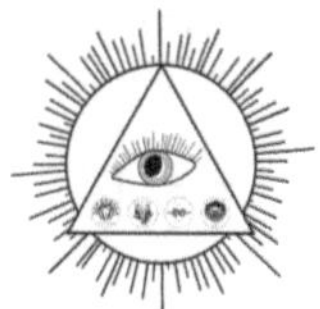

I don't need to be told twice. My heart is swollen to bursting point as we scramble off the couch, hurriedly undressing as if it's an Olympic sport. "You're so fucking sexy," I say, carefully reeling her into my arms when we're both naked.

"I really missed you." Her fingers rub back and forth across the intertwined snake branding over my heart. "What happens when your family allegiance changes?" she asks, looking up at me.

I press a tender kiss to the main Luminary branding on her upper arm, in the same place as mine, and the Sloth branding over her breast. Both are healing well. I peer into her eyes. "I will have the Sloth symbol added at our ascension ceremony."

She rolls her eyes. "Fucking Luminaries and their creepy-ass ceremonies."

I suck my thumb, lathering it with my saliva as I revel in our reunion. I was scared we wouldn't get here, and I'm so grateful for her understanding and forgiveness. In every lifetime, I am unworthy of this woman before me.

Grabbing Ash's ass, I pull her against my straining erection. "Can we stop talking and get to the fucking part now? I need to stamp my claim all over you, Temptress. I miss your pussy. I miss every part of your body." My fingers slide between her ass cheeks, and a tiny gasp flees from her lush lips. I press my mouth to her ear. "I need to fill every hole." I push my thumb into her puckered hole. "I want to bite, lick, and suck every inch of your gorgeous skin. I want to remind you you're mine," I say, toying with her asshole.

"I have always been yours, Jase." Emotion seeps through her words, and her eyes are glassy. "Even when we weren't together, I was still yours."

"I fucking love you," I reaffirm before slamming my lips down on hers. Our hands roam freely as our mouths get reacquainted, and our tongues duel in a feverishly possessive dance.

"Babe, I—"

"Shush, my love." I cut her off with another passionate kiss, as I maneuver us around. I drape her over the arm of the couch. "I know what you need. You don't have to say it." My fingers trail up and down her gorgeous spine as I push her legs apart. Ash bends fully over the couch, twisting her head back to look at me. Her burning gaze begs me to distract her and remove all thoughts from her mind.

"Where does it hurt right now?" I ask, not wanting to exacerbate her physical pain.

"The only place hurting is my cunt." She waggles her brows, and her lips kick up at the corners. "It's crying out for your cock."

Perfect.

She's so damn perfect.

Leaning myself all over her body, I take her lips again, licking and sucking inside her mouth and groaning at the taste of her. She tastes like the most sumptuous chocolate. A heavenly temptation I can't get enough of. "I adore you, Ash. Now and for the rest of my life."

"Vows aren't until Thursday." She grins at me as I wrap my hand around her long pink hair. I straighten up, softly tugging her head back. Normally, I love to yank on it when we're fucking, but she's got a concussion, so I'm extra gentle.

"The vows I make with my body are for us alone." Releasing her hair, I sink to my knees. I can't fuck her until I've tasted her pussy on my tongue. I have been dreaming about this for weeks. Parting her folds, I stare at her glistening cunt and her dripping juices, savoring the moment as I ride an anticipation high. "Always so ready for me," I purr before darting in and licking a line up and down her slit. Ash tastes like the sweetest honey as I lap at her nectar with my tongue.

Whimpers and moans fill the air as I devour her with my lips and my tongue before plunging two fingers inside of her. "Your greedy cunt wants me." I continue pumping my fingers inside her tight walls as my tongue darts out, laving her clit. "Your hungry clit loves my kisses." I suck on her swollen bud, almost coming with the primitive sounds she's making. Smashing my face in her pussy, I stroke my fingers at a more rapid pace, eating her with my lips and fucking her with my hand because I can't get enough.

With Ash, it is always more, more, more.

I am insatiable for her.

If I could spend twenty-four-seven fucking my gorgeous Temptress, I would.

If I could climb inside her, I would.

The need to bury myself deep rides me hard because I need to ensure she never forgets who she belongs to.

"You're mine, Temptress," I growl, adding a third digit in

her pussy and fucking her raw. Curling my fingers inside, I hit her G-spot as I bite down on her clit, and she explodes. Screaming and writhing and bucking against me as I ravage her like a wild beast who can't stop until he has devoured her fully.

"Fucking hell, Jase." Ash is panting when I finally pull my fingers and my mouth away from her stunning swollen cunt.

"You're magnificent, my love." I take a moment to admire her quivering flesh. She is always so responsive and so passionate, and I love it. "Exquisite and beyond comparison." I straighten to my full height, feathering my fingers up and down her spine as I dust kisses all over her back.

"Jase, please." Her body is shivering, her hips gyrating, as I take my sweet ass time loving on her back, her neck, her delectable ass, and her hypnotic legs.

"You want my cock, dirty girl? Was squirting all over my face not enough?" I tease, holding my dick at the base and running it up and down her slit.

"I want to come around your cock next," she grits out, looking back at me. Her face is flushed. Her eyes alight with desire. Her lips curled into a knowing smile. "I want you so deep I feel you in my womb. Imprint yourself inside me, Jase. Stamp your mark as my fiancé and make a promise as my soon-to-be husband." Her eyes burn with need. "Own every part of me the way I own every part of you."

"Goddamn, Temptress," I say, driving into her in one hard fast thrust. "I think I need to pass the dirty-talking crown to you."

Ash moans as I hold myself still inside her for a few beats, closing my eyes and memorizing this moment.

"Destroy me, Jase. Fuck every orifice. Replace the pain in my heart and the heavy thoughts in my head with your cock and your lips and your tongue and your fingers. Wipe it all away. Fill it with you and only you." Tears prick her eyes, and I hate all the shit we are dealing with. I wish I could snap my fingers and take it all away.

Unmoving inside her, I bend down and kiss her slow and deep, pouring everything I am feeling into each brush of my lips. Letting her know we are in this together and we will never be apart again.

Whatever we face, we will face it together.

Tears are streaming silently down her face when I pull back. I swipe them away with my thumbs. Leaning down, I brush my lips gently across her mouth. "My life. My wife." Emotion clogs the back of my throat. "You will never be alone again." I kiss her again. "We're going to burn the world down together."

She sniffles before kissing me hard. "Amen to that, husband."

The word ignites a frenzy inside me, and I start fucking her with no restraint. "If anything hurts, you tell me," I say in between pants and thrusts.

She nods while urging me on with a pointed stare. I fuck her into the couch, rutting in and out of her like a man possessed. Her inner walls squeeze me, and I'm groaning and cursing as I fuck her deep, slamming in and out as I grip her hips and hold her in place. Tilting her ass up, I drive into her at a faster pace, pushing my dick as far as it will go, sliding in and out of her warmth as my orgasm builds. I want to make this last, but I've gone too long without her. Reaching around, I shove my thumb in her mouth. "Suck," I command as I rotate my hips and slow down to stall my impending climax. "Fuck, that feels good," I say as her hot mouth suctions around my thumb and her tongue laves it up and down.

I grope her heavy tit while she sucks my thumb, and I caution my dick to wait a little longer. My fingers flick her hard nipple, and she squirms underneath me, moaning around my thumb. When I withdraw it, I move it to her ass, pushing it in slowly, giving her time to relax and adjust to the intrusion. My other hand moves down to her clit, and I toy with it as I pick up speed, rutting my cock inside her as my thumb presses all the way into her ass. My balls tighten, and a familiar tingly feeling spreads up my spine. I pinch her clit as I fall over the edge. "Come with me now, Temptress. Fall apart on my cock with my thumb wedged in your pretty ass."

Ash screams out her release as I empty inside her, pumping my hips and spilling deep. Visions of filling her with my seed and planting a baby in her womb surges to the forefront of my mind. We're too young, and we have too much shit to deal with, but I wouldn't be unhappy if I accidentally impregnated her.

I can't wait to have babies with the love of my life.

I can't wait to see her stomach rounded with my kid.

"Oh my God." Ash withers underneath me, reminding me she is injured.

Slowly, I pull out. Turning her around, I gather her in my arms, concern rushing through me. I got lost in the moment, and now I worry I was too rough. "Are you okay? Did I hurt you?"

"I'm peachy." She smiles up at me with a lovesick expression, and I wish I could freeze-frame it. Ash leans against me for support, and I lift her up, cradling her against my chest as I hold her in my arms.

"Let's get you into the shower and bed."

Ash insists I fuck her ass when we're in the shower, and after we have cleaned up and are lying in bed, she sits on my face as I make her come for the fourth time. It's not even close to our all-time record, but my wifey is tired. She needs sleep. Ash snuggles into my side as I pull the covers up over us and switch off the lights.

"Babe?" she murmurs in a sleep-drenched tone.

“Yes, my love?” I brush her hair behind her ears before placing a soft kiss to her brow.

“We need to move the mirrors in here.” That’s the last thing she says before she conks out.

I grin at her like a loon, wondering how I got so fucking lucky.

Chapter Fifteen

Ashley

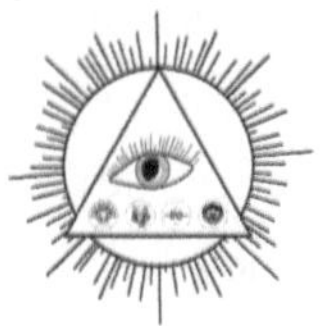

I wake up wrapped in Jase's strong embrace, smiling as the memories of last night swirl through my mind. Heat envelops me from behind, and I twist slightly in Jase's arms, not wanting to wake my sleeping beauty. I look back, startled to find Ares staring at me in that intense way of his. "Hi," I whisper, reaching up to drag my fingers through the growth on his chin and cheeks. "When did you come in?"

He shrugs, his eyes drifting to my mouth as I feel the weight of his hot palm lying low on my bare belly.

"Are you okay?" I whisper, staring at his mouth.

He shrugs again, and I notice he's lying on top of the covers in only his boxers. My libido instantly perks up at the sight of all his gorgeous, toned, tan, inked skin, rippling muscles, and the obvious bulge at his groin.

"Sorry," I mumble, carefully extracting myself from Jase's embrace. "Stupid question." I crawl over Ares. "Don't move," I whisper before I peck his lips. "I need to pee."

Hurrying into the bathroom, I smile to myself when I feel every new ache and pain. Being in love makes everything feel better. Even the shitstorm in my head, and my life, doesn't feel insurmountable this morning.

I take care of business and brush my teeth before climbing back into bed in between Ares and Jase. I half expected my stepbrother to be gone when I came out, but I guess he needs me more than he wants to admit—even to himself.

I feel closer to Ares these past few days despite how he's been keeping me at arm's length. We're like kindred spirits now. Both of us lied to by the people who were supposed to love us. Both of us discovering our true parentage for the first time. Learning about this new secret society and navigating it together.

I'm not even mad about the cameras anymore. I probably should be, but I can't find it in me to care—as long as he hasn't shown the footage to anyone else. Thinking of him jerking off to his "stepsister porn collection" sends a rush of arousal to my core. I'm probably fucked in the head, but the thought of it seriously turns me on.

I thread my fingers through his as he stares at me, his fingers absently toying with my hair. Behind us, Jase is softly snoring, oblivious to the mounting tension in the room.

Taking a chance, I claim Ares's lips in a probing kiss. His arms automatically go around my waist, and he pulls me in against his hard, warm body. His morning wood presses against my thigh through his boxers, and my sore pussy throbs with a new ache. Our hands explore as he angles his head, taking control of our kiss and deepening it. I rock my hips against him, and he clutches my hip, lifting it and repositioning me so his erection is brushing against my pussy.

Delicious tremors rip through my body as it fully comes alive. I want to impale myself on his cock and ride the shit out of him.

Wrapping my leg around his waist, I open myself up. I'm

still naked, and the feel of my bare chest pressed against his elicits a rake of fiery shivers all over my body. I'm already primed and ready for his big fat cock. I'm wet enough he could plunge inside me straightaway.

Ares gets rid of his boxers and nudges my entrance with the tip of his dick as he clasps my face in his large hands and devours my mouth. He pushes inside a little more, and I moan into his mouth as velvety-soft lips kiss my shoulder blade.

"Hmm," Jase murmurs, dotting kisses up and down my neck as his hand moves to my hip. "This is my favorite way to wake up."

Ares turns rigidly still. His dick pops out, and my needy pussy silently wails. His demanding lips retreat from mine as his eyes open and connect with Jase over my shoulder.

"Ares." I touch his face, but I have already lost him.

Sliding out of bed, he pulls his boxers on, then shakes his head and drags his fingers through his hair. He looks at me with a penetrating lens. Lust comingles with a host of other emotions on his face before he spins around on his heels and takes off.

"Shit."

"Sorry." Amusement underscores Jase's tone. "Was it something I said or something I did?"

I thump him in the arm. "You shouldn't wind him up. You know his thoughts on sharing."

Jase rolls on top of me, propping himself up by his elbows. He brushes his lips against mine in a feather-soft kiss I feel all the way to the tips of my toes. "Ares will never volunteer to share unless we start nudging him into it."

"I won't force him, and it's too soon. The timing isn't right." I wrap my arms around Jase's neck. "I don't even know what we are."

His brow puckers. "What do you mean?"

"We have fooled around and kissed a lot, but the only time we had sex was the night of the party, and there have been no discussions or labels or anything."

Shock splays across his face. "Are you saying you haven't been sleeping with him since you broke up with Chad?"

I shake my head. "It hasn't been like that." I chew on the corner of my mouth. "Ares took care of me, and he didn't push me except for his usual outrageous flirting and dirty innuendos. He was actually really sweet."

Jase's brows climb to his hairline, and I get it. Ares would probably throw a hissy fit if he heard me refer to him as *sweet*, but he was. He was incredibly sweet, and my heart swells with emotion recalling everything he did for me these past couple months. "He cooked all my meals and made sure I ate. He held me when I cried and sat through countless chick flicks to keep me company when I was in a pretty bad place."

"Wow." Jase rolls to his side, pulling me with him so we're facing one another. "I never would've thought him capable. But I've seen the way he looks at you. The way he has looked at you for a long time, Temptress." He sweeps his thumb along my lower lip. "I think he's in love with you, and he doesn't have a fucking clue how to deal with it."

I quirk a brow. "Really?"

He nods, looking thoughtful before he asks, "How do you feel about him?"

I worry my lip between my teeth.

Jase loosens my lip. "Don't be afraid to tell me the truth, Ash. I can handle it. I see the way you look at him too."

"I have feelings for him," I truthfully admit. "And I feel even closer to Ares now. I feel very...protective of him. I'm worried what all the revelations are doing to him."

"Do you want to know what I think?" he asks, tucking a piece of my hair behind my ear.

"Always."

His wide smile turns my insides to mush. "I think you love him too."

"It's too soon to say, Jase. I'm not sure how deep it goes."

"I think there was an instant connection between you, but you both fought it. I don't think it's too soon at all. I think it's been a gradual buildup. All that bickering and flirting was foreplay." He waggles his brows, and his grin expands.

"Why are you okay with this? You hate him?"

"Hate is a very strong word. I don't *hate* him, Ash. He irritates me and pisses me off. Mainly because of the way he was with you, and we need to get to the bottom of his animosity for Chad. But he's growing on me. Like mold." He winks, and I bark out a laugh. His expression turns tender as he cups one of my cheeks. "Hearing what you just said helps a lot. He cares about you, and he looked after you when we deserted you. He gets major brownie points for that. And for holding back. For giving you space and letting your needs dictate the pace. I know how hard it is to be around you and not want to nail you to the nearest flat surface."

I burst out laughing again, placing my hands on his chest and marveling at how amazing he is. "God, I love you for so many things, but this is so selfless, Jase. I'm not sure I'm worthy of you."

He pulls my face to his for a loving kiss. "Stop stealing all my lines." He eases back, cradling my face and staring at me like I'm the only person who exists on the planet. "It's always about you, Ash. And it will continue to be so. Whatever you need or want, you got it."

"You really mean it? You would let Ares be with me even after we're married?"

"Absolutely." He kisses the tip of my nose. "If that's what you need." He cocks his head to one side, and his lips curve at the corners. "Of course, I'll have to have a chat with him. Let him know he's dead if he ever hurts you."

I roll my eyes. "I think we're getting ahead of ourselves. We're not even a thing, and Ares said he won't share. If he won't change his mind, that's that."

"He'll change his mind." His tone resonates with confidence I don't feel. "He's already on the same wavelength as me and Chad when it comes to you. It'll be easier than he thinks."

My skepticism still shows on my face.

"I see you don't believe me." His hand traces a path down over my arm, brushing against the side of my breast, along the dip at my waist, and around the curve of my hip. "You underestimate your allure. I'm not just talking about your rocking body." His fingers sweep back and forth across my hipbone, reviving my snoozing libido. "You're intelligent, kind, sweet, funny, and when you love someone, you love them with your whole heart. Once someone comes into your orbit, it's impossible for them to walk away."

"Jase," I croak as tears pool in my eyes. "You're going to turn me into an egomaniac if you keep this up."

"Never, baby." He pulls me into his chest and bundles me into his arms. The steady thrumming of his heart under my ear is soothing. "I speak only the truth." He tips my chin up. "Thank you for giving me another chance."

"Thank you for risking so much to protect me and keep me safe."

We kiss for a few minutes, neither of us in a hurry. His minty breath confirms he must have gotten up at some point before me and brushed his teeth. When we break apart, we stare at one another with shared intensity lingering in the space between us. "You're my world, and I'm going to give that to you."

I palm his face. "You make everything seem better even when it's not."

"You do that for me too." His tongue darts out, wetting his lips. "I want to ask you one final thing before we need to get up."

"You can ask me anything. I'm an open book."

"What about Chad?"

I gulp over the messy ball of emotion clogging my throat. "I want to make things right with him, but I don't know if we can get past everything. And we don't know what state he'll be in when we get him back." Anger surges to the surface. "That woman needs to die," I hiss, clenching my hands at Jase's sides.

"Agreed. And we still need to deal with that bitch Anita too."

"I'd actually forgotten about her, but yes, she needs to be dealt with too."

"Leave Anita to Ares and me, and when Cleo Carter's time comes, you and Chad can handle it."

"I want in on Anita too. She conspired with Julia to murder me."

"I have an idea," he says. "Knight called me late last night after you fell asleep. He's throwing a Christmas party at the Carter residence tomorrow night. I told him we'd all be there. Even if we don't have intel on Chad's whereabouts by then, it's a good opportunity to do some snooping."

"We can test the waters too. See if Rhett has told him anything about me or Ares or his plans."

He toys with strands of my hair. "Exactly, and I'll get Anita there. We can deal with her then."

"Sounds like a plan."

"I'll update the others." He kisses me briefly. "I have some things I need to do this morning, but keep your afternoon free. We're going wedding shopping."

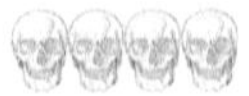

Jase takes a shower while I pull my robe on and slip my feet into my fluffy slippers. Then I head out in search of Ares. I don't like how things were left earlier, and I need to see if he's all right. There is no light trickling out from under his door, so I pad down to the kitchen. The roar of an engine draws me to the front door in time to watch Ares peel away from the curb on his Triumph. Damn it. I really wanted to catch him before he left for work. I can see he's struggling, and I want to be there for him, but he's got to let me in. Tapping out a quick text on my cell, I ask him to call me when he has a break.

Jase, Bree, and I eat breakfast together, and then he leaves. I help Bree with her unpacking, and she fills me in on her escapades last night with Baz. "He knows something is up," she says as we put clothes away in her closet.

"What did you tell him?"

"I only mentioned about Lilianna and arranging that meeting for Ares with Ruben, but Baz isn't stupid. He knows there is more to it. I really think we should bring him in."

"Jase will never go for it." He's always had a fractured relationship with his brother—even more so after Baz fucked me at my initiation.

"He will if you talk to him."

I arch a brow. "Do you think I have a magic wand or something?"

"Magic pussy," she retorts, and a burst of laughter erupts from my mouth.

"I'm not sure I'd go that far, but I'll accept the compliment." We grin at one another, and it's like old times.

"We need all the help we can get, and Baz has a lot of valuable contacts and access to our father's files and key resources within the Lust & Envy Luminary."

"Can we trust him?" I put the last of her sweaters away.

"Yes. Despite what Jase believes, Baz is not our father's mini-me. Far from it. Baz is smart. He knows how to play the game. He has done it so convincingly even Jase believes it. But I see behind that front he wears. Baz doesn't agree with everything. He's not going to blindly continue things the way they are. I'd stake my life on it."

"Okay. I'll work on Jase."

Bree throws her arms around me. "I'm so excited we're going to be sisters-in-law."

"It's all happening so fast it hasn't truly sunk in."

"It sucks that you can't do it your way."

I lean against the doorway. "It's only a piece of paper. What matters is what is in our hearts, and in that, we are finally aligned."

Chapter Sixteen

Jase

I have a productive morning, and I'm smiling like a Cheshire cat when I return to the house. Removing the small black box from my pocket, I secure it in the glove compartment of my Maserati for later. I get out of the car and lock it with the key fob, whistling under my breath.

The sight of Julia's bright pink car parked outside the front of the townhome I once shared with her stops me for a second. Julia got what was coming to her, and I count my blessings I avoided that nightmare. I don't know where things went wrong with her. She was actually sweet as a kid, and there was a time we got along. But not in recent years, and living with her these past few months was a test in patience and self-control.

I make a mental note to get the car towed the second the meeting with the Board of Luminaries ends on Friday. Ash doesn't need a reminder every time she comes and goes from our house. Bree already took Julia's dog to a local place so he can go to a good home. James can deal with the rest of her shit or have one of his staff box up her stuff if he's languishing in the basement at Luminary HQ like I suspect he will be.

I bound up the stairs toward our front door, still grinning like a loon. I dreamed of marrying Ashley, but I was losing hope it would ever happen. I wish we were doing it our way, at a time of our choosing, but I'm not complaining. I hope the things I have put in motion will help it to feel like it's our choice and not something demanded of us by her sociopathic father.

"Honey, I'm home," I holler as soon as I step foot in the hallway.

"I'm in the kitchen," Ash shouts, and I walk in that direction.

My love is sitting beside Bree at the island unit, both of them hunched over a laptop.

Ash lifts her head, and there are tears in her eyes. "We know where Chad is."

"Good." I nod as I come up behind her. Wrapping my arms around her slender waist, I rest my chin on her shoulder.

"She keeps her depravity close to home," Bree confirms, scrolling through the report she's received from the team we assigned to locate Chad. Bree points at an aerial shot of a large building surrounded by woodland. "She had this structure built ten years ago for her charitable 'work' on the grounds of her home."

"Heat signatures confirm she has built her dungeon underneath the building," Ash says, holding on to my arms.

Warmth seeps into my skin as delicious tingles shoot up my arms. One touch from my love, and I'm like putty in her hands.

"Security is a big issue." Bree frowns, reading part of the report. "Our guys tried hacking into her systems to see how easy it was to breach and couldn't get past the firewall."

"I bet Theo could." Ash leans back into me.

"He probably could, but I don't want to involve our friends unless we have absolutely no choice. They don't deserve to get dragged into this mess."

"That's only part of the problem," Bree adds, squinting as she speed-reads the words on the screen. "Armed guards man the exterior and interior twenty-four-seven. Even if we could disable the cameras and security system, we will still have them to deal with."

"Run background checks on the guards," I say, holding Ash closer. "Let's find some dirt on one of them and use him as our way in."

"We don't have the time for that." Ash peers up at me. "We need to get him out of there now, Jase." Her voice cracks, and I know how hard this is for her. I know she is deliberately not thinking about Chad or her father so she holds it together. "I hate the thought of what that bitch is doing to him."

"Our teams are the best in the world at this stuff." I try to reassure her as Bree is already on her cell phone, barking out instructions. "We'll have the intel soon." I swivel her stool around and reel her into my chest. "We'll get him out tomorrow night. The party is the perfect camouflage."

"Her kids must know about it." Ash rubs her hands up and down my chest. "How else would she explain the armed guards?"

"Not necessarily. The Carter property is vast, and they may not even know it exists," I explain.

"She had it built at the very rear of their grounds in a secluded spot that is far away from the outdoor spaces the family uses," Bree says after she ends her call. "Even if they are aware, I'm sure she has made it appear legit. She runs annual fundraisers for a few key charities, and she uses her contacts to exact large donations from benefactors. It's not always cash. People donate priceless works of art, unique pieces of jewelry, and things like cars and boats. I am guessing she stores a lot of that shit in the main area of the building, and it's how she explains the need for such high-level security."

"What a hypocritical bitch. Working for charity and making herself look like an angel when she's clearly the devil. I wonder what her charity contacts would think if they knew she has been kidnapping and abusing men for her own sick pleasure," Ash hisses.

"She's going to pay for it." I wind my fingers through her long, wavy pink hair. "We are going to punish her and put a stop to it. I promise."

Bree glances at Ash, drilling her with some silent command.

Ash clears her throat. "Bree and I have been talking, and we think we need to bring Baz fully in on this."

My fingers stall in her hair. "No. Absolutely not. He can't be trusted."

"I don't agree. Look what he did for us, and he has readily agreed to help with Lilianna and the Ruben meeting."

I snarl under my breath, pulling away from Ash as I drag my hands through my hair. I do not want to think about my brother fucking my woman at a time when I'm planning our wedding. All it will do is put me in a foul mood. Forcing myself to calm down, I blow air out of my mouth before I reply. "Can we not do this today?" I thread my fingers in hers. "I want us to enjoy this afternoon, and that won't happen if I'm thinking about Baz."

Ash shares a fleeting look with my sister over my shoulder before nodding. "Okay." She stands. "We can talk about it later."

I'd prefer to never talk about it, but I can't be stubborn either. I hate we might need him. But I won't sacrifice Chad's welfare or finding Ares's sister for stupid pride or competitiveness or whatever this shit is that has always existed between us.

"PC2." Bree claims my attention, and I look over at her. "Did things go according to plan this morning?"

The stupid smile is back on my face. “They did.” I waggle my brows at her, and she nods, her face lighting up with excitement.

“Then I know where I need to be. I’m out, peeps.” She mock salutes us before skipping out of the room.

“Why does it feel like I’m being left out of something?” Ash slides her hands into the back pocket of my jeans.

“All will be revealed soon.” I lean down and kiss her inviting lips before swatting her delectable ass. “We need to go. We have a lot of ground to cover this afternoon.”

“I’m ready.” She stretches up to peck my lips before looping her arm through mine. “Let’s go.”

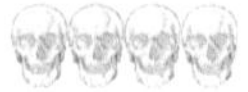

We go to the jewelry store first to pick out wedding bands. I share a conspiratorial look with the woman behind the desk as she places a few bands in front of Ashley. Any of these will work with the engagement ring I purchased earlier.

“These are so pretty.” Ash smiles as she squeezes my thigh. Her eyes are infused with happiness, matching the glow I feel inside.

“Try them on, my love.”

A surge of pride swells my chest as my fiancée slides each platinum band on her ring finger. All have diamonds embedded in the band and are sophisticated in an understated way. Bree offered to come with me to pick out the ring, but I turned her down. I know what Ash would want. She has never been flashy or materialistic despite the wealth she grew up with. Those kinds of things don’t matter to her. While she is very much a girly-girl, she doesn’t need or want a massive rock on her finger. So, I’m not surprised when she chooses the simplest of the bands. The ring is thin, the edges crisp and smooth, with a line of diamonds in the center, running the width of the band.

"This is the one," she says, beaming up at me.

"Are you sure?" I tuck a piece of hair behind her ear.

"One hundred percent."

The woman smiles, setting the chosen ring aside before she puts the others away. She takes out a row of men's wedding bands next and slides them across the desk to me.

"I like this one." Ash points at the same one my eye is drawn to.

I flash her a blinding smile. "Me too."

Ash takes it out and slides it on my finger. The platinum band is wide with two lines of fine diamonds rimming the circumference on both edges. I like the look and feel of it on my finger. As if it has always belonged there. Our eyes lock, and potent emotion charges the space around us. She cups one side of my face, smiling wide, her eyes glassy with feeling.

I place the hand with the ring over her hand on my face as I stare deep into her gorgeous brown eyes. "I love you."

"I love you too," she whispers as a single tear leaks from her eye.

"You two are adorable," the woman says. "You make such a beautiful couple."

Ash's smile expands as we remove our hands from my face and turn to face the jeweler. "Thank you."

"We'll take both of these," I supply, reluctantly sliding the ring from my finger.

She leaves to organize the paperwork and package up the rings, and the second she exits the room, I scoop Ash up onto my lap.

Her hands dive into my hair and she smiles. "I can't believe this is happening. It's like a dream come true."

My eyes probe hers. "I know it's not the way we would have planned it, but are you sure you're okay with it?"

She bobs her head. "I love you, Jase, and I want to marry you. I hate my father is dictating the terms, but I'm not unhappy. Not in the slightest." She presses her lips to mine. "I know we're young, but I don't care. I know what's in my heart, and this feels right."

"It does." I hold her close. "More right than anything else has ever felt in my life."

After leaving the jewelry store, we head to the florist's where Ash chooses a bouquet of white, pink, and red roses with red berry leaves in a nod to Christmas, which is only days away now. We fix on white roses with red berries as boutonnieres. I take pics and send them to Bree on the down-low while Ash is texting with Ares.

Then we head to the bakery to pick out a cake. I had called them yesterday and paid quadruple their normal prices to bake three cakes at short notice. We try the chocolate, lemon, and red velvet samples, both of us agreeing on the latter. The lady shows us pictures in a book, and Ash picks a white-frosted, two-tier cake.

We grab coffee from a local takeout place and when we step outside, Bree is waiting by the wall. "What are you doing here?" Ash asks, glancing suspiciously at her.

"This is where we must part ways, my love." I kiss the tip of her nose. "It's bad luck for the groom to see the bride's dress until the wedding day. Bree is here to go with you."

Ashley grins, looking at something behind me. She pulls my face down to hers for a quick kiss. "Great minds think alike."

When I straighten up, Ares is at my side. He looks uncomfortable as hell. His hands are shoved deep in the pockets of his jeans as he stares at the ground. When she was messaging with him, she must have asked him to go with me to pick out a suit.

"Thanks for doing this," Ash says, rubbing engine oil off his cheek. His eyes lift to hers, and his face instantly softens. Ares has it bad, and it's actually nice to see. I didn't think the asshole was capable of feeling anything for anyone, and I'm glad to be proven wrong. "We appreciate it."

"I'm doing this for you," he grits out, and I bark out a laugh.

"Don't go doing me any favors." Pain tightens my chest. Chad should be doing this with me.

"Stop being a pussy, and let's go."

"Be nice." Ash warns, jabbing her finger in his face. "I know you want us to believe you have no heart in here." She places her hand on his chest. "But we all know that isn't true. I love Jase, and I know you care for me, so don't be a jerk." She stretches up, whispering something in his ear.

He nods before grabbing her face and kissing her hard.

When he releases her, I haul her into my arms and kiss her deeply, uncaring we are drawing funny looks from people passing by. "Have fun, Temptress." I hand her the new credit card I got her on my account. She opens her mouth to protest, but I place my hand over it, muffling her words. "No arguments. What's mine is yours." Withdrawing my hand, I tug her in closer. "I want to buy my bride her wedding dress. Indulge me, baby."

"I love you." Her arms encircle my neck, and she kisses me again before we break apart. "Don't kill each other." She waggles her finger between us. "I need you both."

"You don't have to worry about us. We'll see you at the restaurant later."

Ares and I walk off in one direction while the girls go in the other. I made private appointments at both stores, paying extra to have a tailor and seamstress on hand for immediate alterations.

Ares is silent as we walk the five blocks toward the store. "How are you holding up?" I ask him after a while.

"I'm fine."

"You don't have to talk to me, but you should at least talk to Ash. She worries about you."

"How do you do it?" he blurts, glancing sideways at me as we walk. "Back there, you didn't care that I kissed her." His eyes narrow to pinpricks. "I wanted to knock you into next week when you pulled her into your arms."

"Her happiness is all that matters to me."

He chuckles, leveling me with a look of disbelief. "Come on, dude. Don't spout that bullshit at me."

"I'm not lying." We part ways temporarily, moving to opposite sides of the sidewalk to let a woman with a stroller through.

"You can't tell me you don't get jealous when she's with me," he adds.

"I can." I stop at the pedestrian crossing, and we wait for the light to change. "Maybe it's because I spent two years watching her with Chad while secretly loving her." I scratch the back of my head. "I was very envious of him back then. But why would I be jealous now when I get to have her?" I slap him on the shoulder. "Jealousy is a pointless emotion. I didn't think I would ever get to be with Ash. Now, she's marrying me. She's going to be a permanent fixture in my life forever. If I have to share her with you and Chad, so what? She is still mine, and as long as we keep her happy, we'll never lose her. What's to be jealous about?"

Chapter Seventeen

Ashley

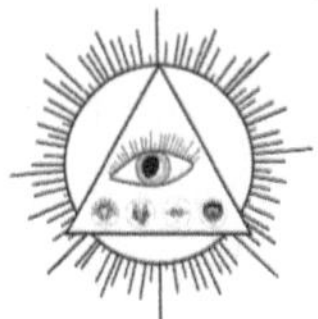

"My brother is going to go crazy when he sees you in that dress," Bree says as we exit the designer bridal store and head toward the restaurant where we are meeting the guys. They have been there for a while since they finished shopping quicker than us. It's dark out, but it's still busy as most of the stores in this exclusive part of Lowell are open late. Light spills out from elegant storefronts as we walk by.

"I hope he won't think it's too plain," I say, thinking of the simple satin dress with the spaghetti straps and ruching over the bust. It is fitted at the waist before flaring out over my hips. The material is in two layers that split as I walk, showcasing a daring amount of my legs and thighs. It is three-quarters length, and I have the perfect silver sandals at home to go with it.

"You look beautiful and sexy, and it's pure you. Trust me, Jase will love it." She loops her arm through mine. "You could show up in a trash bag, and my brother would still be all over you. He loves you like crazy." She pops a kiss to my cheek. "Thank you for loving my brother like you do."

"Gawd," I say, fighting a new burst of emotion. "It's not even the wedding, and everyone is already super emotional. I'm going to be a blubbering mess on the day."

"Weddings are supposed to be like this, and we're latching on to the happy occasion because otherwise we'll be thinking of all the other shit, and I don't think anyone wants to go there."

"I get bouts of guilt," I admit as we round the corner, the restaurant visible up ahead. "It feels wrong to be elated and happy when Chad is imprisoned by a crazy bitch, Ares is retreating into his head, and my dad is dead." Tears prick my eyes as Bree stops, takes my hand, and pulls me over against the wall in between two stores.

"You're allowed to be happy, babe. If we've learned anything recently, it's that life is too short to not celebrate the good things." She brushes tears off my cheeks. "We will get justice for your dad, and we're going to give him the best send-off."

"I wish I could turn back time and do some things differently." I peer up at her through blurry eyes. "Dad tried so hard this past year to make amends with me, and I spent far too long pushing his gestures aside. I wish now I hadn't raced to my room, or rushed out of the house immediately after dinner, eager to avoid him. I wish any of those times he'd asked me to go hunting or fishing with him or to go to a movie I'd said yes instead of turning him down." I can barely swallow over the painful lump wedged in my throat. "I wish I'd told him I loved him more."

She hugs me, running her hands up and down my back. "He knew, Ash. Your dad knew."

I swipe at my tears as we break apart, grabbing a tissue from my purse and wiping my nose. "I wish I knew everything he'd done for me while he was alive. It would have put so many things into perspective."

"He loved you so much, Ash, and he knew what he was getting into when he agreed to marry Pamela and pretend you were his. He knew about The Luminaries. He knew the risks." She clasps my cheeks. "He knew that one day he could lose his life for those choices, and he still did it. He was a good man, and he would not want to see you upset. He sacrificed himself for you so you could live your best life."

My cell rings, and Jase's handsome face stares back at me from the screen. I swipe to answer, speaking first. "We're almost there. See you in a couple minutes."

"Okay, babe. Hurry. I miss you." Ares snorts in the background before Jase hangs up.

I need to pull myself together. This is the last thing I should be thinking about three days before my wedding. Jase deserves more than Melancholy Barbie.

"We are going to come out of this on top," Bree says, dabbing at my blotchy face. "And we're going to change things for the better. I am clinging to that mantra, and you should too. We're gonna get Chad away from that sick bitch tomorrow. We're gonna make it work so he'll be standing at Jase's side as his best man, like he should be."

"We will," I agree, as we begin walking, because there is no other outcome that is acceptable to me. "Thank you for being my maid of honor," I say, watching Jase appear through the doorway of the restaurant. He stands to one side, propping his foot up on the wall as he watches us approach.

"Thank you for asking me." Sincerity bleeds into her tone. "You don't have to say yes, but when it's my wedding, I would love you to be standing beside me. I know it's fake, but I still need you with me. Though I understand if you can't."

I stop a few feet away from the restaurant. "Of course, I'll be there for you. For you and Ares." I feel a little ill every time I think about Bree marrying the guy I'm falling for. But I know it's fake, and it won't be for long. I have to think of the bigger picture and getting Lilianna back will be our main priority after tomorrow night. I won't make things harder for Ares. If he can make the sacrifice, then so can I. It won't be forever.

"You're my best friend," Bree whispers with tears clinging to her lashes. I am still mesmerized by her stunning eyes. One is a silvery blue and the other a striking green. With her blue hair, her stature, and the confidence she projects, Bree claims attention wherever she goes. "I know I don't deserve you, but that's what you are to me."

"You're my best friend too." Now I know she was helping Jase avoid fulfilling his familial responsibilities, it's easier to forgive her for concealing things from me. Her heart has always been in the right place.

"What's wrong?" Jase asks, materializing at my side. He bundles me into his arms, examining my face with a growing frown. "You've been crying." His eyes harden. "Who made you cry, and where are they so I can knock them the fuck out?" He glances at his sister with narrowed eyes, and she glares back at him.

"You're an idiot," Bree snaps, and I giggle.

"No one hurt me, caveman." Hooking my fingers in the waistband of his jeans, I yank him in closer. "I got a little upset about my dad, but I'm okay now."

His eyes flood with empathy as he holds my face in his hands. "I'm sorry, baby."

I shake my head. "Don't be sorry. It is what it is, and I don't want to dwell on it anymore. Let's eat. I'm starving."

Jase reserved a large circular booth tucked discreetly into the back of the restaurant, and I slide in between him and Ares.

Bree sits on the other side of her brother, whispering to him, and I just know they are plotting something. It's nice and private here, with no tables in proximity, so we can talk without fear of being overheard.

"I'm glad to see you're both in one piece," I say to Ares before grabbing a piece of bread from the basket.

"It was touch and go for a while," he admits, sliding his arm over the back of the booth behind me.

"I want you two to get along."

"Jase isn't the problem."

I look up at him as I tear a chunk from my bread. "You could have fooled me."

Ares exhales heavily, and I pop a piece of bread in my mouth while I await his reply.

"I'd like to talk about this too," Jase says, handing me a menu. "But we should order first. I told Carole we'd drop by on our way home."

My brows lift. "When did you arrange that?"

He bops me on the nose. "This morning when I was running errands."

"You're just all kinds of organized today," I say before kissing him. Our kiss deepens. It's completely inappropriate for where we are, but I have been all kinds of needy with him today. We have been kissing and touching all afternoon as we went about organizing our wedding. I have this potent, inherent need to be as close to him as possible.

Jase chuckles against my lips as he breaks our lip-lock. "Always living up to your namesake." He nibbles on my earlobe, whispering in my ear. "Park those desires until later." His eyes flash with wicked intent. "We can fuck in the car. Just like old times."

"Ugh." A scowl washes over Bree's face. "I can hear you,

and I still haven't recovered from that time you fucked in the car in front of me." A shiver crawls over her. "It totally grossed me out, and I still owe you payback."

Ares sits up straighter, looking instantly intrigued.

"You got your payback." Jase waggles his finger in her face. "I still have visions of you bouncing up and down on that idiot's cock on our couch, naked as the day you were born, and the sounds you were making will haunt my nightmares forever."

"Ha!" Bree's grin is smug. "Serves you right."

Jase pins me with a sultry look. "I'm making a new rule. Car sex every time we are in a vehicle with Bree, and we're gonna be dirty and loud." He smirks at his sister as his hand lands on my thigh. "Let her get a taste of her own medicine." A wicked glint appears in his eye as he stares behind my head at Ares. "We could tag team if you were into sharing, but I guess you can watch and take pointers."

"Fuck off, Stewart. I know how to please my woman. If anyone is taking pointers, it'll be you." Ares loops his hand around my shoulder, tugging me in closer to his side. Jase's hand moves higher on my thigh, and Ares clenches his jaw as they face off.

"Oh, boy." Bree giggles as she looks between them. All she's missing is a bucket of popcorn.

Ares turns my head and claims my lips in a passionate kiss that curls my toes and warms up every inch of me. If he's trying to make a point, it's well made.

"Um, ah, are you ready to order?"

I whip my head around at the unfamiliar female voice, not in the least bit embarrassed when I spot her red cheeks and the curious looks from other tables. Grabbing the menu, I order the first pasta dish I see. Our waitress is close to my age, I would guess, and she's having a hard time tearing her eyes away from Ares and Jase. I don't blame her. I suffer the same infliction myself. Her eyes lower to where Jase has his hand high on my jean-clad thigh before darting to Ares's hand curled possessively around one shoulder. I flash her a grin, and her cheeks turn a deeper shade of red.

We are probably traumatizing her for life. Or giving her ideas.

The others order quickly, and the poor girl scurries from the table with her face on fire.

Bree bursts out laughing. "I wish I had recorded that. It was priceless."

I flip her the bird with a wide grin. A girl could get used to this. I'm guessing something went down between the guys, and I would love to have been a fly on the wall for that conversation.

"There will be other opportunities," Jase says, popping a piece of bread in his mouth. "Ares is the competitive type."

Now it's my stepbrother's turn to flip his middle finger up. "You're just jealous my dick is bigger and pierced."

Jase cups his junk. "No dick envy here. I more than hold my own. Just ask Ash."

"Nope." I fix them with a warning look. "We're not comparing dick sizes. Not now. Not ever. All three of you are packing, and I'm never unsatisfied. That's all that matters."

Mention of Chad instantly sours Ares's mood, and he pulls his arm back, letting it hang at his side.

"Okay, that's it." I turn to face him. "It's time to tell us the rest." I cross my arms and slant him with a stern look. I mean business, and he needs to know we are talking about this now. "Why do you hate Chad so much?"

A muscle pops in his jaw as he claws a hand through his hair.

"Ares," I growl a minute later when he still hasn't spoken.

"Why do you think?!" he snaps, earning daggers from Jase.

"I don't know!" I wave my hands in the air. "That's why I'm asking!"

He grinds his teeth and rubs at his tense jaw. "He was in on it!" he blurts. "Chad was involved. Jasper Baldwin was trafficking little kids, and Chad was helping him to do it."

Chapter Eighteen
Jase

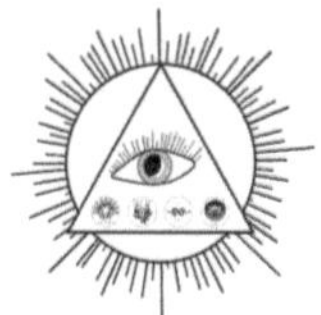

"Are you insane?" I glare at the asshole sitting on the other side of Ashley. "Chad had nothing to do with it! And I seriously have my doubts about Jasper too. If he was trafficking right under our noses, we would've known about it."

"Not if he was working for The Luminaries and they were covering his ass!" Ares slams his fist down on the table.

Ashley covers his clenched fist with her hand, unfurling his fingers one at a time. "Please stay calm. There is no point shouting at one another. We aren't the enemy." She looks at both of us. "You'd do well to remember that. We are trying to get to the truth here. Can we please do it without drawing attention to ourselves?" She subtly nods at our surroundings, and it's a timely reminder. I requested this table on purpose as it's tucked in the back and private. The other diners may not be able to hear what we are saying, but they can still see us. Ares's table-slamming stunt has garnered attention we don't need.

I force the anger to ebb from my veins, resolved to get to the bottom of this. I know Chad isn't involved, and by the time we leave this restaurant, I'm determined Ares will believe it too. "Since his dad was arrested, Chad has been protesting his innocence and claiming his father was set up. I went to my dad, and he swore he didn't know who Jasper was. He had never heard of him, and he was quite sure whatever had gone down was nothing to do with The Luminaries."

Ash emits a shocked gasp, and I arch a brow.

"Shit," Bree says. "I totally forgot."

"So did I." Ash turns to look at Ares, fixing him with a dark look. "I can't believe I forgot."

I can. It's been information overload for weeks.

Ash jabs her finger in Ares's face, looking like she wants to claw his eyes out with her nails. "You and Hera set Jasper Baldwin up!"

"What? Why am I only hearing this now?" I ask, letting my gaze jump between my fiancée and my sister.

"There wasn't any time to tell you," Bree says. "Then all this shit went down."

I lean forward. "What the fuck is going on, Ares?"

"I'll tell you if you'll stop jumping down my throat." Lifting his hand, he calls the impressionable waitress over. "I'll take a beer."

"Make that two," Bree says.

"Make it three," Ash adds.

The waitress looks at me, but I shake my head. "I'm good with water," I reply, lifting the glass to my lips and drinking greedily from it. She chews anxiously on her lip for a second, her gaze darting between Ash and Bree. "Marcus knows me," I tell her, referring to the owner. "It's fine to serve us. You can ask him." My word seems good enough for her, and she walks off.

"We're listening," Ash says, urging Ares to start talking.

Air puffs from his lips, and he leans back into the booth. "I returned to the US after Lilianna was taken. Initial intel pointed to Boston. If you remember, there was a big sex trafficking scandal there recently. We thought the same ring might have been involved. I connected with a guy who had mad hacking skills and hired him to help me. The Boston trail led me to Baldwin. He was in deep with traffickers, and it looked like one of them had taken Lili. My guy found nothing on his computers, but we knew there had to be some records somewhere. I moved back to Fenton, and Mom and I hatched a plan. She would seduce him, gaining his trust, so I could gain access to his home and office."

He stops speaking when the waitress appears with the beers, only resuming his explanation after she has left. "It wasn't difficult for Mom to start an affair with him. The guy was tripping over himself to hook up with her."

I'm guessing the Luminary lifestyle rubbed off on Hera more than she would like to admit. She sounds like a natural. Though, to be fair, she had strong motivation. If I was a father and my kid was taken, I don't think there is anything I wouldn't do to get her back. I'm not going to criticize her for doing what she did when she was doing it for her daughter.

Ash scrunches up her nose but says nothing, sipping from her beer.

"It didn't take him long to trust her either. She managed to make a copy of his home and office keys, and Mom distracted Jasper, on different occasions, so I could snoop in his things."

"What did you find?" I refill my glass from the jug on the table.

"Not a goddamned thing."

"What?" Ash asks, staring at him incredulously. "How can you say he was involved when you found no evidence?"

"That's not what I said."

"You're not making sense," Bree adds.

"I started following him after that. Later, after we became

friends, Shoulders, Rocky, and I took it in turns." Pain flares in his eyes for a brief second at the mention of his dead friends. Both men were members of The Bulls, and they died at the warehouse bombing in Lowell a few months back. Ares shakes the emotion off and schools his features into a neutral expression as he continues. "It became obvious straightaway that Jasper was hiding something. He was cagey and always looking over his shoulder. I watched him burn paperwork and receipts. His actions were not the actions of an innocent man."

"That doesn't mean he was involved in trafficking." Bree picks at the label on her bottle.

"Would you stop fucking interrupting me," he snarls before swigging from his beer.

"Let him speak," Ash says, determined to be the mitigator.

"The floor is yours, Psycho." Bree smiles glibly at him while Ash cautions her with a warning look.

"We took tons of photos. He was always meeting guys after hours in various places. Xavier ran the images for me, and they were always criminals. Gang members, guys involved in the drug trade, or guys suspected of trafficking. It was Jasper who led me to The Bulls. I knew they were involved in some way, and I only pretended to be a high schooler so I could enroll in high school and befriend Shoulders and Rocky. They proposed me for membership, and that's how I was able to infiltrate the gang. Not that it did much good. I still couldn't get near Ruben, and he's the one with all the intel."

"What about Chad?" Ash asks. "Where does he fit in."

"Chad ran errands for his father a couple times a week after school. I watched him hand over envelopes, laugh and joke with these guys." He grips the edge of the table, and his eyes turn black in anger. "I ambushed one of the assholes one time. I needed to see what was in the envelopes." He squeezes his eyes shut for a moment. "It was pictures and details of kids. Boys and girls. Some as young as four and five."

Bile climbs up my throat. Bree and I share a look, both thinking the same thing. How was this happening in our locale without our father being aware of it? It makes no sense. He must have known and lied about it.

"What did you do with that knowledge?" Ash asks.

Ares cracks his knuckles. "I buried that motherfucker alive, and then I sent the information anonymously to the cops with a note."

Silence pervades for a few tense beats.

"Is that why you hate Chad, or is there more?" Ash eventually asks.

Ares glares at her, and I reach forward, grabbing his shirt and pouring venom at him through my eyes. "Knock that shit off right now, or I'll put you through the wall."

He shoves me away, glaring at everyone in the room like he'd love to take out a machine gun and pump us all full of bullets. I have seen a lot of scary assholes in my time, but Ares Haynes is full of pent-up aggression he needs to find an outlet for before he detonates and takes casualties with him.

"Ares. I'm not your enemy." Ash palms one side of his face, forcing his gaze to hers. "I'm just trying to understand this."

"Chad had to know what he was doing, Ash." It sounds like he's trying to convince himself as much as us. I think he hears now how flimsy this evidence is. Unless there is more to divulge. "He was delivering those envelopes for over a year that I watched him. He interacted with those sick perverts like they were best buddies." Her hand lowers from his face, settling on his arm.

"That's his personality. Chad is always the showman," I say. "Always sociable. Football kind of demands it. His dad wanted him to take over the business when he retired, after

Chad's football career was over. He had him working with him on weekends and during holidays since he was fourteen. That doesn't mean Chad was aware of everything he was doing."

"Even if he didn't know," Ares says, his voice dropping a few octaves, "he was an accomplice. He helped to make it happen."

"Chad can't be blamed for something he didn't know." Ash speaks softly, rubbing his arm. "And I'm telling you now he didn't know. Chad wasn't mixed up in this. He wasn't involved in what happened to Lilianna. He was a kid too, Ares. A kid who just wanted to please his dad."

Ares props his elbows on the table and holds his head in his hands.

I reach out and link my fingers in Ash's. This is hurting her.

"I may have overreacted," Ares admits, lifting his head a few minutes later. "Desperation can do that to a person. And maybe something else." His eyes meet mine for a second. He clears his throat, straightening up before he looks at Ash. "In the interests of transparency, I'll admit I stalked you too."

Wow. Way to just put it out there.

More silence descends.

"Explain that." Ash sounds deceptively calm. I wonder if she's reached that place where nothing shocks her anymore because her brain is already too overloaded.

"I was following Jasper for a long time, and then I followed Chad. I watched you with him, and with Jase, and I...fuck it." Air expels from his mouth as he drags his hands through his hair.

"What?" Ash asks, remaining remarkably calm.

"I wanted you," he blurts, looking agitated. "I wanted you, all right? From the first moment I saw you, I felt this pull to you. It was just one more reason to hate Chad."

"Me too?" I inquire because that was the only reason that made any sense to me and Chad.

He nods. "I fixated on Chad after we got rid of Jasper and projected a lot of my hatred onto him. You were his sidekick. It was easy to hate you too."

"And you played with me to piss them off," Ash says, sounding annoyed now.

"Yes. No. Partly." Ares tugs his hands through his hair again.

"He played with you because he wanted you," Bree says, draining her beer. "He wanted to ruin Chad's life because he believed he was somehow involved in Lilianna's kidnapping. Even if deep down, he knew that probably wasn't true. Messing around with you killed two birds. He could hurt Chad and get to keep you. Win-win for Ares." Bree glowers at him.

The waitress stages a timely intervention then, delivering our food to the table. We are all quiet as she distributes plates, a new jug of water, and a bowl of freshly grated parmesan cheese.

"That is seriously messed up." Ash twirls a forkful of spaghetti.

"Told you I wasn't a saint," Ares growls, before cutting savagely into his steak.

"You were really unfair to Chad," Bree says. "He's no saint either, but there's no way he would ever willingly be involved in sex trafficking."

"Absolutely not," I agree. "He adores his sister Tessa. She's only fourteen. He was devastated when he heard what Jasper was accused of, for a lot of reasons, but mainly because of Tessa. He couldn't believe his dad would be involved in kidnapping little girls the same age as his daughter. It's the main reason he believes Jasper was set up. He would never in a million years help sick bastards kidnap kids. Never." I drill a look at Ares as I bite into my shrimp pasta.

"Hera didn't believe Chad was involved," Ash says in between mouthfuls. "I remember something I overheard."

"She thought I was wrong about him," Ares agrees, making quick work of his meal. "But not about Jasper. He was too involved not to know what he was doing."

"That's a valid point," I acknowledge.

"That's why you planted fake evidence on him," Bree surmises. She cuts up her chicken parmigiana into small pieces before scooping a forkful into her mouth.

"We knew he was guilty but didn't have enough concrete evidence. Xavier had other stuff he'd found. We were going to turn it into the authorities anyway, but I planted it in Jasper's office and then phoned in an anonymous tip. The cops and the FBI handled the rest."

"It still doesn't add up," I say, finishing my pasta and reaching for my water glass.

"I don't give a fuck about Jasper Baldwin," Ares spits out, also finishing his meal. "What's done is done. The only thing I care about now is finding Lilianna and bringing her home before those bastards end up killing her."

Chapter Nineteen

Ashley

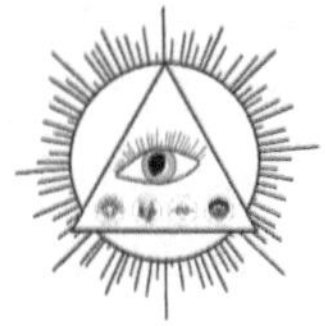

"Ares is full of so much rage," I tell Jase after we wave goodbye to Ares and Bree. "It's going to eat him alive."

"If I was in his shoes, I'd feel the same," he replies, steering me toward the parking lot where his car is parked. "He's going to need all that rage to get his sister back."

"Why do you say that?" I lace my fingers in his as we walk through the quiet parking lot.

"Finding her after all this time will be challenging even with our connections. I wouldn't put it past Rhett to have security on her wherever she is being held as an extra measure to keep us away. Ares will need that rage to fuel him. To push past the obstacles we'll face. He needs to dig deep." Jase presses me up against the side of the car when we reach it. His fingers sweep across my cheekbone. "If we get her back, she's not going to be the same girl. I have seen some of the victims my family have rescued over the years, and it's never pretty. Lilianna will be traumatized, and that won't be easy for Ares. He's going to need you."

"He has me, but he seems determined to push me away."

"Don't give up on him." Jase opens the passenger door. "And don't be afraid to push him. He needs you to break down his walls."

I slide into the car, contemplating his words as he rounds the car. "Did something happen today?" I ask when he climbs behind the wheel.

"Words might have been exchanged."

I beam at him, deliriously happy at the thought of my guys starting to get along. I'm under no illusion about Chad. I don't know if those two will ever be able to set aside their differences, especially when Chad finds out the reasons why Ares has hated him all this time.

Jase chuckles as he powers up the engine and reverses out of the spot. "I can practically see you creaming your panties."

I swat his arm. "Gross, but not completely untrue."

He moans. "Now she tells me." Flooring it out of the parking lot, he pins me with a salacious grin. "I'd pull over, but we're already late to meet with Carole."

Stretching across the console, I reach for the button on his jeans and pop it as Jase maneuvers his Maserati out onto the road. He hasn't replaced his Range Rover since he had to pretend it was stolen that time he and Bree came to rescue me from the crypt.

Man, that feels like a lifetime ago instead of a few months.

I miss fucking around in his Range Rover, but I'm quite partial to the Maserati, and it's time to christen it.

"What are you up to, Temptress?" Amusement dances in his tone.

"Just keep your eyes on the road, and let me worry about that," I tease, lowering his zipper and freeing his semi.

"Thank fuck for tinted windows," he says, cursing when

my hand wraps around his dick, and I begin stroking. He is hard as a rock in record time.

"You're like my own personal energizer bunny," I joke, rubbing my thumb across the tip of his cock. "Always full of life and ready to go at the drop of a hat."

"You turn me on just by looking at me."

"I know the feeling." I squirm on the seat as liquid lust pools south in my body. "Eyes on the road," I remind him as I lower my mouth over his straining erection.

Jase grips the wheel tight as I work him good, dragging my lips up and down his velvety-soft smoothness as my other hand fondles his heavy balls. Hollowing out my cheeks, I suck him down deep and quicken my pace, my head bobbing up and down as he drives.

"Fuck, yes, baby. Suck my big dick. Swallow it all down." He slaps my ass, and he's lucky I didn't bite his big dick.

I faux glare at him with a mouthful of cock.

"Bet you're creaming your panties now, baby. How wet are you for me? How badly do you wish you were bouncing on my dick?"

I flip him the bird because that's just cruel.

He chuckles before pushing my head back down, forcing me to gag on his shaft. I suck him harder and quicker when I feel his balls tighten and I know he's close.

"Jesus, fuck, Ash." Jase roars as he thrusts in my mouth, spilling his hot seed down my throat. The car jerks forward as his foot presses down on the accelerator while I continue to milk every last drop of his orgasm.

"That was something else," he says, grinning like a lunatic when I finally free him, tucking his dick back behind his boxers and jeans. His thumb brushes against the corner of my mouth. "You had a little cum there." He winks as he shoves it back inside my mouth. "Suck my thumb, babe."

I do as he asks, laving my tongue around his hot flesh, and his eyes blaze with fresh need. "You will be the death of me. I'm already getting hard again."

"Good." I look up, spotting we are almost to the apartment building where Chad's mom and sister are currently living. "Pull over. It's time for me to bounce on your cock."

"Whatever you need, baby." Jase pulls onto the shoulder, instantly cutting the engine and scooting his seat back while I wiggle out of my jeans and panties. Not the most accommodating clothing—or car—when you want a quick fuck at the side of the road, but I manage to strip myself from the waist in record time, and we'll make the tight space work.

Jase shoves his jeans and boxers to his ankles as he pumps his dick to full mast. Then I climb on, grab his cock, and situate it at my entrance. I stare deep into his eyes as I lower myself onto him, my natural juices lubricating me as I take his long thick dick into my body. His hands move up under my top and he tugs my breasts free from my bra, groping my sensitive flesh as I start riding him, loving the feel of his cock hugging my tight walls.

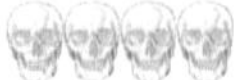

"I'd love to see Carole's face if you turned up looking like this," Jase says ten minutes later when our quickie is over. I check my reflection in the mirror, horrified at my expression. My lips are swollen, my neck is flushed, and my face is blotchy with heavy black marks under my eyes where my mascara is smudged. The lip gloss I put on before I left the restaurant is mostly wrapped around Jase's dick, and my hair is a tangled mess from Jase's hands.

"Geez. I look like I got dragged through a bush."

"Or like you were fucked good with a big dick that isn't her son's."

I roll my eyes. That's not the first time Jase has mentioned his big dick since Ares's comments at dinner. They are so competitive with everything. "I knew you wouldn't be able to let that go."

"Sometimes it's easy to see how Ares got away with pretending to be eighteen last year. He acts more like twelve than twenty-two most days."

"That's not fair or true. Ares works hard to hide who he is. He's a lot deeper and more intelligent than he'd lead you to believe."

Jase shrugs as he turns the engine on. "I don't doubt it, but if he continues to speak to you the way he did back at the restaurant, we're going to have a problem."

"You need to cut him some slack, and I'm capable of handling him myself. He won't be speaking to me like that, I assure you. Not unless he wants to lose me."

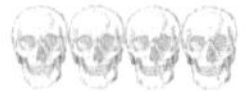

By the time we are standing at the apartment where Chad's family lives, I'm presentable again. Jase takes my free hand, but I pull it away. "I'm pretty sure Carole doesn't know her son shares me with you." Or used to. Since we're officially broken up. "I don't know if she knows we're no longer together. I'd rather not entertain any unwanted questions. We're here for a reason. Let's not distract her."

The door opens then. "Ashley!" Tessa throws her arms around me, hugging me tight. "I have missed you."

"Missed you too, girl. It's been far too long."

She eases back, and I spot Carole behind her. "Chad said

he messed up and you're not his girlfriend anymore. Is that true?" Tessa asks.

Guess the cat is out of the bag. "Yes, but it's complicated."

"He's so sad all the time," Tessa says, pulling me into the house as Jase hugs Chad's mom. Carole looks awful. Even worse than the last time I saw her. Haunting shadows bruise the skin under her eyes. She is in bad need of a haircut, and her clothes hang off her skeletal frame.

"How is school?" I ask Tessa, needing to divert the conversation.

"School is fine." She shrugs, but all the euphoria has disappeared from her eyes. I know it was hard for her to leave Lowell Academy to attend public school. All her friends are freshmen at the private school while she's at a new school without her usual support system. I make a mental note to talk to Chad again about letting me pay her school fees.

"I'm always here if you need to talk," I remind her, pulling her into my side and pressing a kiss to her cheek. She has Chad's big blue eyes and the same shaped face, but she doesn't share his dark-blond locks. Yet they are instantly recognizable as siblings. "Call me anytime."

"Ashley." Carole reaches for me, and she feels like skin and bone in our embrace. "I'm glad to see you."

"I'm sorry I haven't stopped by in ages." I don't offer an excuse because there isn't one.

"Please thank your mother for everything she did for us. I'm very grateful."

"It was no trouble."

"Is there anything you need now?" Jase asks.

"Just my son," she whispers, her voice cracking.

"I can't believe Chad got that bug back again. We had to stay away from him for weeks the last time," Tessa complains, and I wonder who fed them that excuse.

"Your brother will be in touch as soon as he can," Carole says. "Now, it's time for bed young lady."

"Mom." She draws out the word. "It's the holidays, and I don't have school tomorrow."

"You can watch TV in your room," Carole says. "I need to speak with Ashley and Jason in private."

"We'll do something over Christmas," I tell her. We have at least a couple of days where we can't do anything because of the holidays. "I'll call you, and we can go to the movies and out for pizza."

"Yay!" She jumps up and down.

"This is for you," I say, before I forget, handing her the bag with her gifts. I managed to grab a few things for her in between wedding shopping, and the girl behind the counter wrapped them for me. "Merry Christmas."

"Oh my God," she says, peering into the bag. "Thank you so much, Ashley." She envelops me in a hug again. "You're the best."

"No opening them until at least Christmas Eve."

"Go on," Carole urges. "I'll call you to say goodbye before Ashley and Jason leave."

Tessa reluctantly heads toward her bedroom, and my heart hurts for her.

"Thank you for that, Ashley," Carole says, urging us to follow her into the main living area. "That was thoughtful and generous. She was very upset when I told her Chad couldn't be with us for Christmas."

"Who told you he was sick again?" I ask as soon as I hear Tess's bedroom door close and we're assured of privacy.

"No one. I didn't know what else to tell her to explain Chad's absence. Where is he? What's happened to him?"

Chapter Twenty

Ashley

Carole sits down in the recliner chair by the fireplace, gesturing for us to sit on the couch.

Jase and I share a look, and I convey I'm letting him run with this. We sit side by side, our thighs brushing. Jase clears his throat. "What makes you think anything has happened to him?"

"My son calls me every single day. Without fail. Even when he was going through the height of his depression, Chad still called to speak to me and Tess. I last spoke to him on Friday. It's been three days, and I haven't heard a word from him. His cell is off when I call." She slams a hand over her chest as a strangled cry rips from her throat. "A mother knows when something is wrong. I have known something is wrong for some time."

Pity she didn't do something about it then. I still haven't forgiven her for falling apart after her husband died and letting Chad take all the responsibility for his family. That was her job. Not her son's.

Jase and I look at one another again.

"I thought you were here about that, or was I mistaken?" Her gaze flips between us.

"We aren't here about Chad," I say. "We wanted to ask you about Jasper."

Her shoulders stiffen. "Why?"

"A friend's little sister was kidnapped and trafficked a few years ago," Jase explains, resting his hands on his knees. "We are trying to help him find out what happened to her. Jasper's name cropped up."

"Jasper had nothing to do with it!"

"How can you be so sure?"

"Because I knew my husband, Ashley." She pins me with sad eyes. "He was a serial cheater, and our marriage was in trouble a long time before Hera Haynes jumped into bed with him, but he wouldn't hurt children. Jasper was no trafficker."

Shock splays across my face. I wonder if Chad knows his dad cheated a lot and his mom was apparently aware of it? Chad was notoriously tight-lipped about everything after his father was arrested.

I should have pushed him to speak to me.

That was the start of all our troubles.

"Jasper was no child kidnapper," she repeats when we don't respond to her statement. "Jasper could never do that to innocent children."

"He was seen handing information containing details of children targeted for trafficking to known criminals," Jase says, being as vague as he can.

Tears well in her eyes, and her shoulders shake.

Jase and I stare at one another, unsure what to do.

"Can I trust you?" she asks, lifting her head and whispering. She eyeballs Jase. "Chad always said you knew crazy things about people. I know he asked you to look into the allegations against Jasper. I know he told you we believe he was set up."

"I looked into it, and I couldn't find anything to either prove it or exonerate him."

"You can trust us," I add. "Whatever it is, you can trust us."

"I want to, but I'm scared."

Jase sits up straighter. "Scared of who or what?"

"Scared that whoever framed my husband and killed him will come after me and mine if I tell you what I know. If I give you what I have."

My eyes meet Jase's, and we are both trying to hide our shock.

"I can protect you," Jase says. "My father is a very powerful man, and my family has tons of resources. I can move you and Tessa to a safe place. Provide round-the-clock bodyguards and high-level security. Ensure you are both well cared for and that no one can get to you."

"What about Chad? I need to know my son is safe." Tears spill down her cheeks. "Has someone taken him? Is this a warning?"

I didn't want to come here and tell her about Chad, because it'll be a moot point when we get him back tomorrow, but I don't want to lie to her face either. I defer to Jase again.

"There is a bit of a situation with Chad, but we have it covered."

"Oh my God." She begins crying in earnest, rocking back and forth, hugging her knees to her chest. I glance behind me, praying Tessa doesn't hear and come rushing in.

"Carole." Jase sits on the arm of the chair, pulling Chad's mother into his arms. "Chad is my best friend. I'm going to ensure he's safe. You don't need to worry about him, I promise."

I narrow my eyes. That's not something he can promise

with absolute certainty at this time. And we don't know how traumatized he'll be after his ordeal.

"I need you to tell me everything, Carole. If you want to keep your family safe, I need to know it all. I can't help you blindfolded or with my hands tied behind my back."

"You can trust us," I reiterate. "We just want to help."

With more strength than I have given her credit for, she pulls herself together. Accepting a tissue from Jase, she dries her eyes and blows her nose. She clasps her hands on her lap and sits up straighter. Jase returns to sit alongside me. "Jasper ran his own financial investment company, as you are aware," she says. "One of his clients was a top-secret government organization."

That perks both our ears.

"He did highly classified work for them for years and was well paid for it. He was told to keep everything off the books, and he did."

"What kind of work?" Jase asks.

"Setting up offshore investments and hiding money. Sometimes washing cash. He was told when he was recruited never to ask questions and never to talk about it. He had to sign all kinds of confidentiality agreements and make all kinds of promises. He probably wasn't supposed to have told me, but we were actually very close. We told each other everything." She looks at the ground. "We had a good marriage except when it came to sex. I lost interest after Tessa came along, and he found other women to satisfy his needs. I didn't know about it for years. He was always discreet, and I knew none of them were serious. He loved me, but I couldn't give him what he wanted."

I lean into Jase, wishing the ground would swallow me. I do not want to be sitting here with Chad's mom listening to her detailing the problems in her marriage and her sex life. Chad would be mortified if he knew she was telling us all this. But I don't want to interrupt her. I think she needs to get this off her chest.

She should really see a therapist.

Carole shrugs, lifting her chin, looking a little embarrassed, like she hadn't meant to divulge all that. "The money was great, and he felt important to be hand-selected to work for this organization, so he never challenged any of the niggling doubts that plagued him from time to time."

I squirm on my seat. It looks like Ares was correct. This screams Luminary bullshit. It seems obvious now that Jasper was tied up with them.

"We were watching the news one night, and his face paled. A man had been arrested on multiple charges of child rape. He told me he was someone he had dealt with in the past, on several occasions. Someone he gave information to on behalf of the government."

"Did Jasper know what information he was supplying?" Jase asks.

She shakes her head. "He was given sealed packages to deliver. At first, they were irregular, but by the end, it was every week. He had tasked Chad with delivering them, but after that guy was arrested, he assigned Chad other work, and he started delivering them himself."

She gets up, heading over to the bookshelf at the back of the room. "Jasper was troubled for months. He tried to terminate his contract with the government organization, but they wouldn't let him. He realized then he was knee-deep in shady shit and the only way out was to find evidence of wrongdoing and try to use it to prove this organization was corrupt. He suspected it wasn't the government, that he had been tricked all along."

Her fingers move along the spines of books before resting on a thick tome. She pulls it out and walks back toward us.

"That is when he started actively investigating." She sits down with a copy of *War and Peace* on her lap. "I was terrified. I begged him to stop. He wouldn't tell me anything about his investigation. He said if I was questioned it was better I knew nothing." She opens the book, revealing a chunk cut out in the middle housing a sealed glass case. She takes it out, opens it, and extracts a thumb drive. "A week before he was arrested, he gave me this book. He told me to hide it someplace it would never be found, and to only give it to someone I trust. He made me promise not to give it to any cops or FBI agents or anyone claiming to be the government or from that organization that had hired him."

She is crying again. "I wanted to hand it in after he was arrested, but he had made me promise. I knew if he wanted them to have it he would have told the officers or his lawyer or the prison warden to come and ask me for it. No one ever did."

"Does Chad know about this?" Jase asks.

She shakes her head. "I have tried to keep him out of it. I let him believe I fell apart because of the affair with Hera, but the truth is, that barely even registered."

"You've been living in fear," I say, seeing it so clearly now.

"I am terrified, Ashley. They killed my husband, and I'm so scared my children and I will be next."

Chapter Twenty-One

Jase

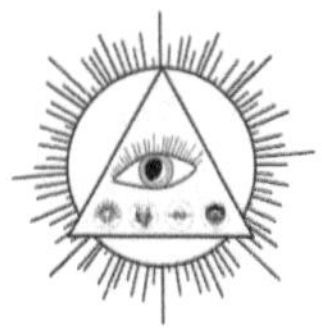

"Was Hera a spy?" Carole asks, shocking both of us.

"Why would you ask that?" Ash inquires.

"Towards the end of their affair, Jasper thought she was digging for intel. He feared she was a plant from his client. That they were on to him and knew he was trying to gather evidence against them."

"Did you share that suspicion with Chad?" I ask. It would explain why he loathed Hera with every fiber of his being.

She shakes her head. "Jasper didn't want Chad to know about his involvement with the client or the part he unwittingly played in helping them to kidnap kids. I didn't mention anything to my son in case he drew conclusions. Instead, I let him believe Hera was the reason our marriage ended and I fell apart."

"Hera isn't a spy," Ash supplies. "Though she *was* looking for evidence she thought Jasper had."

Carole's lips pull into a thin line.

"Her daughter was kidnapped and sold," Ash adds.

Carole's eyes pop wide.

"She's a year younger than Tess, and she's been missing for over two and a half years."

Carole covers her mouth with her hand.

"Hera thought Jasper was involved in her abduction. That's why she was with him. She needed to get close to see if he had any evidence that could point to where her daughter is being held."

"Oh my God." Tears glisten in Carole's eyes. "I had no idea. The poor woman. That is...There are no words." Sadness cloaks her like a shroud. "It makes so much sense now. I wish she had just asked. Perhaps Jasper might have been able to discover something about the kidnapping."

As if Hera or Ares could just walk up and knock on their door and ask Jasper if he was involved in sex trafficking and could help them to find Lilianna.

I resist the urge to roll my eyes at her naivety.

Leaving Ash to talk to Carole, I head outside to make a few calls. I return fifteen minutes later with an update. "I have a couple of bodyguards on the way over to watch your place," I tell Chad's mom. "They will rotate shifts every twelve hours. I advise you and Tessa to stay home unless it's absolutely necessary to go out. Then one of the men will go with you while the other will stay to guard the apartment. I have spoken to my father, and he'll prepare one of our safe houses tomorrow for your arrival. I will call you when it's arranged, and we'll send a car to take you there. I suggest you pack whatever you need to bring with you ASAP. The house will be fully stocked with groceries, so just clothing and personal belongings."

"We'll bring Chad to see you as soon as we can," Ash adds.

"Thank you." Tears pool in her eyes again. She pulls Ash into a hug and then me. "I can't thank you both enough."

"Chad is our family, and you're his," I say, taking Ash's hand. "We look after family."

After saying goodbye to Tess, we head to the car in silence. Before she buckles her seat, Ash leans across the console and kisses me.

"Not that I'm complaining, but what was that for?" I ask, securing my seat belt and kick-starting the engine.

"You're amazing. What you just did is amazing."

"I meant what I said." I drive out onto the road. "Carole and Tessa are important to Chad, and he's important to us. It's only right we take care of them when he's not here to do it himself."

"Yeah," she whispers, biting on the corner of her lip and averting her eyes.

"Hey." I glance over at her as I head in the direction of the lake. "Look at me, baby."

Ash wears her heart on her sleeve, and I can see everything she's thinking. "It's not your fault Chad was taken. The person responsible is Rhett Carter. That's not on you, and Chad would not want you taking that burden on."

"It isn't easy to ignore the guilt. If he wasn't messed up with me, this wouldn't have happened to him."

"Temptress, stop. Please don't do this to yourself. If you need to blame someone besides Rhett, blame me. I was the one who first brought this shit into his life."

The seat squelches as she turns to face me. "No way. You did everything to protect us. This isn't on you."

"Exactly." I pin her with a knowing look. "You need to take your own advice."

Slowly, she nods. "I know you're right, but it's hard to let the guilt go."

"Carole just told us Jasper was either a grunt or an expert.

Chad wasn't dragged into this world because of us, baby. His father did that."

"God, it's so fucked up."

"I know." I'm wondering why my father didn't know Jasper was working for The Luminaries. He said he checked it out—unless he was lying. Surely someone must have known? "By the way, I have a meeting at my house in the morning with my father."

Her brows climb to her hairline. "How come?"

"He agreed to provide the safe house, but he was hinting at other stuff that makes me nervous. He insisted I come over to talk."

"Do you think he knows something is going down?"

I swallow heavily, fearful he has gotten wind of something. "I don't know. Guess I'll find out tomorrow."

"Rhett said we can't tell anyone. I would think that especially means your father."

"Yeah. I'd think so too." I press my foot to the accelerator when we hit the main road, trying not to overreact until I know what we're dealing with. "No matter what he thinks he knows, we can't confirm it."

We arrive at our destination twenty minutes later. The moon is out, casting flickering shadows on the lake in the near distance. Stars scatter across the sky, shining clearly and brightly, as I drive the car up the winding driveway to the Stewart vacation house at Clear Lake. My parents also have a luxury cabin at Tahoe, but this place is homier and where Ash, Chad, and I spent several weeks every year during summer breaks.

Ash eyes me curiously. "What are we doing here?"

I press the button to pop the trunk. "I wanted to spend

some time alone with you, and I didn't want to head back to the house yet. I thought we could sit out on the dock, watch the stars, and reminisce about the good old times." I flash her one of my signature smiles before jerking my head behind me. "Grab the blanket from the trunk, will ya, babe?"

Ash gets out, and I swing into action, grabbing the ring box from the glove compartment and the bag with the champagne and glasses from the back seat. Slipping the box in the pocket of my jeans, I hold the bag and climb out.

"We had so many cool summers here," Ash says, coming up alongside me. The thick blanket is draped over her arm, and a content smile graces her gorgeous mouth.

Snaking my arm around her shoulders, I reel her in close while I hold the bag in my free hand. "We did. Coming here always felt like a different world. It was easier to leave all the Luminary bullshit at the front door."

We stroll along the side of the house, heading toward the large dock at the rear of the property. It faces directly onto the lake, and at this time of night, and this time of year, it's deserted. Just how I want it.

"Is someone else here?" Ash asks, spotting the lit firepit as we approach the end of the dock.

"I had someone swing by and light it. They should have left supplies to make s'mores too, and I have champagne," I add, lifting the bag up high.

Ash pins me with a dreamy smile, rendering my insides to mush. "This is very romantic. I think you're spoiling me."

"I think you deserve it." I kiss the tip of her nose. "You deserve to be spoiled every day of your life, and I intend to follow through."

We sit in the two gray Adirondack chairs in front of the firepit overlooking the oldest lake in northern Cali. Popping the cork on the bubbly, I pour two glasses while Ash fixes the blanket over both of us. We roast marshmallows and make s'mores, talking and laughing as we eat and drink. I take sips of my champagne, letting Ash have most of it, because I've got to drive us home.

"It's so peaceful here." Ash leans her head back and stares at the smattering of stars overhead. "I could happily live here full-time and be a recluse."

"Shutting the world out is hugely appealing, but we won't have that luxury when we are in charge of the Sloth Luminary."

"Ugh. I don't want to talk about that tonight. Not here." She turns on her side, snuggling under the blanket. "It's magical here, and we're getting married in three days." She beams at me, and my heart pounds to a new beat.

"Are you happy?"

"To be marrying you? Absolutely." She leans over and kisses me softly. "There are no cold feet here if that's what you're asking. I love you, and I can't wait to be your wife."

There will never be a more perfect moment. Setting my glass down on the ground, I slide out from under the blanket and go down on one knee in front of Ash's chair. Her eyes startle, instantly flooding with emotion. I take her hand in mine. "I know this isn't the way we would choose to get engaged and married, but I need you to know you mean everything to me, Ash, and I wouldn't change a thing because it's led us here to this moment. A moment I dreamed of and wished for, for so long, but I never thought it would come true."

My heart swells with love as she stares at me like I hung the stars in the sky. When Ash looks at me like this, there is nothing I would deny her. She stares at me with so much trust, so much devotion, and so much love I am almost speechless. Clearing my throat, I shake myself, determined to do this one thing right for the love of my life. "I loved you from the first moment I met you, Ashley Shaw, but you were not mine to love. So, I shoved my feelings down, tried to be happy for my friend, and told myself if it was meant to be it would happen. And it did. The day you agreed to be mine was the happiest day of my life. It sounds cheesy, but that was the first day I felt complete. I have been walking around with this void in my chest for so long, but you fill it up, Ash. You fill it completely, and no matter what obstacles life throws at me, I know I can surmount them if I have you by my side."

Removing the box from my pocket, I pop the lid and present the ring to her. "I couldn't let things go without doing this right because you deserve everything, Ash. I love you and I promise to take care of you and worship and cherish you every day for the rest of our lives. I know you have already agreed to marry me, but this one is for us. This is the story we will tell our kids and our grandkids when they ask how we got engaged."

Emotion clogs the back of my throat, and I'm struggling to continue. Tears are streaming down Ash's face, but I know they are happy ones. "You're the love of my life, Ashley Shaw, and I never want to spend another day apart. Marry me, my love?"

"Yes, Jase." She's crying and laughing, and my eyes are suspiciously damp as I slide the ring on her finger. "Nothing would make me happier or prouder. I cannot wait to be your wife."

Chapter Twenty-Two

Ares

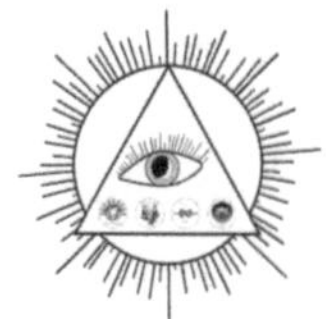

I watch Bree gushing over the rock on Ash's finger with conflicted emotions. The girls are seated on stools at the bar in the basement room, fawning over the ring Jase gave her and giggling like they're five. At least he knows her well. It's not some massively expensive over-the-top gaudy diamond. It looks elegant and pretty on her finger, sparkling under the bright lights. She can't stop looking at it, and she has the biggest smile on her face. Jase hands them a glass of champagne each, wrapping his fiancée in his arms as he bends down to kiss her. Ash tilts her head up, staring adoringly at him as she flings her arms around his neck and kisses him deeply.

Things start happening down south, and I silently caution my dick to calm down. Watching someone else kiss the girl I have feelings for should not be a turn-on.

What the fuck is happening to me?

Leaning back in my chair, I avert my eyes and try to focus on the TV rather than attempt to decipher my twisted feelings.

I'm a fucking mess right now.

Bree and I waited up for Ash and Jase to return, not realizing they would be gone for hours. Bree has an update from her contact she wants to share, and apparently it couldn't wait until tomorrow.

"Got something on your mind?" Jase asks, handing me a fresh beer. He flops down on the couch beside me, bringing his own bottle to his lips.

Ashley giggles, narrowly avoiding falling off the stool she's sitting on.

"Is she drunk?"

"She's a little tipsy, but she's fine."

I harrumph, switching my gaze back to the TV as I drink from my beer.

"Are you jealous?" I feel Jase's eyes boring a hole in the side of my skull.

As if I'm answering that. "Don't try to psychoanalyze me or pretend like you know me."

"Not sure you got the memo, dude, but we're on the same side."

"Not sure what fucking side I'm on anymore," I blurt.

He sighs heavily. "Yeah. I know. It's a shitshow."

"What happened at Chad's place?" I ask, wondering what his mother had to say.

Jase fills me in. The girls are giggling and drinking in the background.

"How the fuck did you not know his old man was involved in Luminary bullshit?"

"It's not exactly something that is openly talked about, and he's not part of our Luminary family. If he was, my father would have told me," he replies.

I kick my bare feet up on the coffee table. "I'm betting he's Carter's."

"It would make sense." Jase purses his lips before pulling out his cell. His fingers fly over the keypad. He looks up and answers my unspoken question. "I asked Knight to check it out for me."

"Is that wise?" Ash asks, tumbling onto Jase's lap with a giggle.

"I doubt it will raise any red flag or warrant him mentioning it to his father."

"We need to see what's on that flash drive," I say before I get up and stalk to the refrigerator behind the bar, grabbing two bottles of water. I toss one to Bree and hand the second one to Ash. "Drink." I pin her with a sharp look.

"Aye, aye, Captain." She smirks as she salutes me, and I flip her the bird. She cracks up laughing, smiling at me like we're not in the middle of Armageddon and the world hasn't gone to hell in a handbasket.

Snatching up my beer, I drain it in one go.

Bree lifts her palm. "Hand me the drive, and let's see what's on this baby." Jase gives her the thumb drive Carole handed over to him and Ash. She slots it into the side of her laptop, instantly cursing.

"What?" Ash asks, immediately sobering up.

"It's password protected."

"I suspected as much." Jase runs his hand up and down Ash's spine.

"Should we ask Carole if she knows the password?" Ash asks before knocking back a mouthful of water.

"She would've told us if she had it. Jasper knew whoever ended up with this file would be able to crack the password."

"I'll take it over to my guy first thing in the morning," Bree says.

"Have we made any headway with the men guarding the building where Chad is being held?" Ash asks.

Mention of his name has me grinding my teeth. I hate admitting I'm wrong, and nobody can convince me Chad didn't suspect his dad was up to something shady, but I believe Ash and Jase when they say he wasn't involved in the trafficking. Doesn't mean I like the dude or we'll be holding hands around the campfire any time soon.

"We have an in," Bree confirms. "Our team found some dirt on one of the guys, and we can use it to our advantage. The good news is, he's on the roster for tomorrow night."

"Yes!" Ash leans her head on Jase's shoulder. "Thank God."

"Is he on shift tonight?" Jase asks Bree.

"No. They alternate days and nights. Weeks where they are on nights, they do one day on, one day off."

"Good." Jase lifts Ash off his lap, placing her down on mine. "I'm going to grab a few guys and pay him a visit tonight."

"It's after midnight," Ash says as she snuggles into me. The scent of her perfume seeps into my pores like a magic potion, adhering to my skin and calling to me like an enchantress. My arms automatically band around her, and I hold her close, pressing my nose to her hair, inhaling the peachy smell with hints of vanilla.

Jase smirks, and I glare at him.

"This needs to happen now. I have that meeting with Dad in the morning, and then we need to plan a strategy for tomorrow night. We don't have time to waste."

"Hold tight for a sec, PC2." Bree closes her laptop and sets it down on the coffee table. "I have something I need to tell you all." She sits sideways, tucked into the end of the couch, toying with strands of her long blue hair.

Jase sits back down, giving her his full attention.

"You need to know what happened in South America, and I think it could be connected."

"We're listening." Ash sits up a little straighter in my lap. Her arms curl around my neck, and she tucks her knees up closer. I cling to her like she's the oxygen I need to breathe, and it's troubling.

What is this girl doing to me?

Why am I falling harder when I should be pushing her away?

Bree clears her throat and starts explaining. "When I was in South America, I worked for a time at a rape support center. One day, this young girl came in, screaming hysterically that her friend was in danger, and she needed help. When we eventually calmed her down enough so she could explain, she told us her friend had gone to meet an American man who promised her she could be a model in the US."

Goose bumps sprout on my arms, and I have a sixth sense what she's going to tell us *will* make a difference.

"This girl had a bad feeling about it. She'd read about other young girls going missing from the area and she smelled a rat when the man told her not to tell her parents. She begged her friend not to go, and she promised she wouldn't, but she lied. As soon as the girl found out, she tried to tell the girl's parents, but they were at work, and she couldn't reach them, so she came to us for help."

"Shit." Ash shivers in my arms. "I'm guessing this story doesn't have a happy ending."

"It doesn't." Bree gulps before wrapping her arms around herself.

"The girl knew where she was meeting him, so we got a crew of eight together, and we went after them." Bree drinks from her water, her hands shaking so badly it's a miracle she doesn't spill it. "The guys we were with were local vigilantes. They told stories on our way there. This wasn't anything unusual for them. It happened all the time." Her voice wobbles, and her lower lip trembles.

My heart thuds painfully against my rib cage, thinking of all the Liliannas out there.

Jase slides over beside his sister, circling his arm around her shoulders. "Whatever it is, you can tell us."

"No judgment," Ash adds. "You were trying to do a good thing. If it went wrong, that's not on you."

Bree draws in a sharp breath before continuing. "When we got to the location, it was an old factory building in a remote part of town. We heard screaming and crying, and the guys rushed in without hesitation. I entered the building in time to see the doors closing on a large van. There were at least ten young girls inside. Gunfire broke out, and it was a free-for-all. I tried running around the edge of the building, hoping I could shoot out the tires and stop the van from leaving, but I didn't make it in time. The van got away. At that exact moment, a man crept up behind me, and we fought. He had me pinned from behind, but I managed to stab him in his thigh and push him away. I turned around and shot him, riddling him with bullets until he fell to the ground. By then, the gunfire had stopped all around me. We had lost one man but taken out five kidnappers. Two got away with the van."

Jase hugs his sister as she shakes. "The vigilantes were checking through pockets, looking for wallets and IDs to dispose of separately before they burned the bodies. That's when I saw it." Her face pales. "The guy I had killed had the Luminary branding on his upper arm."

"You think it was a sting operation?" Jase asks.

Bree shrugs. "I don't know what to think. I know this is what Lust & Envy does. I know we have teams in the field who set up situations to trap these perverts, but it was happening all the time, Jase." She looks up at her brother. "If they were there to stop it, why hadn't it stopped?"

"Which Luminary family was the guy from?" Ash asks.

"I panicked when I saw the arm branding and ran without checking. All I could think was I killed a member of a Luminary family and I would be murdered if anyone found out. Especially if I had interfered in an official mission and taken out one of our own. I didn't even stop to check if any others had the branding."

"It doesn't make sense," Jase says. "A Luminary family member would not be involved at that level. At most, it was someone from a master's family. You would be punished but not killed for that."

His words incense me. "So, it's okay to kill one man if he's of a lower social standing as long as we don't touch the precious Luminaries?" I hiss, finding little comfort in the fact I apparently can't be murdered without consequence.

Jase nods. "It's a toxic system, and it shouldn't be okay to kill anyone, but murder is a normal way of life in our world. I'm just stating facts. Not saying I agree because I don't."

"It's such bullshit anyway," Ash says. "The Luminaries break the rules all the time. Look at what Rhett has done and is planning. It's clear there are loopholes and ways around that rule. The man came up behind you with the intent to kill you. I'm betting he knew who you were. It's a clear case of self-defense, and we could argue that if we had to." She tilts her head, her features hardening as she looks at her friend. "But I get why you're worried. That fucking prick who gave me life could hand whatever evidence he has over and land you in a world of trouble."

"It would be his word against mine, and he has the upper hand because he's one of the most powerful men in the country and I'm a known 'problem child.' It's not hard to imagine who they'd believe."

"How did Carter get his hands on evidence?" Jase scrubs a

hand along his jaw, looking worn out. "Why is that asshole always ten steps ahead of us?"

"He's been plotting this for a long time, and we're playing catch-up," Ash says.

It might seem insurmountable, but I'm determined we are going to win this battle. "That bastard is going down, and we're going to be the ones to do it," I say. Steely resolve resonates in my tone.

Jase nods. "Nothing less will be acceptable." He looks over at his sister. "Do you have a theory on how Carter knew about this?"

Bree bobs her head and wets her lips. "I was living with a photographer and his girlfriend at the time. We were all fucking, and while it started out amicably, the dude couldn't handle it when his girlfriend grew closer to me. Turns out, he followed me that day and took pictures. He used them to blackmail me into leaving." She barks out a laugh. "The irony is, he didn't need them. I was terrified of repercussions and knew I needed to come home. I figured if shit was going to rain down on me, I would be better off under the protection of my family."

"You told Baz," Ash surmises.

Bree nods, and Jase curses. She turns to her brother. "I know you don't trust him, but you are wrong. Baz is on our side."

"I am," Baz says, entering the room from the bathroom where he has clearly been hiding this entire time.

Jase looks furious as he glares at Bree. "Are you for real right now?" he yells, standing and pacing. Ash gets up, grabbing his hand and threading her fingers in his. She whispers in his ear, calming him down.

"If you're on Bree's side, how did Rhett Carter get his hands on this evidence to blackmail her with?"

"He didn't." Baz takes a few photos from a large brown

envelope. "I buried it and covered the tracks. No one should have known, but that prick Carter didn't need it." Baz holds up a photo and I rise, moving with Ash and Jase to inspect it.

"Fucking hell." Ash looks between me and Jase. "The guy Bree killed had the Greed & Gluttony brand on his chest."

"Meaning he was a Luminary, and I'm standing in an ocean full of hot water," Bree says, sliding her arm around her older brother's waist.

"Why would a man of his status be involved in a low-level sting operation?" Jase asks, frowning as he looks at Baz.

"A better question is, why would the Greed & Gluttony family be anywhere near an operation that falls solely under the responsibility of Lust & Envy?"

"He's running a side hustle," I say, connecting the dots. "Rhett Carter has his dirty hands all over this, and I'd bet my life he gave the order to take my sister. He didn't investigate to find out where she is. He's known all along."

Chapter Twenty-Three

Ashley

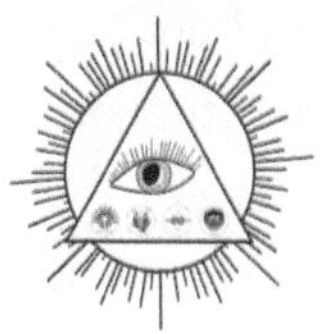

"Jase is back," Bree says as I pull my Lexus into my parking spot in front of our townhome and kill the engine the following afternoon. Her brother's Maserati is at the end beside a sleek black Bugatti that has me salivating and creaming my panties.

"I wasn't expecting him back so soon," I admit, grabbing my workout bag from the back seat and hopping out of my SUV.

"The meeting must not have gone well." Bree purses her lips as she slams the passenger door shut.

"Who owns this?" I ask, running my fingers reverently along the side of the coveted Bugatti.

"Baz," she confirms as I lock my car with the key fob.

"Do you think Jase is talking to you yet?" I loop my arm in hers. "He was hopping mad last night. Really angry you blabbed to Baz without consulting him. I had to fuck him into a virtual coma to get him to shut up."

Bree's pretty face contorts into a grimace. "Ugh. I definitely did *not* need to know that."

I grin. Can't help it.

Bree flips up her middle finger. "You're wicked."

We climb the steps together, both of us hot sweaty messes after our workouts at Fox Fitness. Vincent put us through our paces, and it shows.

We enter the house to the sound of shouting and roll our eyes. "I thought love and marriage might mellow PC2, but he's as argumentative as usual." We dump our bags in the hallway and make our way into the kitchen.

"Can you both chill the fuck out," Bree says, storming over and pushing herself in between her brothers. They are in a tense face-off, looking like they want to knock the shit out of one another.

"Can we at least try to discuss this like civilized adults?" I ask, punching digits in my cell phone. Ares picks up on the fourth ring. "Can you feign sickness and come home now?"

"I'm on my way," he says before hanging up.

I love that he just accepts me at my word. There is no questioning it. If I say I need him here, he'll drop everything to be here. The thought sends a flurry of warmth charging through my veins. Ares might still be trying to keep me at arm's length—my offer to sleep in his bed last night was instantly shot down, proving my point—but I know I am under his skin in the same way he's under mine. After we get through the wedding and the board meeting, I am pinning him down and making him talk to me. He can't avoid me forever. And he cannot continue to bottle his feelings up and pretend like he doesn't care about me.

I'm worried about him. He's carrying a lot on his shoulders, and I want to share the burden and help to lighten his load.

"We're going to grab showers and freshen up," I say, pulling Bree back from her warring brothers. "Make yourselves useful and fix lunch while we're gone. Ares is on his way home, and then we're all going to sit down and talk in a nonconfrontational manner." Narrowing my eyes at the guys, I warn them with a pointed stare. "Quit this shit." I jab my finger between them. "Let's harness all that pent-up testosterone and point it at the enemy." I lean in and peck Jase's lips quickly. "News flash, it's not your brother."

Unless something transpired at the meeting this morning that contradicts that assertion. But I'd bet my inheritance Baz hasn't betrayed our confidence, and my gut tells me he's on our side.

"Sure I can't tempt you to elope with me?" Baz rakes his gaze over me while licking his lips and grinning.

"Knock it off!" Bree thumps him in the arm as Jase clenches his fists, looking ready to swing at his brother.

I slide my arm around Jase, plastering myself to his body. "Nothing or no one could tempt me to walk away from Jase." I stretch up and kiss him. "He's my man." Clinging to his arm, I watch the aggression slowly ease off his face. "Soon to be my husband, and I love him with an intensity I can't put into words."

"Love you too, Temptress," he says before slamming his lips down on mine in a kiss far too passionate to be shared with an audience.

When we separate, all tension is gone from his face, and my work here is done.

"Behave and play nice. That's an order." I shoot them one final warning look before Bree drags me away.

"Damn girl," she says, smothering a laugh as we back out of the kitchen. "That was some slick skillful manipulation. I'm thinking you're way better suited to Lust & Envy than Greed & Gluttony."

I snort out a laugh as we climb the stairs. "A woman has to use every weapon at her disposal, and I've spent years honing my craft. How else do you think I've successfully navigated a relationship with two men?"

When we return downstairs twenty minutes later, Ares has arrived, and the guys are finishing setting up lunch on the long table.

"Hey, sexy." I saunter up to Ares, fling my arms around his neck, and smash my lips to his before he can utter a word or attempt to reject me. He doesn't disappoint, wrapping his arms around my back, lifting me off my feet, and kissing the shit out of me. I am red-faced and panting when he puts me back down a few minutes later.

"Holy shit," Bree mouths behind his head, fanning herself. "So freaking hot!"

Baz sidles up to me, tugging me into his side. A flirtatious grin dances across his mouth. "Where's my kiss? I'm feeling left out." He puckers up, and I duck out from underneath his arm before Ares or Jase takes a swing at him. Both my guys are glaring at him like he's the devil and it's their mission to eradicate the world of his evil.

Ares doesn't even know about my initiation.

The thought reminds me we need to have a conversation about his. I wonder if Jase has mentioned it to him yet.

"Quit stirring shit." I level Baz with a dark look.

"I hear there's a vacant spot in this little harem of yours." Baz grabs a grape from the fruit bowl, popping it into his mouth. "How does one go about applying?"

I thump him in the arm, and he almost chokes on the grape. "Seriously, asshole? We are in a world of shit, and you have to keep goading them?"

The humorous expression drops off his face. "You're right. Sorry. This is just what Jase and I do."

"I suggest you both get an attitude adjustment." I whip my gaze to a smug Ares. "You can stop gloating. You need one too. How many times do I have to remind you knuckleheads that we don't stand a chance at beating the enemy if we are not united? We need to be a team in every sense of the word."

Baz opens his mouth to say something, and Bree thumps him this time. "Don't even go there!"

"What the fuck is with you two and violence?" He rubs at his upper arm. "That actually hurts."

"Pussy." Ares grabs a bowl with chips and walks toward the table.

"They just came from a session with Vincent," Jase says as if that explains it. He reels me into his arms. "Sorry, baby." He nips at my earlobe before whispering in my ear. "Your bossiness is such a fucking turn-on. You make me so horny, Temptress." Angling his hips, he nudges me with his boner.

"You have sex on the brain," I whisper back. "Not that I'm complaining, but time and place. We need to have a serious conversation."

"We can hear you," Baz deadpans.

"And you have sex on the brain too," Bree adds, quirking a brow at me.

I shrug and grin. "I have three men to satisfy. It's impossible *not* to have sex on the brain."

"Three?" Ares inquires from his seat at the table. The plate in front of him is loaded with sandwiches, fruit, and chips. A look of displeasure is etched upon his face. "Tell me you don't mean Baldwin. I thought you had more self-respect, or have you forgotten how he taunted you and pushed Julia in your face?"

I stomp over to the table, instantly livid. "*You* rubbed Julia in my face."

"I wasn't your boyfriend." He shrugs before stuffing a sandwich in his mouth.

"Neither was Chad when that happened," I remind him even though it didn't make the pain any less. "It's none of your business, and you don't get to tell me what to do."

"It is if I'm also fucking you."

"I'm not having this conversation now."

"I love some light entertainment with lunch," Baz unhelpfully adds as he slides onto a chair across from Ares.

"Oh my God, get over yourselves already!" Bree throws her hands in the air before claiming the seat beside Baz. "It's like trying to wrangle toddlers at a kiddie party."

"Preach, sister." I sit beside Ares, and Jase sits on my other side.

"We have a lot to discuss and plan before the party tonight. Can we at least try to stay focused?" I ask, adding a couple of sandwiches and a piece of chopped-up apple to my plate.

Jase pours ice water from the large jug we always keep in the refrigerator, and finally everyone settles down.

"Vincent had an update for us," I say in between mouthfuls of chicken salad sandwich. "Your mom is settled," I tell Ares. "For now, they think it's best we have no contact as we don't know exactly what access Rhett has. We don't want to compromise her."

"And that doesn't make me suspicious at all," Ares snarls. "I'm not sure I trust these guys."

"Your dad did," Baz says. We updated him fully last night after the bathroom reveal. There didn't seem any point not to. He has promised not to breathe a word, and he instantly said he was in. Jase is still wary, but I believe Baz is sincere, and we need as many hands on deck as possible. "They are one of the most respected master families out of all the Luminaries. Victor is a man of his word. If he told your dad he'd keep his family safe, he meant it. You can trust him."

"I doubt Hera would've gone with him if she had any doubts," I say.

"Either way, we have no choice but to trust them," Jase supplies. "Unless they give us a reason not to."

I take a drink of my water. "At least he is following through on his promise."

"We'll see." Ares is tense as he devours the rest of his sandwich.

"I arranged a prison meet for you with Ruben," Baz says, eyeballing Ares across the table. "It's for two days after Christmas."

Ares nods, and that's the closest Baz will get to an acknowledgement of thanks. I roll my eyes, adding another item to my mental checklist for my convo with Ares—how to be gracious and show gratitude.

"Thanks, Baz. We appreciate it," I say, shooting daggers at the man sitting beside me.

"You're welcome, beautiful." Baz's grin is downright wicked, and if I don't shoot this down now, World War Three will break out. "What happened at the meeting with your dad?" I blurt, looking between Baz and Jase.

Baz drops the flirty smirk in a nanosecond. "He suspects something. He was sniffing around, asking questions about Carter and Salinger."

"Well, shit." I turn to face Jase. "What did you tell him?"

"I played dumb and deflected all his questions." His eyes lift to his brother's. "I don't think he would have bought it if Baz hadn't backed me up."

"So what was all the shouting about when we came in?" Bree asks with a frown.

"Baz thinks we should tell Dad everything," Jase replies.

"No way." Ares slams his fist down on the table. "We've already taken a massive risk bringing you in and planning to rescue the jock." Frustration seeps from his tone as he glares at Baz and then Bree. Jase wasn't the only irate male in this house last night. "My sister's life is at stake here! We can't take any more chances. She could die if we make one wrong move and Carter finds out about it. I haven't come this close to finding her just to lose her."

The gravity of the situation hits home at his heartfelt words, and tension bleeds into the air.

"I understand," Baz says. "I would feel the same way if it was Jocelyn. She's the baby in our family, and we wouldn't want to do anything to risk her safety, but I know my dad. I have worked closely with him for years. I have his trust, and he has mine. He doesn't always confide in me, but I have known for some time that he's up to something. I think he suspects Carter and Salinger of plotting something. I think he would side with us if we told him."

"And I told you it's too risky." Jase leans across the table. "I don't happen to share that same level of trust. I don't trust him."

"If you knew the lengths he's gone to in order to give you as much freedom as he can, you would. He's not your enemy, Jase. He's not any of our enemy. I know the reputation he has. He has cultivated it to be so. But he's a good man, and he wants change as much as we all do."

"If that's true, he'll agree to help us once Walter Salinger and James Manford are out of the picture. If he sides with us on the vote and agrees to help us kill Carter, then I'll believe you." Ares crosses his arms over his broad chest. "But not before then. We can't risk it. We can't risk him warning Manford or Salinger or going head-to-head with Carter on his own. Unless you can tell me with absolute certainty that that wouldn't happen, we say nothing to him now."

Baz rubs the back of his head, looking torn.

"Exactly," Jase says. "You may know him, but you don't know exactly how he'd react. For now, we continue deflecting. In the coming days, we'll see if Eric Stewart is the good man you consider him to be."

Chapter Twenty-Four

Ashley

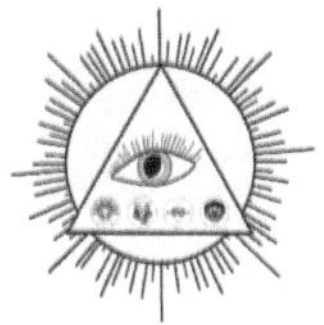

"I'm trying to keep my head in the game," Jase says, sitting alongside me in the back of the limo taking Bree, Baz, Ares, Jase, and me to the Christmas party being held at the Carter mansion. "But it's challenging when you look sexy as sin, and all I want to do is peel that dress off and fuck you six ways to Sunday."

"We can hear you," Bree drawls, fiddling with the hem of her sparkly, purple dress. We both opted for minidresses and sky-high ankle boots. Where Bree's vibrant dress is one shoulder, my black, silver-sequinned gown has spaghetti straps and a crisscross feature at the back. It only reaches mid-thigh when I'm seated, so I'm flashing a lot of flesh. Jase isn't the only one feeling frisky. Ares's eyes are like laser beams on my body, undressing me with every heated look he sends my way. He's sitting directly across from me with Bree beside him. I might have parted my legs, offering him a tantalizing glimpse of the flimsy lace thong I'm wearing, on purpose.

"I don't care," Jase retorts as his fingers glide up and down my thigh.

His touch sends scorching heat racing across my exposed flesh, and I'm not exactly opposed to his sexual overtures. Especially when he looks good enough to eat in his Prada tux. His wavy, dark hair is tamed back off his face, highlighting those gorgeous green eyes and the dimples I love. Jase is sex on a stick, and my libido is itching to climb on to his dick and ride him into oblivion.

But sex will have to wait.

We are on a mission, and we can't get distracted.

"Get Chad out, and I'll be your reward later," I say, cupping his junk and squeezing gently. Ares's eyes flare with fresh heat. Tracing the edge of my boot up the side of Ares's leg, I add, "The same applies to you."

"I don't share," he grits out predictably. It's like a mantra these days.

Baz chuckles. "You're such an idiot."

Ares turns venom-filled eyes on Jase's older brother. "Fuck off."

"Only a guy who has never had group sex or experienced DP would spout that shit."

"Screw you, asshole. I've fucked multiple girls at once. By myself and with other guys. It's—"

"You have?!" I blurt, instantly lowering my foot to the ground. Leaning forward, I glare at him. "So, what, it's good enough to share them but not me?" I shoot daggers from my eyes as hurt slays me on the inside. Crossing my arms, I glare out the window at the dark landscape as it flashes by.

"Stop being so fucking sensitive." Ares grips my chin, forcing my face to his. "None of them meant anything. *You do.*"

That helps a little. But only marginally. Now my head is filled with images of him fucking other women, and I'm consumed with jealous anger and frustration. I open my mouth to rip him a new one before clamping my lips shut again. I swore to myself I wouldn't pressure him, and if I spew the thoughts currently in my head, it will come across like that.

When Ares joins us, I want it to be his decision and his alone.

"You all have serious issues." Baz smooths a hand down the front of his expensive suit jacket. Like his brother, he's wearing a designer tux, and he looks hot. His rep on campus is no surprise, and I doubt he had to work hard for it. He only has to smile at a girl, and she drops her panties for him.

"Fuck you," Jase and Ares say in unison. "Mind your own business," Jase adds. His eyes narrow to slits as he eyeballs his brother. "What we do doesn't concern you."

Baz opens his mouth to retaliate, but Bree gets there first. "We're here," she says, looking out the other window as the car turns into a long, wide driveway. "It's time to put our game faces on."

Jase helps me into my silver faux fur coat before we emerge from where the limo is parked at the front of the extravagant Carter mansion. It's a sweeping two-story redbrick building set on acres and acres of landscaped grounds. Stone steps lead up to the entrance, facing an ornate fountain. Partygoers are lined up on the steps and in front of the grand double doors, talking and laughing, and everyone appears to be in good spirits.

It's hard to feel in the mood when I know Chad is being caged and tortured somewhere on the property. The desire to rampage is riding me hard, but I remind myself we have a plan, and we need to stick to it. Baz and Jase personally put the screws on Cleo's guard, and whatever shit they are blackmailing him with must be good as he readily agreed to our demands.

"What if the guy double-crosses us?" I ask, licking my lips and squeezing my thighs when Ares climbs out of the limo behind Bree and Baz. Ares looks edible, and I'm salivating for a taste.

There was an almighty argument when Ares showed up in the kitchen wearing biker boots, jeans, a black shirt, and his battered leather jacket. He looked hot as fuck—like always—but Baz and Jase forced him into one of Jase's suits, saying he would stick out like a sore thumb if he didn't present at the party suitably attired.

I had to sweet-talk Ares into wearing it and I'm so glad I did. The fitted black suit hugs his ripped body in all the right places. It's a little snug across the shoulders and biceps as Ares is a bit broader and more bulked up than Jase, but it only draws attention to his best assets. His dark hair is slicked back, and the scruff on his chin and cheeks has been trimmed to a stylish layer of stubble. With his piercings and the ink creeping up the side of his neck and out from under the cuffs on his hands, he is garnering more than his fair share of admiring glances.

Jase snaps his fingers in my face, pinning me with an amused expression. "You haven't heard a word I've said, have you?"

"Nope." I grin at him as I pull Ares in close, lacing my fingers in his, while snuggling into Jase's side. Fuck what anyone thinks looking at us. "Can't help a girl for zoning out in the face of such hotness." I waggle my brows, and Jase chuckles.

"I was telling you we took the guy's fiancée as insurance," Jase explains. "He'll toe the line."

Nausea swims up my throat. "I hate that. We're no better than Carter."

"We didn't exactly have a lot of time to plan this," Ares says, looking equally uncomfortable.

"And she won't come to any harm." Jase looks around before pressing his mouth to my ear. "Even if he crosses us, we won't hurt the woman. We aren't like him."

"Okay." My tongue darts out, wetting my lips as I glance over at the large house. A shiver works its way through me, and I cling tighter to Jase, siphoning some of his warmth. "Are Rhett and that bitch here?"

"They won't be here," Baz says. "Knight has thrown this party the past three years, and the rents always make themselves scarce."

"Cleo is at the building," Jase says, showing me his phone. The screen displays an image of the underground of the building with several red dots. Some are moving, some are stationary.

"Are those people?"

"Yes. Our contact has helped us to identify every heat signature." He points at a dot in the middle of the structure. "That's Chad." He drags the tip of his finger along the map. "And that's our route to get him." His cell pings, and an incoming message lights up the screen. His eyes scan over the text. "It's break time." Jase looks up and grins. "That gives us about an hour for the sleep sedative to work."

The plan is for our contact to drug everyone but Chad. Then he'll log into the security system and let Bree's guy hack in. When we're a few minutes away, he'll disable all the cameras, wall-mounted keypads, and alarms so we can get in and out undetected. Our biggest issue is getting to the building at the far perimeter of the vast property. We intend to steal a few four-wheelers and hopefully use the cover of the forest that surrounds the vast estate on all sides to conceal our movements.

Baz is going to create a diversion at the house to distract the guards Carter has manning the house tonight. Hopefully, we can slip away unnoticed. It's not without risk, but it's the best our collective brains could come up with at such short notice.

"Come on," Baz says. "Let's not hang around outside and draw attention. We'll join the party and mingle."

Baz leads us up the steps, past the line, gesturing at the man at the door who is checking names off a clipboard. There's no doubt the children of the Lust & Envy Luminary are known to all in our circles, which is why we are ushered inside with no issue.

Laughter, loud music, and a potent floral scent greets us when we step into the capacious entryway. Marble floors run the length of the space. Exquisite side tables housing enormous vases filled with flowers and antique lamps are dotted around the perimeter of the room. Ornate chandeliers hang overhead, raining glistening light down upon us. A sweeping staircase extends from one side of the hallway in a curve that leads to the upper level. Giant gold-framed and silver-framed mirrors compete with expensive paintings on the walls. Wide corridors exit both sides of the space, and the walls are adorned in a rich gold-patterned wallpaper and painted wood panels.

It's a mix of old and new that meshes well. I'm guessing an interior designer worked on the house because I can't see that depraved bitch having such good taste.

A man in a stiff uniform steps forward, gesturing toward our coats, but Bree and I shake our heads. There won't be time to come back for them, and we'll need them outside. We follow Jase and Baz down a long hallway in the direction of the music. Light and laughter spill out of other rooms as we pass. I catch glimpses of people congregating in side rooms, drinking, snorting coke, and cavorting semi-naked in couples and bigger groups.

"Fucking Luminaries." Ares snarls under his breath, taking my hand and holding it tight.

We enter the main ballroom where a DJ is spinning tunes on an elevated dais at the top of the room. To the left is a large bar, swamped with partygoers eager for the free booze. On the right, copious seating areas are curled around a circular dance floor. Beats thump out of humongous wall-mounted speakers, making conversation difficult. Waiters flit around the room with trays carrying flutes of champagne and hors d'oeuvres.

"Might as well drink the bastard's champagne," Ares says, stopping a waiter and distributing glasses to me and Bree. Ares drains his in one go, snagging another flute before the waiter walks off.

Jase and Baz are talking to a group of guys and girls. A few of them look vaguely familiar from campus. A simpering blonde with massive fake boobs and a short, skimpy, strapless red dress is hanging off Jase's arm, batting her eyelashes and smiling seductively at him. He shoves her arm away, paying her zero attention, as he talks to the guy in front of him. Undeterred, she clings to his arm tighter, winding her hand around his back to land just above his ass.

Excuse-fucking-me?!

"Hold this," I say, handing my champagne to Bree. Slipping my coat off, I shove it at Ares before pushing my shoulders back.

"Go get her, tiger." Bree's eyes alight with glee as I stride toward the crew in front of me.

The girl doesn't see me approaching. She's too busy pawing at my man. Jase is trying to be polite, removing her hands every time she puts them on him. If we weren't trying to keep a low profile, I'm betting he would be ripping her a new one.

But fuck not drawing attention.

I'm not going to stand by and watch some stuck-up Barbie wannabe hit on my man.

Grabbing the hand that is placed precariously low on Jase's back, I dig my nails into her wrist as I pull her away.

"Get your hands off me," she screeches, yanking her hand back. Whipping her gaze to mine, she plants her hands on her scrawny hips. "Who the fuck are you?"

"Your worst nightmare, bitch." I move around so I'm blocking Jase at the side and facing off with her. "Do you always put your hands where they're not wanted?" I cock my head to the side. "If any man did what you just did, women would be up in arms and demanding he be thrown out. What gives you the right to put your hands on any man without permission?"

She scoffs, her eyes roaming my body in a derisory fashion. "I don't know who you are and why you think you can talk to *me* like that, but you know nothing. Jase loves my hands on him. Isn't that right, baby?" she purrs, licking her lips as she attempts to flirt with him over my head. My eyes narrow on her arm and chest, only spotting the flesh-toned patches covering her brandings because I know now to look for them and Bree and I are wearing them too.

So, she's a Lum.

I couldn't give a flying fuck.

No hussy is putting her hands on my man ever again.

"Nope." Jase wraps his arm around my chest from behind. "If my removing your hands was too subtle for you, let me spell it out. You're vile, Ember, and no part of me has ever wanted any part of you touching me."

"I'm telling Julia. Where is she anyway?" She scans the room.

I want to shove my engagement ring in her face, but we

can't let that cat out of the bag yet, so I left it back in the limo.

"Good luck with that plan," I say as a tall man with silver hair, wearing a butler's uniform, approaches.

"Gentlemen. Ladies." He nods respectively at us. "If you could please come with me. Mr. Carter would like a word."

Chapter Twenty-Five

Ashley

My palms are sweaty as I walk in between Ares and Jase, following the butler as he leads us through the mansion toward my father. Fuck, fuck, fuck. I thought he wasn't going to be here. If he has summoned us, I hope it's not because he's discovered our plan. Pain slices across my chest at the thought we may not be leaving with Chad. To have him so close and yet so far is unbearable. I can't leave him in that bitch's clutches any longer. I don't know how to convince my asshole sperm donor to let him go, but I'm hell-bent on giving it my best shot if that's what he wants to talk to us about.

Jase squeezes my hand as he stares straight ahead, offering what little comfort he can.

The butler stops at a closed thickset mahogany door, rapping on it three times before the command is given to come in.

Jase and Baz share a look as the door is opened, and the butler ushers us inside. My brow scrunches as we step into the room and are confronted by Knight Carter—Rhett's son and heir and my half-brother. My shoulders relax a smidgeon, but it doesn't mean we're not in danger. We don't know Knight's motives or his allegiances or how close he is with Rhett. Tension bleeds into the air like a tangible substance as we line up in front of him.

Knight is alone, standing in front of a roaring fire with his hands clasped behind his back. Like Jase and Baz, he's clothed in a custom-fit tuxedo. His dark-blond hair, identical to the shade of his father's hair, is gelled to perfection, and he carries himself completely still. "That will be all, Benson. Thank you."

"As you wish, sir." The older man backs out of the room with a bow, closing the door behind him.

Knight's gaze rests on me. He must have gotten his piercing blue eyes from his mother because he doesn't share the brown eyes I inherited from our father. His probing gaze is intelligent and compassionate as he stares at me. I return his stare with confidence, wondering how long he has known about me. "I don't know why I didn't see the resemblance before," he says eventually, breaking the fraught silence. "You look so much like my youngest sister, Paisley." He clears his throat. "*Our* sister."

"He told you then." I school my features into a neutral line as I hold his gaze, trying to guess where he is going with this and what he wants.

Knight shakes his head, stepping away from the fireplace and coming closer. His posture loosens, and his facial expression floods with warmth. "He hasn't told me anything. I figured it out for myself."

"Figured what out exactly?" Jase asks, sliding a protective arm around my shoulders the same time Ares steps in closer to my side.

"All of it." He stops a few feet away, his eyes still drawn to my face. Dragging a hand through his hair, he messes up his careful styling. "Well, I think all of it."

"Let's cut the bull and lay our cards on the table," Baz says as his head whips around the room. "Unless it's not safe to talk in here?"

The room is small with a velvet-backed couch and two chairs positioned in front of the old-fashioned fireplace. To the left, propped against the wall, is a desk and chair. The large window on the right faces the side of the gardens. I glance over my shoulder, noting the floor-to-ceiling fitted shelving on the back wall. Every row is filled with books arranged in alphabetical order.

"There is no surveillance in here. It's why I chose this place," Knight says. "We have privacy to talk openly."

"Excuse me if I check." Baz pulls out a small rectangular device, and we are all quiet as we watch him activate it and scan the room. When he's satisfied it's safe, he nods.

"What do you know?" Jase asks. "And what is this about?"

"Why don't we sit?" Knight gestures toward the seats in front of the fire.

Bree and I sit on the couch. Baz takes one of the chairs, and Knight takes the other. Ares and Jase stand behind the couch like sentinels primed and ready to strike at the first sign of trouble.

"I have suspected something since your initiation." Knight leans forward and clasps his hands on his knees. "Father only shares what he wants to share with me, and it's always in a controlled manner, so I did some snooping, but I had to be careful."

"That doesn't surprise me," I admit.

"I spied on him during meetings and when he was making important phone calls, and I started to piece things together. Then I overheard him and my mother arguing about you." He clenches his hands into fists, and pain flares in his eyes. "I didn't know. I swear I did not know about her dungeon or the twisted shit she's into."

"I find that hard to believe," Ares interjects. "She's doing it from a building at the back of your house. Surely you must have spotted something over the years?"

"The estate is huge. What you refer to as "the back of our house" is a structure that is over a mile away. We never have reason to go back there. As far as we know, it's where she stores donations for her charity auctions. There are underground tunnels running underneath the entire property. She uses them to get in and out, so we don't know how often she goes there."

"Who is *we*?" I ask, cursing myself for not asking Jase or Bree more about my father's family. It wasn't a conscious decision to not think about them but a subconscious one. I'm not yet prepared to accept what the revelation of my paternity means, and we have enough on our plate. I have been trying to compartmentalize.

"We have three siblings. Daria is sixteen, Kylo is fourteen, and Paisley is twelve."

I already know Knight is only eighteen, which makes me Rhett's oldest child. That we know of. Who knows how many other women he raped who gave birth to his kids? There could be a whole colony of Carter bastards in the world.

"Please tell me you haven't shared any of this intel with Daria or Kylo?" Jase asks, landing his hands on my shoulders. I reach up and grip his fingers.

Knight watches my every interaction with avid interest. "I'm not an idiot." He pins Jase with a narrow gaze over my shoulders.

"Why are we here?" I ask, wanting to cut to the chase. We'll need to make tracks soon.

"I want to help," Knight says, and I see no lie on his face. "I'm sickened at what my mother has done to countless men while I was sleeping soundly in my bed only a mile away. I spoke with Chad a couple of times at parties, and I know how much he means to you." His troubled blue eyes pin mine in place.

"You know she has him?"

He nods. "I snuck into the basement yesterday for the first time. I saw him."

"Is he okay?" I blurt, leaning toward my half-brother. "How does he look? Is he hurt? Did you tell him we'd get him out of there?"

"He was asleep...in his cage." He hangs his head, blowing air out of his mouth. When he lifts his head again, a few seconds later, apology is etched across his face. "I am so sorry, Ashley."

"No!" I vigorously shake my head. "You don't apologize for her actions unless you knew about it and did nothing."

"I swear to you I didn't. I only found out about it two days ago when I overheard my parents arguing over you, your mom, and Chad." He looks behind me at Jase. "I texted you immediately to ensure you were coming to the party." He stands. "I'm going to help you get Chad out. Tonight. Now."

"Why?" I ask, rising to my feet. "Why would you help us?"

"Why?" He looks incredulous. "My parents are monsters! My mother has been abusing men for years right under her kids' noses. My father is a fucking psycho who intends to rule the world and slaughter thousands and thousands of innocents in the name of The Luminaries because some sick pricks years and years ago thought it was a great idea to eradicate sin and sinners from our world."

He claws his hands through his hair again. "I know you don't know me, but Jase, Baz, and Bree do. I'm not that guy. I'm not the guy who wants to hurt others. I'm not the guy who flippantly agrees with everything our teachings say."

"How are we to know that?" Baz props his right foot up on his left knee. "You look like the guy who does what he's told and never ruffles feathers."

Anger flashes across Knight's handsome face. "It's called playing the game and biding my time. I think you know all about that, Balthazar, or have I pegged you all wrong?" Knight arches a brow, and Baz smirks, slowly nodding.

"My gut tells me we can trust you," Jase says. "But we have a lot at stake here. Several lives are on the line. Your father is blackmailing us and holding our loved ones hostage so we'll do his dirty work for him. How do we know you're not in on this with him? That this isn't a test of how true we are to our word?"

"Nothing I can say will prove that to you. I can tell you I'm not working with him. That I would rather side with you because it's the right thing to do." He slams a hand over his chest. "That my gut tells me I'm right to risk my life by coming to your aid."

"Why would you betray your father?" I ask. "You risk being ostracized or punished if he discovers you are working against him. Make me understand why you would do that?"

He leans forward, shielding nothing from his face. "Because you're my sister and he kept us apart all this time."

"That's not enough," Bree says.

"No, it's not." Reluctantly, he drags his gaze from mine. "There are multiple reasons, but the main one is, he's got to be stopped. Things need to change. And if I have to sacrifice myself for change, then fine, I'll do that because I'm done playing a waiting game. Finished standing at the sidelines and watching in desperation as his insanity and thirst for power increase."

His Adam's apple bobs in his throat, and his features harden. His jaw tenses. "Father hates I'm his heir. He would much rather it be Kylo or even Daria. They both share his coldhearted disregard for life and his cruel streak. Unless he kills me, he's stuck with me. I haven't rebelled. I have done what he's asked of me because I want to take control of the Greed & Gluttony Luminary. I want to be in charge so I can try to change things." He places his palm to his chest. "Hand on heart, I swear that's the truth."

Subtly, I glance at Bree. His words have got to resonate with her. Their goals are aligned, and I know how passionate my friend is about exacting change. Bree is devouring Knight with her eyes, looking at him as if she's seeing him for the first time. A sheen of interest mixed with respect glimmers in her eyes, and she licks her lips as her gaze rakes over him from head to toe.

Knight rubs at his temples. "I do what I must to show him I'm good enough, but I'm not bloodthirsty about it, and that's why he holds stuff back from me. He doesn't quite trust me. I wouldn't put it past him to have plans to murder me so he can put one of my siblings in my place."

Knight's eyes dart to mine. "I heard him talking about you. He's in awe of your spirit. He likes when you fight him. He loves to see that fire. I wouldn't be surprised if he's doing all this so he can mold you into his successor."

"Hell will freeze over before that happens."

"He already has plans for Ashley," Jase supplies.

"I know." Knight resumes standing in front of the fire, with his hands behind his back, as if he's chilled all over. "I know about Julia. I knew he was fucking her. She made one too many cryptic remarks to me." He shakes his head, a look of disgust creeping over his face. "She tried seducing me so many times." He shudders. "It makes me ill just thinking about it."

"She was always hitting on guys," I say because it was the truth. "It doesn't surprise me she was trying to entice you into her bed at the same time she was fucking your father. She wanted bragging rights, and no doubt she planned to use it to hurt Rhett." Not that he would have cared. He didn't give a fuck about my cousin. She was a pawn in his game, and he killed her when she finished her part.

"She was a nasty little bitch, but she didn't deserve to be murdered," he replies. "I think she really did love him."

"There is no accounting for taste," Bree says. "And let's not pretend any of us care. Julia was poison, and she got what was coming to her. I know I won't be losing any sleep over it."

"We need to go," Baz says, eyeballing Jase.

"I can take you to Chad." Knight calmly walks toward the row of books behind us. Pressing a switch tucked discreetly at the back of the shelving unit, he stands back as it parts in the middle, revealing a set of steps leading to a hidden passage. "I came down here earlier and left some weapons, tear gas, and some clothes for Chad. We can smoke the place out and hopefully not have to kill too many of the guards."

"I'm down for killing the lot of them," Ares says, practically sprinting toward the steps. "None of those men are good people. They knew what she was doing. They aided and abetted her. As far as I'm concerned, the whole lot of them can rot in hell." He drills a look at Knight. "Your mother included."

Knight grabs his arm. "You don't touch my mother."

They face off for a few tense seconds. We all gather behind them.

Knight pulls his gaze from Ares and looks between Baz and Jase. "I know she's a monster, but she's still my mother. I promise I will handle her and the fallout. Don't kill her. Just concentrate on getting Chad out alive."

I want that bitch dead for what she's done to Chad, but we're not stupid. We know we can't kill Carter's wife. She's a Luminary, and he might go nuclear on our asses if we took it that far. Everyone was already in reluctant agreement on it. But

I want to bury her when the time is right. That bitch *will* be punished. "Okay." I reply for everyone. "We won't kill her, but she must pay for this, Knight. We can't allow her to continue to do this."

"I agree, and it stops now. I swear it ends tonight. I'll find a way."

"We're one step ahead of you," Jase says, flipping the switch on the wall and illuminating the narrow passageway.

"What do you mean?" Knight asks, frowning.

"We have a plan."

Knight stares expectantly at Jase.

"We'll tell you when we get there."

"You don't trust me," Knight deduces as he starts going down the stairs.

"This could be a trap," I say, voicing my concerns out loud. I really don't think it is. I think Knight is sincere, but it's so hard to know who to trust, and these Luminaries are skilled at manipulation. We have to play it smart.

"It could," Knight says, looking back at me as I descend the stairs behind him. "But it's not. I understand trust is earned, and I plan to do that. This is just the start." Determination exudes from his tone and the expression on his face. "Whatever you're planning, I'm all in."

Chapter Twenty-Six

Ashley

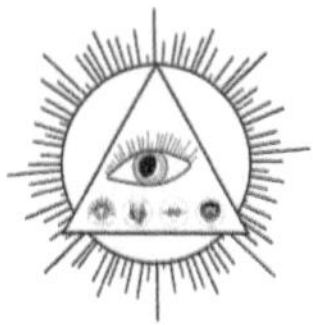

Knight fills us in on everything he knows, which is pretty much the same as us, as we race along the tunnel infrastructure underneath the Carter house and grounds. He tells us how his—*our*—great-great-grandfather built all of this in the late eighteen hundreds so his family would always have a way of escaping should they come under attack. Right now, I could kiss that man—if he were alive—because his actions are bringing us closer to rescuing Chad.

When we reach the end, the farthest-most point of the tunnel, we are all panting and sweating despite how frigidly cold it is down here. Knight pulls a couple of stones out of the wall, revealing a stash of handguns. "I know it's not much, but it's all I could safely stow. Mom uses this tunnel, and I didn't want her finding anything that would give the game away."

"We shouldn't need it," Baz says, accepting one of the weapons. "But we're grateful."

"Are you still not going to tell me what the plan is?" Knight asks, distributing the rest of the guns.

"The less you know, the better," Jase says, before adding,

"and it's not solely that we don't trust you. If you mean what you say, that you're on our side, you need to stay out of this. We shouldn't compromise your position."

"Jase is right," I say, curling my fingers around the handgun Knight hands me. "Rhett can't know you're helping us. You're more valuable on the inside."

"I'll send you the coordinates to the back gate and the code to get out. I'll have your limo waiting there for you," he adds, punching digits into the wall-mounted keypad. The door pings open. Knight holds us back, popping outside to check the coast is clear before we pile out.

Dense forest surrounds us on all sides, and up ahead, just visible in the distance, is the building we need. A chilly breeze wafts around us, lifting strands of my hair. I hemmed and hawed over how to wear my hair tonight, but I'm glad I chose not to wear it up. At least the long length protects my neck from the cold.

"Stick to the edges of the forest," Knight says. "It will conceal you as you make your approach."

"We've got it covered," Ares grits out, rubbing his hands and itching to get on with this.

I was happy when he readily agreed to come tonight. He's not exactly a fan of Chad, but he hasn't wavered in his support. He isn't only here for me. Trafficking is something Ares feels very strongly about because of what happened to his sister. He's motivated to put a stop to this, and I think he's angry on Chad's behalf, and he wants to see those who did this to him punished.

Maybe, just maybe, he's rethinking his stance on my ex now he knows Chad wasn't involved in trafficking or Lili's kidnapping. At least, I really hope he is.

Bree and I hand Knight our ankle boots. We swapped them out for the ballet flats we stashed in our purses when we first came down here. Neither of us wanted to slow things down by attempting to run in heels. "Can you hold on to these for me?" I ask my brother, a little thrill running through me at that word.

"No problem."

"Thanks." I smile at Knight as Jase comes up behind me, covering me with his warmth. Nighttime in December in Cali is *cold*.

Knight returns my smile. "Good luck and be safe. You have my number." He looks over my head. "Use it if you need backup."

"We'll be in touch," Baz says as Jase takes my hand and turns us around.

"Ashley. Wait."

I turn back and face Knight.

"I know this isn't the time or place, but I was hoping we could spend some time together over the Christmas break. I'd like to get to know you."

Warmth spreads across my chest, and my answering smile is genuine. "I would really like that. We'll set something up."

"Cool. Okay. I'll see you then." His smile falters. "I hope Chad is all right. If I can do anything to help, just ask."

"I will."

I won't.

I know Knight means well, but the last person Chad needs to be around is the son of the woman who incarcerated him. Even if Knight wasn't involved and didn't know, he will still be a reminder. Not sure how I'm going to manage it with both in my life, but it's a problem for another day.

On instinct, I reach out and hug him. "I always wanted a brother or a sister," I whisper in his ear. Of course, I have Emilie. But my cute little sister is only a baby. It'll be nice to have siblings closer to my age. There is only a year between Knight and me, and I hope we become close. I like the idea of it a lot. "At least something good has come out of this whole mess."

He hugs me close. "Now I know, you'll always have me," he whispers, and the warmth in my chest spreads to my entire body. "If there is anything you need, call me. Any time."

I whisper another request. One the others had put the kibosh on. I figure it can't hurt to ask.

"I'll see what I can do," he says.

"I hate to break this up," Baz says, "but we're on the clock."

"Go." Knight releases me. He fixes Jase with a stern look. "Keep her safe."

"Always." Jase grabs my hand, and we set out running after the others as they dart into the forest.

Jase casts quick glances at me as we run.

"What?"

"You like him."

"I do. I know we don't trust him yet, but my gut tells me he's sincere."

"I have always liked Knight, and I want to trust him, but we need to be careful. This could still be part of Rhett's game plan. I really don't think it is, but until we know for sure, we need to be smart."

"You don't think I should meet him?" I pant out, watching Ares reach out to steady Bree when she almost trips and face-plants the ground.

"I'm not saying that. Get to know your brother. Just be careful." He chuckles when he sees the instant smile appearing on my face again. "You like having a brother."

"I hated being an only child. You know this." I often lamented to Chad and Jase how I wouldn't feel so alone when Mom and Dad were off traveling if I'd had a sibling or two.

"You might change your tune when you meet Daria and Kylo."

"They're that bad?"

"Yes, but Paisley is a sweetheart. She's most like Knight, and those two are close."

"I can't wait to meet her." Not sure how I'm feeling about the other two, but I guess I'll be meeting them at some point as well.

We slow down as we catch up to the others. Baz has his cell phone at eye level, and he's looking through it as if it's binoculars.

"What's he doing?" I whisper, purposely keeping my voice low in case there are any guards prowling the vicinity.

Jase is typing out a message on his cell. "Scanning the area for guards," he explains, chuckling when he spots the look of confusion on my face. "We have high-tech phones with tons of gadgets. It doubles up as binoculars when we need it."

"I want one of those," Ares says, taking the words right from my mouth.

"I'll hook you both up with one." Bree blows on her hands, rubbing them together as she jumps up and down to keep warm.

"The coast is clear," Baz says, slipping his cell back in his pocket.

"Our contact has not responded to my last two messages." Jase shares a troubled look with his brother.

"What does the heat signature show?" I ask.

"The only movement appears to be coming from the room the prisoners are in."

"We can't back out now," Baz says. "Send the word to Gregor to disable the security systems. We'll handle whatever comes our way." We check our weapons and remain quiet as we wait for the go-ahead from Bree's IT guy. When it comes a few minutes later, we emerge from the trees in front of the building and jog toward the door.

Baz insists on entering first, giving us the okay a few seconds later. Jase and Ares flank Bree and me on both sides as we step inside the building. It's a vast open space with tons of high shelving, crowded with boxes of various sizes. A couple of cars, a boat, a vintage motorcycle, and a children's treehouse occupy the corner space at the rear. On the other side is an office, the glass walls revealing the desk, chair, and filing cabinets inside.

Jase leads us into the office, cautioning us all to be quiet as he presses his ear to a section of the carpet and listens. You could hear a pin drop in the eerie silence. Ares moves in closer, linking his pinkie with mine.

"I don't hear anything," Jase whispers.

Baz steps forward, pushing his brother back.

The more I'm around Balthazar Stewart, the more I like him. He's a natural leader, and he puts himself before others all the time. I imagine that probably grates on Jase's nerves, but I'm not going to criticize Baz when he protects my fiancé at every turn. I think Baz has been doing that a lot. Eric Stewart isn't the only one trying to shield Jase.

Ares and Jase crowd Bree and me, pushing us back as Baz pulls up the hidden opening in the floor, revealing the steep steps underneath.

We file down the stairs, one at a time, and I'm afraid to even breathe. My heart is thumping wildly against my chest cavity, and I grip my gun tighter, trying to prepare myself for what we might be facing.

When we reach the bottom, we crowd into the space behind Baz as he curls his hand around the door handle. "Wait," Jase hisses under his breath, his eyes flitting between his phone and his brother. "I swear I just saw movement in the hallway."

"Give me that." Ares swipes the phone, examining the

screen carefully. "It shows five heat signatures in the hallway. Surely that's excessive." He curses under his breath. "You weren't wrong. I just saw that person move." He taps at the screen.

"You can't go out there," Bree says. "They'll shoot the instant someone shows their face."

"We need a distraction," I whisper. "Get your guy to set off the alarm. It should startle them for a few seconds and give us enough time to make the first move."

"Good thinking, Batman." Bree lightly punches my arm as she taps out the instruction to Gregor.

"Okay." She looks up. "Get ready. He said ten seconds."

"You two stay back." Jase warns Bree and me with a look. Ares shakes his head when he sees the intent on my face. I want to tear into them for treating me like some prissy princess, but there's no time.

We ready our weapons as Baz whispers a countdown.

Adrenaline pumps through my veins, and blood rushes to my head.

The second the alarm goes off, Baz and Jase rush out into the hallway and instantly open fire.

Chapter Twenty-Seven

Chad

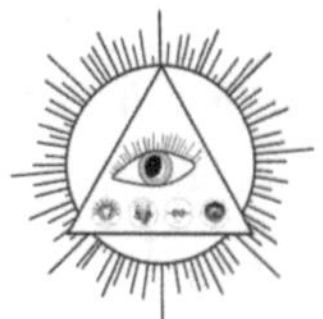

The unmistakable sound of gunfire reverberates in the hallway outside, followed by shouting, and it drags me from the drug-induced haze that twisted bitch put me in before she collapsed on the ground. I was hoping she'd had a sudden coronary, but the rise and fall of her semi-naked chest confirm she's still breathing. She's just sleeping. Unfortunately.

My dry lips part as I move my furry tongue, desperate for water. Pain shoots up my arms when I attempt to move. It's a futile exercise anyway. She has me strapped into her favorite contraption, and I can barely move. I don't know how long she's been unconscious or how long I've been dangling here, but my arms throb from the unnatural stretching, and I can hardly feel my legs, the limbs turning numb from the angle I'm at.

The walls outside rattle and shake, and there's more yelling. A glimmer of hope rises to the surface at the thought it could be my friends, but I'm reluctant to place too much faith in it until I know more.

The door handle rattles repeatedly, and the door shakes as

someone tries to open it. But it's bolted on the inside. "Chad! It's me. We're going to get you out!" Ash's voice is like music to my ears despite the clear desperation lingering behind her words.

"Siren," I croak, the word barely more than a whisper. Clearing my throat, I try again. "Ashley!" I shout with as much energy as I can muster.

"I'm here. We're here. Hold tight."

There's a bit of commotion and then a loud blast, and the door swings open as someone shoots out the lock.

Ash rushes into the dimly lit room followed by Jase. Her eyes dart to the prone body on the floor before swinging to me. Horror washes over her face as she takes the scene in.

I hate my girl has to see me like this.

Exposed, weak, vulnerable, and completely at the mercy of others.

Shock splays across Jase's face too, and I know what it must look like. Me strapped to this sex device, arms stretched over my head, legs spreadeagled, clamps on my nipples, and an electrostim cock cage wrapped around my dick. I've been in a constant cycle of hell as electrical shocks are delivered at regular intervals from the automated device. My dick has been hardening to the point of pain. My orgasm is denied every time, and it's the most brutal torture. They can't see the vibrating butt plug shoved deep in my ass from this angle or know how bad the pain searing me from the inside is.

Jase darts back to the doorway. "We've got this," he says before closing the door.

I see the transformation in Ash. The horror is quickly replaced with rage as she looks at the bitch passed out on the floor. Emitting a high-pitched roar that resembles a war cry, she launches herself at the woman, dropping to her knees and slapping and pummeling her face. Jase watches her for a few seconds before walking over to me. "Hey, man. Just hold it together for a little longer," he says, working quickly to unstrap me.

"I don't think I can stand," I say, hearing how my words slur.

Jase curses, tilting my head up and peering into my eyes. "What did she give you?"

"Don't know."

"You fucking cunt!" Ash yells, claiming our attention. Jase continues unstrapping my aching body from the machine as we watch Ash rip the bitch's flimsy clothing apart, exposing the older woman. All the time, she's voicing threats and cursing obscenities at the sleeping woman, promising bloody retribution. "You disgusting nasty perverted piece of shit!" She punches her in the stomach and the ribs, growing frustrated. She looks up at Jase. "Please tell me you have a knife? I want to gut the bitch until she bleeds out all over the floor."

"Temptress, remember the promise you made outside," he cryptically replies.

"I promised not to kill her," she hisses, dragging her manicured nails down the woman's cheeks and across her collarbone, drawing blood. "I didn't say I wouldn't hurt the sick bitch."

My arms flop down at my sides as Jase releases my upper body, and I sway forward. My buddy catches me, holding me upright.

"A little help, baby?" he asks, looking over at Ash.

She seems reluctant to leave the sick bitch on the floor, but she gets up and comes over to us. "She's going to pay for this." Ash presses her body weight against me, holding me up, as Jase sinks to his knees to untie my legs and feet. The familiar scent of Ash's perfume swirls around me like a safety blanket and I could cry.

The ordeal is over.

They came for me like I knew they would.

Murderous intent is written all over Ashley's face, and if my dick wasn't so overworked and traumatized, I'd probably get hard. The ferocity of her response proves she still cares for me. I know it doesn't necessarily mean anything, and it's not what I should be focusing on now, but I was afraid I'd never get to see her again. Never get a chance to make amends. "I love you," I blurt because it's been on my mind the entire time I've been locked up here. "I'm sorry about everything. I'm so sorry, Ash. More than I can explain," I choke out over the lump in my throat.

The promise of violence fades from her face. "Love you too," she whispers, fighting tears. Gently, she cups my cheek with one hand while supporting me with her body. "I'm so sorry you got dragged into this mess."

"Not your fault," I pant, trying to straighten up so I don't crush her. "Your dad," I add, remembering Doug being executed at gunpoint in the middle of the street.

"I know." Pain skates across her face before she composes herself. "Don't worry about anything for now. We need to get you to safety. There'll be time to talk later."

Jase releases the last of the straps, and they both hold me up, carrying me over to the couch. Ash kicks the bitch in the side as we pass. "I wish I'd kept my boots. I'd stomp all over her with my heels."

They lay me down, and I attempt to move my arms, wanting to remove the nipple clamps and the cock cage myself, but my limbs won't cooperate. Whatever that bitch gave me has taken away normal bodily function. "Let me," Ash softly says, sweeping her fingers along the thick growth on my chin and cheeks. "I'll be careful."

Jase walks back to the woman, kicking her in the ribs and

the cunt while Ash frees me from the nipple clamps and removes the painful cage from my dick. "My ass," I say, feeling heat creep up my face.

I have done a lot of kinky shit with Ashley in the past, but having her do this for me because I can't get my fucking body to work long enough to do it myself is humiliating. I don't want her to know what went down in this place. I don't want her thinking less of me or treating me with kid gloves. I don't want her pity. I only ever want her to see me how I used to be. The sociable guy who loved football, his girl, his family, and partying with the only woman who has ever mattered. The guy who loved her with his body, heart, and soul. The guy she explored her sexuality with. The one who was up for anything in the bedroom and willing to share her with his best friend.

Ash fights to rein her anger in as she slowly removes the vibrating butt plug from my ass. Pain radiates from her eyes as she flings it away. Clasping and unclasping her hands, she averts her gaze as her chest heaves up and down.

I hate this. I don't want her feeling bad for me. I don't want her to look at me and see me as damaged or broken. Even if that's what I am right now. I want her to look at me with love in her heart and desire in her eyes.

But I'm realistic enough to know that may all be in the past, and I could've lost her long before today.

Ash forces the grief from her face when she turns back to look at me. She's purposely keeping her gaze focused on my upper body, but I know she's seen my erection. I'm painfully hard, which is humiliating. Every time that bitch forced my body into a state of arousal and she made me come, I felt ill. I threw up a couple times. I tried to stop it from happening, but I couldn't. She never forced my hands on her or touched my dick with anything other than her fingers or her mouth, but the things she did to me were intimate and felt like the ultimate violation. It only happened a few times. I wasn't here long enough for her to truly ruin me, but I can't deny the things she has done have altered me.

Will my girl ever be able to look at me as a man again?

Will I ever be able to forget the things done to me in the short time I was here?

I hope so, on both accounts, because I don't want this to define me.

"I wasn't into it," I rush to explain. "I swear. But it's a powerful stimulation, and I couldn't stop my body from reacting." Shame washes over me, threatening to drown me.

Ash threads her fingers in mine. "Just because your body reacted naturally does not mean you wanted it or liked it. It wasn't consensual, and that bitch had no right to touch you. I understand, Chad. You don't need to explain it."

Behind us, Jase is going to town on the bitch, and I only wish I had the strength to join him.

"Do you think you can stand?" Ash asks.

"Help me up."

Jase comes back over, and together they help me to stand.

Ash guides us to the woman's side, glaring at her. She has gouge marks down her cheeks and across her chest, and bruising is already appearing around her ribs and on her arms. One eye is swollen from Ash's fist, and there's a small cut on her lip. I bet when she wakes she still won't feel half of the pain I've felt at her depraved hands.

"Piss on her," Ash says, her gaze darting between Jase and me. "Piss all over the bitch. It's nothing less than she deserves."

Jase grins as he lowers his zipper. Ash moves me to the left a little, angling my hips so my erect dick is pointing right at her. Then we let go, relieving ourselves all over her. Ash barks out a laugh, and there's a wicked glint in her eye. Jase and I share a look, and I swallow heavily over the lump in my throat.

Jase holds me upright when we're done as Ash moves to the door. She opens it a smidgeon, talking in hushed voices to whomever is outside.

"No one is to know how you found me," I say in a low tone, averting my eyes in embarrassment as Jase supports me while I hobble back to the couch.

"You can trust Ash and I to keep it to ourselves." Strain is clear in his eyes as he looks at me. "You have nothing to be ashamed about, Chad. If you want to talk about it, I'm here for you."

Yeah, no. I won't be telling anyone the shit that bitch put me through. I flop down on the couch. "You came through for me. That's all I need. Thanks, man."

"I'm sorry we didn't get here sooner," he adds as Ash closes the door and walks toward me, carrying a bundle of clothes in her arms.

"These should fit." She sets socks, boxers, gray sweats, and a black hoodie down on the couch beside me. Ash and Jase help me to get dressed, which is a slow, awkward, embarrassing process.

There's a rap on the door just as I'm dressed.

"Guys. We need to go."

Ash rushes over to the door, pulling it open, revealing Balthazar Stewart. His eyes dart over her head to mine. "Good to see you, man. It's time to bounce."

"Did you get the others out of their cages?" Ash asks, eyeballing him.

"We already talked about this. It's too risky."

She shakes her head. "We're not leaving those men behind. I don't give a fuck how risky it is."

"I know how you feel," Jase says, "but Chad is our priority. That and getting in and out without drawing attention to ourselves." He lifts his gaze to his brother. "Is everything cleaned up?"

"We took care of all the guards and wiped any and all trace evidence. I'll sweep this room before we go."

"I'm with Ash." I stand on wobbly legs, clutching Jase's arm before I face-plant the ground. "We can't leave them here with this bitch. She'll kill them all. She was going to kill me." She wouldn't have spilled her guts to me if she thought I was ever getting out of here.

"We're taking them with us." Ash levels a stern look at the Stewart brothers, daring them to challenge her.

Baz shares a look with his brother.

"How can we pull this off?" Jase asks.

"I asked Knight to procure a van. I trust him to come through for us. It should be waiting beside our ride," Ash says. "We need to move fast if we're to get them all out in time."

Does she mean Knight Carter? She must. It's not a common name. I was told he's the bitch's son. I'm confused as to why he's helping, but now isn't the time to start questioning my friends. I trust them.

"I'm already ahead of you," a man with a gruff familiar voice says.

I'm surprised by my lack of feeling when Ares Haynes appears behind Baz in the hallway. He has an unconscious naked guy flung over his shoulders. When I think about it now, our feud was immature and pathetic. Our differences don't matter when you consider the big picture. Investing time and energy in hating one another is stupid. I have no feelings about Ares either way right now.

"Ash is right," Ares says, casting a quick glance over me. His nod of acknowledgment is subtle, but it's there. I return the gesture, grateful he came. "We're not leaving them behind. I don't care what we previously agreed or what the consequences are. We're setting them free."

Ares and I share a look, and for once, we appear to be on the same page.

Jase relents. "Okay. It's agreed. Let's move out then."

Chapter Twenty-Eight

Chad

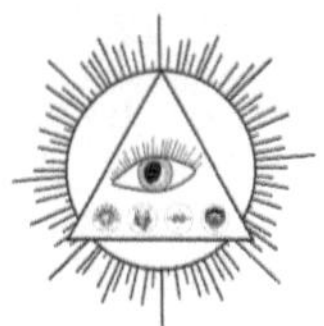

Ares strides down the hallway with the naked guy on his shoulders. Baz and Jase each take one of my arms as I stagger unsteadily from the room. Some feeling is returning to my legs, but I can't yet walk unaided, and I fucking hate it. The man's dead eyes look straight at me over Ares's shoulder, and I wonder if he's even aware he's been rescued. His frame is skeletal, and the haunted look in his eyes tells its own tale. He must have been here quite some time, and it's obvious his spirit is broken. I hope he gets help on the outside so he can reclaim his life.

How do you do that after such a prolonged ordeal?

I'm pondering that question as Ares hands him over to whomever is standing behind the side door. Ash rushes past us, checking on me with a brief look of concern as if she needs to confirm it's really me. She shares a look with Ares as they race off down the hallway in the other direction, heading toward the room I was incarcerated in. I have zero desire to ever set eyes on that space again.

Armed guards lie motionless on the hallway floor, shoved

over to the side. A couple are dead. The round holes in their skulls and bloody pools under their bodies give it away. The rest appear to be unconscious. Tape covers their mouths, and their hands and feet are tightly bound.

A growl slips from my lips when I come face to face with the man behind the main door. He's one of the guards. Not one of the nastier ones, but he's still a perverted prick in my eyes. Anyone who was a party to this and did nothing is an asshole. Blood seeps from a small injury to his head, trickling down his face.

"Go help the others with the cages," Jase snaps at him.

Avoiding my gaze—because he's a chickenshit—the guard walks around us, following orders without hesitation. I have a ton of questions. A ton. But it's not the time to ask them. They can keep until we're back home.

After all the prisoners are safely evacuated from the basement, they are taken away in a large black van while we get into a limo. I must have fallen asleep immediately because I don't recall the journey. I only recall waking up in this strange bed, in an unfamiliar room, with jackhammering pain rattling around my skull and seriously sore limbs. A doctor was here at one point. I have a vague recollection of him checking me out, but I must have fallen back asleep before he left.

I stare out the window, trying to work out where we are. There are no curtains on the window and it's pitch-black outside, making it hard to determine my location.

"We're here," Ash says.

I roll onto my side, in the direction of her voice, wincing as my body protests the motion. Ash and Jase are slouched in uncomfortable-looking chairs, pulled up close to the king bed I'm lying in. They both have blankets draped over their laps and tired expressions.

My eyes adjust slowly to the semi-darkness. A small lamp

emits dull spurts of light from the bedside table it resides on, bathing the room in an eerie glow. "Where are we?" I rasp, yawning and rubbing my eyes before I pull myself up against the headboard. I'm glad my limbs are cooperating again. It must mean the effects of the drugs are wearing off.

"You're at a safe house in Tahoe," Jase explains, leaning forward with his elbows on his knees. "I'm making arrangements to move you to a property my family owns where your mom and Tessa are staying."

Panic is instant, spreading through my veins like fire. "What's happened? Are they okay?"

"Relax. They're both fine." Ash reaches out, taking my hand. Warmth seeps into my skin from her touch, immediately soothing me. "It was a precautionary move. A lot has happened while you've been gone."

"Like what?"

Jase and Ash trade looks, silently communicating.

"Tell me."

Ash squeezes my hand, peering at me with sympathetic eyes. "You've been through a lot, Chad, and it's only four thirty a.m. You should try to go back to sleep."

Peeling the covers back, I swing my legs to one side, noticing I'm only in my boxers. My ass hurts, and my cock throbs with the need to ejaculate, but I bite on the inside of my mouth and adjust my hard-on before standing. "I'm awake now. I'd rather take a shower, grab something to eat, and catch up on everything I've missed."

"Why don't I run you a bath?" Ash suggests, climbing out of the chair. "You're still weak, and submerging your sore muscles in warm water will help. Or I can get you something to eat first, if you prefer?"

"I'll take the bath. I want to scrub that bitch off my skin and clean every last trace of that place from my body."

Her hands clench into fists at her side, and her soft smile seems forced. "Stay in bed. Keep warm. I'll call you when it's ready." She ducks into a side door, which I presume leads to an en suite bathroom.

I crawl back into bed, pulling the covers up over me as I fight another yawn. Scrubbing my hands down my face, I scratch my fingers through the thick growth on my chin. "Does your father own this place?" I ask, needing to break up the tense silence. I get the sense my friends are tiptoeing around me, unsure what to say or do, and I hate it.

I just want things to go back to normal.

Whatever *normal* is now.

Jase shakes his head. "Friends of the family own it. Try not to worry. You're safe here."

I jerk my chin up at that. "Do I *need* to worry? What's going on, Jase?"

Dragging his hands through his hair, he sighs, and it's a tormented, exhausted sound. "I can't tell you not to worry, but we *will* keep you safe."

"What are you and Ash mixed up in?" I ask as the sound of running water filling the tub filters into the room.

"I would rather have this conversation with Ash, and truthfully, there isn't much we are permitted to say."

That is as close as my buddy has come to telling me he's mixed up in some crazy insanity. I probably would have let it go. Like the other times when Jase was vague or dismissive, but after the shit that sick bitch divulged, there is no way I'm letting it go.

Whether I like it or not, I'm involved now, and I'm not shying away from it.

But I'll park it for the moment. I want to speak to both of them about it.

"I want her back," I say, changing the direction of the conversation.

"I know."

"Be honest. Do I stand any chance with her?"

There's a pregnant pause. "This isn't a conversation you should be having with me. You need to talk to Ash."

"Come on, man. I'm not asking you to betray her confidence. Just give me something."

"She came with us to rescue you, and you watched what she did to that twisted bitch. She's in there running you a bath, and she's been pacing this floor for hours watching you sleep with fear in her eyes. What does that tell you?"

"I know she still cares, Jase. The same way I still care. You don't just switch off feelings overnight. But that's not the same as her being able to forgive me for the horrible things I've done. You haven't exactly been Prince Charming, but you guys seem to be okay."

"We're together again," he confirms before averting his eyes. Briefly, I wonder where that leaves Ares. But I push that thought from my mind. I don't want to think about him now.

"That's good." I mean it. "I'm glad she has you. That you were there for her when I couldn't be. I'm just hoping I get the same chance. I know our situations are different, but do you think she's open to trying?"

He drags a hand through his hair again. "I can't get involved, Chad. It's between you and Ash. It's not for me to decide if you can forgive one another. That's got nothing to do with me."

"What's got nothing to do with you?" Ash steps into the room and looks at Jase. "The bath is ready," she adds, swinging her gaze to me while she dries her hands with a small white towel.

My eyes are drawn to the sparkling diamond on her ring finger. My breath stutters in my chest as my eyes lock on what is clearly an engagement ring. "You're engaged?" I splutter, looking between them, because the alternative doesn't bear thinking about. I'm presently indifferent to Ares, but that would all change if I find out that ring on her finger was put there by him.

"Yes." Ash tucks her hair behind one ear in an obvious nervous tell. "We're getting married on Thursday."

My eyes pop wide, and my tone carries my considerable disbelief. "*This* Thursday?"

"Yeah." Jase stands, moving over to Ash and pulling her into his side. He presses a kiss to the top of her hair while studiously avoiding eye contact with me. What's that all about?

There is more to this than meets the eye, but I'll have my bath, eat, and then pepper them with questions. A maelstrom of emotions twists and turns inside me, but I'm not ready to confront them yet. And I won't make things difficult for them either. It is what it is. I had my chance—when Ash's mom asked me to marry her—and I blew it.

I understand it better now.

I sensed Pamela was desperate that day, and I should have just agreed. Who the fuck cares about money? It's what Ash has been trying to tell me all along, and I'm an idiot because I couldn't see it.

I can't get mad at Jase for doing what I failed to do. If this is about Ash's protection, then I won't fault my buddy or raise any selfish concerns.

"Wow." I get out of bed again. "I guess congratulations are in order."

"You're...okay with this?" Ash's warm brown eyes probe my blue ones, and her brow scrunches up.

"I'm a little in shock," I admit. "I'm still processing, but I'm not, *not* okay, if that makes sense."

She nods. “We can talk about it in a bit.”

“Can we talk while I’m in the bath?” I ask because I’d like some alone time with her. I don’t think Jase will mind. But...the dynamic of our relationship has changed. And things are a little weird with him. Is this why? I eyeball my buddy. “If that’s okay with you?”

“Don’t look at me,” he replies. “It’s up to Ash. She knows I’m cool with it.”

“Sure,” she says before stretching up and kissing Jase. “Can you make us something to eat?”

He bobs his head and walks away, stalling at the bedroom door. He looks over his shoulder, drilling a look at me. “Nothing has changed, man. Everything is still about Ash. Whatever she wants and needs.”

Unspoken words charge the space between us, but they don’t need to be said. I can read between the lines. All is good with my buddy where Ash is concerned, and a layer of stress lifts from my shoulders. “Good to know.” I know he said that for my benefit, and I’m grateful.

“Come on.” Ash gently takes my hand. “Let’s get you in the tub before the water turns cold.”

Chapter Twenty-Nine

Ashley

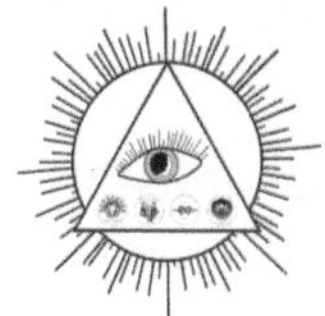

Chad winces as he eases himself into the tub. I'm doing everything I can not to cry at the state of his bruised body. The shock of seeing him tied up like that hasn't left me. Since we rescued him, my emotions have been veering back and forth like a yo-yo. Thankfully, the doctor confirmed there is no serious injury or permanent damage. He took blood and urine to test as a precaution and to confirm what drugs he was injected with. He'll also be tested for STDs.

I still want to cut the bitch.

Anger is ever present.

The she-devil is lucky I didn't have a knife because I would have shredded her to pieces until she was a messy bloody puddle on the floor and enjoyed every second of carving her up.

I'm pissed at Rhett too. How the fuck was this keeping his wife on a leash?

The prick lied to me. I shouldn't be surprised, and it's just extra incentive to murder him.

A grimace spreads across Chad's face as he sits. I stuff my clenched fist in my mouth to smother the scream building inside me. I saw how red and sore his ass was when I was helping him back at the house of horrors, and I know he must be in pain. I found some Epsom salts and added it to the water, which might help. Walking to the cabinet over the sink, I remove the small medical kit tucked inside. Pulling out a couple of pain pills, I set them to one side of the sink. "I'll be back in a sec," I say before exiting the room.

"What's up?" Jase asks when I enter the kitchen a few moments later.

"I'm just getting a glass of water for Chad to wash some Advil down." A thought occurs to me. "Or should I not? We don't know what shit she gave him."

Jase stops slicing tomatoes and wipes his hands on a kitchen towel. "The drugs seem to be gone from his system, and I doubt a couple of pain pills will cause any damage." Reaching overhead, he extracts a glass from the cupboard and hands it to me.

"I'll let Chad decide," I say, filling the glass with water. "Have you heard anything from the others?"

He shakes his head. "Not since the last message Ares sent me. I'm sure they're sleeping. Carter must not know or he's decided after-hours house calls are rude."

I snort out a harsh laugh. "As if. That prick never considers any other person."

We chose to split up in case Rhett showed up demanding to know where Chad is. We covered our tracks, and we're confident there is no evidence confirming it was us. The men we rescued are on a plane right now. They are being taken to a private hospital in France for treatment and rehabilitation. Bree spearheaded that operation using her contacts to set it up at short notice. In time, we'll have to give the guys' new identities and impress on them the urgency of keeping what happened a secret.

Their survival relies upon it.

Rhett has his hands full planning his hostile takeover, so we think he'll let it be for now. However, when he finds out what happened last night, his finger will point in our direction first. We thought it'd be suspicious if no one was home, so the story is Jase and I are staying at the Stewarts' residence overnight. We know he won't check up on us if we say we're there as it would only arouse suspicion.

I was going to say we were at my mom's, but I called her several times on the way here, and she didn't pick up. I didn't hear from her on Sunday either after I messaged her to confirm the wedding was on Thursday. I get she wants to keep a low profile until her injuries heal, but she could at least pick up her fucking phone and acknowledge my existence every now and then. I have no clue if she's going to show up on Thursday or not.

At this point, I'm not sure I care.

Mom has reverted to form, and I might as well be invisible.

"If he's going to confront us, I'd rather just get it over with," I say, pushing away from the sink.

"He's got to know we'd attempt this, and he must have known we'd be at Knight's party."

I arch a brow as I round the island unit, anxious to get back to Chad. "You think it was a test or something? Like he wanted us to rescue him?"

Jase shrugs. "Who knows what goes through that psycho's mind." He jerks his head. "Go on. I'm sure he's waiting on you."

I nod and walk off.

"Ash?"

I turn back around.

"I don't think this needs to be said, but I'll say it anyway." He props a hip against the counter, flicking his head and tossing waves of messy dark hair to one side. His clothes are wrinkled from hours forcing his long broad body into a too-small chair, there are shadows under his eyes and extra growth on his jawline, but he's still one of the most beautiful men I've ever seen. His piercing green eyes are sincere when he says, "I'm okay with whatever you decide with Chad. Same goes for Ares too."

"I know." I blow him a kiss. "But thanks for confirming it." I blow him another kiss before I walk back to the en suite bathroom.

Chad's arms are resting on either side of the tub and his head is back, his eyes fixated on a tiny crack in the ceiling, when I reenter the room. Tilting his chin down, he swings his gaze on me. The shorter cropped bleached-blond style he was sporting a few months ago has been replaced with a look I'm more familiar with. His hair is darker with fading blond streaks, and it's longer all over. He looks more like the boy I fell in love with in high school. Though that version of Chad didn't have ink covering one arm and part of his chest.

"Do you want some pain pills?" I ask, hovering by the sink where I left the Advil.

"Yeah. I think I need them." He tries to hide a grimace as he sits up straighter in the tub, water sloshing around him with the motion.

Kneeling beside him, I pass him the pills, and my skin tingles when our fingers brush in the exchange. His eyes lift to mine when he feels it too.

Attraction was never an issue for us.

We didn't break up because we weren't into one another anymore.

We broke up because communication broke down between us and I betrayed him with Ares. It doesn't hurt any less acknowledging it to myself. Even when I know our breakup wasn't just my fault. Wordlessly, I hand him the glass, watching as he swallows the pills.

"Can I wash you?" I reach for the soft white cloth and body wash.

He nods, turning his head to the side to look at me. "Why are you so good to me?"

"You're in pain, and you need my help. I would never deny you that." I dump a load of body wash on the cloth and dip it in the water, getting it all sudsy.

Sadness shrouds his face, and I know that's not what he was hoping to hear. "I'm sorry, Ash. I'm so sorry about everything. Shutting you out, getting lost in my own head, refusing to listen to reason when you told me not to get involved with The Sainthood. Letting my stupid pride get in the way when you and Jase offered financial support. It's *my* fault you ended up in bed with Ares. I pushed you into his arms. I wasn't the boyfriend you deserve or need. I stopped being that guy the minute shit went down with my dad, and I wish I could go back and do it all differently."

I sweep the cloth back and forth across his shoulders, chest, and arms before moving it lower. His hard-on juts out from his body. Long, thick, and leaking precum. It seems he's been painfully hard since we rescued him from that horrible place. Tears stab the backs of my eyes when I think about all he's endured. My hand stalls on his lower abdomen, and I lift my face to his. "I wish I'd done some things differently too. We both made mistakes."

"I don't blame you for what happened with Ares. He shouldn't have taken advantage of your vulnerability, but I knew there was chemistry between you. I chose to ignore it because burying my head in the sand seems to be my go-to motto these days."

I move my other hand to his face, gently palming his cheek.

"Don't be too hard on yourself. You were shouldering a lot of responsibilities."

"It's not an excuse. I should have leaned on you and Jase. Instead, I hid shit from you, and I created space between us. I didn't even tell you how badly my mom had fallen apart."

"We spoke with your mom. Tessa too. You need to have a conversation with her, Chad. With Ares too. All is not as it seemed."

"I don't want to talk about that now. I want to talk about us. If there is still the potential of an us."

"You really want to talk about it now?"

"Probably the only good thing to have come out of the past few days is the realization that I was focusing my energies on all the wrong things. Worrying over stuff that doesn't fucking matter. And life is too short." He reaches out, water dripping down his arm, and brushes wet fingers across my face. "I was terrified I would never get the chance to tell you how sorry I am or how much I am still in love with you. My biggest regret is leaving you that day instead of staying and talking it through. Trying to find a way to get past what had happened with Ares. I let my personal feelings about him get in the way, and I lost you in the process." His blue eyes are troubled as they pin me in place. "I love you, Ash. I never stopped. I love you so much. You are my world, and I should never have lost sight of that."

Pain stabs me through the heart as unwelcome images pop into my head. "You hurt me, Chad. What you did with Julia, it hurt so damn much. It still does."

Removing both hands from the tub, I lower to the floor on my butt, raise my knees and rest my head on them. My chest is heaving with remembered pain.

A wet hand lands on my arm. "I did it to hurt you," he softly admits. "I was in so much pain, and then you showed up with him, and I'd had too much to drink, and I just wanted you to feel what I did."

"Do you think I wasn't hurting?" I lift my heavy eyes, staring at him. The pain in my throat is so extreme I can scarcely force the words out over the messy lump clogged there. "You were my everything, Chad, and I tried so damn hard to get through to you, but you refused to listen. I could see what you were doing, and I had to stand by and watch it all go down!" I move into a kneeling position, resting my butt on my heels. "Have you any idea how horrible it is to watch the man you love self-destruct and push you away? At a time when I needed you most! I had lost Jase, and I needed you to be there for me, and you were emotionally unavailable. I didn't mean for things to happen with Ares. I swear I didn't, but they just did."

A pregnant pause ensues. "Ares was there for you when Jase and I weren't," he admits after a few silent beats. "I can't blame either of you for what happened. You didn't purposely set out to hurt me. Not in the way I did to you. It's unforgivable. I know that. I know I have no right to ask for forgiveness, but I'm going to because what we have is too special to lose." His voice cracks. Tears roll silently down our faces as we look at one another.

We are shielding nothing now.

"This is the conversation we should've had back then," I whisper, fighting to trap my sobs inside.

"I know, but I was too hurt to have it. I lashed out at you instead." Tentatively, he reaches for my face. I let him. Chad palms my face in his warm, wet hands. "I said this to you at the hospital, but I don't know if you heard it. I didn't have sex with her. What you saw in the hallway was the extent of it. It was all for show. When we got upstairs, I went to my bedroom and slammed the door in her face. I didn't want her. I have never wanted her. You're the only woman I love and desire, and even if you can't forgive me, that won't ever change."

"I want to," I say, sniffling as I lean into his embrace. "I want to forgive you, but I don't know if I can. Those images are so vivid in my mind. I don't know if I can get past them, but I will try because I'm not over you. The feelings are still there."

"I want you back, Siren." Determination is etched all over his face. "I want a chance to prove I can be the man you need. That sorry version of myself this past year is not who I am. The boyfriend you knew before that is the real me. If you give me another chance, I promise you won't regret it. I will make it up to you. I swear."

"What about Jase? And Ares?" I wind my fingers through his on one side of my face.

"Not gonna lie. Always thought I'd be the one to marry you, but if it can't be me, I'm glad it's Jase. Especially if it's happening like this to protect you."

My eyes startle at his astute observation, but I don't want to cut this conversation short as it's been a long time coming. So, I park that thought for now. "And Ares?"

"Are you saying you're with him too?"

"We haven't put any labels on it, but yeah."

He looks contemplative for a few seconds. "I'm willing to mend bridges with him if he's willing to meet me halfway."

You could have told me angels just flew down from heaven, and I wouldn't be any more surprised than I am right now.

Chad chuckles at whatever expression is on my face. "I know what you're thinking. We hate one another, but it's connected to things that our parents did. Things I suspect neither of us fully grasped. I projected a lot of my anger onto Ares, and I suspect he did the same with me. If he can set that aside so you get what you need, then so can I. Can't say we won't ever fight, but I will make peace with him if that's what you need." He laces his fingers through my hair. "You are all that matters, Ash. Everything else is insignificant now."

I place my brow against his. "That means a lot." We don't speak for a few beats. "I can relate a little. I'm not saying everything is perfect. We still have stuff to work through, but I spent the past few days worrying I'd never see you again. That I'd never get to hold you again, and that thought gutted me, Chad."

An errant sob travels up my throat as I lift my head up and stare into his gorgeous face. "We got you back. You're safe, and we have a chance to fix things between us. I'm not going to let fear or shame or stubborn pride get in the way of that. Hurt is a different matter. I need to work that out of my system, but I want to try. I don't want to lose what we have because of our mistakes and the things others have done to try to keep us apart."

"I'm so not worthy of you." Emotion floods his face and dampens his eyes. "I didn't dare to hope you'd be willing to give me another chance. That you have means everything to me. You are one in a million, Ash. I promise I will spend the rest of my life making it up to you and proving you made the right choice. You won't regret this."

An overwhelming desire to kiss him washes over me, so I do—softly brushing my mouth against his. I'm conscious of the ordeal he's just been through, and I don't want to do anything that could trigger him.

Chad kisses me back, slowly and softly, and emotion flays me on all sides. I burst out crying, and he holds me to him, whispering soothing words as he cradles the back of my head and clutches me to his chest.

Neither of us care he is naked, wet, and in a tub.

All that matters is we seem to have found a way back to one another.

The road will be bumpy, and things are far from resolved, but there is a righteousness to being in his arms I cannot deny.

Some girls might say I'm a fool.

Some guys might tell him he's an idiot.

But all that matters in this moment is what is in our hearts, and for the first time in a long time, I feel like things are going to be okay.

Chapter Thirty
Ashley

"Let me finish washing you before the water turns cold," I say a few minutes later when I have stopped crying enough to compose myself.

"Are we going to be okay?" he asks, reluctantly letting me go.

"I hope so." My smile is genuine as I snatch the washcloth again. Deliberately bypassing his swollen cock and sore ass, I wash his thighs, his legs, and his feet. "I just need some time and to take it slow."

"Whatever you need," he readily agrees before adding, "You've always been too good for me. I have missed you so much, Ashley. I had a physical pain in my heart every day we were apart."

"Me too," I admit, placing the cloth on the side of the tub as I finish washing him. Tilting his head back, I wash and rinse his hair.

"Thanks, sweetheart." He kisses my cheek with tenderness. "Thanks for getting me out of that hellhole too. I knew you would both come for me."

His words, his touch, and his adoring smile take me back in time, and my heart thuds to a new beat behind my rib cage. "No matter how things were between us, I would never have abandoned you, Chad." My eyes drift to the straining elephant in the room. I'm not sure how to broach this or whether I should. I just told him I want to take it slow, but it's clear he's in need, and I have always liked looking after my men. I fix my gaze on his cock for a few seconds before looking deep into his eyes. "Want me to take care of that?"

"Yes." His answer is immediate and decisive. "But you don't have to unless you want to. I can take care of it myself."

"I wasn't sure if you'd want anyone touching you," I truthfully admit because I don't think we should shy away from talking about what happened to him. I know he was only there for a few days, but she abused him and hurt him, and I don't know how that's going to affect him in the days, weeks, and months ahead.

"I always want your touch, Ash. I still crave it as much as I always did, and that won't ever change because I love you." He pauses to draw a long breath. "You can help me to forget too. Your touch will help to block out the memory of hers." His large palm covers the back of my neck. "I need to feel like me again, and you're an intrinsic part of my soul, Ash, but I won't lay that burden on you. You said you need time, and I'm more than fine with that. I would wait forever for you."

"I want to touch you. I've missed you. I've missed the closeness we had when you were my person, and we were so entwined I barely knew where I started and you ended. I want us to get back to that place."

He presses his forehead against mine. "I must have done something right in my life to deserve you." He kisses me more forcefully this time before pulling back. There is barely any space between our faces as he peers deep into my eyes. "Don't hold back, Ash, and don't treat me with kid gloves. You know my body as well as I know it. You know what I like and how to work me up. If it triggers anything, I'll tell you."

"I don't want to hurt you or cause you further pain." My fingers move carefully across his broad wet shoulders.

"You won't—unless you plan to not kiss me or not wrap your skillful fingers around my dick."

"Promise you'll tell me to stop if you need me to," I say as my fingers trek lower across his collarbone and down to his chest.

"I promise." He seals it with a loving kiss, clasping my face in his hands as he kisses me deeply and passionately, and I'm drowning in bliss and a whole host of emotions I'll need to decipher at some stage.

Leaning down, I kiss the spot over his heart where my name is etched in permanent ink. "I love you," I whisper.

"I love you more," he says, and we both grin. It's what we used to say to one another all the time before things turned to shit.

This time when Chad grips my hair, it's his usual firm hold. He angles my head, devouring my mouth and controlling our kiss, as I circle my hand around his cock and stroke him the way he likes. I pull his flesh down tight, stretching the skin as I brush my thumb over his crown, swiping the precum sitting there. His flesh is slippery, hot, and velvety soft against my hand, and I curl my fingers more tightly around his shaft as I pick up my pace, pumping him in hard, fast thrusts.

Chad moans against my lips, tangling his fingers in my hair and sweeping his tongue into my mouth, as I jerk him off. It doesn't take him long to find his release, and he kisses me the whole way through it. Ropes of salty cum spray over his abs and up to his chest as I finish him off. When he's done, I gently release his cock as he slows his kisses. We break apart, gazing at one another. His lips are swollen, his cheeks flush with color, and his eyes seem more alive. "Are you okay?" I ask.

"Yeah, babe." He pulls my forehead to his. "I needed that in more ways than one. Thank you."

Grabbing the cloth, I clean him up quickly before helping him to climb out of the tub. I hand him a large fluffy white towel as I grab a hand towel and dry my arm. Chad drapes the towel over his shoulders, and it's large enough to cover from his torso to his upper thighs. I lean carefully into him. "I know your ass is sore. I saw petroleum jelly in the cupboard. Let me put it on. It'll help."

Heat flares on his face.

I know this is difficult for him, but if we're doing this, he can't shut me out again. "We've explored every part of one another, and you're intimately acquainted with my ass," I remind him with a small smile. "You shouldn't be embarrassed about this. It's just me, and I want to help." I don't know how much it will help. He probably just needs to let it heal naturally, but I wanted to offer. "I want you to know you can talk to me about anything. Ask for my help in any way. I don't want you to bottle anything up, Chad. Look where that got us the last time."

"I know, but this is humiliating. It makes me feel..." Pain contorts his handsome face before he lowers his eyes to his feet. His chest heaves painfully. "It makes me feel like less of a man."

"Chad." I place my hands carefully on his towel-covered chest, waiting for him to lift his head before I continue speaking. "You aren't less in my eyes. Would you feel *I* was less of a woman if I'd been assaulted?" Technically, I was. Though Baz was considerate during my initiation, I was still forced into having sex with him. Chad doesn't know about it though, and it's not like I can mention it now to prove my point.

Chad will *never* know about that.

He shakes his head, like I knew he would.

"Then please try not to feel like that. What happened is all on her, not you. Don't let her take anything else from you."

"I don't want anyone looking at me differently or treating me differently."

"They won't."

"Jase can barely look at me."

"It's not what you're thinking. There's a lot of stuff going on in his head, and I know he feels like it's his fault you were in this situation. I have similar feelings."

I blow air out of my mouth. I need to be careful because I can't tell him too much. It kills me that I can't, but it's only short-term. When we are married and officially part of the Sloth Luminary family, we can bring him into our confidence. Until then, we can't divulge anything for fear of it getting back. We swore an oath of loyalty and secrecy, and we can't break it without repercussions.

Chad has already suffered through his association with us.

We're not putting him in the line of fire again.

"There's a lot of stuff going on. Some is stuff we can share, but there is plenty we can't. Not yet anyway."

He opens and closes his mouth in quick succession. Like he was going to say something but thought better of it. Instead, he nods, opens the cabinet, and hands me the petroleum jelly. Placing his hands on the edge of the counter, he drops the towel and spreads his legs.

After I've helped him, he pulls me into his arms, and we hug it out in silence for a few minutes. "Thanks, sweetheart." He presses a fierce kiss to my temple.

I wash my hands as he dries off and gets dressed.

"I think Jase feels bad about the wedding too," I admit, turning around as I dry my hands. Maybe I shouldn't interfere, but there can't be secrets between us. Chad and I aren't the only ones who need to repair their relationship. "He hasn't said it to me, but I know him. I think he thinks you might feel like he's stolen your girl. He wants you standing there as his best man, but he won't ask you. He doesn't want to put that on you if you're hurting about it."

"I'll talk to him." He drags a towel back and forth across his hair before tossing it in the basket just inside the door. "Would you want me standing at his side?"

"Yes. Having both of you there would be perfect, but I won't force you to do something if it feels awkward or it would hurt you."

"It wouldn't." He takes my hand. "I won't lie and say I'm not jealous when I am, but I don't resent my buddy or you. As long as there's still a place for me in your lives, I will make my peace with it. I wouldn't want to miss out on your special day and live to regret it because I know I would."

Warmth blossoms in my chest. Both my guys are prepared to go to considerable lengths to make things up to me, and it buoys my spirits. It's remarkable when you consider how much danger we are all still in. That I can feel anything close to elation is a miracle. But as I walk out of the bathroom with Chad, I am feeling the same sense of righteousness I was feeling a short while ago. Like we are all where we should be and things are going to work out.

Jase has made sandwiches and soup, and we eat in comfortable silence. After, we head out to the sunroom to watch the sun rise. I sit on the couch in the middle of the two guys with a blanket thrown over us. Chad sits on a pillow to cushion his sore ass, and every time I see him wince, I want to go back to that building and murder that fucking bitch. Jase grips my hand, and I know he's having the same murderous thoughts.

We fill Chad in on his mom and Tessa, the things we

discovered about what went down with Jasper and Hera, and the encrypted drive Carole gave us. We tell him about Lilianna, careful to leave out all mention of Luminaries and who Ares really is. We don't mention Rhett is my bio dad or the sick bitch who kidnapped him is my stepmother.

"Jesus." Air whooshes out of Chad's mouth. "I knew my dad wasn't a willing sex trafficker, but he still aided and abetted them."

"He was trying to fix it, and he was killed for it," Jase says, wrapping his arm around me.

Stifling a yawn, I rest my head on his shoulder.

"I knew there was something shady about some of those guys I made drops to." Chad stares off into space with a deep furrow in his brow. "I mentioned it to Dad several times. Sure, I laughed and joked around with them, but it was only to mask my discomfort. Dad stopped asking me to do it after that. I should have followed up. Should've asked him before about it, but I was relieved not to have to make bullshit talk with assholes." He cracks his knuckles, and his jaw pulls tight. "If I'd known what was going on, I'd have murdered them with my bare hands."

"We both would have, brother." Jase leans across me, squeezing Chad's shoulder.

"It's no wonder Ares acted like he did." Chad kicks his bare feet up on the coffee table. "He must have been going crazy knowing his sister was out there somewhere with sick pricks." His face pales as he rubs a hand across his chest. "I would leave no stone unturned trying to find her if that had been Tessa. I know how it must have looked to him about Dad and me. It makes so much sense now."

"He knows it's not the truth," Jase says. "He's trying to come to terms with a lot of stuff that has come to the surface, and I think he feels bad now for how he treated you and your mom."

"I think it's time to let the past stay in the past." Chad eyeballs us. "I want to help to find Ares's sister, and I want to clear my dad's name."

"Do you think your comments were the reason your dad looked into it and discovered the truth?" I probe in a soft tone. It's bound to be a sensitive subject with everything that went down.

Chad shrugs. "We'll never know now, but I guess it's possible." Pain skates across his face, and I regret asking the question.

"Don't feel guilty. What happened was not your fault. We don't know that your dad wasn't already suspicious. Even if he hadn't started digging, he still could've ended up in the same place. These men are dangerous, and everyone is expendable."

"I wish he'd never gotten mixed up in it. He'd still be alive if he hadn't. I hate how his name has been tarnished. It's not fair."

I lace my fingers in his. "It's not, and you were right. You were always insistent he was innocent."

"I suspected he was cheating on my mom before," he blurts.

"When?" I ask, lifting my head from Jase's shoulder. "You never said."

"It was before you and I were together. I was fourteen, and I saw him one day at a café around the corner from his work with another woman. He was holding hands with her over the table. As soon as he spotted me, he dropped her hands like a hot potato. Fed me some bull about her being a work colleague and he was consoling her because she was upset that her cat died." He rolls his eyes. "I didn't buy it. I asked him outright if he was having an affair, and he denied it to my face, but I sensed it was a lie." His tongue darts out, wetting the small cut on his lip. "I thought of telling Mom, but I hadn't seen enough. I didn't want to upset her if I was wrong. I watched him more carefully after that, but he must've taken extra precautions. I never saw anything again, but I always suspected. Poor Mom. She didn't deserve to be treated like that."

"He was a shitty husband, but he wasn't a sex trafficker," Jase says.

"No, he wasn't." Chad sits up a little straighter, moving his body in slow careful motions. "I'm going to make amends with Hera," he promises, looking me straight in the eye. "Now I know why she did it, I can't continue to hold it over her. Losing a child in that way must make you desperate, and I understand it better now." He scrubs a hand down his face. "You care for her, and I want to patch things up."

He really seems sincere about turning over a new page and I'm thrilled. Not just because it will make my life easier. Harboring all that hatred and guilt and anger was consuming him. He needs to let it go for his own sake.

"She's overseas right now, but I'm sure she'll love that, Chad. She has never held anything against you."

Turning sideways, he takes both my hands in his. "I'm sorry about your dad, Ash. Poor Hera. I bet she's devastated." His eyes widen, and his face floods with alarm. "They were carrying you out of the ambulance! And you got shot! Shit! I can't believe I forgot that!"

I can. He was drugged repeatedly from that moment until last night, and he's been abused and assaulted. It's no wonder his brain is scrambled.

"Are you okay?" His frantic gaze roams over me, checking me for injuries. "What happened? Where did they take you, and what did they want?" It's as if a light bulb has just gone off in his head, and he's remembering everything.

Panic jumps up and bites me. We had hoped he didn't see

all that or wouldn't remember. I know Ares did, but he felt sure Chad was unconscious before that went down. I guess he was wrong. Looking over my shoulder at Jase, I wonder how the fuck we can explain it. I don't find the answer on Jase's face. He looks as unsure as me.

Forcing my panic aside, I turn around and face Chad, purposely only answering one of his questions. "I'm fine. I had a concussion, but I'm okay now." With everything going on, I haven't had the time to feel any pain. Apart from conking out the second my head hits the pillow at night, I haven't felt the aftereffects of my injury. I pop some pills daily that conceal any lingering aches in my hips and my legs from the fall. I was lucky the bullet only grazed me slightly. I lift my hair. "I still have a mark here, but it's healing well."

The panic eases on Chad's face, quickly replaced by fear. "You need to tell me what's going on."

"We have told you as much as we can for now. In a few weeks, we'll be able to tell you more," Jase says. Chad opens his mouth, and Jase raises his hands. "Please, buddy. If we could tell you, we would. We need you to trust us."

It's a tall order. Especially when we've agreed there will be no more secrets. But this is about keeping Chad protected until it's safe to tell him.

"This is about The Luminaries, right?"

My mouth falls open, and I hear Jase suck in a gasp. "What?" I stutter. "Where did you hear that?"

His mouth purses. "*Madame* X. That bitch who kidnapped me," he clarifies. "She had no intention of letting me go, so I guess she thought it was safe to spill her guts while she was abusing me." A muscle pops in his jaw as he drills us with a look. "I know it all. I know who you all are and what's expected of you."

Chapter Thirty-One

Ashley

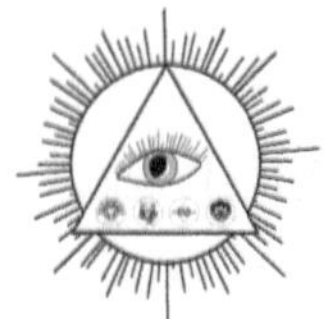

Cleo Carter just signed her own death warrant. That's what I'm thinking as Chad tells us everything she blurted to him. He knows it all. What the Luminary society is, the current structure of Luminaries, masters, experts, and grunts, and how it came to be. He knows each of the four families—the current Luminaries, their heirs, and their areas of responsibility, and he knows about initiations and the tasks Jase and I have to uphold as part of our commitments.

She blabbed it all.

And now she's going to pay for it.

"Rhett either lied to us or lied to her." Jase looks as shell-shocked as I feel when Chad finishes talking.

"She hates him," Chad adds while smothering a yawn. "She knows he cheats on her, and she's mad."

I scoff. "They all do. Not sure why she's so mad when it's the norm."

"With that generation." Jase holds me tighter as he dots kisses into my hair. "Not with ours. Not with *me*." He drills me with a pointed look, making sure I understand the promise behind the words.

I wasn't worried. I already knew he'd be faithful to me.

"That's one of the first things we will insist is upheld when we're in control," he says.

"Thank fuck, our responsibilities will change after we're married and in charge of the Sloth Luminary. I don't know how your mother has put up with the things your father has to do."

"It hasn't been easy."

"She hates you and Pamela too." Chad tightens his hold on my fingers. "Like really hates you."

It's not like I've ever done anything to her but exist. "I'm sorry she used you to get back at me and that Rhett took you as insurance. Your association with us put you in harm's way," I add, "and that doesn't sit right with me."

"Or with me." Strain is etched upon Jase's face. "If I wasn't such a selfish asshole, I would have cut you loose years ago, but I valued your friendship too much. I tried to keep you out of this, but you got sucked in anyway."

"If I'm not to blame myself for my dad, then you're not to blame yourselves for this." Chad drills us with a look.

"You're right. The blame game does none of us any favors." I stare off into space as I mull over our options in light of Chad's revelations. We can use this, but it all depends on what Chad wants. I focus on his gorgeous, tired face. "What do you want to do? This can go two ways. We stick to our original plan, and you go live at the safe house with your mom and Tessa until we fix this mess, or we use this situation to our advantage. We tell Rhett his she-devil wife has loose lips and redirect his rage onto his other half. He can't punish us, and we have a legitimate way of pulling you into the ranks now."

Bree's guy, Gregor, hacked into the system, and he took a copy of everything. If we needed it, I'm sure we could get proof of Cleo's betrayal. Jase has already made it clear all copies are to be handed to him and only him. We don't want these tapes falling into anyone else's hands. And I don't want Chad knowing they exist. We have no plans to look at them or let anyone else look at them. We just want to hold them in case we ever need to fall back on the evidence.

"I want in." Chad doesn't hesitate, and determination resonates in his tone and on his face. If anything, he almost looks at peace.

"You need to think about it," Jase cautions. "This is a lifelong commitment, Chad, and these people are dangerous. This Luminary society is seriously fucked up. Even with us in control, your life will not be your own. We have a responsibility to our people and the world at large. It's a massive undertaking and a giant burden. You don't have to be sucked in. You can walk away."

"No, I can't." He shakes his head. "And I don't want to. My life is with you. I'm not going to change my mind, and I can't unhear all the things I've heard. It's crazy shit, and I'm still wrapping my head around it, but I'm going nowhere. I'm all in." Resolve shines in his eyes as he looks between us. "I've known you were both keeping stuff back from me. It's actually a relief to have no more secrets between us. I don't need time to consider it. I had days where all I did was think about it after Cleo blurted the truth. I know what I want, and it's you guys. I want to help Ares find his sister, and I want to help you take Carter down."

I lean in and kiss him. Just 'cause I felt like it. "Are you very sure, Chad? There can be no going back."

He brushes his lips against mine. "I have no doubts. This is what I want."

I look up at Jase. "So, where do we go from here?"

His lips kick up at the corners. "I have an idea if you're both on board," he says before he proceeds to tell us his plan.

My chest heaves with emotion, and tears glisten in my eyes as I stare at Chad, nodding the same time he does. They gravitate toward me as one, and we wrap arms around one another in a group huddle, letting the magnitude of the moment settle between us. Nothing has ever felt more right, and it feels like everything has been leading to this moment. My only concern is, how do I tell Ares?

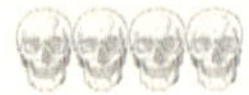

Now that Chad is all in, there's no need to hide, so we call the pilot and charter the helicopter to take us back to Lowell. When we reach the compound we call home, Jase goes with Chad to the old townhome to pack up his stuff. I wander inside the house in search of Ares, but he's already left for work. "He was on an early shift," Bree says from her perch at the kitchen island. She's dressed in sleep shorts and a hoodie with fluffy slippers on her feet and her blue hair tied into a messy bun.

"What are you working on?" I ask, coming up alongside her.

She slams her laptop closed before I can see the screen. "Nope. You're not ruining your surprise. I'm making some alterations now the plans have changed a little." Her eyes light up, and she squeals as she bundles me into a hug. "I'm so happy for you." She eases back. "I take it things went well between you and Chad?"

"We still have shit to work out, but we're on the same page. We're both determined to fix our relationship and move forward."

Her smile fades. "Is he okay?"

"He will be," I say with confidence.

"Good." She glances at her phone. "Shit, we need to get changed."

I'm still wearing my party clothes, and my dress is crumpled from hours sitting in an uncomfortable chair. "Changed for what?" I ask as she loops her arm in mine and drags me toward the stairs.

"We're booked in for a bunch of treatments at the salon." Her wide grin is back. "I can't believe you're getting married tomorrow!"

"I know!" We walk up the stairs. "Is there time to drop by my mom's house? I want to see if she's coming to the wedding." I received a cryptic text an hour ago telling me she was lying low and she'd reach out to me soon. That was it. No mention of my wedding or anything. She's so damn frustrating to deal with at times.

"We have time for a quick visit," she confirms.

When we stop by Mom's house, Richard opens the door with Emilie in his arms. "Pamela isn't here." A flash of annoyance crosses his face before he hides it. "I haven't seen her in days. Something urgent cropped up with the business, and she had to go overseas. I'm surprised she didn't tell you."

So much for not keeping secrets from her husband.

Mom clearly doesn't want him to know she suffered a beating at her ex's hands. I'm tempted to spill the beans, but I've got enough drama in my life and zero desire to interfere in my mother's marriage, so I keep my lips zipped. "She sent me a brief message, but she didn't mention she wasn't at home."

"You're welcome to come in for a coffee." Richard steps back to let us in.

I wish I had time to spend with my baby sister, but Bree cautioned me we're on a tight schedule, so I have to pass. "We've got salon appointments, but I'll definitely stop by over

Christmas to play with this one." I take Emilie's chubby little hand in mine as I lean in to blow kisses on her cheeks.

"Lee, Lee," she babbles, pulling on my hair and giggling.

"Love you, princess." I shower her with kisses, as she wriggles and writhes in her father's arms, before we leave.

Bree and I spend most of the day at the salon getting waxed and buffed and preened to perfection. I spent half my time snoozing and catching up on a missed night's sleep while the staff stripped all the hair from my body, gave me a mani and pedi, applied a facial, and tidied up my brows.

I check my phone again, but Mom hasn't replied to the message I sent her after I visited Richard, and I'm all out of patience. Bree drives us home while I place a call to Knight, pleased when he readily agrees to my request.

Ares's motorcycle is parked beside my SUV when we pull up at the house a few minutes later, and I'm relieved. We haven't spent any time alone these past couple of days, and we need to have a conversation. I plan to pin him down tonight, and no excuses will get him out of this discussion. I'm not getting married tomorrow without knowing where I stand with him and checking he's okay.

I'm pleasantly surprised when Jase tells me Ares and Chad have been locked in the basement for the past hour talking things through, but there's apprehension there too. Circling my arms around Jase's waist, I peer up at him. "Are you sure they're not beating the crap out of one another down there?"

He chuckles before pressing his lips to mine. "I'm sure. Things are different now the truth is out. They both have bigger things to worry about than a petty feud."

"Can it work?" Sliding my hands up his chest, I curl them around his neck. "Can the four of us really make this work?"

"If that's what you need, we'll make it happen."

I worry my lip between my teeth because Ares is still the wild card. The thought of losing him tears me to shreds on the inside.

There is no denying the truth any longer.

I love him and want him too.

There, I've said it.

Jase chuckles. "You love him." I'm not surprised he read it on my face. I'm a terrible liar. Something I will probably have to get better at.

"I do," I quietly admit.

"Good."

I still struggle to accept it's this easy. "You're sure you're okay with all this?"

"Baby." Jase pulls me in tight to his body. "What makes you happy makes me happy. Having three men to protect you is better than two. I'm cool with Ares, and I think Chad will be too."

"It's not you or Chad I'm worrying about."

"Ares will come around. He loves you too much not to."

"I need to talk to him. I haven't given him any of my attention in days, and I need to have an honest chat with him before tomorrow."

"You'll get your chance. Chad, Bree, and I are staying at my parents' place tonight."

"Why?"

He tweaks my nose. "It's bad luck for the groom to spend the night with his bride before the wedding."

I roll my eyes. "You're not the superstitious type."

"Some traditions should not be broken."

I sense there is more to it, but I won't argue. Time alone with Ares is much needed. "Okay."

"Consider it a wedding gift." He waggles his brows as he swats me on the ass. Grabbing me by the butt, he lifts me up. My legs automatically wind around his waist. "But I need a going-away gift." He nips at my earlobe as he walks us toward the door. "I need to be inside you, Temptress. When Ares is fucking you later, remember you belong to me too."

Jase might be okay with it, but he's still possessive.

Not that I'm complaining when he carries me into the downstairs bathroom and locks the door. Placing me on the counter, he strips our clothes away and impales me on his dick. My walls hug his hard cock as he plunges in and out of me, rocking my world and tipping me over into pleasure in record time.

No, I'm not complaining at all.

Chapter Thirty-Two

Ashley

When we emerge from the bathroom after our energetic quickie, Ares and Chad are in the hallway waiting for us, standing beside a collection of bags on the floor. Ares pouts as he watches me straighten my clothes and attempt to tame my hair so it doesn't look freshly fucked. Chad smiles. No trace of envy is on his face.

"Did you two work things out?" I ask, looking between them.

"We're figuring it out," Chad confirms.

Ares folds his arms over his chest and crosses his feet at the ankles as he leans against the wall. "We have a mutual purpose and goal." His eyes bore into mine. "And we've called a truce. We have much bigger fish to fry."

"Thank you." My heartfelt gratitude is sincere. "This means a lot to me."

"I'm still not sharing," my grumpy man says because, of course, that relief could only be fleeting.

"You're convincing no one," Jase drawls, lifting his head as Bree comes scrambling down the stairs.

Ares scowls. "Don't tell me what I'm feeling."

"Work your shit out." Jase narrows his gaze on him. "Ashley needs to talk to you, and we're all giving you the space to do it. Don't be a jackass."

Ares flips him the bird.

Jase just smiles. "You're welcome by the way," he adds, lifting a brow. Then he reels me into his arms, dips me down low, and kisses me passionately, knocking all the air from my lungs. When he pulls me back up, I can barely breathe. "Love you, Temptress." He hugs me to his chest, and I inhale his scent and savor his warmth before he pulls away.

"I love you too." I grin at him. "I'll see you tomorrow. I'll be the one in white."

He reels me back in, kissing me again. Heat sears me from behind as hands land on my hips. I know it's Chad. His touch is as familiar to me as breathing. Jase lets me go, and Chad spins me around, holding my face in his warm palms and kissing me. He takes his time, carefully exploring my lips and my mouth as if he thought he'd never get to do it again. "Love you," he whispers in my ear the same time Bree says, "I am so turned on right now."

She huffs out a dreamy sigh. "I need my own harem."

Resting my cheek on Chad's chest, I look over at my friend. "I highly recommend it, and you totally should."

Ares scoffs, and I know my work is cut out for me with him.

"Sleep well, Siren." Chad pecks my lips. "I'll see you tomorrow." Excitement dances in his eyes, and I'm sure the sentiment is mirrored in my own.

"No marking the bride." Jase jabs his finger in Ares's direction. "Keep it vanilla."

I snort out a laugh. Ares doesn't know the meaning of the word.

Walking up behind me, he wraps an arm around my chest and tugs me back against him. Ares tilts my head to one side and grazes my ear with his teeth. "My little slut likes it when I bite, and I'm making no promises."

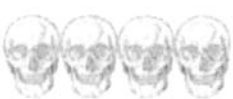

"We need to talk." I spin around in Ares's arms the instant the door is closed after Bree, Chad, and Jase leave.

Ares grabs my ass and pulls me up against him, pivoting his hips so I feel his hard-on digging into my stomach. "Talking was not what I had in mind, dollface." His mouth lowers to my neck, and he plants a slew of drugging kisses along my skin that almost works.

Snapping out of my instant sex haze, I shove at his chest and wriggle out from his hold. "Talking first. Fucking second."

"I've had my fill of talking for today," he grumbles.

"Tough shit, psycho. You're not avoiding me any longer."

The pout returns to his face as he purposely fixes his erection behind his jeans. "Fine, but you let me tie you up and do whatever the fuck I want to that sexy body."

He says that like it's a negotiation. But hello?! I'm me. There is nothing to negotiate because I'll gladly submit to him in the bedroom. "Deal. Now get your grumpy ass in the living room."

He mumbles under his breath again as he slings his arm around my neck—caveman style—and walks us into the living room. Ares pulls me down on his lap on the couch, fixing my legs so I'm straddling him. I arch a brow as I attempt to slide off. "This isn't conducive to talking." I'm working hard to ignore the bulge pressing against my ass from underneath.

His hands glide down my sides as he smirks. "If you want to talk, this is how we do it." His fingers creep under my top, and he trails them across my lower belly, igniting a rake of shivers in their wake.

"Ares, be reasonable," I protest, fighting the urge to push myself into his hand as it explores the flat planes of my stomach.

"This *is* me being reasonable."

I narrow my eyes at him.

"What?" He feigns innocence as his fingertips creep higher. "Sue me if I'm horny. I've had to watch and listen to you and Stewart going at it for days."

"You could have joined in," I remind him.

He opens his mouth to say it, and I slap my hand over his lips. "Nope. Do not spout that bullshit at me. If you have shared other women before, you can learn to share me."

He nips at my palm, and I shriek, pulling it back as I fix daggers at him.

"You're the most frustrating woman. I told you those others meant nothing and it's not the same with you."

"How is it with me?"

"You tell me. You're the one getting married tomorrow."

"Ugh." I slap his hand away from under my top. "You're the most frustrating man. I'm trying to have a conversation, and you're not treating it seriously."

"I'm trying to get laid, and you're not treating *that* seriously."

I bop him on the nose, and it catches him off guard enough to let me slide off his lap. I storm off. "Forget it. This is pointless. I don't know why I bother trying."

I don't get very far before I'm lifted and tossed over his shoulder. "Stop being so dramatic." He stalks back, dumping me unceremoniously on the couch.

"I'm dramatic? Have you looked in the mirror, pal? If you're not throwing punches, you're stirring shit or swinging your big dick around."

A laugh bursts from his mouth, and it helps to lighten the moment. Scooting back into the corner of the couch away from him, I snag a cushion and press it to my body as if that will hold him off. "I need to know where we stand," I say in a calmer, softer tone, letting my emotions show on my face. "And I'm worried about you. I need to know how you're handling everything. I'm not trying to be a bitch. I'm just concerned. Concerned about your mental state and concerned I'm losing you."

My phone vibrates in my pocket with the worst timing ever. Looking at the screen, I sigh. "I need to take this." I hold up a finger, cautioning him to be silent as I put it on speaker. "Uncle James. To what do I owe this pleasure?"

"Have you seen my daughter? I have been trying to get a hold of Julia all day, but the little bitch just keeps sending me terse replies." Mom has her phone, so she must be the one replying.

Oh, look. She *is* capable of responding to messages.

Just not mine.

"Julia's at a frat party," I lie. "Can I pass on a message to her?"

"Get her to call me, and, Ashley?"

"Yeah?"

"I hope your injuries are healing. I want you back in the saddle the day after Christmas. This is a perfect time to trap sinners, and you can't shirk your responsibilities any longer." I flip him the bird even though he can't see me.

"I'll be ready to return to work," I lie. I don't doubt Rhett will have him locked up in the dungeon at HQ by then, and we'll be in charge. He can't force me to do jack shit anymore.

"Good girl," he says before hanging up.

"What a fucking prick." Ares pulls his knees into his chest as he settles at the other end of the couch. "What did he mean by responsibilities?"

"He had me and Julia attending parties so we could spy on the weak and the lazy. I had to send a monthly report of people they should be watching."

"That's seriously fucked-up shit."

"I know, and it's not the worst of it. They are developing some virus they plan to infect people with." I get mad every time I think about Julia using Chad as a guinea pig and how Mom agreed with the plan. He could have died!

"What the fuck?" Ares's eyes pop wide. "These people are insane."

"They think they have a God-given right to do whatever the fuck they want. It's so wrong, and we have to stop it." I'm not sure how we can completely transform the organization, but we're determined to do it. "All of the heirs are on board with change, so it's possible even if it's a massive endeavor. We must convince millions of Luminaries and masters around the world there is a better way. It won't happen overnight. It will be piecemeal change, and we'll have to suck it up and accept we'll need to do things we don't like until we can completely alter it."

"Or we just completely throw out the rulebook."

I shake my head. "I wish it were that easy. These people, these traditions, are entrenched. If we try to evoke drastic change, people will rebel. We'll be killed, and others will be inserted in our place. We need to be super smart about how we do this. Anyway, that's a conversation for another day. Right now, I want to know where your head is at with all of this. It's been a lot to take in. I know. I've been in your shoes."

"I'm still processing. The Luminary bullshit is the least of it." He scrubs his hands down his face. "I can't believe Mom lied to me. About so many things."

"I can relate to that too."

"I have tons of questions, but I can't ask them yet, Ash. You need to let me process this my way."

"Promise you'll come to me with those questions. I might not have all the answers, but Jase will. You, me, and Chad are in the same boat. We're all playing catch-up."

"Have you really patched things up with the jock?"

I crawl down the couch and kneel in front of him. Reaching out, I take his hands in mine, admiring his long slim fingers and the ink etched on his skin. "We still need to work through things, but we both want to. Chad has been a big part of my life. You've only seen him at his worst. You didn't see him when he was at his absolute best. Chad was my rock for years when I had no one else. He valued and loved me. He encouraged my hobbies and my ambitions. He made me laugh when I didn't feel like laughing. He was my first lover. My first everything. He has held me while I've cried myself to sleep on more occasions than I can count and cheered me on when I needed to be supported. He's my family, and I can't walk away from our past or the future we had planned. He lost his way this past year. His dad's death hit him hard, and he took on responsibility for his family. He pushed me away when he should have held me close."

I drag my lip between my teeth. "I haven't been an angel either." His amber gaze pins me in place as I move in closer so our legs are touching. I stare straight into his eyes. "I was hiding feelings for you and acting on them when I shouldn't have."

Chapter Thirty-Three

Ashley

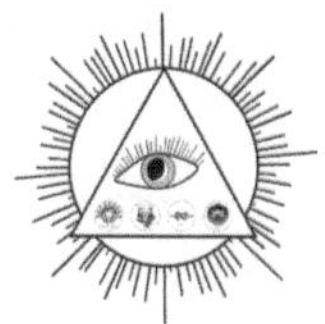

"I manipulated you, Ash. It says way more about me than it does you," Ares replies.

"It takes two to tango." My lips fight a smirk, but it's no laughing matter. "And I wanted it. I wanted you. I just couldn't admit it to myself."

He hauls me back into his lap. This time, I'm sideways with my legs draped over him and the side of the couch. Banding his arms around me, he holds me in a solid embrace. "What do you want now?"

"Nothing has changed, Ares." I wind my fingers in his hair and tip his face up. "I want you. I want us."

His eyes dart to my mouth, and his pupils darken with desire. "I don't know how to do this. I've never had a relationship, and I can't stand the thought of sharing you."

"So, you'd rather lose me?" The words stab my throat as they exit my lips, but it needs to be asked.

"No, fuck no." He rests his brow against mine as his arms tighten around me. "I don't want to lose you. Not before I've even had you, but I don't know how to navigate this."

"Babe." I pull my face back from his brow, peering deep into his hazel eyes. He's an open book to me now. "I think the sharing will help." He goes to speak, but I shake my head. "Hear me out. I understand you can't share me in the bedroom." I try to keep my disappointment from my tone.

It's not as if I've been fantasizing about all three of them filling me at once.

I haven't been dreaming about that at all.

"Could you try sharing me in a relationship? This way, it'll ease us into things. If you're not used to sharing your life with a woman, this will give you your own space, and I'll still be here when you need me. We keep our sexy times private, and I will never force you to change your mind unless it's something you come to want."

"Adding me to the mix messes up the dynamic." He threads his fingers through my pink hair. "You three have worked for years. The guys and I only have a tentative understanding. What if we can't make it work?"

"We won't know if we don't try." I cup his gorgeous face. "I have faith in us. This could be a really good thing for you, Ares. I understand how you've grown up. My situation wasn't the same, but I was alone a lot too. I don't know what I would've done if I didn't have Chad and then Jase. You don't need to rely on yourself for everything anymore. You have all of us now. You just need to let us in."

"It's not easy for me."

"I know. I'm just asking you to try."

His Adam's apple bobs in his throat before he slowly nods. "Okay. I'll try, but what about the marriage situation? Yours and mine."

I hold his face more firmly. "Our relationship will be equal. It doesn't matter whether there's a piece of paper between us or a verbal commitment. It's all the same to me. You won't be treated any differently than Chad or Jase. And about that..." Anxiety pricks at my nerves, but I forge on. "You should know I'm marrying Jase *and* Chad tomorrow."

He stares at me blankly for a few seconds before his brows climb to his hairline. "Say what?"

My hands drop down to my sides. "It's the best way to protect Chad and keep him with us. As my husband, he will have immunity from whatever punishment the Carters might have planned for him."

"But you're marrying Jase. What am I missing here? You can't marry two men. It's not legal."

"It's not, but I'll only be legally marrying Jase. I will be marrying Chad in a religious ceremony. There is nothing in the Luminary rulebook that specifically states you cannot be married to more than one spouse at a time. In fact, Jase told me it was very common when the society was first founded, and it was one of the ways they grew the Luminary population. Custom within general society has changed over the years, and the organization has moved with the times."

I don't state the obvious, which is that I could marry *him* in the future if that is something he desired. Like I haven't told him I love him yet because I don't want to spook Ares. I need to tread carefully where he's concerned.

"Then I definitely don't see how things are going to work out if they're your husbands and I'm just—"

"You will be my partner, Ares, in the same way Chad and Jase are. I don't care about a marriage certificate or labels. I only care about what's in my heart." Emotion clogs my throat as I take his hand and press it to my chest, over the spot where my heart beats steadily. "The three of you are in my heart. That is all that matters."

He claims my lips in a searing-hot kiss, and I melt against him.

"One more thing," he says before pressing his lips to that sensitive spot behind my ear. "What about my marriage to Bree?"

"What about it?" I force my head back so he stops kissing me. I cannot think straight when he's kissing me like that.

"Are you telling me you're okay with it?"

"It will be fake, and I trust you both."

"We might be forced to do stuff neither of us wants to do." He grips my hips and repositions me over his crotch. "How will you handle that?"

"I will deal. It's a complicated situation, and it won't be forever. You can get the marriage annulled when this is all over."

"Are we really doing this then?" he asks, rolling me back and forth over his erection.

The feel of him pulsing against me is more than I can handle, and I'm ready to be done with the conversation. That's enough of the heavy for one night. I just want to reconfirm one thing. He told me before I was his and he believes we were meant to find one another, but I don't know if he still feels like that. He said those words at a time when it was just him and me, and it's no longer like that. "Is this what you want, Ares? Am *I* what you want?"

Tension bleeds into the air as he stops moving underneath me and captures me with an intense look. My chest heaves as I wait for him to answer. He clears his throat and wraps his hand around the back of my neck. "No woman has ever made me feel the way you do. You're my pretty little dollface." He buries his face in my neck, inhaling deeply. "You're under my skin, Ash," he whispers into my ear, and I shiver all over. He takes my hand and puts it on his chest. "You wormed your way in here. It terrifies me." Lifting his head, he stares deep into my eyes. "But not being with you terrifies me more, so yes, this is what I want. I want you. Though I must warn you that I'll probably fuck it up."

"You won't." I sweep my lips back and forth across his lips. "I won't let you." I wind my legs and arms around him, letting a happy smile loose on my face. "You are making all my dreams come true."

"Does this mean we can progress to the fucking part now?"

"Yes, baby. Take me upstairs, and show me what it means to be yours."

"Be careful what you wish for," he says, smirking as he stands with me in his arms as if I weigh nothing.

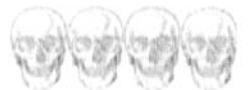

"Oh my God." Sliding down Ares's body onto the plush carpet in his bedroom, I spin around, drinking it all in. It's the first time I've been in here. When we were together on other occasions, it was always in my room. This is the first time I've *seen* in here because he always keeps the door locked, and now I know why.

Lighting is low, and it casts a subtle red haze around the room. A heavy gold, red, and black gothic-style patterned wallpaper covers the walls, contrasting with the black silk sheets on his large bed. But it's the bed itself that has my jaw trailing the ground. It's a four-poster monstrosity with steel ends to accommodate all the cuffs and hooks adhered to it. Hanging on the wall beside his bed is a vast array of whips, chains, and ties. A leather box is open on his bedside table, displaying a myriad of sex toys and aids.

I twirl around, taking the rest of the room in. A large gold-framed floor-to-ceiling mirror is mounted to the wall at the far end. Suspended from the ceiling in front of it is a bondage sex swing. An elevated table with a cushioned leather covering and multiple restraints rests against the wall.

"Changing your mind?" he asks, coming up flush behind me. Grinding his hard-on against my back, he brushes my hair to one side so he can gain access to my neck.

"Are you kidding me?" My voice comes out all squeaky. I arch my neck and tilt my head so I can look at his face. "Put your hand inside my panties and tell me if I've changed my mind."

With his arrogant smirk firmly in place, he pops the button on my jeans and lowers the zipper before sliding his large palm inside my silk panties. Two long fingers push inside me, gliding in effortlessly because I am fucking soaked.

"I knew you were kinky, but I didn't know you were into all this," I rasp as he pumps his fingers in and out of me. Chad and Jase like to tie me up and spank me, but this is a whole other ball game.

"I needed to know you were all in."

It's the first time he's alluded to it, and I know now I wasn't the only one hoping we would get to this point. My pussy pouts when he removes his fingers. "I'm all in," I blurt in case he needs to hear it verbalized.

"I know." He spins me around. "I see it written all over your face, and I think I know this side of you better than you know yourself." Wrapping my hair around his fist, he tugs my head back. "Do you trust me with your pleasure and your safety?"

"Completely," I say without hesitation.

"Good." He leans in and bites my neck.

So much for no markings. Jase really should have known better than to throw down the gauntlet. My guess is Ares is going to go to town on my body, stamping his mark all over me in as many places as possible.

I hope the woman Bree has hired to do my makeup tomorrow brings some heavy-duty coverage because I think I'll need it.

"I'm not formally trained, and I don't give a shit about it," he explains, grabbing the front of my blouse and ripping it open with his hands. "I know what I like and what you'll like."

"I trust you."

"Good little slut." He rips my bra off with his bare hands too, feasting his eyes on my breasts before he roughly grabs them. He tweaks my nipples painfully, carefully gauging my reaction as I cream my panties. "Get naked," he demands, slapping my tits before he turns and walks away.

I yelp from the stinging pain zipping across my chest, but I do as I'm told, kicking off my ballet flats and shedding my jeans and panties until I'm standing buck-ass naked before him. "On your knees, dollface." He stalks toward me holding a black collar with an attached silver chain in his hands. He's naked, his clothes in a messy ball on the floor by his bed. His hard-on juts out strong and proud from his body, and the glistening metal from his piercings has me licking my lips in anticipation.

Ares has a body carved from stone. He trains religiously every day, and he has a physical job. It shows in every curve and dip of his magnificent body. The ink covering his arms and a portion of his chest and back only adds to the appeal along with the heated promise in his eyes.

"I won't ask you again." He pulls the chain taut between his hands, and I realize I've just been rooted in place, ogling him with no shame.

I lower to my knees on trembling legs. Adrenaline courses through my veins, and I'm so turned on already I could come with the barest touch. Ares moves behind me and scoops my hair up into a loose bun on the top of my head before securing the leather collar around my neck. The vein in my neck throbs, and my nipples are so hard they could cut glass. Tugging on the chain, he yanks my head back at an awkward angle until I'm halfway upside down. Then he shoves his cock in my mouth and fucks me like an animal.

"Touch your cunt," he instructs, slamming in and out of my mouth. "But you're not to come. I own your orgasms, and I'll tell you when you can let go."

Ho. Lee. Fuck.

I slide my hand down my body, touching my swollen clit and moaning around my mouthful of dick. There is no illusion I'm in charge of any of this, and I fucking love it. Ares has complete control of my mouth as he tugs on my neck and forces his cock deeper past my lips. I concentrate on stretching my mouth as wide as it will go and loosening my jaw. Tears stream out of my eyes, and saliva drips from my mouth as he fucks into me.

"Put your fingers in your pussy," he grits out, pressing his groin to my face so his dick is all the way to the back of my throat and I'm struggling to breathe. I slide my fingers in my wet pussy, not pushing too deep because I'm at the edge of the precipice, and it won't take much for me to fall off the ledge.

Without warning, Ares pulls out of my mouth and yanks me to my feet. He pushes me down on the middle of the bed before hooking my wrists to cuffs secured on the bedposts. An unwelcome thought enters my mind as he's tying me up. He stops what he's doing, studying my face and whatever expression he sees there. His slick cock is right by my face, covered in precum and my saliva, and my core aches with raw need as my head wars with my libido. Leaning down, Ares kisses me softly. "No one has been in this room, or this bed, but you."

His words soothe me, and I force all fears from my mind.

When he has my wrists restrained, he moves down my body, pushing my knees up to my chest and applying a spreader bar to my feet. Positioning himself between my legs, he pushes my feet up higher, resting them on his broad shoulders and exposing everything to him. The lust-drunk look on his face as he stares at my most intimate parts almost makes me come undone. My pussy throbs with need, and if he doesn't fuck me soon, I'll die.

"Look at how stunning you are." He shoves three fingers into my pussy before pulling them out and pushing his thumb inside. "Look how wet you are." Removing his thumb, he slides his fingers back inside my cunt the same time he thrusts his thumb into my ass.

I explode, shattering into pieces as I scream out his name, and my limbs convulse with the most intense orgasm. He works his fingers into both holes as I writhe underneath him, consumed with blissful tremors. With my legs elevated like this, the orgasm is much more extreme, and I feel it pulsing and twitching in my leg and stomach muscles as I surrender to him.

Extracting his fingers, Ares stays kneeling between the apex of my thighs, staring at me with a dark unreadable expression.

Fiery tremors zip over my skin as I stare up at him. "What?"

"Did I say you could come?" He arches a brow, as I make an O shape with my mouth.

Oh shit.

He slaps my pussy, and I yelp. "Bold pussy." He slaps it again. "But such a pretty pussy. I can't stay mad at it for long." That's the only warning I get before he rams into me in one hard thrust, and I scream again. At this rate, I won't have any voice left to make my vows tomorrow.

Ares fucks me like a savage, pounding into me with force, and I can only hold on for the ride. He stops abruptly, removing the bar and unhooking me from the restraints before flipping me onto my stomach. Raising me to my knees, he spreads my legs wide. Pushing my head into the pillow, he drives back inside me from behind, and I immediately see stars. Another orgasm is building, and when he shoves his thumb into my ass, I detonate again. This time, my punishment is a succession of hard slaps against my butt cheeks.

Ares shoves his dick back inside my cunt before grabbing the chain at my neck and tugging hard, pulling me up so I'm sitting on him with my back against his chest. I love the feel of his pierced cock at this angle as he hammers into me. "Fuck, you drive me insane, dollface," he pants into my ear. "In the best possible way. I'm insatiable for you. I won't ever get enough."

"Don't stop." I moan as he grabs my tits, groping them violently. He continues thrusting into me from behind before one hand roams lower. Finding my clit, he rubs circles against my swollen nub while he quickens his pace. I sense his impending release, and he confirms it when he pinches my clit and roars, "Come!"

I explode around his dick, writhing and moaning as he roars out his release, driving into me so deep I can feel his sperm unleashing inside me. I offer up silent thanks to whomever invented the IUD. When we're both done, he lets me go, and I flop forward onto the bed, spent and deliciously achy all over.

But my lover is far from satisfied.

And we're far from done.

Chapter Thirty-Four
Ashley

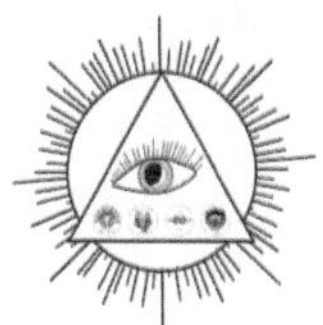

"Ares Haynes!" Bree yells. "Get your stupid grumpy ass in here right now!" She spins around to stare at me with a fresh bout of rage. I'm standing before her in my bridal underwear—a strapless lacy white teddy bodysuit—and she's cataloguing the myriad of bruises and teeth and finger marks on my body with mounting horror.

I smirk as the door opens and Ares sneaks inside.

His eyes devour me on sight, and I squeeze my thighs together as my body reacts instantly to his rabid attention. My pussy throbs in a combination of need and slight pain. I applied an aloe vera gel earlier this morning before we left our townhome to meet Bree at this beautiful private home where the wedding is being held. My grooms were already here hiding from me because it seems they are both taking this tradition seriously.

My eyes welled up when I realized how hard Bree and Jase have been working these past few days to give me something special. I'm betting Rhett is throwing a hissy fit right about now when his car showed up at the house to collect me to find I'm already gone. Jase has messaged him to confirm the venue has changed and he'll send the coordinates in due course.

No one wants him turning up until the last possible moment.

If I had my way, he wouldn't be attending at all, but we can't forget the things he's holding over our heads.

With Mom's lack of recent communication, I don't know if blackmailing me with her life is an effective strategy anymore. I'm finding it hard to care when she clearly doesn't. But Lilianna is important. We can't push the Greed & Gluttony Luminary too far because we need him to keep Ares's sister safe until we discover where she's being held.

Looking out over the grounds of this exquisite private home, which caters purely to weddings, I know I will remember today every day for the rest of my life.

"Don't you dare smirk," Bree snarls, dragging me out of my head.

She's in a stand-off with Ares, and he's fixing her with one of his cocky signature special grins.

"Look at the state of her body! My brother warned you!" She flings her arms in my direction. "He's going to kill you!"

"Bree, relax. They are mostly contained to my body and will be concealed." There are a couple of fingerprints on my chest that need concealing with makeup, but the rest are mainly centered on my upper thighs and my hips, which will be covered by my dress. The small bite mark and faint bruising at the sides of my neck will be curtained by my hair.

"You can't even walk properly!" she screeches. Fixing her hands on her hips, she glares at him. "What the hell did you do to her?"

"Nothing she didn't fucking love." Ares's sultry deep voice is like a caress against my skin, and I shiver all over. Visions of him fucking me relentlessly for hours resurface in my mind, and I'm seconds away from coming on the spot. My pussy aches for attention, it's thirst for cock knowing no bounds.

It doesn't matter that I'm sore.

I want more.

More. More. More.

Fantasies of sharing my marital bed with all three of my guys flood my mind, but I force them aside before I come on the spot. It would be a dream come true, but I already know it won't happen. Ares has made his thoughts clear, and I won't force him. Chad and Jase will more than take care of my needs, and perhaps its only right that it's just the two of them and me tonight.

I send Ares a heated look as I walk over to Bree. She's practically hyperventilating at this point. "Calm down. Take nice deep breaths."

Ares continues smirking, his eyes trailing over every mark on my body with abject pride.

"You should go," I say. "Because if you keep looking at me like that, I'll never make it up that aisle in time."

Ares stalks toward me, pulling me into him by the hip. "I haven't had my fill." He nips at my earlobe. "I doubt I ever will."

"Okay, that's it. Out." Bree grabs his arm and tugs hard, but she's no match for his physicality and his strength.

"You're the one who called me in here." He speaks to her while looking at me. His eyes drag slowly down my lacy one-piece, and I'm tempted to say fuck it and indulge in a quickie.

"To rip you a new one!" Bree growls, still tugging on his arm. "Not so you could slaughter her pussy even more!"

I burst out laughing. Bree is normally so laid-back, and this is a side of her I haven't seen before.

"Go." I press a quick kiss to his lips. "Go help the guys."

Chad and Jase are in a room on the other side of the house

getting ready. There are seven en suite bedrooms in this three-story Victorian-style Queen Anne mansion. It was built in 1904, and it's actually called The Christmas House Inn, which is fitting for our wedding. It's been lovingly restored, and the interiors are stunning with original stained-glass windows, refurbished wooden floors, a multitude of grandiose mirrors, and several Victorian fireplaces with wooden surrounds and Italian tiles. There is a hugely romantic feel about the house, and I haven't even seen The White Garden where the ceremony is being held yet because it's being kept a secret until it's time to say I do.

As Bree gave Ares and I a tour earlier, my heart was so full it felt like it would burst out of my chest. I can't wait to get to the consummation part of the day so I can worship Jase and show him with my lips, my fingers, and my pussy how much I adore him for going to so much trouble.

Ares kisses me deeply, and it's a kiss that is equally tender and brutal. Grabbing my ass, he squeezes my cheeks as he moans into my mouth.

"You're going to be the death of me," Bree complains, and I push Ares away.

Something that takes enormous willpower because all I want to do is pull him closer. "Later, sexy." I swat his ass as he turns to walk away, and he pins me with a dark look over his shoulder. It promises payback for the daring move, and I cannot fucking wait.

"You are so in love and lust with him it's sickening," Bree exclaims after Ares has exited the room.

"I am. This all feels like a dream. Like it can't possibly be real because I couldn't be this lucky."

"I'm happy for you." She pulls me into a hug.

"Thank you." Tears pool in my eyes. "Thank you so much for doing all of this. I suspected you guys were up to something, but I never imagined you could pull off something of this scale at such short notice."

"Never underestimate the power of Luminary connections or the devotion of a man deeply in love." She squeezes my hand. "Jase didn't want to marry you at city hall. He wanted something special so you can see how much you mean to him."

"I already knew it, but if I ever had doubts, this slays them." Tears bubble up in my eyes. "I'm so happy to be marrying him. To be marrying both of them."

"And this way, Chad's life is protected."

"It's not just about his protection, Bree. It feels right to be marrying him too. Even if we still have shit to work through." I wet my lips. "I know you're pissed Ares marked me up, but I let him because I want to have his stamp on me when I'm marrying the other two loves of my life. He needed to stamp his claim, and I'm A-okay with it."

"I'm sorry for freaking out. I just want today to be perfect."

"It will be. You have both seen to that." I hug her again. "Love you."

"I love you too."

The makeup and hair people arrive then, and we let them work their magic. I opted to wear my pink hair down in soft waves with some strands pinned back with blue bejeweled hair clips. They belong to Bree, so it ticks the borrowed and blue boxes. The new is my dress, and the old is my strappy stiletto sandals that wrap around my ankles. My makeup is soft and natural even if it feels like I have a ton of product on my face.

Bree is zipping up my dress when there's a commotion outside in the hallway.

Three loud raps sound on the door accompanied by "Ashley" in a familiar deep, gruff voice. Rhett sounds irritated, and I'm glad we've managed to piss him off.

"Hell." Bree's lips pull into a tight line.

"We can't avoid this. Let him in," I say as I turn to admire my reflection in the mirror.

I can't hold back my smile.

I feel pretty, and I'm excited.

I can't wait to get married.

Happiness is oozing out of my every pore.

Not even my asshole sperm donor can dampen the euphoria I feel.

Bree opens the door to let Rhett in, talking in hushed whispers to whomever else is out in the hallway.

"What is the meaning…Oh, wow. You look stunning, Ashley." Rhett stares at me with approval, and he looks sincere in his praise. Pity it has no effect on me. Nothing this man could say would ever resonate with me. He's poison, and I hate that I came from his nefarious loins. Still, I have a part to play.

I smile sweetly at him as I stride toward him, keeping my shoulders back and my head held high. "Thank you."

"I can't believe you're getting married with pink hair." My mother slips into the room behind my father before Bree closes the door.

"What's wrong with her hair?" Bree side-eyes my mother. "Ashley looks beautiful."

"I'm not saying she doesn't." Mom glares at Rhett as she bypasses him, making a beeline for me. "But you have gorgeous natural blonde hair most women pay a fortune to achieve. Blonde is much more elegant," she adds, touching her coiffed golden-blonde hair. Whoever did her makeup has done a good job concealing the bruises on her face and neck.

"If you came here to insult me, you can leave." I challenge her with a narrowed look. Nothing or no one is going to put a dampener on today for me.

"Don't be overly sensitive. It's not an insult. Merely an observation." She casts a quick glance over my dress, and I can tell it doesn't meet her exacting standards either. It's probably far too simple and casual for Pamela Stewart. If it'd been left up to her, she'd have put me in some monstrosity with layers and layers of tulle and a demure neckline. Whatever her thoughts, this time, she keeps them hidden. "You look beautiful. Jason is a lucky man."

"I'm not impressed by my plans being hijacked at the last minute," Rhett says, apparently done with the pleasantries.

Clearly, he doesn't know how to play nice either.

Anger rises to the surface without coaxing. "We're doing what you want," I snap. "The least you can do is let us dictate how we say I do." I glare at him with unconcealed venom.

"There is no need to take that tone with me, young lady."

"There is every need, and you know it."

"We should leave," Bree says, not lifting her head from her cell phone. "The ceremony is due to begin shortly."

"I'm proud of you," Rhett says, smiling at me as if a switch has just flipped in his head. He can transform from sour to sweet in a split second, and he gives me mental whiplash. He really is psychotic, and it's scary. A full-body shiver washes over me at the thought as he offers his arm for me to take. "It's my honor to give you away."

Bree gives me a subtle nod as the door opens, and I breathe a sigh of relief when I see my brother.

"I believe that's *my* honor." Knight steps right up, and I loop my arm in his, leaving Rhett with his arm suspended in the air looking like the fool he is.

"You are the most beautiful bride." Knight kisses my cheek. "Jase is going to go crazy when he sees you."

"What are you doing here?" Rhett pins suspicious eyes on his son.

"Giving my sister away," Knight coolly replies, guiding me past my parents.

Pamela looks as shocked as Rhett. I had considered asking Mom to give me away, but when she refused to even answer my calls, I quickly gave up on that idea. Knight agreed before the words had even left my mouth, and I'm so glad it's him.

I already love my brother, and I barely know him.

A person can tell when someone is good, and Knight Carter is a good man.

"Don't look so shocked," I say as we pass by Rhett. "Knight is my brother, and he's an heir. I find it insulting you hadn't confided in him about who I am, so I filled him in at the party on Tuesday." Rhett hasn't told Knight anything, and it's important we protect him so he can spy for us from within. I snuggle into Knight's side. "I always wanted a brother, and now I have one." My smile is for Rhett's benefit, but it's genuine as are my words. "He is here as my guest."

I threw out the party reference on purpose to see how Rhett would react. He didn't come near us about Chad's disappearance or what went down, and we all find that strange and alarming. He has to know by now that his wife's dungeon of horrors was attacked and the prisoners all freed, so why hasn't he accused us? Cleo may not know who was behind it, but Rhett would suspect us first.

Rhett gives nothing away in his expression. "The timing of these things is important." The double meaning is clear. "I had no intention of keeping you from your siblings. I was merely waiting for the most opportune time to tell my wife and my children about you."

He is such a liar. Cleo most definitely knows who I am because Knight overheard them arguing about me and Chad said she hates me.

"Well, I saved you at least one conversation," I toss out over my shoulder as we reach the door. "You can thank me later."

Chapter Thirty-Five

Jase

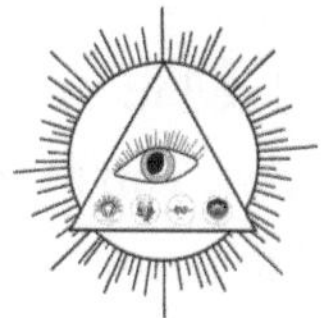

"What the hell do you think you're playing at?" Rhett Carter barks, sending daggers over my shoulders at Chad. If he didn't know we were the ones to rescue him before, he sure knows it now.

Chad and I are standing at the top of the aisle in the beautiful surroundings of The White Garden, on the grounds of The Christmas House Inn, waiting for our bride. Rhett came charging out a few seconds ago, and he looks like his head is about to explode. Knight is keeping Ash back, out of sight, until Bree gives them the signal, and I'm grateful he's here. I know he'll protect her from any ugliness.

I want nothing, and no one, ruining today for her.

Rhett is close to losing it, and it's a welcome sight.

The man is unhinged, and that is something we can work with.

"You'll have to be more specific," I say, smoothing a hand down the front of my tailored black Armani suit. Chad and I are wearing similar suits. He's currently standing beside me in his capacity as best man, but when it's time for him to say his vows, we will switch roles. I'm glad he's on board and that Ashley is happy with the arrangements. It finally feels like we are in the right place.

"What is *he* doing here?" He points in Chad's direction.

Chad stares coldly at him but says nothing, leaving this up to me, like we agreed.

"He's my best friend and Ashley's boyfriend. Chad was always going to be here."

Rhett is apoplectic and red in the face as he huffs and puffs in front of me. What a pity we can't just blow him away. "Don't be facetious," he snaps. "You know what I mean."

"Surely Cleo has informed you by now?" I straighten my red and gold tie. "Did you really think we wouldn't rescue him?" We have no choice but to fess up. However, we decided it's no harm to show Carter he's not fully running this show. This demonstrates we're resourceful and not afraid to test him like he's testing us. It's risky with Lilianna still out there somewhere, but we're playing a cunning game of chess, and we must make carefully planned strategic moves to draw him out while not pushing his boundaries to extremes. "The fact it makes your daughter happy should be all that counts," I tack on the end for good measure.

"You're skating on thin ice," he warns in a threatening tone. "Continue to push me, and see what I do."

I level him with a dark look. "We don't respond well to threats. We are doing what you ask of us. We're facilitating your takeover. A little give-and-take is how these things usually work. I'm sure I don't need to school you on the subject."

We face off for a few tense moments before he collects himself. "I'll let the rescue operation slide, but he can't be here." His eyes swing to Chad for a second, and I have no doubt he's already plotting ways to murder him. "He can't be privy to anything we have planned. You swore an oath, Jason."

"And I haven't broken it," I say as the female officiant emerges from the house. "Your wife is the one who broke the oath."

I watch his face pale and his hands ball up at his sides.

Good. Let him stew over that during the ceremony. "We can finish this conversation later. Now isn't the time." I step in closer, enjoying the extra couple of inches in height I have over him. "Don't do anything to upset my bride. I have gone to a lot of trouble to make today special for her. If you care about Ashley, as you claim, you will make today about her."

He is incandescent with rage as he turns on his heels and stomps over to the seating area, plonking his surly ass down in the chair beside Pamela. Pamela flinches, staring straight ahead with an expressionless look on her face that is familiar.

She's a cold fish, that one.

It's a miracle Ash is so amazing with their DNA floating through her veins. I think it's a combination of her inherent goodness and Doug's positive influence that has won out. I know Ash didn't have the best of upbringings, but it sure beats what it would have been like if she'd grown up with Pamela and Rhett for parents.

Rhett casts my own father in a good light.

And speak of the devil.

I whip my gaze to Rhett when I spot Baz approaching, noticing my parents and Jocelyn hanging back, to speak to Ashley, presumably.

What. The. Hell?

"Are they supposed to be here?" Chad whispers in my ear as I watch Rhett react to my family's arrival. Carter narrows his eyes at me, and he's practically shaking with rage now.

"What the fuck have you done?" I hiss when Baz reaches me.

Ares gets up from his seat just behind us and approaches.

"I'd like the answer to that question too. Have you forgotten about my sister?" he whisper-barks. "You being here jeopardizes her safety." He looks two seconds away from breaking my brother's neck.

"Relax, you are all way too wound up." Baz smirks as he fiddles with my tie. I swat his hands away and glower at him. "It's your wedding day, little brother. You're supposed to be smiling not frowning." He cocks his head to the side. "I'd sure have a big smile on my face if that hot, sexy little—"

I swing my arm to punch him, but my brother has awesome reflexes, and he ducks down before impact.

Baz straightens up and lifts his palms. "I'm not here to cause trouble." The smirk is gone from his face.

"Why are you here?" Bree snaps, coming up behind us. She looks as pissed as me, and I'm glad she wasn't a part of this. My sister looks very pretty in her ankle-length silvery gown. Her blue hair hangs down her back in soft waves, and she's wearing more makeup than usual. I owe her a lot for today because she pulled out all the stops to make it happen. I couldn't have done it without her help.

"I didn't tell the folks anything that could get you in trouble. Dad will talk to Carter and smooth things over. He's going to say I overheard you and Bree planning the wedding last night and I told them because I knew they'd want to be there. I'll feign innocence in relation to all the other stuff if Carter corners me," Baz says.

"What did you tell Dad?" I ask, watching Ares silently plot ways to murder my brother. Ares is seething, and I don't blame him.

This.

This is why I didn't want Baz involved.

If anything happens to Lilianna, I will personally help Ares to slit my brother's throat.

"I told them you found a way to avoid marrying Julia and you couldn't wait any longer to marry Ashley. I knew Mom would cry if you got married without her here." He clamps a hand on my shoulder. "Jocelyn too. We both know you're her favorite brother. You shouldn't get married without your family by your side."

Of course, I want them here. I'm sure Chad wishes his mom and Tess could be here too, but it's too fucking dangerous, and we're already risking too much. I shake Baz's hand loose. "How did you explain Carter's attendance?"

Baz runs a hand through his hair. "I didn't need to explain that part."

A chill creeps up my spine. "What do you mean?"

"Dad already knows Ashley is his daughter. The first thing he asked me is if Rhett or Doug was giving her away."

"How the fuck does your father know about that?" Ares grits out, folding his arms across his chest.

"I don't know. He wouldn't say."

"Well, that's just swell." Bree looks over her shoulder to where Rhett is staring at us. She prods her finger in Baz's chest. "I went out on a limb for you, and you shouldn't have done this without talking to Jase or me. You're on my shit list now."

"You have a cover story to protect you. You're not responsible for the fact Dad already knows about Ash. Let them figure that out together." Baz flips his head to the side. Dad is now seated beside Rhett, and their heads are bent together, and they are deep in conversation.

"You need to go smooth things over with him," Bree tells me as we watch the men talking. "Explain we had nothing to do with this and Baz did this behind our back. Then we need to get this show on the road." She subtly nods in the direction of the officiant. The woman is looking at her watch with a frown.

"Jason." Mom comes up to me, wearing a huge smile. "Look

how handsome you are." She draws me into a hug. "I'm so pleased for you, honey." She holds my face in her palms. "I'm thrilled you're getting to marry for love, so I'll overlook the fact you were keeping this from us."

"There were reasons, Mom." I kiss her cheek.

She sighs. "Yes. I'm sure there were. Isn't there always?" Taking my hands, she says, "You'd better still be spending Christmas with us. Ashley is invited."

None of us have given a second thought to what we're doing Christmas Day. It's not like it's been a priority. I doubt Ash will want to spend it with Pamela, but I'll check. "If Ashley is okay with that, we'll be there."

Mom looks over at Chad, leaning in to kiss his cheek. "You too, Chad. I already invited your mom and Tessa, and Eric has made plans to transport them safely." Dad obviously told her he'd put them up in one of the safe houses.

Chad looks to me, and I read the silent question. "They'll be safe at our house. Dad has huge security."

His shoulders relax. "I'd love to join you. Thanks for the invite."

"Good." She turns to Ares. "That invitation extends to you too. The more, the merrier."

"Thanks, Mrs. Stewart," Ares says in a polite tone that earns my respect.

"Call me Anna-Lynn." Mom smiles at him and then squeezes my hand before stepping aside to let Jocelyn through.

"Favorite brother." Jocelyn flings her arms around me as Baz arches a brow in an "I told you so" look. "I'm so happy you're marrying Ashley. We talked with her inside. She looks stunning. You're going to die when you see her."

"I hope not, pipsqueak," I quip. "I have lots of plans for her later." I waggle my brows, and Jocelyn laughs.

"Jason!" Mom shrieks. "That is wholly inappropriate."

"She's sixteen not six, Mom, and have you forgotten what our familial responsibilities are?" My little sister is far from innocent, and we all know it. It sickens me whenever I think about it, so I try not to. That's something else I want to change. Kids should be kids for as long as possible. Initiations at ten are going to be a thing of the past if I have my way.

A throat clearing breaks up the conversation. "I have another appointment after this," the officiant says. "We really do need to get started if we're to fit everything in." She looks pointedly between Chad and me.

"Apologies for the holdup," I say. "We'll move things along now."

Ares returns to his seat, and Mom, Jocelyn, and Baz claim the chairs beside him.

"I'll head back to Ash," Bree says. "You need to say something to that psycho before he takes out a gun and shoots the lot of us," she whispers in my ear.

"Stay here," I tell Chad before I walk toward Rhett.

My father approaches, having ended his convo with Carter. He stops me, leaning in for a hug. "I don't know what's going on here, son, but I have my suspicions." I go rigidly still in his embrace as he whispers in my ear. "I didn't say anything to Carter. He knows how and why I'm here. I suspect a lot of things will be clearer after the board meeting tomorrow." He straightens up, clasping my shoulders. "We'll talk at Christmas, and this time, you *will* tell me the truth."

Well, shit.

Dad squeezes my shoulder. "I'm pleased for you, Jason. I know you love her, and she's a great girl. I hope you'll be very happy together."

Me too, but right now, that depends on how long we get to live.

My father walks off, and I head toward Rhett, dropping

down on the seat beside him. "We had nothing to do with my family showing up. Nothing." I drill him with a look, and I hope he sees the truth in my eyes because we haven't confided anything in my father.

"I believe you." He puts his hand on my shoulder, much like my father just did. He digs his fingers in as he pins me with a warning look. "Ensure it stays that way."

Chapter Thirty-Six

Jase

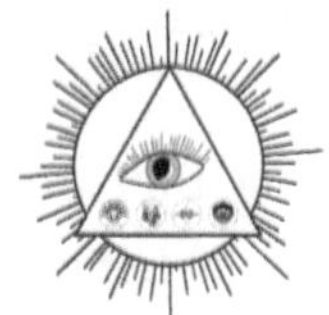

As I return to my place beside Chad, the harpist starts playing, and Ashley appears from the house on Knight's arm. My heart stutters behind my chest wall as I drink her in. Chad sucks in a gasp. She is so fucking beautiful. More exquisite than anything I've ever seen in my life. I don't have the words to adequately describe the woman striding confidently up the aisle toward us. Her long pink hair tumbles over her shoulders in soft waves with sexy strands curving around her stunning face. Her makeup is subtle, and she glows.

But the dress.

Holy wow.

"Fucking hell. We're so not worthy," Chad whispers, and I'm betting his eyes are glued to our bride like my eyes are.

"We're not."

Ash is a vision in white.

She is truly spectacular.

Her dress is temptation on a platter. The thin straps showcase her tan skin and the elegant curvature of her collarbone and her regal neck. It dips a little low on top, enough to expose a hint of cleavage without giving too much away. It's fitted around her middle, and then it flows more softly over her hips. Flashes of toned leg emerge from the daring split up one side. Again, it is sexy without exposing too much. It's a perfect dress for a California wedding, and it works perfectly with the unprecedented sunshine we're enjoying today.

It's as if the heavens are beaming down on us, bathing us in approval.

As much as I'm loving the dress, I'm already counting down to the moment I can peel her out of it.

Tears glisten in her eyes, but she's wearing a wide smile as she approaches on her brother's arm.

"My love. You are more beautiful than I can describe," I say when they reach us. "You are stunning."

"You look incredible," Chad adds, earning a slight frown from Knight as he releases Ash into my care. Knight has no clue he's looking at the other groom, but he does know they used to date. "You are truly gorgeous." Chad's fingers twitch at his side, and I know he's craving to touch her, but he'll have to wait his turn.

"Thank you. You both look hot and totally fuckable," she replies in a low voice so only we can hear.

Knight's brows climb to his hairline, and I can tell he's wondering what the fuck is going on. I had been forced to keep my relationship with Ash a secret, and Knight wasn't in our company much to know that was a lie. He has no idea Chad and I shared Ashley for the better part of two years, so I know where the confusion lies.

I wonder what he will make of his sister marrying both of us.

Guess we'll find out soon.

Threading my fingers in Ash's, I lean down and kiss her cheek. "Ready to make this official, Temptress?"

"I was born ready." She squeezes my hand and dazzles me with an expansive smile. Happiness radiates from her every pore, matching my own. She turns to her brother. "Thank you, Knight."

He kisses her cheek. "It was my pleasure." Knight walks off to take his seat beside his father.

Ash and I stand facing one another before the officiant as the ceremony begins. We clasp hands and lock eyes the entire time, and I barely even register the words, our surroundings, or the other people around us.

I only have eyes for my gorgeous bride.

When it's time to say our vows, we repeat the standard vows first. The Luminaries are traditionalists, and I didn't want to give anyone any reason to claim this marriage isn't legitimate or real. After, we make our own personal vows, which are similar to the promises I made Ash the night I proposed and the ones we both made later with our bodies.

We pledge our love, exchanging rings as we vow to love, honor, and obey, in sickness and in health, for the rest of our lives. My hand is shaking as I slide the ring on my bride's finger, and my heart is pounding in my chest. Potent emotion sweeps through me when the officiant pronounces us husband and wife. I don't wait for her to tell me I can kiss my bride, reeling Ashley into my body, dipping her down low, and pressing my lips to hers.

I kiss her passionately and deeply, pouring all my emotions into every sweep of my lips and every brush of my tongue as our guests clap and whoop and holler. When I straighten us up and break our lip-lock, Ashley presses her brow to mine. Tears are glistening in her eyes again, and her chest is heaving. "I love you," she says. "I love you so much, Jase."

"I love you too, my love. My wife." I can't contain the grin on my face from finally getting to say that word.

Snaking her arms around my neck, she kisses me again, and I hold her tight, savoring this moment.

Ashley is my wife.

She is finally mine for all eternity.

There is no better feeling.

We circle our arms around one another as the officiant wraps up this ceremony, and then we sign the necessary paperwork to make it all legit and legal.

With a discreet nod, the officiant conveys we are ready for round two.

I kiss my wife one more time, and then I release her hand and trade places with Chad.

"Please remain in your seats," the officiant says over our heads. "We have another ceremony to conduct."

Hushed chatter rings out behind us, broken by Rhett Carter. "What do you mean? What other ceremony?"

Ashley grabs Chad's hand and turns them to face where her father is standing and staring. "Chad and I are getting married too."

"That's...that's preposterous! You can't legally marry two men."

"I know, but it doesn't need to be legal to be legitimate in our society, now does it?" She fixes Rhett with a smug look. "We have done our research. There is nothing to stop me marrying Chad as long as we pledge our love to God. Our ancestors married multiple partners, and if the commitment was made with God's blessing, it was recognized and honored."

"That was hundreds of years ago," Rhett retorts, stepping up to the aisle.

"That may be so," I interject, "but there is nothing written into our laws that says this can't happen."

"They speak no lie," the officiant says. She is from a master's family and well aware of our customs and traditions. "I have conducted many ceremonies like this." I was intrigued when we first spoke to her, and she shared that little nugget of information. We are definitely not the first marriage of this kind within Luminary circles, so there is nothing Carter can do to stop this.

"This is happening." Ash's tone brooks no argument as she stares at her bio dad. Pamela has yet to say a word or show a flicker of emotion, so it's hard to know what she's thinking. Ash's mom had asked Chad to marry Ashley before, to try to circumvent Ash's initiation, so I know she approves of him. Whether she approves of both of us marrying her daughter is another matter.

One I couldn't give a flying fuck about.

Pamela Stewart is insignificant in all this.

"He's not worthy of you!" Rhett barks. "He isn't the right pedigree to marry a first daughter and an heir." Guess that confirms what my father and Rhett were just discussing.

Ash leans in closer to him so only we can hear what she says. "You should be thanking me. Your wife told Chad everything about The Luminaries and who we all are. She told him his father was an expert working for you. She also hurt him. So much for keeping that bitch on a tight leash," she tacks on the end, under her breath.

Of course, Carter ignores that part. Chad and I exchange a look. Cleo didn't mention anything about Jasper Baldwin. Baz confirmed that information to us last night, and Bree filled Ash in this morning. I know why she has brought it up now, but I'm not so sure it's wise. Although it won't matter if he can't prove it wasn't Cleo who told us. Cleo is going to lie through her teeth when he accosts her anyway because she knows her life is at risk.

Maybe it's a good thing Ash brought it up like this. It's a threat without being the obvious threat. He's arrogant enough to think we know nothing deeper than he hired Chad's father to work for him. But he will wonder. It should make him stop and think, but I doubt it will. He doesn't see us as adversaries, just pawns to move around his chessboard.

Hopefully, by the time he realizes, it will be too late.

Carter knows he should be nowhere near sex trafficking. If he was sending jobs to Jasper Baldwin that related to the trafficking of young kids, he is breaking several rules. He has no jurisdiction, and facilitating the abuse of innocent children is intolerable.

It's enough for us to hang him. If he realized we know exactly what Baldwin was doing for him, which he doesn't. We also need proof, and until someone can crack that drive Carole gave us, we can't do much with it.

For now, Ash's words are enough to force him to back down. "Very well. If this is what you want."

"It is."

Rhett eyeballs Chad. "There are rules you will have to abide by as my daughter's husband."

"I have no problem in agreeing to whatever is required of me. I love Ashley, and I want to spend my life with her. I will do what is necessary."

Rhett offers him a terse nod. "You will be required to attend mandatory training and lectures. We can discuss it in the new year."

Ares captures my eye, and we exchange a look. Rhett backed down rather quickly. Either he didn't want to draw attention to his wife's predicament or he's panicking a little. I consider either a win.

Rhett returns to his seat, and Ash and Chad turn back around. Ash's smile is wide enough to split her face in two. We all expected that to be more difficult. Seeing her obvious delight swells my heart to bursting point. Chad squeezes her hand, and they smile at one another, their expressions full of relief, adoration, and love. I couldn't be happier for my best friends as the officiant begins their wedding ceremony.

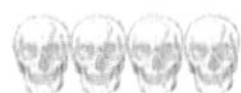

Chad

Ashley's hand is warm and soft in mine, her smile beaming, and her face glows with happiness as the officiant conducts our ceremony. I barely hear what she's saying because I can't take my eyes off my bride. My heart is brimming over, full of so much emotion. I thought this was lost to me. To us. And now we have come full circle.

"Chad Lucas Baldwin," the officiant says. "Do you take this woman, Ashley Eloise Stewart for your wedded wife? To have and to hold from this day forth, now, and forever?" She continues with the traditional vows. The same ones Ash just made with Jase.

My heart thuds as I say, "I do."

Ash repeats the same words, and then it's time for our personal vows. I stayed up late last night writing them, wanting to get them perfect.

Taking her hand, I raise it to my lips for a soft kiss as I keep my eyes locked on hers. Ashley has the most gorgeous brown eyes. Big, warm, and expressive. She looks at me with so much love, shielding nothing. My heart tries to beat a path out of my chest as butterflies swoop into my stomach. I wet my dry lips and clear my throat. "My heart has belonged to you from the very first moment we met. I took one look at you and knew I was staring into the face of the woman I would love forever. We were only fifteen. It was crazy, but I just knew."

I squeeze her hands, fighting to keep my composure. "We were inseparable from the very start, growing closer every day, and I constantly pinched myself because I couldn't believe a girl as amazing as you could love me back. Your heart is so pure, Ash. I love the way you love with your entire being and how you go to war for those you care about. Loving you, caring for you, supporting you, is what I've been put on this earth to do. I failed you this past year, but I make a solemn vow to you now, in front of our guests and in the eyes of God, that I will never fail you again."

A sob escapes her mouth the same time a tear leaks from the corner of her eye. "You are so beautiful, so kind, so intelligent, so loving. I could live a million lifetimes and never come close to your goodness, but I will try. For you. Because you deserve the best husband, the best lover, and best friend, and I will be all that for you." I wipe the tear as it rolls down her cheek, careful not to ruin her makeup. "There is only you for me, Ash. For now, and always, until we draw our last breath. I promise to love, cherish, honor, obey, and worship you all the years we'll be together. Thank you for giving me a second chance, and thank you for loving me."

"Chad," she croaks as tears spill out of her eyes.

Ignoring protocol, I pull her gently into my arms and hug her while she tries to compose herself. Jase hands her a tissue, which she gratefully accepts. After mopping up her tears, she pulls back a little. I place my hands on her hips and smile at her.

"It wouldn't be a wedding without tears, right?" she asks.

"You're allowed to cry at your own wedding, sweetheart."

"Thank you for those beautiful words, babe." She cups my

cheek briefly, taking an extra couple of seconds to gather her thoughts before saying her vows. "I felt an intense connection the moment we met, and something clicked into place inside me that first time I saw your face. As if the universe was realigning and our souls were reconnecting. I have loved you from that day. I never cared we were young. I always knew what was in my heart. You were there when I needed you, and you always stepped up for me. When your arms are around me, I feel like I'm indestructible. You put my needs first, selflessly sharing my heart when you realized I loved another. I don't have the words to express how much that means to me. How much *you* mean to me."

Her words wrap around my heart, helping to paper over the tiny fissures still there. The love I feel for this woman is indefinable. There isn't another soul on this planet I love more than my Siren. I pull her a little closer, wishing I could kiss her now.

"We lost our way for a little while, but my love for you never died," she says. "I can't ever imagine my life without you in it, and now I've experienced it, I know for sure. Chad and Ash are always meant to be. I love you, and I promise to show you every day through my actions and in my words."

Ash sniffs as we exchange rings, and I slot a thin band alongside Jase's band on her ring finger. It's only a placeholder until I get a custom fit one to sit perfectly in between her other rings.

Her hands are shaking as she slides a black tungsten band on my finger. I'm trembling with powerful emotion when the officiant says, "I now pronounce you man and wife. You may kiss your bride."

Without wasting another second, I sweep Ash into my arms, lifting her up as my lips press to hers and I can finally breathe.

Chapter Thirty-Seven

Ashley

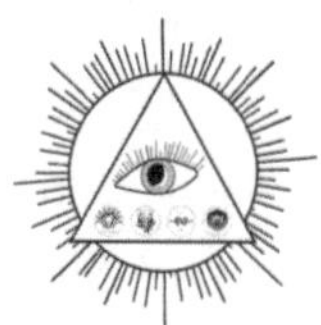

Our guests crowd around us, offering congratulations, hugs, and kisses. Rhett is brief in his congratulations, still pissed at being one-upped by us. He makes an excuse and leaves, and there's a collective sigh of relief. Mom quickly follows suit. I hate the disappointment that flows through my veins. When will I get the memo she doesn't care? It seems so obvious now, and I wish it didn't hurt. But it does.

"Fuck her." Chad pulls me back into his chest, wrapping his arms around my waist from behind. "She's a shitty mother, and we don't need her here."

Ares hangs back behind Jase's family with his head bent and his hands shoved deep in the pockets of his dress pants. He looks lost, and my heart instantly aches.

"Can you take everyone inside?" I ask as Jase swipes a flute of champagne off a tray a waiter is carrying and hands it to me. "I need a moment with Ares."

"Of course, wife." Jase flashes me a blinding white smile, hypnotizing me in his usual way. He chuckles before leaning in to my ear. "I will never tire of saying that." He pecks my lips. "Love you, wife."

I stretch up and kiss him. "Love you too, husband." I grab a second glass of champagne from the waiter before he walks off.

Angling my head, I press my lips to Chad's inviting mouth. "Love you."

"You're my world," he simply says, returning my kiss with longing. He nuzzles his nose into my hair before walking off with Jase.

I take a sip of my champagne before walking toward Ares.

Everyone else walks around the side of the house toward the other veranda, where the small dining room opens out onto the gorgeous grounds.

"Take a walk with me?" I ask, handing Ares a flute.

He jerks his head as he accepts the drink. I slip my free hand in his as we set off.

We walk along the small stone path leading through the rose garden. Every color and type of rose imaginable surrounds us, grouped in pretty designs and situated around stone features and wooden decorations. We don't talk at first, but the silence is comfortable. Ares's hand is solid and warm in mine, and I'm more content than I can ever remember.

"You look stunning," he finally says, ushering me toward the gazebo at the back of the garden.

"Thank you." I beam up at him as we enter the gazebo and sit down on the cushioned love seat. It sways gently as we sit side by side drinking our champagne, admiring the stunning view, and swimming in a myriad of emotions.

"Was that hard for you?" I ask, tipping my face up to his.

He shrugs before sliding his free arm around my back.

"Talk to me," I implore in a soft voice. "Please don't shut me out."

"This is your special day, Ashley. I don't want to sully it."

"You being here means so much to me, Ares." I move closer and twist my body so I'm looking at his handsome face. Butterflies run amok in my chest, and my heart beats erratically as I pull my big-girl panties on and admit my truth. "I wish I could have married you too."

His Adam's apple bobs in his throat as his fingers toy with the ends of my hair. "I'm so fucking jealous," he blurts after a few beats of silence. "I want to hate those motherfuckers for taking what's mine, but I can't. Not anymore. Especially when they make you so happy."

"They're not the bad guys," I say, placing my hand on his thigh.

"I know that now." Taking my half-empty flute, he sets it alongside his on the small end table. His fingers curl around mine, and he wears the most intense expression on his face as he stares at me. "You're so fucking beautiful, Ash. Inside and out."

"You don't look so bad yourself." My flirtatious smile is an attempt to lighten the heavy tension, but it's no lie. Ares in a suit is an ovary-pounding experience. He is so goddamned hot. All three of my guys are today, and I'm a lucky bitch.

"I love you," he whispers, still staring at me intensely.

The world stops spinning, and the only sound is my heart thrashing around my rib cage and the blood thrumming in my ears.

"You love me?" I whisper, needing to be sure I heard him right.

"I fucking love the shit out of you, dollface." He cups my face in his large palms. "I have for a while."

Happy tears prick my eyes as I place my hands on his waist. "I love you too. So much, Ares."

We move as one, like magnets, and the universe explodes when our lips meet. This kiss is the kiss to end all kisses as he worships me with his lips and his tongue in an unhurried fashion that is not his usual style. Ares makes love to my mouth while cradling my face, and he has never made me feel more cherished.

When we break apart, we are both panting and flushed and wearing the biggest smiles.

"Fuck me, Ashley. What are you doing to me?" He rests his brow against mine. "You're turning my insides into mush. I'm becoming the biggest pussy."

"Pussies get bad press, and it's not fair or true." I sweep locks of dark hair off his brow. "Pussies bring men to their knees and deliver babies into the world. Pussies symbolize strength not weakness." I can't keep the smile off my face. "It's not a bad thing if you're a pussy. Not at all."

"My pretty little doll." He nibbles on my lower lip. "So fucking smart too." He stands, pulling me into his arms. I sway in his embrace, loving how safe I feel when he holds me. "One day, this will be us too." He grabs a handful of my ass through my dress. "That's a fucking promise, my little slut." This time, his kiss is hard, punishing, and possessive, and I feel the promise he just made in every glide of his lips.

"I want that for us," I tell him when we break apart. I don't want there to be any doubt.

"It's a given." Taking my hand, he leads me out of the gazebo. "I better get you back to your husbands before they send out a search party."

"You know they are okay with this." I squeeze his hand as we walk back through the garden. "They're okay with all of it."

"I know. We have spoken in depth about it." He stops as we reach the house, pulling me into his chest. "I said I would try, and I will, but I can't promise any more than that."

"That's enough." At least for now.

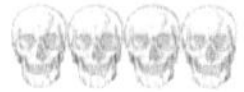

We have a gorgeous dinner with Jase's family and my brother, drinking copious cocktails and glasses of champagne. When the sun sets, Jase's parents leave with Jocelyn—much to her disgust and dismay—and we close the double doors, knock back shots, crank the music up high, and dance the night away. I dirty dance with all three of my men, grinding up against them and groping them without shame, barely conscious of the fact Knight and Bree are doing the same in the other corner of the room. Baz is very vocal about the unfairness of the situation, and after another failed attempt to join my harem, he leaves to hook up with some sorority girl he has on speed dial.

When it's time to call it a night, I'm unsurprised to see Bree leading my brother by the hand toward her bedroom when we reach the upper level of the house.

"She's going to eat him alive," Ares says, chuckling, as we head in the opposite direction.

"Don't underestimate any Luminary." Jase slings his arm around my shoulders. I'm in my bare feet, and Chad is carrying my stilettos. "Knight will give as good as he gets."

"Enough about them." Chad loops his fingers in mine and flashes me a dirty look. "I'm more invested in how I'm going to eat *you* alive, wifey." He nips at my earlobe, and I jump a little.

"You won't get any complaints from me." I fix him with a flirty smile.

Stopping at the door to the bridal suite, Jase and Chad release me and step inside, leaving me in the hallway with Ares. I don't need to ask permission. I already know the guys won't mind me saying this. Cocking my head to one side, I grip Ares's hip and fix him with my most seductive smile. "Join us? Please?"

It would be the best wedding gift, but I won't beg, and I won't pressure him.

Torment flits across his face as he shakes his head. "I can't, Ash. I'm sorry." He presses his lips to my cheek before walking off down the hallway toward the other two bedrooms.

A heavy weight presses down on my chest for a few seconds, but I force it aside. Ares loves me, and I firmly believe he just needs time.

"He'll come around," Jase says, coming up behind me. Brushing my hair to one side, he places a lingering kiss on my neck.

"I hope so." Turning around, I circle my arms around his neck and press my body against his bare chest. In the time I was talking to Ares, he has removed the clothing from his upper body and his socks and shoes.

"Don't worry, sweetheart," Chad says, walking toward me in only his boxers. "We'll give you a night to remember."

I don't doubt it. Every nerve ending in my body tingles in anticipation as Chad closes the door and presses himself up behind me, so I'm sandwiched between both my husbands.

Chapter Thirty-Eight
Ashley

The beautiful suite barely even registers except for the giant four-poster bed covered with a heavy gold-embossed quilt and strewn with rose petals. "You were stunning today, Ash," Chad says, peppering my neck with kisses. "And I love this dress."

"But it's time to lose it, Temptress," Jase continues, sinking to his knees in front of me. His warm hands glide up the insides of my thighs as I lean back against Chad. Chad lowers the straps on my dress and pushes the top and the lace teddy down, exposing my bare breasts.

Jase's hands stall on my skin. "I am going to murder the bastard," he grits out, staring at the bruising on my upper thighs, and I can't help smiling.

"It was consensual, and I loved everything he did to me," I say around a moan as Chad cups my breasts from behind and fondles them. His long fingers tweak and tug on my nipples, and they instantly harden. "Besides, it's not like you guys haven't given me bruises before."

"Not like this." Jase softly brushes his fingers over the

bruises and marks Ares left on my inner thighs. Wait until he gets a look at my hips and the teeth marks on my neck and my breasts currently concealed with makeup. "These are hard-core."

"Ares is hard-core and kinky. He likes it rough, and I fucking love everything he does to me." I look down at Jase. "You don't get to be mad at him for giving me what I wanted."

His chest heaves as he pins me in place with piercing emerald eyes. "How kinky?" He arches a brow, and I grin.

"Extremely. He has a bondage bed and the accessories to match. He even has a swing mounted to the ceiling in front of a large mirror." My pussy gushes with liquid warmth in anticipation.

Chad whistles low on his breath as he continues playing with my tits and grazing his teeth along the column of my neck. "No wonder he always keeps his door locked."

Now isn't the time to mention the cameras or his stepsister porn collection, but Chad will need to be made aware at some point. Jase forced Ares to transfer all the files to our secure cloud file. He wanted him to delete them, but Ares point-blank refused, and honestly? I don't want him to delete them. I want to watch them, and I think Chad will too—when he gets over his initial rage.

Lifting one arm, I reach around for Chad's neck and pull his mouth down to mine. We kiss passionately as Jase buries his head under my dress, pushes my teddy to one side, and parts my pussy folds. I whimper into Chad's mouth when Jase takes a swipe up and down my slit with his skillful tongue. Chad's arm tightens around my waist as my knees threaten to go out from under me when Jase drives his tongue inside my pussy and goes to town on it. Chad continues groping my tits and pinching my nipples, and I'm so wet it's a miracle Jase isn't drowning.

I cry out when Jase pulls his mouth away and stands. "Fuck, you taste so good, wife," he says before pulling my head to his and smashing his lips down on mine.

Chad lowers the zipper on my dress, and it pools at my feet. His fingers tiptoe up and down my spine before he slowly peels the lacy teddy from my body. Jase breaks our kiss to lay both items of clothing carefully across a chair before coming back to me. "On the bed, Temptress," he growls, picking me up and throwing me down on the mattress.

Jase's eyes rake over my naked body as I scoot up the bed, propping my head on the pillows.

"He's a dead man." Jase removes his belt, pants, and boxers as he catalogs all the finger marks and bruises on my body while Chad grabs some lube and a couple of silk scarves from his bag.

"We already talked about this, and neither of you are mentioning it to Ares." I fix them with a warning look. "Unless you don't want to get laid on your wedding night."

Chad drops his supplies at the end of the bed, standing before me buck-ass naked and stroking his erect cock. "It's between you and him as long as you promise you'll tell us if he ever hurts you."

"He won't hurt me. He loves me." A wild grin runs rampant across my face.

Jase's expression softens as he comes up to stand alongside his best friend. Jase smiles at me as he takes his heavy cock in his hand. "He told you?"

I nod. "I told him I loved him too," I add so there is no doubt where my feelings lie.

"I'm happy for you, babe." Chad crawls onto the bed, pushing my legs wide.

I can tell he means it, and I don't want to talk any more. My pussy is slick with need, and I want them to satisfy it.

"Pull your knees up to your chest, Temptress." Jase fists his dick in his hands and pumps it hard. "Show us how badly you need us to fuck you."

"Damn, Siren." Chad slides one finger inside my pussy, and my walls grip his digit. "You're fucking soaked." Chad repositions himself, gliding up alongside me. His mouth finds mine, and he kisses me deeply as his finger slowly eases in and out of my cunt.

"Hold still for me, baby." Jase settles in between my thighs, pushing my bent legs back farther before he parts the cheeks of my ass.

I almost arch off the bed when his wet tongue circles my puckered hole. Chad adds a second finger in my pussy and moves his thumb up to rub my clit. They worship my body like pros, fitting seamlessly together to work me into a frenzy. They know what I like, and they are in sync as they pluck and tweak my body like a violin.

Chad moves his lips from my mouth to my jawline, my neck, down along my collarbone, and to my chest. His greedy mouth covers first one breast and then the other, and his hot tongue licks and circles my nipples as his finger plunges in and out of me. Jase licks my ass with teasing strokes before he adds one lubed finger into my tight hole.

The only sounds in the room are our mutual ragged breathing, heavy panting, and the slickness of my body as my husbands bring me to the brink. It doesn't take long for me to fall apart, and I'm whimpering, moaning, and writhing as I come with Jase's fingers in my ass and Chad's in my pussy.

They stay with me through it all until I collapse into the bed, my limbs a quivering mass of spent muscle. I'm aware of the guys holding a silent communication and I let them do their thing. This isn't our first rodeo, but it's the first time in months we've had sex together.

I have missed this.

Missed them.

They always make me feel so good and so adored.

"All good, sweetheart?" Chad asks, hovering over me as Jase covers his dick in lube.

"Better than good." I grab his head and drag his lips to mine, shoving my tongue into his mouth and devouring him as fresh need builds inside me. "Are you okay?" I whisper in his ear, not wanting to make a big deal of it, but it needs to be asked. Chad has been through an ordeal this past week, and I want to make sure he's comfortable.

"I'm good, Siren." Lying flat on his back, he pulls me on top of him. "I promise I'll tell you if I'm not."

I nod as I straddle his thighs, roll my hips, and move my pussy back and forth across his dick. Thank God, the doc confirmed he is clean and STD free. I would have hated having to fuck him with a condom on our wedding night.

"Ride me, Siren." Chad grips my hips. "I need to feel your pussy strangling my cock."

Taking his hard length in my hand, I hold it steady as I slowly lower on top of him. We both groan when I'm fully situated. Emotion stabs me in the heart when I look at him. From his expression, I can tell he's feeling the weight of this moment too. I don't move except to lean down and kiss him. "I love you," I say breathily over his mouth. "I love you so much, Chad."

"Love you too, babe." He grabs my head and plants a sweltering kiss on my lips. "I'll love you more if you move."

A laugh bubbles up from my throat, and I ease back, dragging my mouth down his chest. I kiss the ink over his heart—loving seeing my name on his body—before moving lower. My tongue flicks at his nipples, and I love how they harden instantly. Knowing my touch does this to him empowers and emboldens me. I sit up on him and begin to move as the bed dips behind me. My hands fall to my breasts as I toss my hair over my shoulder, and I grope my tits as I bounce up and down on Chad's hard shaft.

"Fuck, you're so sexy like this," Chad says as his fingers sweep across my stomach and move down.

"Our wife is sex on legs." Jase pushes his body against my back, and his hands cover my hands over my breasts. "So fucking sexy." He drags his teeth along the column of my neck, and I moan as fiery tingles shoot across my skin.

I continue riding Chad while Jase pushes his hard-on against my back, and he gropes my tits and bites at my neck. "Are you up for trying something, baby?" he murmurs, nuzzling my neck just behind my ear in a sensitive spot.

"Always," I rasp, crying out when Chad's thumb starts rolling circles around my clit.

"Lean down," Jase demands with a gentle push on my back.

I plaster my chest to Chad's, and he immediately claims my lips in a hard, hot kiss. I'm expecting Jase to take my ass, so I'm surprised when his dick nudges my pussy. "Relax, baby, and let me in too."

"It won't fit." I'm temporarily panicked.

Jase chuckles. "Trust me, it will."

"It's gonna be so good, sweetheart." Chad winds his fingers in my hair as he peers deep into my eyes. "We will look after you, like always."

Clearly, they have discussed this in advance, and I love they put thought into making this night extra special. I don't need to worry. They always take care of my needs. "I know." I let go of my anxiety and trust my guys.

Jase slowly inches inside my pussy alongside Chad, and I hold still, barely even breathing as they both fill me up. I feel impossibly full in the best way. "Oh fuck," I cry out when Jase bridges the last gap and thrusts inside me to the hilt. "That feels unreal."

Chad pushes me up a little, and their dicks twitch inside me causing my pussy to clench around them.

They both groan and curse.

"Hold steady, Temptress. We've got this." Jase wraps an arm around my waist from behind. Then they both start moving, thrusting in sync, and I hold still, letting them do all the work as they fuck in and out of my cunt in long deep drives.

I'm crying and screaming and blurting out nonsense as they fuck me and grope my body. Chad's fingers are at my clit, and Jase is fondling my tits as they ruin my pussy for all time. How will I ever go back to single sex after knowing how amazing it feels to have two cocks in my cunt at the same time?

The bed creaks, and the headboard bangs against the wall as we fuck like it's going out of fashion. My eyes are closed, and I'm savoring every thrust, every touch, every kiss, committing it to memory. I wonder what it feels like for the guys. The sensation of their cocks gliding side by side inside my pussy. We have never done this before, and I wonder if that's why? They aren't into crossing swords—much to my disappointment—and I think this is as close as I'll get.

I know they have given this to me tonight to make today even more special, and I couldn't love them any more. They are so selfless when it comes to me, and I'm such a lucky bitch.

"I'm close," I yell. "Oh fuck, yes! Keep going! Don't stop." The sounds coming out of my mouth are not human, and I know I'm loud as fuck, but I don't care.

"I'm gonna come," Chad grunts, thrusting up deeper inside me as Jase plasters himself to my back.

I scream from the top of my lungs as the most intense orgasm crests over me. I almost black out from the intensity of the pleasurable waves rolling over every inch of my body. I'm shivering and shaking, and it doesn't seem to be stopping anytime soon. Chad roars out his release next, spilling inside me, and all I can think is how hot it will be if they remove their dicks and they're covered with each other's cum.

I think I'll climax on the spot if that happens.

Before I can think another thought, the door slams open with a loud crash, and Ares enters the room with wild eyes, looking hell-bent on destruction and living up to his namesake.

Chapter Thirty-Nine

Ares

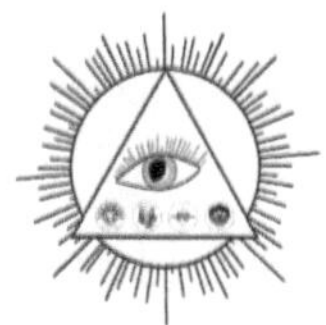

My nostrils flare, and I clench my fists into balls as I stand in the doorway of the bridal suite exuding rage and pent-up lust. My dick throbs behind my boxers, and I can't stand it a second longer. If there was an Oscar for the loudest screamer in the bedroom, my pretty little dollface would win it hands down.

Ash is currently impaled on both their dicks, and it's hot as fuck. Precum leaks from my cock as blazing need rampages through me. Stomping across the room, I grab her off them and toss her over my shoulder. Chad lets loose a string of expletives, reaching for her as his shaft jerks with the final thrusts of his orgasm. Jase roars and ropes of cum spurt from his dick, going in all directions, as his climax erupts violently all over the bed.

Oops.

Bad timing. Or perfect, depending on your perspective.

The look he gives me is murderous as I flip them both the bird and stride out of the room.

Ashley is screaming bloody murder and thrashing around over my shoulder. My hand comes down in a loud slap across her ass before I clamp my arm firmly around the back of her legs to hold her in place.

Hearing footsteps behind me, I run down the hallway, picking up speed. Ashley is yelling, and the dicks behind me are hurling insults as they race after us. But I got a head start, and even with the aggressive beauty wriggling on my shoulder, I beat them to it, skidding into my bedroom and slamming and locking the door before they can stop me.

"Put me down, you fucking degenerate!" Ash screams, beating on my back.

I throw her down on the bed as the door rattles from angry fists.

"What the hell is wrong with you?" Ash demands, sitting up on the middle of my bed and scowling at me. "You can't just do that! It's my wedding night!"

Shoving my boxers down my legs, I grab my straining cock and tug on it hard. "This." I prowl toward her with hungry eyes, my gaze roaming over her gorgeous body. "This is why I'm doing it, and don't pretend like you didn't know what you were doing." I bet she thought I'd come and join in despite me telling her I won't share her in the bedroom.

She scoots up the bed, pressing into the headboard, and her chest heaves up and down as her eyes darken with lust watching me crawl up the bed toward her. "I don't know what you mean."

"You're going to pay for that, little slutster."

"Pay for *what*?" she hisses, jutting her chin out and reclaiming her defiance.

"Teasing me and driving me insane." Grabbing her ankle, I pull her toward me.

She shrieks, lashing out with her other leg, but I snatch it, hauling her toward me with one hand around both ankles.

"I was fucking my husbands and you...you...you had no

right to do what you did!" She tries to fight me as I kneel and drag her up onto my lap.

"This is your fault," I say, banding my arms around her back to hold her against me. Her skin is warm and slick with sweat, and it only turns me on more. "Do you have any idea how loud you are when you're fucking?" I bite down on her neck and grab her ass, kneading it in my meaty hands. She stops fighting, and her breathing accelerates. "Your screams and sexy moans do something to me. It's like a calling card. I couldn't stop this even if I wanted to, and I don't."

Without giving her a chance to respond, I crush my mouth to hers in a punishing kiss that will never be enough because I want to crawl inside her and never leave. My dick is painfully hard and throbbing against her stomach, and I can't take it any longer. Lifting her up by the hips, I position my erection at her entrance and drive inside her in one brutal thrust.

Ash screams, and the two pussies pounding on my door go crazy. The door rattles and the walls shake, but this house is old as dirt, and there's no way they're breaking that solid door down. I laugh against her mouth as that thought lands in my mind.

Let them know what it's like.

I spent months listening to them fucking her—jacking off so much I almost gave myself wrist strain.

I don't care she married them today.

She loves me.

She wants to marry me too.

And she told me we're equals, and she won't force me to share.

They had their fun.

Now it's my turn.

"Ares." Ash tries to speak, but I shut her up with my mouth. If I was in my bedroom, I'd gag her so she couldn't talk. The thought gives me an idea. Carrying her, I stand and climb off the bed.

"Ares, please. Just open the door and let them come in."

I push her to her knees.

"Open your mouth. Nice and wide, my little slut."

"No." She moves to stand, but I push her back down.

"They have had you all day. Now it's our time."

Her hands glide up my thighs as I wrap my hand around her hair and tug her head back. "I want this with you, but I'm not excluding them. It's not fair. It's our wedding day."

The second she stops talking, I shove my dick in her mouth and fuck her face, ending all conversation.

A brief crisis of conscience hits me, but I swat it away.

Deep down, she knows she wants this.

I'm not giving her anything she doesn't want or need.

Ashley glares at me, and for a few seconds, I'm concerned she might bite my dick, but she loves it too much to damage it. She's fuming. I can see it in her eyes, but she wants this. I see that written there as well. She can't help herself as much as I can't. The chemistry between us is too combustible, and we're both slaves to it.

I see the moment she succumbs, and I go for it.

Ashley relaxes her jaw and sucks me down as I thrust savagely into her mouth. We fucked for hours last night, but it has only dialed up my desire for her.

I'm insatiable when it comes to my dollface, and she's the same for me.

It's gone suspiciously quiet outside. I'm not naïve. They haven't given up, but I don't want to think about my competition right now. Not when my slutty stepsister is on her knees and sucking on my dick like a champ.

"You're so perfect, dollface," I murmur, tightening my hold

on her hair as I press my cock all the way to the back of her throat.

She makes a choking sound, and tears leak from her pretty eyes as I hold myself still. "Breathe through your nose," I instruct, taking a mental picture of this image for my spank bank. "That's a good girl." As much as I'd love to come down her throat, I need to fuck her pussy, and I can't wait a second longer.

Easing my dick out of her mouth, I help her to her feet. Ash glowers at me, and I chuckle as a noise vibrates off the window. Ignoring it, I pull her into my arms and sweep the moisture under her eyes away with my thumb. "Are you okay?" I know I can be a selfish prick in the bedroom. I always make sure my lover is satisfied and has multiple orgasms, but I'm demanding, and it's a lot to take. It can seem like I don't care, but I do.

With Ash, I always want her to know I'm taking her needs into account too.

It might sound hypocritical, considering I just kidnapped her from her marital bed and stole her away to mine, but I know she needs me too. She wants me as much as I want her.

"You're an asshole." She glares at me, thumping me in the chest. "But I'm okay." She looks angry with herself as she takes a bite of my chest. Pain spreads across my skin, and my dick twitches with renewed need.

Pings bounce off the window, and I can't believe the idiots have gone there.

They must be desperate.

I don't think Ash has noticed yet. She's too busy biting and glaring at me.

"I'm going to fuck you now," I tell her, dragging her over to the window. I push her up flat against it and spread her legs. "I used to fantasize about this." I bend her over slightly and jut her ass up.

"You're a sick bastard," she says, finally noticing Chad and Jase outside.

The idiots are standing in a spot with a sensor, and the lights are on, highlighting them standing in only their boxers. The security team Jase hired to guard the property during the wedding and overnight are outside protecting the grounds. A couple of armed guards walk past, pretending they aren't looking at them, but I see their lips twitching. Chad and Jase glare up at us, at *me*, their mouths moving, but I can't hear what they're saying.

"I am," I agree, holding my cock and leading it to her entrance. "But you love that about me."

She heaves out an aggrieved sigh, not confirming or denying it. Ash screams when I jam my dick inside her pussy from behind in one aggressive move.

"I used to jerk off in the shower imagining this very scene," I explain, rutting in and out of her like a madman as Jase and Chad watch from outside. They're not throwing stones anymore. I wonder if their juvenile action was more to get eyes on Ashley. To ensure she is okay.

Briefly, a surge of remorse sweeps through me, but it's fleeting.

They know I would never hurt her.

They fucking know.

I flash them a smug grin as I pound into her harder, moving one hand around to the front and finding her clit. I am rough as I rub at her swollen bundle of nerves with urgency. Plastering my front to her back, I slide my other hand up her body and squeeze her tit. "You have the best fucking tits, baby. I can't wait to fuck them." We haven't done that yet. Haven't done a lot of things, and I can't wait to check off a few more items on my list.

The dicks watch me groping and pleasuring their wife as I

ram my shaft in and out of her. Ashley cries and screams and bucks as she detonates around me, and I have to slow my movements and squeeze my eyes shut to stave off my own release.

I want to come all over her ass and then fuck her there.

Every woman deserves anal on her wedding night, right?

When I open my eyes again, the pussies are gone, and I hope they got the message.

Ash is mine for the rest of the night.

One round will not be enough, and I have plans to ravish her body all night long.

Sue me if I'm selfish.

I don't fucking care.

"Oh my God, Ares." Ash is panting, and I think she'd be on the floor if I wasn't holding her up. I slide out of her, both hating and loving the heavy pressure in my cock and balls. The need to come is extreme. But the need to make this last as long as possible is stronger.

Carrying her to the bed, I set her down, kissing her lips softly as I hover over her. "I love you," I whisper. I feel them all the time—the words and the emotions attached to them—whenever I'm with her and when she's not around. Saying them is still hard, because I have no experience with this, and it makes me feel vulnerable.

But I can't control it any more than I can control my dick or my possessive selfish need for her.

She melts before me. "God, Ares. I love you too." Her fingers dig into my scalp and she yanks on my head, glaring at me with red heat in her eyes. "You're still a fucking dick though, and I'm super pissed at you."

I chuckle as I remove her hands and flip her onto all fours. "Like I said, I never claimed to be a saint." My hand comes down on her ass in a few cracking slaps, and she yelps. I caress her pink skin with my palm as I slide my cock up and down her ass. She goes deathly still. "I'm fucking your pussy," I tell her, driving three fingers inside her wet cunt. "Then I'm gonna come all over your ass before taking it."

A shudder rocks her body as a whirring noise emerges from the hallway, claiming our attention. "What the hell?" Ash says, looking and sounding confused.

I notch my cock at her entrance, my shoulders shaking with laughter when I realize what her husbands are up to. I push my dick inside her slowly, an inch at a time, as I listen to the sound of the electric screwdriver. "They're taking the hinges off the door," I say, digging my fingers into her hips and pivoting my pelvis. "I didn't think they had it in them to be this inventive." I groan as I rut into her, feeling her tight walls hug my dick. I know I'm not going to last much longer. "I'm quite impressed."

"They're going to kick your ass," she rasps over a moan.

"They can try, but we both know who always gets the upper hand."

To be fair, both guys are built and fit. I have fought Chad a few times, and it's always close. I've never fought Jase, but he has Luminary training, so I figure he'd be a worthy adversary.

A familiar tingle starts at the base of my spine as my balls tighten. "Hold on, baby." I hold her hips steady and rock into her, gritting my teeth and cursing as warmth spreads over me.

The drill stops, and the guys grab the door before it falls inward, carrying it between them.

"Oh fuck," Ash says when I press down on her clit. I pinch it hard, and she comes apart again, crying and whimpering as another orgasm rips through her.

The guys place the door against the wall and advance on me just as I pull out, spread her ass cheeks, and come all over them.

"You selfish motherfucker!" Jase yells, grabbing me by the

shoulders and pulling me off the bed. The jocks have reversed roles, it seems.

I stumble back, laughing and ducking as his arm swings for me. My reflexes are dulled by the alcohol sluicing through my veins, and I'm guessing the guys are the same. We all consumed a lot of booze today. We throw a few sloppy punches, and then Chad joins in, and it's kind of a free-for-all as Ashley stands behind us, yelling at us to stop.

"What in the actual fu—" Bree stops mid-sentence in the doorway when she sees what she's walked in on. Her eyes flit between us, the screws, hinges, and screwdriver on the floor outside, and the door propped against the wall. A bare-chested Knight Carter slams to a halt behind her, cursing and covering his eyes when he spots his naked sister.

"You see what I have to deal with?" Ash asks, rubbing at her temples.

"Welp," Bree says, grinning wide. "I'll leave you to it."

Chapter Forty

Ashley

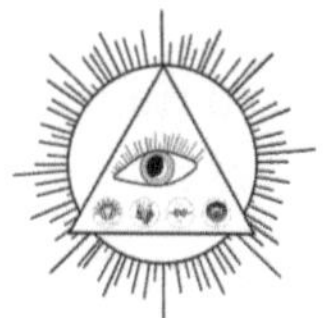

I'm yawning and struggling to walk in a straight line as we follow the guard along a wide hallway at Luminary HQ the next morning. To say I had an eventful wedding night would be an understatement.

After Knight and Bree left, I took Jase's and Chad's hands and led them out of Ares's bedroom. Ares was calling after me, but I ignored him. After the stunt he pulled, he's lucky I didn't let the guys beat the absolute shit out of him like I know they wanted to.

The guys wouldn't let me apologize. They are laying all the blame squarely at Ares's feet. I wanted to get the night back on track, so we locked the door, and then I made sweet, sweet love to them, one at a time, until we collapsed in a sweaty heap of tangled limbs sometime after four a.m.

Jase and I woke first this morning, and I fucked him in the shower. When we stepped out, Chad was jerking off against the wall, having watched us together, and it felt like old times. Chad took me on the counter in the bathroom, and then I needed another shower.

Rhett sent a car for us, along with a couple of his goons, to take us to Luminary HQ for the board meeting, and there wasn't time to even grab coffee let alone discuss what happened last night. It's a conversation we'll be having when we're all back at the townhome later. Ares does not get to do that. I know he doesn't have experience with relationships, and he doesn't want to share, but this will not work if he continues to be a selfish motherfucker.

As much as it hurts me to think it, I don't know if Ares can handle this.

I won't let him manipulate or monopolize me.

If he can't change, there is no future for him in our relationship.

Pain tightens my chest even thinking about letting him go, but I won't have Chad and Jase undermined because of Ares's jealous possessive streak.

I deliberately push those sentiments to one side and get my head in the game. Today is too important to let our personal issues get in the way. At least on the outside, we need to look like a team. Everyone understands, and our shit has been parked until later.

Chad isn't permitted to attend the board meeting. He hasn't sworn an oath yet, and we know Carter wouldn't back down, so we don't protest. Pick your battles and all that. Chad will take our bags back to the townhome and wait for us there. Jase has hired a couple of private security guards to travel with Chad to ensure he is safe. None of us trust Carter not to pull something.

The ride over was silent for the most part with lots of looks being traded and tension thick in the air. Bree is dying to know what happened, and I need to quiz her over my brother. Knight was gone this morning when we all came downstairs, but it seems obvious they slept together. I wonder if it was just a casual one-night-stand, or if there is more to it.

"Wait here," the guard says, opening the door to a small room and ushering us inside. A wide rectangular window resides in front of two green leather couches. A couple of end tables and a coffee machine and water cooler dispenser are the only other fixtures in the room. "Mr. Carter will be with you shortly," he says before leaving and closing the door behind him.

Jase steps up to the window and looks through it. "That's the boardroom down there." He taps on the glass. "This is the observation room. We can see them, but they can't see us."

Joining him at the window, we look down at the room below. It's a long, wide rectangular space with a glossy mahogany table in the center. Twelve high-backed black leather chairs are evenly spaced around the table, all currently vacant. Various plaques and framed photos adorn the walls. Wall hangings with the various Luminary symbols drape from the ceiling at the far back of the space. A side table holds tea and coffee along with bottles of water, plates of pastries, and bowls of fruit.

Two women in gray-and-white uniforms enter the room and begin setting it up, placing coffee cups, glasses, and other supplies on the table along with pens and pads.

Jase removes a small black device and scans the room for bugging equipment. He doesn't find any but still cautions us. "It doesn't appear to be bugged, but I suggest we keep talking to a minimum." He reels me into his arms, and I rest my head on his chest as Bree and Ares fix coffee for the four of us. Tension is evident on our faces and in the bleak silence. We know what

Rhett hopes to achieve today, but none of us know exactly how he plans to go about it.

I sit beside Jase on one couch while Ares and Bree sit on the other. Jase has his arm around my shoulders, and we are nursing coffees and our thoughts when the door opens and Rhett steps inside. Our heads move as one to look at him.

"I need you to remain here until I signal for you to join us. I have a guard stationed outside the room to escort you when the time comes."

"What role are we to play?" I hate being blindsided.

"You will say nothing unless asked to speak. For the most part, your presence will be there to prove you are in agreement with the plans and willing to do whatever is necessary to ensure there is no disruption to Luminary control." He drills us all with a look. "Do not step out of line or attempt to pull any funny business." His gaze dances between me and Ares. "I assume I don't need to remind you of the consequences if you cross me."

"I want to see my sister." Ares stands and folds his arms across his chest. "I need to know she's okay."

"I already proved she was okay, and this was discussed previously. When you have played your parts and I'm satisfied, I will give you her location and help you to retrieve her. Until then, just shut up about it and do what you're told."

I shake my head at Ares in silent warning. His entire body is shaking with pent-up rage, and I know he wants to rip Rhett's head from his shoulders. I get it. We all do, but we have to bide our time. Ares stares back at me, and we hold eye contact for a few brief tortured moments.

"None of that down there." Rhett points in our direction before swinging his gaze to Bree and Ares. "I will be announcing your match, and you need to show a united front."

"We won't let you down," Bree says, tugging on Ares's hand. He drops down beside her again.

"See that you don't." Carter drills us all with a look before striding from the room.

"Cheery, isn't he?" Jase says, and a laugh erupts from my chest.

"I think you had a lucky escape." Bree looks over at me. "Imagine having to grow up with him as a parent?"

"Pamela was bad enough," I say, and isn't that the truth.

We sit up a little straighter so we can see into the room below from our seated position when the four Luminaries enter the space. Conversation filters into this room through two speakers built into the wall. We can hear everything as clearly as if they were standing beside us. They shoot the shit for a few minutes as they enjoy coffee and pastries before taking their seats, and the meeting is called into session.

"What is this about, Carter?" Salinger asks, drumming his fingers impatiently on the table. "It's Christmas tomorrow. Surely this could have waited?"

"I'm afraid not." Rhett stands, placing his hands behind his back. "It is with a heavy heart I must report a breach of Luminary protocol of the highest levels. A breach that jeopardizes everything we, and our forefathers, have built."

"What breach?" James Manford—my uncle—asks with a frown.

Rhett pierces him with a look. "Why don't you tell us?"

Walter Salinger, Ares's murdering uncle, and Eric Stewart, Jase's dad, sit up straighter in their chairs, wearing similar puzzled expressions.

"Cut to the chase, Carter," Stewart says. "None of us have time for games."

"I have a daughter."

Panic courses through me at the words. "I thought that was supposed to be a secret?"

"Maybe my father knowing changed things," Jase replies, running his fingers up and down my arm.

"You have two daughters," Salinger says, looking at Carter like he's lost his mind.

"I have another daughter. My firstborn. A first daughter."

I watch all the blood drain from my uncle's face.

"A daughter denied to me and hidden from me by *him*." He points at Manford, glaring at him with unconcealed hatred. "Him and his sister."

"What the fuck?" I jump up and stalk to the window, wishing I had laser beams for eyes so I could zap my bio dad out of existence. "He promised he'd keep my mom out of this." I know my mother is a shitty mother, but I don't want her to die.

"What are you talking about, Rhett?" Salinger stops drumming his fingers on the table.

"Pamela's daughter, Ashley, is my flesh and blood." He thumps his hand over his heart. "She's my daughter too, and they've gone to considerable lengths to hide the truth from me. James, Pamela, and Doug conspired to keep my daughter from me for nineteen years."

"What proof do you have?" Salinger asks.

Eric is quiet because he already knows it's the truth.

"Pamela tried to switch out the blood sample before Ashley's initiation. I caught her and had it tested." He hands out papers, which I'm guessing are the same blood test results he showed me.

"That was months ago." Salinger skims his eyes over the report. "Why are we only hearing about it now?" He scrubs a hand over his fleshy jawline. "And while it's reprehensible she would be kept from you, and Manford will have to atone for his actions, if he's responsible, I don't see where the urgency is? Or am I missing something?"

"You are well aware of why I went to those lengths," James says, spitting fire from his eyes as he glares at Carter. "Don't pretend you're the injured party here."

"We should have brought popcorn," Bree whispers.

"It's no secret there is little love lost between James and I," Carter replies, speaking to the room and ignoring James's outburst. "It is also widely known he was opposed to the match between his sister and me. Pamela and I were in love, and it broke my heart when she cheated on me with Douglas Shaw. If you remember, Doug was James's best friend at LU, and he conspired with him to entice Pamela away from me." He glances around the room, rubbing a hand across his chest as if he's in pain. "When I discovered Pamela was pregnant, the first thought I had was that the baby was mine. I was devasted when the medical reports proved otherwise. But they were all fraudulent." His gaze narrows on my uncle. "James bribed the medical personnel and had fake reports delivered confirming the baby was Doug's, and you all know the rest."

"I fail to see where you're going with this, Carter." Eric drills him with a look. "Get to the point."

"James was threatened by my relationship with his sister because he's in love with her himself. He didn't want Pamela marrying me because she'd be lost to him, so he set this all up to keep her by his side and under his control. Doug never loved Pamela. Their marriage was a sham. Keeping my daughter from me was another way to stick the knife in my back."

James scoffs. "You're reaching, Carter."

"I'm inclined to agree," Stewart says.

"Perhaps this will change your mind." He flings more papers down on the desk.

James lifts a page with trembling hands, and a horrified look washes over his face as he reads whatever it says.

"What does he have on him?" Jase murmurs, tapping his knee up and down.

"Julia wasn't your daughter?" Jase's dad says, probing Manford's face as he lifts his head from the paper in his hand. "And you knew?"

"He didn't know at first," Carter continues explaining. "His slut of a wife concealed the truth, didn't she?" He tosses a grin at my uncle.

James is gripping the table with a death grip.

Holy shit. If this is true, Julia wasn't really my cousin, and if she knew, it was all the motivation she needed to hate me. It makes a lot more sense to me now.

"But Lucille paid the price for it. Isn't that right?" Carter adds. You can tell he's really enjoying this, and he has a natural flair for the dramatic.

"You killed her?" Salinger surmises, eyeballing Manford. He licks his lips, slowly nodding as he connects the dots in his head. "You killed your wife and staged it as a skiing accident to hide the truth about Julia instead of coming to us as you should."

"Fucking hell." Jase absently presses a kiss to my temple.

"These people are the worst sinners of all," Ares snaps. "And they have the nerve to punish others for a lot less? Bloody fucking hypocrites."

"Preach," I say.

"Oh please." James composes himself. "As if we haven't all taken matters into our own hands. As if *you* haven't." He quirks a brow and levels a challenging look at Salinger.

"That is exactly why he did it," Carter says. "James fully intended for Julia to be his heir, even though she was only a plebeian, because the alternative was admitting he had committed treachery against another Luminary and hidden my daughter out of spite. He knew if we discovered the truth my Ashley would have been instated as the rightful heir of the Sloth Luminary, and he did everything to stop that from happening."

"*My* Ashley." Ares growls, echoing the sentiments in my head perfectly.

How dare that bastard try to claim me as his own when he's using me and throwing my mother to the wolves despite claiming he would protect her if I went along with his sick plan.

"Is this true?" Stewart asks.

Manford's jaw clenches, and I can almost see the wheels churning in my uncle's head as he tries to worm his way out of it.

"It gets worse." Carter smothers a grin as he reclaims his seat. He's only short of rubbing his hands in glee. "He suspected I'd discovered the truth after Ashley's initiation, and he colluded with his daughter to put a hit out on Ashley's life. My daughter was shot at in the parking lot at LU a week ago. Thankfully, her injuries weren't serious, but one poor innocent lost her life that day. I know you have all read that report."

It's hard to believe that was only a week ago because so much has happened in the intervening period.

"Do you think it's true?" I ask Jase. "Do you think my uncle was behind it? Not Julia?"

He shakes his head. "Carter's lying to suit his agenda, but I can't say for sure that James wasn't also involved. Julia was behind it for sure. There is no doubt in my mind about that. Anita admitted it and the part she played before we took her out."

I twist around to face him, the leather underneath me squelching with the motion. "Wait. What? You killed Anita?

Why is this the first time I'm hearing about it?! I told you I wanted to be involved!"

"The plan had been to handle her after the party, if you remember, and after we'd gotten Chad out, but she was a no-show. I'm sorry we didn't involve you, but she was a loose end we needed to tidy up ASAP. Chad and I paid her a visit the night before last. We didn't want you to have blood on your hands the night before our wedding. I'm sorry if that upsets you, but I don't regret our choices. She was a nobody, Ash. Not worthy of any more of your headspace."

"I knew nothing." Bree holds her hands up, stabbing me with a pleading look.

I nod, believing her. It seems clear the guys did this themselves. I swing my gaze around to Jase. "You didn't even fucking tell me! We agreed no more secrets."

"We planned to tell you today." He tips my chin up. "We didn't want to tarnish our wedding day by mentioning that bitch."

"I wanted to be a part of it. That cuntface helped Julia. She wanted to kill me."

"Guys, we're missing this," Bree says. "Surely you can park this argument for later?"

Her words are a timely reminder. We have bigger fish to fry, and Anita Hoare no longer matters. The guys took care of it. I don't want to fight over this. Not when we have a much bigger argument brewing over last night. "It's fine," I tell Jase. "As long as you promise never to exclude me again, and Ares and I get the next promised kill." We all know who I mean without needing to elaborate.

Jase nods, and we refocus on the conversation happening in the boardroom.

Carter is still speaking. Still loving the sound of his own voice. "I received intel confirming James and Julia were trying to take Ashley out of the equation, to end the threat she represented, after James had arranged transport for her to Luminary HQ to receive medical attention. Except that's not what he had planned. The first assassination attempt failed, so he planned to kill her himself. I sent a team out to stop them. There was an altercation on the street and some casualties. Douglas Shaw was one of them. Julia got away, and she had taken Ashley, Jason and Bree Stewart, and Ares Haynes with her."

At the mention of Ares's name, Walter Salinger bolts upright in his chair, a look of sheer panic crossing his face for a split second before he gets himself under control.

"He knows." Ares takes the words out of my mouth.

"Fuck." Jase scrubs his hands over his face.

"What happened?" Stewart asks.

"Julia took them to the crypt. I barely got there in time. She was about to shoot Ashley, but I shot her first."

"What?" James jumps up, looking wild-eyed.

Carter presses a switch on the table and the door to the room opens. A line of armed guards piles into the room in single file, taking up position at the walls. Tension bleeds into the air down below, and you could hear a pin drop in here.

"He should start writing fiction," I say, breaking the heaviness. "He's so good at telling stories."

"He has twisted everything," Jase agrees.

"To the point where I can't tell which is truth and which is lies," Bree adds.

"He has had years of practice," Ares grits out.

"And plenty of time to line this all up," I supply.

"What did you do to my daughter?" James yells, lunging across the table at Carter.

Carter flicks his head at two guards. "Seize him."

The other three Luminaries don't stop him.

"Your daughter is dead. I had no choice but to kill her."

"You lying bastard!" James yells, thrashing against the hold the guards have on him. "We only have your word for it!"

"No, we don't." Carter glances up at us, and that's our signal.

We stand as the door opens, exchanging wary looks as we quietly leave the room.

Chapter Forty-One
Ashley

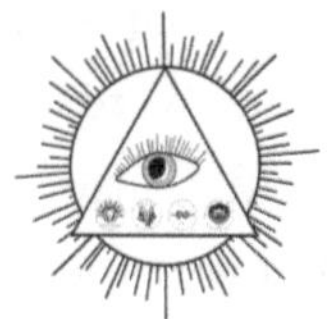

We file into the eerily silent boardroom behind the guard, and the atmosphere is so heavy you could cut it with a knife.

"Sit." Carter gestures toward the empty chairs, and we all sit down. Ares and Bree on one side of the table. Jase and me on the other.

"He can't be here." Walter Salinger points his finger at Ares. Steam is practically billowing from the Pride & Wrath Luminary's ears he's that enraged. Behind the anger is fear, and it's palpable in the room. "This is no matter for a plebeian."

"He's already involved if he was at the crypt," Manford says. "I'd like to hear what they have to say." My uncle has schooled his features into a neutral expression, giving nothing away now. Surely, he knows we are here to corroborate Carter's version of events. Like he must know this is all a setup. My uncle is not a stupid man.

"And we all know he's no pleb," Eric Stewart adds. I'm not altogether surprised Jase's dad knows about Ares. He clearly knows a lot more than we were led to believe. More than I think

Rhett Carter realizes. I'm itching to talk to him tomorrow now, dying to find out what he intends to say. Somehow, I feel like it's going to be a turning point.

Jase stiffens in his seat beside me, and I thread my fingers through his. My uncle notices, looking at our conjoined hands, his eyes fixating on the wedding bands on our fingers.

"Let's not get ahead of ourselves, Stewart." Carter pins him with a look, and I wonder what agreement was made at our wedding yesterday when they were huddled in conversation.

If Jase's dad partners with Carter, we're all fucked.

But my gut tells me that isn't the case.

Eric Stewart is playing Rhett Carter.

I'd stake my life on it.

"What happened at the crypt with my daughter?" James asks, staring me straight in the face.

I glance at Carter, and he nods. Clearing my throat, I tell my uncle the concocted version of what went down that day, spouting the same bullshit as Carter.

James nods, and his eyes look sad, but that's the only emotion playing out on his face.

"You know this leaves us no choice," Stewart says.

"I'm aware." James wets his lips and sits up straighter in his chair as two guards move up behind him. "Pamela had nothing to do with any of this," he volunteers. "It's as Carter explained it. I have always hated him, and he wasn't good enough for my sister. Doug and I came up with a plan. Pamela was innocent and naïve. I'd sheltered her, and it didn't take much for Doug to seduce her."

We all know this is a lie, but we remain expressionless, letting him spin his web of lies. I can only assume he's doing this to protect my mother. If he told the truth—that Rhett raped and tortured Mom—it would implicate her in the subterfuge. He has no choice but to confirm Carter's version is the true one.

"I doctored the medical reports. Pamela had no clue until Ashley's initiation, and I had to confess."

"That's why you fought so hard against it," Salinger says. He's been casting sly looks at Ares when he thinks no one is looking. He isn't fooling anyone.

James bobs his head. "I didn't want it to come out. I knew Pamela would never be able to forgive me."

"It's a moot point now." Stewart clasps his hands on the table in front of him.

"I know I have no authority to ask for anything, but I would like to make a request." James's eyes harden as he looks at Carter. Carter nods, urging him to make his request with a flourish of his hand. "Let Pamela take over as CEO of Manford Media. It needs a Manford at the helm. She has the business acumen, skills, and experience to lead it competently."

Carter's lips briefly kick up at the corners.

James nudges his head in my and Jase's direction. "I see they are married, and I know your intent is for Jase to be anointed the Sloth Luminary. He has always been my choice, but he's too young to take over the media corp. It is as much my life's work as my Luminary responsibility. We employ hundreds of thousands of people all over the world. People who rely on us. My replacement needs to be someone capable of running the business and leading it into the future. There is no better choice than my sister."

"We will discuss it and take your suggestion under consideration," Carter says, before snapping his fingers at the guards. "Take him to the basement and confine him."

"Give me your word my sister won't be harmed," James says, not protesting when the guards pull his arms behind his back and cuff him. "She is innocent in all of this. Everything I did was for her, but she never knew."

"Pamela won't be harmed," Stewart says, lifting a glass of water to his lips.

James looks over at me, his eyes boring into mine, as he's led out of the room. He doesn't fight. He just accepts his fate.

Walter stands. "If that's all, I need to be on my way."

Ha! I'm sure you do!

"Sit down." Carter drills him with a look. "We have other matters to attend to."

There's a knock on the door, and a man wearing a silver robe enters. Carter gets up and comes around to stand behind Jase and me. He places one hand on each of our shoulders. "Our most pressing matter is ensuring these young people are sworn in. We cannot leave the Sloth family without a Luminary leader. Stand."

"I thought we had to attend an ascension ceremony?" I ask as Carter steers us over toward the dude in the silver cloak.

Rhett looks like he wants to murder me for speaking out of turn. It is my husband who responds. "A Master of Ceremony can perform essential ceremonies at times of grave urgency. They have the authority to anoint heirs, administer oaths, and invoke initiations without resorting to the ritualistic ceremonies."

"Jason is correct," Rhett says, digging his fingers into my shoulder in silent warning as we come to a stop in front of the man. "We will conduct a celebratory ceremony in the new year, but it will only be a formality. Today will make it official."

Rage charges through me, and I can't help myself. Shucking his hand away, I spin around and shove his chest. "You mean to tell me I could have just done this instead of being forced into that invasive, abusive, archaic initiation ceremony?"

Rhett grips my arm painfully. A vein pops in his neck and he looks like he's seconds away from slapping me. "Our ceremonies take precedence as it is the traditional way our forefathers made their commitments. It is only in extreme emergency situations we allow this to happen. That was not the case with your initiation." He digs his fingers into my arm, and I wince. "This insubordination has been noticed. You are about to ascend to the highest position a woman can hold in our society. Show some goddamned respect!"

Jase grabs hold of his wrist and pulls on it. "Get your hands off my wife." He levels him with a lethal look that has all the tiny hairs lifting on the back of my neck. A tense standoff ensues as Carter makes a show of gripping my arm tighter while facing off with my husband. "I would not underestimate me right now, Carter. Back away from my wife, or I'll make you."

Eric Stewart walks over to us. "Everyone, back down. Remember the greater good. We are not enemies."

Oh, the irony.

I want to tell Jase's dad to fuck off, but he's right. I let my anger get the better of me. I can't forget Lilianna. Angering Rhett risks her life. I'm instantly chastised. "I apologize," I say through gritted teeth. "I was disrespectful. It won't happen again. I am ready to commit."

Carter removes his hand, and Jase pulls me into his side, still glaring at my bio dad. Eric fixes his son with a warning look as I squeeze Jase's hand, and he backs down.

We turn around and the Master of Ceremonies speaks, first in Latin and then English. We repeat our vows after him, and then we are formally announced as the Sloth Luminary and his wife.

After we have reclaimed our seats, Walter moves to stand again. Carter lifts one hand, and two armed guards move over and stand behind the Pride & Wrath Luminary's chair.

"We are done when I say we're done," Carter grits out.

"You're not in charge," Walter spits out. "We are all equal, and you can't keep me here." He stands, glancing over his shoulder at the guards and scowling. His fingers move to his hip, clutching thin air. Everyone who enters HQ must hand over their weapons, so the only people armed in the room are the guards who are all clearly under Carter's thumb. Salinger is panicking and making bad choices. He knows what's coming next. He knows he's screwed, and there is nothing he can do about it.

"Judgment day has arrived," Ares says, shooting his uncle a look laced with venom. A smug grin washes over his face. "It's time to pay the consequences of your actions."

A muscle clenches in Walter's jaw as he glares at his nephew.

If Rhett is surprised we know more he doesn't show it. "Sit down, Salinger, or my guards will make you."

Reluctantly, Walter drops into the chair, looking agitated and defeated.

"Before we get on with this, we have the matter of Pamela Manford to discuss. Although James would do and say anything to protect his sister, I believe she is innocent," Carter says, and I breathe a sigh of relief. I'm guessing he knew James would take all the blame, so him looking like he was throwing Mom to the dogs was all for show. "Doug and James manipulated Pamela her entire life. She doesn't deserve to be punished." I hate my dad is being thrown into the mix, but I know if he was here he would do this for Mom.

"I agree," Stewart says.

Both men turn to look at Jase. "I agree." He squeezes my thigh under the table.

Every set of eyes turn to Salinger.

He growls. "You don't need my vote. It's already agreed."

"You are still, at this moment, the Pride & Wrath Luminary. You must cast your vote," Carter says.

"Remember your responsibility," Stewart adds.

"Fine. I agree." Walter tosses it out there like a toddler throwing toys out of his stroller.

"Are we in agreement to appoint Pamela Manford as CEO of Manford Media?" Carter asks next, and one by one, the four Luminaries agree. "Very well. On to the next matter at hand." Carter removes a new set of papers from his briefcase. He moves around the table, handing out the pages.

"What are we looking at?" Jase asks as we skim down the report.

"Walter Salinger's plan to kill me, Stewart, and Manford so he can gain control of the board and The Luminaries."

Walter barks out a laugh. "You were always delusional. You can't prove that."

"It appears he can." Stewart lifts his head, leveling a dark look across the table. Jase's dad looks over at the guards. "Seize him."

"You can't do that!" Salinger roars, jumping up in his seat and swinging at the guards as they reach for him.

Around the room, every guard raises their weapon and points it at Salinger.

"I would advise you to cooperate," Carter says in a calm tone.

"Or what? You'll shoot me?!" Walter flaps his hands in the air, and he really is an idiot. It is clear there is no way Walter would've been able to usurp his older brother–Ares's dad, Clinton–without Carter's help. Carter was the brains behind the operation. My guess is Carter did that already knowing this moment would come in the future.

"You have committed grievous treachery," Stewart says, also standing. "The evidence is irrefutable." He slaps the report down on the table.

"It's not the first time." Carter distributes a second report with obviously doctored evidence confirming Walter Salinger murdered his brother, in broad daylight, in front of his young son, and planted evidence on a zealot religious group.

"I knew you would turn on me!" Walter shouts, wrestling with the men as they grab his hands behind his back. "It was his idea!" Walter's desperate gaze lands on Eric Stewart before swinging to Ares. "It was Carter's plan to kill your father and put me in his place. He was the one who came to me with it, not the other way around."

"No one believes your lies," Eric Stewart says.

I want to hold up my hand and say, "Eh, yeah, we believe him."

But, obvs, I don't.

This must play out the way it needs to. I hope Jase's dad is executing a cunning plan and not believing the bullshit Carter is peddling. The smug look of delight on Carter's face tells me *he's* buying it, and that's all that matters.

"Take him downstairs too." Stewart commands the guards. "I want two men standing guard outside Manford's and Salinger's rooms," he says, sweeping his gaze around the room. "And no one speaks of this to anyone. Ever. Even after the official communication has been released."

Heads bob around the room.

Walter roars and shouts and wrestles with the guards as they drag him from the room. The silence after he is gone is golden.

"You knew about me." Ares directs his question to Jase's dad.

Eric sits, opening another bottle of water for himself, looking like he wishes it was something stronger.

I can relate.

I feel like I need vodka, chocolate, and popcorn for this meeting.

"I had my suspicions. You look too much like your late father for it to be a coincidence, but it wasn't until yesterday that I knew for sure when Rhett confirmed it."

Ares props his elbows on the table and looks down the table at Carter. "What about Toby, the rest of Walter's family, and the extended family?"

"Walter's family is being picked up right now and anyone in the extended family who may oppose your right to rule or present a threat. They will be incarcerated here until we decide what to do with them. You do not need to worry. I have it covered." Carter walks over to Bree and Ares. "It is time."

"What, now?" Bree sighs.

"I'm sorry I can't give you a lovely wedding like your friend." Sarcasm underscores Carter's words as he flicks his gaze to me. "But you need to be married now. After, Ares will be initiated and anointed as the Pride & Wrath Luminary." He shrugs as he straightens up. "You can always plan a big wedding for the new year." Carter said previously Ares would have to be initiated first, before getting married, but it doesn't surprise me he's switching up the rules. It seems to be his M.O.

Bree looks across at me, and I nod.

We all knew this was coming.

Not today, obviously. While this needs to happen because men can't be anointed as Luminaries if they are unmarried, I can tell the prick is enjoying this. He considers it punishment because we outsmarted him with our wedding yesterday, and he's not going to let it happen again.

Rhett Carter is a petty prick.

As well as a psychopath.

It's nothing new.

The Master of Ceremonies conducts a quick wedding ceremony. When he says, "You may kiss the bride," Ares pecks Bree on the cheek, both of them clearly uncomfortable.

"You must kiss her on the lips," Carter says, and I imagine sticking a knife between his shoulder blades.

Ares presses an awkward kiss to Bree's lips as Jase links his fingers in mine under the table.

"Happy?" Ares snarls, glaring at Carter before glancing in my direction. I keep a neutral expression on my face. It's only one fleeting kiss, and it doesn't matter.

Rhett takes over from the MC, conducting a shortened initiation ceremony. He has Ares kneel and repeat the same vows I did the day at the crypt, first in Latin, and then in English. The MC passes around a gold chalice, and we take turns making incisions in our palms and dropping some of our blood inside. After we have all drunk from the chalice, Rhett announces Ares is now a Luminary. I'm surprised I wasn't asked to fuck him in front of everyone. As the only other woman in the room—Bree can't do it as Ares's wife—I had anticipated it was coming. But Rhett makes no mention of that or the branding part of the ritual, and no one raises the topic.

The final part is the anointment of them as the Pride & Wrath Luminary and his wife, which the MC conducts.

Eric Stewart passes around Band-Aids, and we all apply them to the cuts in our palms.

After everyone is seated again, Carter hands out more paperwork. No one can say he didn't come prepared. "That is the proposed communication announcement. Please read it and confirm if you agree. We need to get ahead of this now before rumors start."

Jase and I read it together. It's pretty basic. Just confirming Manford's and Salinger's arrests for high treason and the new appointments.

"What about Salinger Finance & Investment Banking Ltd. Who will take over as CEO in Walter's place?" Eric Stewart asks after we have all approved the memo for distribution within Luminary circles.

"Ares and I will speak with the board after Christmas and ask them to appoint an interim CEO while Ares is being trained to take over his family business."

Ares opens his mouth—to tell him to go fuck himself, I assume—but then he clamps his lips shut again. Thoughts of Lili overrule any natural reaction he just had.

Carter purses his lips and looks down the table at Ares. "Do you have something to say?"

Ares smirks at him as he leans back in his seat. "What about my name?"

"You read the communication. Your birth name is Blade Salinger, and that is the name you will go by. We'll sort out your official paperwork in due course."

"What about our branding?" Bree asks.

"That will be taken care of before you all leave," Carter says, proving he has left no stone unturned. Rhett looks over at one of the guards standing by the door. "You can let our first guest in."

I suck in a gasp when Chad is led into the room. He looks furious and rattled. I get up and go to him immediately, pulling him into a hug. "Are you okay? Did they hurt you?"

He shakes his head before taking my hand.

"What is going on?" Jase asks.

"He needs to swear the oath and be initiated into the Sloth Luminary unless you'd prefer his life to be at risk?" Carter gloats as he runs a hand through his hair. The prick could have told us this was all going down.

"Let's just get it over with," Chad says.

Jase and I stand beside him as the Master of Ceremonies conducts the short ceremony, and just like that, Chad is one of us. I'm a little confused over exactly what his status is as you can't be initiated into a Luminary family unless you are blood. Carter previously mentioned the possibility of Chad being initiated into a master's family, and my dad was brought in as an expert. Rhett didn't conduct an initiation like he just did with Ares, so I'm not sure how this works or if it's legit within the Luminary world, but if it protects Chad and means I can keep him, I'll keep my mouth shut.

At least for now.

"Is that it?" Ares asks, drumming his fingers on the table. "Can we go?"

"We have one last matter to attend to." Carter snaps his fingers at the guard by the door. "Escort our last guest inside."

Chad turns rigidly still at my side, and Jase turns his head, feeling his reaction too, before the door is even opened.

But when it is, I understand.

My fangs come out, and my fingers curl into claws as a guttural snarl rips from my throat when Cleo Carter is ushered into the room.

Chapter Forty-Two

Ashley

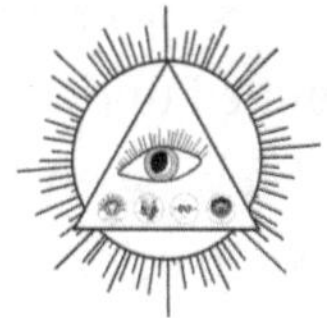

My brain switches off, everything inside me replaced with a red haze, and I shove past Jase and Chad and lunge at the woman who hurt my husband. The guards step back, not understanding the protocol for this. I am the wife of the Sloth Luminary, and they witnessed how Jase reacted earlier when Carter put his hands on me.

I tackle Cleo to the ground, and the only thing I register is her startled expression before the rage takes control. Straddling her hips, I land punch after punch to her face and her upper body, unleashing all of my frustration and anger as I pound her until she's an unrecognizable, bloody mess. I don't feel the ache in my arms, the throbbing in my shredded knuckles, or the pain as the small incision in my palm reopens and blood seeps through the Band-Aid. I just keep hitting her, consumed in a fugue state where all I see is her violating and abusing my man and other innocents.

"I think that's enough," Carter says, and my surroundings come back into focus.

Jase lifts me off her, and I'm thrashing around, adrenaline still coursing through my veins as I kick and scream like a madwoman.

The guard helps Rhett's wife to stand as Jase hands me off to Chad with a knowing look.

Chad grips my face in his hands and kisses me. Hard and deep and passionate, with lots of tongue, until I come back to myself. "Okay?" he whispers, peering into my eyes when we stop kissing. Concern is etched upon his face.

"I'm okay." I rest my brow against his. "Or at least as okay as I can be until we unalive that sick bitch."

"I love you." Chad kisses me again before pressing my head to his chest.

"Aw, how sweet," Cleo says, spitting blood onto the carpet. "But does she suck your dick as well as I do? That's the million-dollar question now, isn't it?"

The strangled, enraged noise that travels up my throat doesn't even sound like me. Anticipating my move, Jase darts over, trapping me between him and Chad. "As much as watching you go all She-Ra on her ass turned me on, we need to deal with this formally."

"She needs to die," I hiss, trying to see past the wall of solid male muscle shielding me.

"For what?" Eric Stewart asks. I hear the confusion in his tone. This is something he doesn't know.

Jase quickly fills his dad in while holding me in between him and Chad. I clutch Chad tightly, hating he has to share air with this soul-sucking oxygen thief.

"Is this true?" Eric asks Carter.

"I'm afraid so."

"I'm okay," I say, grabbing both my guys. "I won't go for her again. Let's sit down."

I ignore Cleo, holding hands with Jase and Chad as they lead me back to the table. They sit on either side of me while the others reclaim their seats. The Master of Ceremonies has left the room now he's attended to all his duties, so the only people left standing are the guards and a restrained Cleo Carter.

"I was unaware of any of it." Carter shakes his head, looking sadly at his wife.

"Bullshit," she barks, fixing her gaze on Eric Stewart.

Wow, I really did a number on her face. Both eyes are swollen. A fresh, large bruise is already mushrooming over one cheek. Her lip is split, and blood covers her face, dripping down onto her chin and over the short black minidress she's wearing. From the way she's hunched over, I can tell I at least bruised some of her ribs.

All my sessions with Vincent have started to pay off. The murderous rage helped too.

"Rhett has known all along. He helped me to set up the operation," she confirms. "Actively encouraged it. He has helped me to bury the bodies all over the grounds of our property. It was Rhett who kidnapped the boy and handed him over to me." Her depraved grin lands on Chad, and my guys set their hands on my thighs, holding me in place. "Such a pretty little pup and so virile." She licks her cut, bloodstained lips as she eye-fucks Chad, and I'm done.

"Are you going to shut that bitch up, or am I?" I glare at my sperm donor.

"Oh, if you insist." In a move none of us predicted, Rhett raises a gun, points it at his wife, and fires.

Cleo's scream dies in the air as the bullet finds true aim, lodging in the center of her skull. It's lights out immediately for the sick bitch, and I'm suddenly sorry I enticed Carter to kill her. She didn't deserve to die so painlessly. We should have had hours with her in a torture chamber to inflict as much pain as possible before we snuffed out her existence.

"Carter!" Eric slams his clenched fist down on the table. "What the fuck are you doing?" Jase's dad is livid. "You cannot take matters into your own hands, and how did you get that weapon past the guards at the entrance?"

That part is easy. He has all these men in his pocket. It's a scary truth. Carter has possibly made more inroads than we imagined. As for why, that is easy too. He had to shut her up. She was going to blab all his secrets. I curse my misguided anger. I played right into Rhett's hand, and I didn't even stop to consider Knight or my other siblings. No matter what, she was their mother. She still had to die, but I would rather I hadn't played such an active part in her demise. Maybe her painless death was for the best. Not sure my siblings would forgive me if I had mercilessly tortured their mother for hours.

Fuck.

Rhett calmly sets the gun down on top of the table before pouring himself a glass of water. Like he didn't just murder his wife in cold blood in front of an audience. "She was my wife. She was my responsibility to deal with."

"So why even bother bringing her here?" Eric asks, clenching and unclenching his fists.

To torment Chad and remind us of our place.

I think it, but I don't say it.

"I needed witnesses to her confession."

Eric barks out a laugh. "You barely let the woman speak."

"Trust me, she had little of value to add." Carter sips from his drink, a look of disgust washing over his face when his gaze roams over the dead body of his wife on the ground. Blood is trickling out of the hole in her skull and pooling under the back of her head. "Deal with that," he says, lifting a hand toward one of the guards. "And call in a cleanup crew. We're almost done here." He speaks so flippantly about the woman he shared his life with. The woman who bore him four children. I hated Cleo Carter with a passion, but this man was married to her, and he has no emotion about her death.

A shiver works its way through me. I sometimes forget how dangerous Rhett Carter is, and it's a mistake I can't afford to make again.

After the meeting is formally ended, I go with the others to a room on the upper level to watch while they get their brandings done. Jase and Bree are getting their new Luminary symbols added to their chests while Ares and Chad are getting branded for the first time. We are all silent as we make our way upstairs with a couple of guards and Eric Stewart. Everyone is kind of numb after all that's gone down.

There are two men in silver cloaks awaiting us in the room upstairs. A nurse is also there, and she treats the open cut in my palm and my torn knuckles. Jase and Bree lie down on two raised cots as the men apply the branding. When I am patched up, I hold Jase's hand in mine while his branding is done, and Eric Stewart holds his daughter's hand.

Ares and Chad remain stoic but pale as they watch and wait their turn. Ceremonial music filters out from wall-mounted speakers, and it's very out of place in the cold clinical room with the white walls and functional furniture.

When Jase and Bree are done and are swapping the cots with Chad and Ares, Eric Stewart pulls me aside to whisper in my ear. "I'd like you to come with me. You need to speak to your uncle."

I arch a brow. "Why?"

"He has things to say you need to hear."

I turn to look at Jase, but Eric shakes his head. "Just you," he says in a low voice. "Let Jase and Bree stay here to help Blade and Chad through it."

"What's going on?" Jase asks, coming up behind us.

"I am taking Ashley to speak to her uncle," Eric says.

"I'm coming."

Eric shakes his head. "Stay here, son."

Jase's jaw locks tight.

"I promise I will stay by her side and ensure she is safe." Eric smiles down at me. "Ashley is not just your wife. She is our daughter-in-law. I will protect her with my life."

I know Jase has issues with his dad, but no one could listen to those words and deny the sincerity of them. It bleeds from his tone and the expression on his face.

"I'll kill you if anything happens to her."

"Jase!" I hiss, cautioning him with my eyes. "You don't need to threaten your father. Nothing is going to happen to me."

Eric smiles at his son. "You'll make a great husband and Luminary." His eyes soften a little. "I'm proud of you and the man you're becoming."

Shock registers on Jase's face. "Keep my wife safe" is all he says in reply a couple of beats later.

Eric nods and steers me out of the room.

Chapter Forty-Three

Ashley

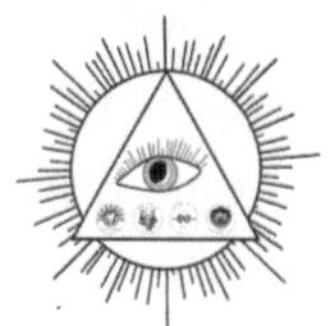

"You can wait outside," Stewart tells the guard as he steps into the room behind us in the basement cell where James Manford awaits.

"My instructions are to remain in the room at all times when visitors are in attendance," the guard replies while looking straight ahead.

Eric doesn't hesitate, shoving the man up to the wall and pressing an arm underneath his chin. "I am the Lust & Envy Luminary. Ignore my direct command again, and it will be the last thing you ever do."

The man gulps, nodding as fear enters his eyes. Eric releases him, and he scuttles out of the room like he has a rocket up his ass. James is sitting on a single bed by the wall, just under the camera. He lifts a finger to his lips, cautioning me to be silent. Beside me, Eric discreetly removes a black device from his pocket and presses it.

What the fuck is going on?

I wet my dry lips, feeling like I've stepped into the middle of a James Bond or Jason Bourne movie.

"Okay, we can talk, but we don't have long," Eric says, spinning around to face James.

James motions for me to sit beside him on the bed, and I walk toward him as if on autopilot.

"The cameras are scrambled," he confirms. "This conversation is private, but it won't take long for them to fix the technical glitch. I know you must have lots of questions. I wish I had time to answer them. Eric will be able to answer some."

"Are you two working together?"

"I'll discuss it with you tomorrow," Eric says. "Listen carefully to what James has to say."

I bob my head and wait for my uncle to speak.

"Firstly, I had nothing to do with that attempt on your life, and I had no idea Julia was behind it if she was."

"She was."

His chest heaves, and sadness washes over him. "She was so troubled and always so jealous of you."

"Doesn't mean I deserved to die."

"Of course not." He takes my hand, and I let him, only because I'm curious to see where this is going.

"I only found out my wife had been cheating on me, before and during our marriage, when Julia was ten. I was devastated. I loved her. I understood the implications, and I was prepared to bring it to the board when your mother stepped in and pleaded with me not to. She had worked so hard to keep you from this life, and she knew things would change if the board became aware Julia was not a pureblood."

"That must have hurt so much, especially when you didn't have any other children."

"It did." James scrubs a hand down his face. "I contracted a deadly virus while on a business trip to Africa in my twenties. I was on death's door for a week, but I recovered. It was only later I discovered it affected my fertility. I couldn't father any children."

"I'm sorry. I didn't know that."

"It's not something I publicize."

"James." Urgency threads through Eric's tone, and my uncle nods.

"Anyway, I chose not to say anything for your and your mother's sakes. Julia was matched with Jason, and I knew he would make a fine Luminary one day. Having a pure-blood in control of the Sloth Luminary helped to appease my guilt. It was the best way to protect everyone and keep the sanctity of our society intact."

If you say so. Whatever you need to tell yourself to sleep at night.

"Everything had settled down, and then Pamela killed my wife."

I perk up at that news. "What?" My eyes startle wide.

"Your mother staged it to look like a skiing accident, but she broke down a couple of weeks later and admitted the truth to me."

"Why would my mother kill your wife?"

"Pamela was furious on my behalf, especially when she discovered Lucille in bed with another man." His Adam's apple bobs in his throat. "I loved my wife, but she was jealous of the close relationship I had with my sister, and she had affairs to punish me." He claws a hand through his hair. "Or maybe it was a cry for attention." He shrugs. "I don't know." His eyes are sincere when he looks at me. "Lucille knew I would take a bullet for Pamela. That I would choose my sister over her, no matter the circumstances. And she knew Pamela felt the same. She couldn't handle that truth."

Not sure I can either. This is all sounding very *"Flowers in the Attic"* like, and a little puke fills my mouth. I don't ask the question that's burning inside me even though I am kind of intrigued in a grossed-out way. Pamela and James have a fucked-up relationship, and it's better I don't know the specifics. It's not like I need more reasons to despise the woman who gave me life.

"Pamela flew into a rage when she discovered Lucille with another man and killed her." I'm reminded of how I attacked Cleo upstairs, and though I don't regret it—that woman was due a beating and some—I hate the thought I got my fiery side from my mother. It's not a side of her I have seen often, but from what's been said lately, she has that streak in her.

I hate I have two psychos for parents. What does that say about me and what I could be capable of?

"That's why you took responsibility in the boardroom?" I say, slotting it all into place.

James nods. "Your mother must be protected at all costs, Ashley."

"I have my issues with Pamela, but I would never hand her over to be punished or killed."

"I'm glad to hear it."

"Hurry it along," Eric says, glancing at the device curled around his palm.

"I know Pamela was there in the crypt. I saw what Carter did to her." He grinds down on his teeth and grips the edge of the bed. At least I know where my mother was lying low. Did she tell him everything? Did he come here today already knowing how it was going to play out? If that was the case, and he's clearly been working with Stewart, why didn't they stop this? Why not come to us and get us to side with them over Carter? It makes no sense, and my head is about to explode trying to decipher all the lies and betrayals.

"He still wants her," James says. "He will go after Richard next and try to take him out so he can have her." James takes my arm. "Your mother won't let that happen, Ashley. Do you understand what I'm saying? She will kill herself before she lets that happen."

"What do you want from me?"

"I want you to promise me you'll look after your mother. That you'll work with Eric to stop him. I'm not going to make it out of this alive, so I can't be here to protect her."

"You're really prepared to die for her?"

He stares at me like I've got ten heads. "I have made my peace with it. Your mother is my sole reason for existing, and I have always been prepared to die for her. She would do the same for me."

Gross, and honestly? I'm not so sure she would, but I keep that thought to myself.

"My dying wish is that you keep her safe. Can you do that for me?"

Chapter Forty-Four

Ashley

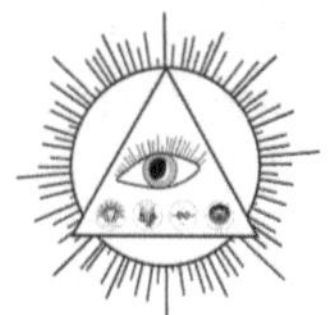

"I need a drink or ten," I say when we walk through the front door of our townhome a couple of hours later. "My head's about to burst." I filled the others in on my little tête–à–tête with my uncle. The knowledge Jase's dad is more clued in than he has led us to believe seriously pissed Jase and Bree off. At least it appears he's on our side. I tried to draw him out in the elevator after we left my uncle's cell, but he warned me of the cameras and said we would discuss it at dinner tomorrow. Ares is grumpier than usual, for obvious reasons, and Chad is quiet. Seeing that bitch again must have been hard.

We could all use a drink or ten.

"That was some heavy-duty shit," Bree agrees, heading into the living room and making a beeline for the liquor cabinet.

"I'm out," Ares says, heading toward the stairs.

"Like fuck you are." Jase takes the words right out of my mouth. "Get your selfish grumpy ass in the living room right fucking now."

"Screw you, jock. I don't take orders from anyone."

"Do you love me, Ares?" I ask, putting him on the spot. Planting my hands on my hips, I drill a look into the back of his head until he turns around.

He looks uncomfortable as fuck, but I don't give a shit. "You know I do," he admits after a few tense beats.

"Then get your ass inside. We have shit to resolve, and it can't wait. Unless you've decided you don't want a relationship with me." I gesture toward the stairs, moving my fingers in a stepping motion. "In that case, carry on."

Ares stares me down for a few intense seconds before expelling air from his mouth. Without saying a word, he moves into the living room.

Sitting beside Chad on the couch, I accept a vodka cranberry from Bree. Jase plonks his butt on one of the recliner chairs while Ares takes the other. When Bree has finished distributing drinks, she sits cross-legged on the floor, resting her back against the couch. Technically, she's not part of this relationship, and maybe she shouldn't be here for this conversation. But she's involved. She lives with us, and she's now married to Ares. It doesn't feel right to exclude her unless she chooses not to stay. That's her call.

Clasping my hands on my lap, I channel inner calm. I am determined to have this conversation in a civilized manner. "What you did last night, Ares, was supremely selfish, and we are angry with you."

"I know." Ares takes a mouthful of his beer as he eyeballs me. I'm glad he's not attempting to make light of it.

"I understand you don't want to share me in the bedroom. We have already discussed it. While it is disappointing for me, I would never force the issue. We had an agreement. You said you would try. I spelled out what that would mean. You know how important Chad and Jase are to me and how special yesterday was. I asked you to join us. You declined, which was your call. You didn't have the right to barge in later and take *my* choice away from *me*. My husbands went out of their way to give me a memorable day and night, and you tried to shit all over it." I'm not going to say he succeeded, because the truth is, he didn't. What happened put a dent in it, but it didn't take away from the overall experience.

"I told you I'd fuck it up." A muscle tenses in his jaw.

"That's a cop-out," Jase says. "You knew what you were doing, and you did it anyway."

"I was jealous, all right!? Is that what you want to hear?" Ares guzzles half his beer after that little outburst.

"You were selfish," I say.

"I'm not denying it." His tone is growing argumentative. "And I'm not excusing it, but I had drank a lot, and it somewhat impaired my judgment."

"You're right," Jase deadpans. He sinks onto the couch on my other side and unfurls my tense fingers. "It's not an excuse."

"Look, I'm sorry. Okay?" Ares looks like the words pain him to say, and I know they kind of do. He's so stubborn and not very self-aware at times. "I agree it was a shitty thing to do, and I feel bad about it."

That helps. Maybe all isn't lost.

"It's always about Ashley," Chad says. "That's how we have managed our relationship with her. It is all about doing what is best *for her*."

"Well, aren't you fucking selfless saints with perfect impulse control?" he snaps, glaring at Chad.

And just like that the switch is flipped.

Ares's mood swings give me mental whiplash at times.

"God, you're such an asshole." Jase jabs an angry finger in Ares's direction. "Grow the fuck up, man. You're twenty-two, and you're acting like you're two and we've stolen your favorite toy."

Bree is slurping on her straw, lapping all the drama up.

I take a healthy gulp of my vodka, needing alcohol to get through this conversation.

"This isn't easy for me," he replies, making an effort to keep his tone level. "You all have an established pattern, and it works. I'm trying to slot in around that and navigate my way in a relationship for the first time. I'm also a naturally jealous person."

"Do you think I didn't get jealous at the start with Jase?" Chad says, managing to remain calm, which is a miracle because he is the one who had the most grievance with my stepbrother. "Because I did. A lot. I had to learn to rein it in. To look at things from a different perspective. What I didn't do is act like a fucking Neanderthal, busting into the room during their private time and kidnapping her straight out of his arms."

"That was not cool," Jase says, slinging his arm around me. "It was selfish, arrogant, and controlling."

"It was manipulative," I add because I need to get this out too.

"You wanted it." Ares is getting on the defensive now, and one part of me understands it. He feels cornered and attacked even though we are all trying to keep calm and discuss this like adults.

"I did, but not like that." I lean forward, straining toward him, carefully considering my words. "I love you, Ares, and I love what you do to me in the bedroom, but you can't use sex to manipulate me. It's not healthy. It is already causing problems, and it makes me feel guilty after the enjoyment has gone." It was the same the night we first had sex, when he tricked me into thinking he was Jase. And yes, I know deep down I knew he wasn't, but I was vulnerable, and he used that to his advantage. I had forgiven him for it, but last night, he used my attraction to him against me, and I'm not okay with it.

"I should not have had sex with you last night. I should have insisted you let me out so I could return to Chad and Jase. I didn't do that. I got caught up in the sex, and it was amazing, but it left me with a sour aftertaste, and that is not what I want for us."

"I can't help my jealous possessive streak, Ash. Nor can I help how much I want you."

"You have to try harder," Chad says. "You have to push your own selfish needs aside and put Ash's first. It's the only way it will work."

"And if I can't?" he asks, finishing the last of his beer.

"Then I don't know if we have a future," I say with a pain in my heart.

"Are you okay?" Chad asks later that night as we are lying in my bed together.

"I'm shattered. Emotionally and physically drained," I truthfully admit.

"Do you ever wish we could return to high school, before all the shit went down, when we had it so easy and didn't even realize it?"

I roll onto my side, and he does the same so we're facing one another. "All the damn time."

"There is a lot of the heavy right now." He brushes his fingers across my cheek. "I'm worried about you."

"I'm worried about you too." I place my hand on his bare chest, careful not to touch his new branding. "I hate you had to see that bitch again today."

"She's dead now. It helps a lot." His lips curl into a smile. "You going apeshit on her ass helped a lot too." His grin expands, along with the bulge in his sleep pants. "That was so hot, Siren."

I move in closer, pressing my hips against his growing erection. "I barely remember it. This red haze came over me, and I just lost it. I think I could have killed her."

"I'm not going to tell you it's wrong when that's not what I feel. She was an evil monster. She deserved to die. My only regret is how easy her death was."

"Same." I rub my crotch against his hard length through his thin pants. "She should have suffered."

Chad presses a kiss to the corner of my mouth. "I don't want to talk about her anymore."

"What do you want to talk about?"

He kisses the other side of my mouth. "I don't want to talk at all," he whispers over my lips before claiming them in a hot kiss.

We don't do much talking after that, slowly undressing one another, and then he's thrusting inside me, and we're both groaning as we rock together, hips and mouths aligned as we make love.

After, we lie sweaty and sated in each other's arms, our legs entangled and our hearts in sync. My head rests on his chest. "I love you, Ash. I'm so proud you're my wife."

"Love you too, babe, and I'm happy you and Jase are my husbands. It's more than I ever dared to dream." I move my head, careful not to touch the patch over his chest and on his arm. "Are you in pain?" I ask, gesturing toward the brandings.

"Nah." He toys with my hair as I prop up on one elbow and stare down at him. "Those pain pills you gave me worked a charm. I only feel a twinge."

"Good." I peck his lips. "What are you going to tell your mom tomorrow?" I brush strands of hair off his brow as I peer into his gorgeous blue eyes. Chad is so handsome, and he's all mine. Forever.

We have slotted back into our relationship easily, and I'm pleased. Our trust issues are still there, but they don't seem insurmountable. That's the only good thing to have come from everything else. Chad has put his animosity toward Ares aside, forgiven me for my betrayal, and I'm learning to forgive him for the things he did.

I'll probably need a whole heap of therapy by the time this all plays out—Chad too—so I'll just add this stuff to the mental list I'm keeping in my head.

"Not a lot. I'll tell her we got married, and that'll distract her from asking questions. I don't want to involve her or Tess. I want to keep them safe."

"Now that we know Jase's dad is on our side, I have a feeling this is all going to get resolved a lot quicker."

"Let's hope so." He reaches up to kiss me. "We could all use a little normalcy."

Chapter Forty-Five

Ashley

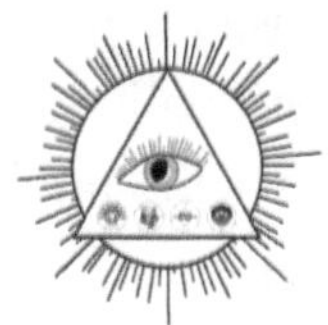

Ares is quiet Christmas morning, and I don't know if he's retreating or licking his wounds, if he has come to a decision, or he's still mulling it over. Maybe it's a combination of all of that plus missing his mom and Lili.

"Penny for your thoughts," I say after we have all exchanged token gifts. It's all there was time for us to get yesterday afternoon when we headed to the mall for some last-minute panic shopping.

He shrugs, looking so sad and lost. My heart aches for him as I lean into his side. He looks down at me, a look of surprise on his face, and I wonder if I was too harsh yesterday. Should I have said nothing until after Christmas? I know he must feel so alone, and I don't want him to feel like that when I'm here. "Are you thinking about Hera and Lili?" I ask.

"Always." His smile is strained.

"Tell me about Lili," I ask, clinging to his arm.

A rare softness materializes on his face. "She's a sweetheart." He looks down at me. "You remind me of her sometimes. She has long blonde hair and brown eyes just like you. She also has a short fuse and gets riled up about the things she's passionate about." He eyes me knowingly, and I flip him the bird.

He tweaks my nose, and I swat his hand away. "She loves fiercely too. But she has a shy side, and she struggles to open up to people." He squeezes his eyes closed for a few seconds. "I used to think it was because of the way we had to live, but I think now it's just her personality. She's quiet and observant most of the time, but she will stand up for herself and her beliefs when the need arises."

His eyes turn glassy. "I miss her, and I'm so fucking worried, Ash. What has she been through? And will I even know my little sister when we get her back?"

"Let's worry about one thing at a time. We'll focus on getting her back, and whatever she needs then, we'll get it for her." I run my fingers through his hair, dragging my nails gently through the shorn side parts. "She's lucky she has a big brother like you. She'll be fine as long as you're there."

His eyes shine in gratitude, and he doesn't need to say the words for me to hear them.

"I love you," I say before brushing my lips against his. "What's happened the past few days doesn't change that." I feel that needs to be stated. I hate seeing how lost and vulnerable he looks right now.

Carefully, he circles his arm around my shoulders. "I love you too, but I don't know how to do this, Ash." His voice cracks a little, along with my heart. "I don't know what the rules are now and whether I'm still allowed to touch you."

"Ares." I choke out the word over the lump in my throat. I cup his face. "You need to decide whether you can do this with us, but I didn't mean for you to feel I have pushed you away.

We can still be us while you're figuring it out, as long as you are respectful to my other relationships. I'm still here for you if you need me."

"I know what I want, Ash." He rests his brow against mine. "I want you." His chest heaves, and I close my eyes, absorbing the smell and feel of him against me. "I want to make this work too. The guys are trying. I want to try too. I just don't know if I can." Agony is threaded through his tone, and it guts me inside.

Tears stab my eyes, but I push them back down. I refuse to cry on Christmas. "Take your time to think about it. I'm going nowhere." I lean back and peer into his beautiful hazel eyes. They are more green than brown today, and it makes them seem more earnest somehow. "Just don't pull any more stunts."

"I promise I won't." He nuzzles his face in my hair, and we cling to one another until Jase approaches.

"We're leaving in five," he says, scrutinizing my face, checking to see I'm all right.

I give him a thumbs-up. "We'll be ready."

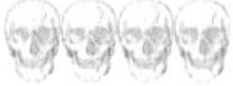

I have never been to the castle Jase calls home before, and it's stunning. Mrs. Stewart gives us a quick guided tour, explaining how the castle was modelled after the original Stewart residence in Europe and that a lot of the original features have been replicated inside. She points out pictures of Stewart ancestors, hanging in frames on the walls as she speaks passionately about her husband's background. She is more reserved when I admire the colorful paintings hanging alongside them, reluctantly admitting those are the fruits of her labor. She is very talented, and I wonder if that's where Bree gets her creative flair from.

Anna-Lynn—Jase's mom—has the house beautifully decorated for Christmas with candles, garnishes, and lights adorning the hallways and the rooms we pass. Traditional Christmas music follows us through whatever high-tech sound system they have installed all over the house. It's warm, welcoming, and Christmassy in a way our home never was.

We congregate in the living room, enjoying glasses of champagne and canapés while we catch up with everyone. Chad's mom and Jase's mom aren't what you'd call best friends, but they know one another because the guys have been best friends since they were little. There is no awkwardness, and the vibe is chill. It's exactly what we all need after an extremely stressful couple of weeks.

Chad has a tearful reunion with his mom and Tessa. Carole then proceeds to hug the shit out of Jase and me, thanking us profusely for looking after her son. Tessa squeals when she discovers I'm married to her brother, taking my hand and gushing over the rings on my finger. If Carole is startled to hear I'm also married to Jase, she keeps those thoughts to herself, and I appreciate it.

Eric Stewart chats casually with everyone, pulling Jase and me aside to say we will talk privately later. He wants everyone to enjoy the day before we get into all the heavy Luminary shit. I can't say I disagree with his logic. We could all do with a break from it today.

Dinner is an elaborate affair with a large turkey and all the trimmings. Bree came over earlier to help her mom, Carole, and Jocelyn with the prep. I would have helped out too, but I went over to my mom and Richard's to give them their gifts and spend a little time with my baby sister. Mom was melancholy and not very talkative. Carter had called her yesterday to tell her about James and her new CEO position at Manford Media.

She didn't ask me anything, and I didn't volunteer it. I was glad when it was time to leave.

After dinner, Jase and Chad take Tessa to the home movie room to watch *The Polar Express*. Ares goes off somewhere with Baz. They were seated together at the dinner table and spent a lot of it with their heads bent together in conversation. They're close in age and share similar personality traits, so I'm not that surprised at their burgeoning bromance. I like it for Ares. He's seemed lost since Rocky and Shoulders died, and now with his mom overseas, he's more than a little adrift. Baz is one of the good guys, and I would welcome it if they became friends.

While my husbands get the movie set up, Bree and I make popcorn and grab some snacks before joining them. I had promised Tessa pizza and a movie before I knew they had to be moved to a safe house, so this is the best alternative I could come up with. I doubt I can fit another morsel in my mouth after that dinner, but Tess is a growing teen, and I'm sure she can find some room.

Chad's sister is a sweetheart and full of enthusiasm, never once complaining. She's just happy to be here with all of us. The obvious joy on her face confirms it. She sits snuggled into her brother, whispering and giggling with him throughout the movie, and my heart swells with love watching them together. I imagine this is what Ares is like with Lili. My heart pings with sadness this time, remembering our earlier conversation.

Carter said he was making sure Lili was okay. I'm hoping this is one time he's not lying.

When the movie ends, Tessa and Carole have to leave. Tessa sobs, clinging to her brother, and I notice Ares watching their interaction avidly. Chad and Ares have so much in common. It's probably why they have clashed the most in the past. I'm hopeful we have turned a corner and that has changed. Only time will tell.

After Chad's family leaves, Eric asks me, Jase, Chad, Ares, and Bree to join him and Baz in the library. "Oh my God. I feel like Belle from *Beauty and the Beast*," I say, twirling around when we enter the large space, my eyes lighting up in glee. It's one of those old-fashioned libraries. All done in dark wood with row upon row of shelving on all sides of the room, stretching upward and touching the ceiling. A rolling ladder affixed to each wall of shelving is the only way to reach the books at the top. A large desk sits propped in front of a window facing the grounds. On each side of it is a window seat and reading nook. In the center of the room is a seating area positioned around a firepit that is encased behind glass. It must be one of those modern electrical fires that looks like a real fire, but I have never seen one that shape.

It's to this area that Eric leads us. Baz closes and locks the door behind us as we all take seats. I'm sandwiched between Ares and Jase on one side, and heat from their bodies mixes with the heat from the fire, cocooning me in a warm bubble. I stifle a yawn and the urge to curl up on the comfy couch with two of my guys for a cuddle.

Bree tops off our flutes with more champagne while we wait for Jase's father to speak. Expectation is rife in the air along with a hefty dose of trepidation. "We have a lot to discuss," Eric says, sitting comfortably in a high-backed red leather chair. He has his feet crossed at the ankles, looking like the epitome of calm and relaxed. Only the slight tapping of his foot gives his anxiety away. "I asked Baz to tell me everything he knew this morning, and I have been fully briefed on everything."

Jase explodes, and I jump up and sit on him before he can go nuclear on Baz. "Stop. Wait a second." I wrap my arms around Jase's neck as I look at Eric. "Are you on our side, Mr. Stewart? Do you want to stop Rhett Carter from becoming Lord of The Luminaries?"

"I am most definitely on your side, and that monster needs to be stopped before he destroys our society and the world as we know it."

I look down at Jase. "I know you're mad, but don't be. Carter needs to be stopped, and Lili is out there somewhere, and we need to find her. Baz didn't betray our confidence. He told your father what he needed to know so we could accelerate this conversation." Pressing my mouth to his ear, I whisper, "He's not our enemy. Please, babe, just let it go."

Jase stews for a few seconds before blowing air out of his mouth and nodding.

"That is true talent," Baz says, grinning from his perch on the arm of the chair Bree is sitting on.

"Don't you start." At some point, I am going to knock Jase's and Baz's heads together and put some sense into them.

"Can we get on with things," Eric says, looking between his children. "I don't want to be away too long. Your mother has gone to lots of trouble today, and I want to spend the night snuggling with her on the couch and sneaking a few Christmas kisses."

Baz, Bree, and Jase all stare at their father as if he's grown wings.

Eric chuckles. "You should see your faces."

"Where's my father gone, and how did you take control of his body?" Jase asks.

"There are many masks we need to wear as Luminaries," Eric says, his gaze softening as he looks upon his second son. "You will discover that truth now and how nothing is ever as it seems."

"It sounds and looks exhausting," I truthfully admit.

"It is, Ashley. It really is." His voice heaves with a tiredness born of years of hiding in plain sight.

"Can you help us find my sister?" Ares blurts, and the conversation turns heavy.

"I can and I will. After Baz and I spoke, I talked with Gregor and put him in touch with my own personal IT team. If anyone can crack that password, my guys can. From what I have learned about Jasper Baldwin, I am confident the information we need is on that drive."

"What have you learned about my dad?" Chad asks. "I need to clear his name. He's not a trafficker."

"I know that, son, and we will clear his name and get back everything that was taken from you and your family. Our first order of priority is finding Lilianna Haynes and evidence to take Rhett Carter down."

"We need to kill the motherfucker," Ares says, cracking his knuckles.

"And we will." Eric swirls the Scottish whisky in his tumbler before taking a sip. "But we can't just kill a Luminary without proof to justify our actions."

"Why not?" I ask. "Look at what he has done."

"We all know what Rhett Carter has done, but he had evidence or witness testimony to corroborate his actions."

"Half of that is bullshit," Jase says.

"And he was blackmailing us into lying for him," Bree adds.

"I am well aware. Like I'm aware Carter is behind the separatist movement, the killing of Blade's father, and a whole host of other atrocities. He will be chairing a motion to have Walter Salinger and James Manford killed for their gross treachery. There is nothing Rhett Carter does without some form of justification and a hell of a lot of planning."

"How long have you known he was planning this?"

"It's always been evident Rhett was hungry for more. He is

the Greed & Gluttony Luminary, after all." He gives us a wry smile, and Jase's mouth slackens a little. I know he sees his father as cold and emotionless, but he doesn't come across like that to me.

It appears Rhett Carter isn't the only one playing a long game.

"But it's only in recent times that James and I realized he was getting ready to strike. He has always been one step ahead, and we need to overtake him."

"We already have," Ares says. "We control three of the four Luminaries now. That gives us the most power."

"The fact Carter isn't concerned about that tells me there is something we don't know."

"He's too arrogant to consider us a threat," I say. "And too focused on his own plan to notice things under this nose."

"I would like to believe that, but we should never underestimate a man like Carter. He has amassed huge global support. That is of grave concern. You saw how all the guards at HQ are on his payroll. It's the reason I took out a few of them before I left yesterday and replaced them with men loyal to me. Walter and James would not have survived the night otherwise."

"Walter doesn't deserve to survive," I snap. "He deserves to die for what he did."

"He does, and he will when the timing is right. It serves us to keep him alive. Carter has pinned Clint's murder on him, but Carter was the one in the driver's seat. I don't need Walter to convince me of that. I want to find the real proof and use that as one of our reasons for deposing Carter."

"I still don't understand why we need a reason? The man is a monster," Bree says. "And our word is law. We just take him out after we get Lili, and we can manufacture evidence if we need to explain it."

"You would stoop to his level?" Eric asks her. "I thought my daughter was more principled."

"You can't fight someone like Carter with principles," Baz says. "You have to beat him at his own game."

"If we want to effect change, we need to hold ourselves to the highest accountability. We don't need to manufacture evidence against Carter when he has broken so many rules. We need to find irrefutable proof of his crimes, and we present that in an honest light, and no one can argue against it. If we don't do that, if we are seen to treat him unfairly, his supporters will move against us. We need to present enough evidence to make them stop and think."

"We don't have the luxury of time," I say. "He's going after world domination."

"And he plans to elevate a master's family to Luminary status," Ares says. "I'm thinking that's his next priority."

"Do you know who it is?" Eric asks.

"We were hoping you would have ideas." Jase rubs the bridge of his nose.

"I don't. That is his most closely guarded secret."

"I need to see Ruben now," Ares says to Baz. "Can you move that meeting forward?"

"You don't need to see Ruben," Eric says, draining the last of his drink. "He can't tell you anything I don't already know."

Stunned silence greets his statement until Ares finds his voice. "Then tell us. I know The Bulls were heavily involved in sex trafficking, and they started selling kids around the same time my sister went missing. I know in my gut they were involved in it."

"I suspect they were," Eric says. "Like I suspect the intel on Baldwin's drive will prove it once we have accessed it. But Ruben couldn't tell you that. He was smart enough to outsource the operational side of their new business to someone else, so if shit went down, his fingerprints weren't on it. Ruben is a shrewd player."

"Not shrewd enough to avoid getting arrested and thrown in jail," Ares says in a snippy tone.

"The Sainthood set them up with a little help from VERO. Whether Ruben was smart or as dumb as a bag of rocks didn't matter. He was still going down because he was a scapegoat."

"For the sex trafficking?" I ask, starting to lose the train of this conversation.

Eric shakes his head. "That was a drugs sting, but it was to get The Bulls out of the way while VERO went after The Sainthood."

"Who is VERO, and what does this have to do with my sister?" Ares asks, sounding as confused as I feel.

"VERO is a secret organization that takes on high-level projects for the government and private clients," Baz explains. "They are government funded, but if you investigated them, it would look like they are privately funded."

"It's all a smoke screen," Eric says. "They have a number of Luminary investors on their board, and VERO does a lot of the dirty work for The Luminaries."

Lo's friend D pops into my head, and I wonder if this is the organization he works for. My eyes meet Chad's, and I can see he has the same thought. It's not that far of a stretch. Not when VERO and The Sainthood have just been mentioned in the same breath.

"If Ruben wasn't the guy on the ground, who was? And can you get me a meeting with him?"

"The guy running the operation for The Bulls was a man named Luke McKenzie."

"Was?" I ask.

"He's dead. Gunned down outside a burned-out meth house last year."

Ares curses and buries his head in his hands.

Eric stares at me strangely for a minute. "I thought your friend Harlow Westbrook might have mentioned him to you."

"Why would Lo mention some dead trafficker to me?" I frown. Am I missing something here?

"Because Harlow Westbrook is the person who took McKenzie down."

Chapter Forty-Six
Ashley

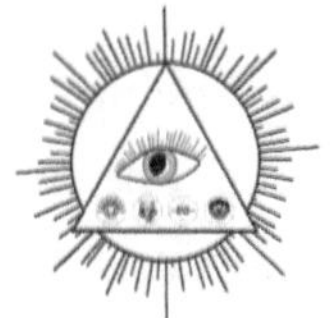

"It feels like I've never really known my dad," Jase says when we're alone in bed that night. Chad was with us for a while, but he's gone to sleep in his own bed now. Ares has been sullen since Eric confirmed The Bulls angle is a seemingly dead-end. My heart hurts for him, and I hope we get a breakthrough soon. He is losing hope of ever finding his sister.

"Not if he's been wearing so many masks." I tuck into his side, and his arm slides around my naked body.

"I feel foolish. Like I should have known."

"I get it, and I'd feel the same way," I say, tracing circles on his chest with the tip of my finger. I stay away from the healing brand on his chest. "But at least you know he was trying to protect you and he's not the coldhearted bastard you've always believed him to be." I sit up, staring down into his gorgeous face, sweeping my fingers across his cheeks. "And the best news of all is he's on our side. He's known some of what Carter was planning, and he's already made his own chess moves."

Jase had a long talk with his father before we left, and they got a lot of stuff out on the table. Eric isn't privy to everything

Carter has done or planned, but he knew enough to formulate his own plan. He has his own trusted men within the Luminary inner circles, and he's been infiltrating the separatist movement for some time. All of this will help after Carter is eliminated and we're trying to root out his supporters.

"I wish my father and James weren't so *noble*." He curls his fingers into little air quotes. "Carter plays dirty, and you need to fight dirty with dirty."

"I don't disagree," I say, laying my head down on his arm and snuggling back into him. The instant my bare flesh meets his, my libido wakes up again. I'm insatiable these days, it would seem. "But your father's argument has merit. We can't present as the better alternative if we're sinking to Carter's levels, and James had already taken plenty of risks with his actions. He couldn't risk more."

Their plan had been similar to Carter's. They were working to build evidence against Carter and Salinger and were planning to use it to oust them from the board and replace them with their heirs. They weren't aware of the Ares connection, and they hadn't been planning on using me. But they were too late and too many steps behind Carter because he got there first.

"My father deserves an Oscar for the way he handled Carter yesterday."

"Truth," I say, sliding my leg in between Jase's. "He played it perfectly, and I think Carter fully buys into it."

"Let's hope so." Jase rolls me onto my back and moves over me. "But enough Luminary talk." He pushes my legs wide with his knee as he grins down at me. "Now it's time to give my wife her private Christmas gift." He waggles his brows as he slips two fingers inside me to check I'm ready for him even though he knows I always am.

As he slides his cock deep inside me, a content sigh escapes my lips, and I forget everything Luminary as my husband makes love to me.

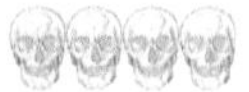

The days that follow are strange. The official Luminary announcement is now public, and everyone knows about the new Sloth and Pride & Wrath Luminaries. Gossip is rife about Salinger and Manford being arrested, Salinger's heir and family being locked up, and the shocking death of Cleo Carter for high treachery.

Knight came over with our youngest sister, Paisley. She is super sweet, and we clicked instantly. I look forward to getting to know her. Daria and Kylo were a no-show. Knight cringed telling me they refuse to have anything to do with me, in part because they blame me for the circumstances of their mother's death. Which is grossly unfair, but whatever.

Carter gave them an altered version of the truth. Of course, he did. We told Knight how it really went down, but Jase insisted I omit the part where I attacked their mother and the sick things she hurled at Chad before her demise.

I don't like keeping anything from my brother, but Jase made a valid point. What I did had no bearing on her death. Carter killed her, not me. My siblings don't need her reputation tarnished any more than it already has been in recent times. And why risk damaging my burgeoning relationship with my brother by revealing something that ultimately made no difference to the outcome?

So, I kept that part to myself.

It seems obvious now that Carter let us rescue Chad on purpose. It explains why he didn't show up at our townhome afterward. I'm betting he hoped we would kill his wife and save him the trouble. It would have been a win-win for him. Get rid of her like he wanted and have something additional to hold over our heads. I'm glad we didn't give him the extra ammunition and he had to kill her himself. I doubt my brother would have been willing to overlook me murdering his mother.

Knight is now firmly on our side, and he's promised to keep tabs on his father and let us know of anything he overhears or any suspicious activity.

I still don't know what went down between him and Bree because I have barely seen my bestie. Between training sessions with Vincent, attending Luminary training and meetings with senior Sloth officials about the transfer of responsibilities to Jase and me, sessions with Carter as he outlines how things are going to work, fielding calls from nosy assholes, and avoiding the funny looks people are throwing our way, we have had minimal downtime. Most nights, I flop into bed exhausted.

But I'm determined to talk to her today. Today is my dad's funeral, and we have cleared our schedules so I can give my dad the send-off he deserves.

Chad and Jase support me through the church ceremony, and they flank me at the graveside as I finally succumb to my grief and sob my heart out. Ares hovers near me, but he's been keeping his distance, and I don't know where his head is at. Richard holds Mom upright as she wails and sobs and clings to him in an uncharacteristic display of emotion. I don't know what to make of it. My parents may not have been in love, but they shared a genuine friendship, and they were a good team. I want to believe Mom is sincere, but I'm having a hard time with her recently. Everything just seems so...fake.

Our townhome is crowded with people when we return. Bree and her mom organized all the food and ensured we were stocked up on drinks. Jase heads into the kitchen to see if he can help, and Chad goes off to fix me a drink. Ares headed straight for the bathroom when we arrived.

"Ashley," my beautiful cousin Sydney calls out to me as I step foot in the living room.

She looks happier and healthier than the last time I saw her. With her slim figure, long blonde hair, and stunning face, she is turning heads as she walks toward me. Living independently in Europe obviously agrees with her. I know she was back in the US for the holidays, and she changed her return flight so she could attend Dad's funeral. I appreciate that so much.

"How are you holding up?" she asks when she reaches me. "I'm so sorry for your loss." Tears prick her eyes as she pulls me in for a hug. "I can't believe it. I loved Doug. He was always so kind. He took an interest in me in a way my own father didn't. I always loved that about him."

"Where is your dad?" I ask, easing out of her embrace and scanning the room for Herman Shaw.

"He had urgent business to attend to. He's already on his way back to New York." Her tone is clipped, her jaw tight.

I noticed she wasn't standing by her father at the funeral either. "You're still estranged from him?" I ask.

She nods. "I'm not sure I can ever forgive him for the things he's done to me."

"I know you." Ares steps up beside me, glancing at my cousin with a slight frown. "You're Sydney Shaw, right?"

Sydney tilts her head to the side, studying Ares's face with a furrowed brow. "Have we met?"

I move in closer to his side. Please, God, let Ares not have fucked my cousin. I like Sydney, and I don't want reasons to dislike her. Not sure what it says about me that my mind has instantly gone there, but I'm trying to imagine how they might know one another, and it's the obvious reason.

The thought sits in my stomach like a lead balloon.

Ares presses his mouth to my ear. "You're cute when you're jealous."

He smirks, and I almost cry in relief. It's been a while since I've been on the receiving end of one of them, and it's comforting. He has seemed so out of sorts lately, and I hate it. I miss the cocky arrogant jerk.

Ares's arm slides low around my back, and he pulls me flush against him, seemingly pleased with my little territorial display. Refocusing on my cousin, he shakes his head. "We haven't met, no."

Relief shuttles through me.

Sydney's brow puckers, and I'm not surprised. One, she's trying to figure out how he knows her when they've never met. And two, she's confused over the status of our relationship. Sydney has met Chad in the past, and I introduced her to Jase briefly outside the church. She saw the rings on my fingers, and I explained I was married to both my guys.

I can tell she is now wondering who Ares is to me. I open my mouth to explain, but I'm not sure how to introduce him. Calling him my stepbrother isn't right, and is he even that anymore now my dad is gone? Besides, that's not who he is to me. I can't call him my boyfriend because it doesn't seem like enough, and with things hanging in the balance right now, I don't want to go there.

Thankfully, Ares saves me from further indecision by redirecting the conversation. "I'm friends with Xavier Daniels. I'm aware you were married to Sawyer Hunt for a brief period."

Sydney's eyes pop wide. "Oh. I can only imagine how that conversation went."

Ares smiles. "Xavier and Sawyer only ever have good things to say about you."

Her cheeks flush. "That's kind. I'm happy it's all working out for them. They deserve it."

"Ash."

I spin around after hearing my friend's voice. I knew Harlow and the guys were coming because she had messaged me for the funeral details. I asked her to come back to the house to talk.

"Lo." I fall into my friend's hug, holding her tight. "Thanks so much for being here."

"I'm really sorry about your dad, babe." She squeezes me tight. "I know what it's like, and I'm here whenever you want to talk about it." Lo lost her dad about eighteen months ago, and she was super close to him, so it hit her hard.

"Thank you. That means a lot."

Galen, Saint, Caz, and Theo come up to me one by one, offering hugs and sympathy, and I'm appreciative they all traveled to be here. I'm super grateful for their friendship.

When I turn back around, Sydney has disappeared, and Ares is standing warily to one side. A tense silent face-off ensues between Ares and Lo's four husbands. I'm not surprised after what happened the last time they visited.

Reaching out, I grab Ares's hand and pull him toward me. "Babe. Stop with the looks. Let's go talk in private."

Chapter Forty-Seven
Ashley

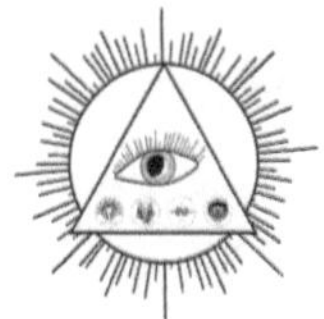

The guys are aware I am married to Chad and Jase, and I'm sure Lo told them in recent months I am with Ares too, but it's clear from the hostile looks they are throwing his way as we walk out of the room they don't trust him.

My husbands materialize in the hallway, and they make quick hellos before I lead everyone down to the game room in the basement. Chad locks the door so we have privacy, and Jase fixes drinks for everyone while we get settled on the couch and the chairs.

When everyone is ready and it's quiet, I clear my throat and begin explaining. I tell them about Lili and Ares's reason for coming to Lowell and how his investigations led him to The Bulls. I don't mention anything about Luminaries, keeping it strictly focused on Ares's missing sister and the sex trafficking Bulls connection. Then I come to the punchline.

"We are aware the man in charge of running the sex trafficking ring for The Bulls is dead, but we were wondering if you knew anything that might help."

Out of the corner of my eye, I notice Saint and Galen sharing a troubled look. Lo sits up straighter. Her sharp expression tells me she knows exactly who I'm talking about. "Why would you think I'd know anything?" she asks, being extremely guarded.

Setting my drink down, I take her hands in mine. "Let's cut the bullshit. You're my friend. I trust you with my life, and I hope you'd say the same."

"Goes without saying," Lo immediately replies.

"Then you know whatever is shared here will be kept strictly between all of us. We will never breathe a word of this to anyone else. You can trust us. I promise you."

Lo's husbands all turn as one, as if it was coordinated, and stare at Ares.

For once, Ares doesn't scowl or give them any of his usual passive-aggressive bullshit. "I understand your hesitation when it comes to me," he says. "I know I have deserved it, but everything I have done has been for my sister. It's all been about finding Lilianna."

"That's why you asked for a list of Sainthood members last time," Lo says, remembering our conversation in the study at the party.

Ares nods. "Marwan wouldn't organize a visit for me with Ruben in prison until I jumped through a bunch of fucking hoops."

"It was The Bulls who set up the ambush at the warehouse?" Saint surmises, arching a brow.

"It was their idea, but The Sainthood knew. They were lying in wait for us," Ares explains.

"That whole situation was orchestrated by higher-ups," I supply. "Both were pawns who were always going to be taken out."

Silence descends as we all contemplate the things we know

and can't say. I know Lo is mixed up in some shit, possibly with VERO, if my assumptions about her friend are correct, and I know she knows we are mixed up in something too. I wish we could trade secrets, but it's too risky. We are already risking enough even having this conversation.

Lo and Theo have some kind of silent communication before she turns her attention back to me. "What do you want to know?"

"Anything you can tell us about Luke McKenzie. We have been told you were the one who killed him, and we'd like to know why." Our guess is it's something connected to sex trafficking because Lo and the guys were pivotal in smashing a massive sex trafficking ring orchestrated by The Sainthood, and The Bulls were their rivals, so it doesn't take much to connect the dots.

"How the fuck do you know that?" Saint stands, looking agitated as he cracks his knuckles.

"My father told us," Jase confirms. "He has powerful connections, and he's helping us to trace Lili."

Lo looks seriously shell-shocked as her gaze bounces between her husbands before swinging back around to me. "No one is supposed to know about that! The evidence was buried."

I shift uncomfortably on my seat, locking eyes with Jase.

Jase clears his throat. "There is a lot we would like to say but can't. My father is part of a very powerful organization. They are all-seeing and all-knowing. I don't know how it went down with McKenzie, but you have nothing to fear. There is no interest in you. This is us purely trying to find out how involved that prick was and whether he is the one who took Ares's little sister."

"You even asking us this places Lo in danger," Galen says, standing. "We're leaving." He drills Lo with a deadly look.

Lo rolls her eyes. "Sit your ass down and stop overreacting.

Ash and the guys would not put me, or any of us, in harm's way. I don't see how answering their question makes any difference."

Lo's husbands trade worried expressions, but ultimately, they don't fight her.

It's totally clear who wears the pants in their relationship!

"This is probably not what you want to hear," Lo says, squeezing my hands. "But I didn't know Luke McKenzie."

"None of us did," Caz adds.

"We were on a job to burn a meth lab belonging to The Bulls, and he was there," Lo says. "He was taking potshots at us as we were leaving, and I ended up killing him accidentally."

"We had no dealings with the prick up to that point. We didn't even know who he was." Saint glances at Ares. "I'm sorry, man, but we have no information on what he was up to or the trafficking he was involved in."

"Well, shit." Jase scrubs a hand across his smooth jawline before taking a swig of his beer.

Ares's shoulders slump in defeat, and I get up, dropping into his lap and wrapping my arms around him. His head falls to my shoulder as he clings to me.

"I can do some digging," Theo offers, his eyes glistening with compassion.

"If we can help now, we'll do it," Galen says, staring at Ares with a strange look on his face.

My heart swells with emotion. "I appreciate that so much, but we can't involve you. It's too dangerous."

"We have contacts," Lo says.

"We know," I say, smiling softly at my friend. "But that contact will tell you not to come a million miles near this, and he'd be right. You can't get involved."

"We have the best resources at hand," Jase says before adding, "No offense, man. I know you're a dope hacker, but we don't want to put our friends in harm's way."

"We just thought you might know something," I say. "That's the only reason we brought it up."

"I'm sorry we don't," Saint says, looking and sounding sincere.

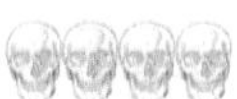

"Are you sure we can't do anything to help?" Lo asks an hour later as we say our goodbyes in the hallway. The guys are all shoving and pushing one another in good humor, riling one another up over the competitive games of pool they played after our tense conversation ended. Lo, Bree, and I caught up over a few vodka cranberries while the testosterone-fueled idiots played pool and video games.

"I'm sure, but thanks for offering."

Lo unbuckles a belt from around her waist and hands it to me. My brow puckers as I accept it. "I want you to take this." She presses in on the center of the belt, and it pops open, revealing a hidden compartment inside. I remove the sleek, slim dagger inside, admiring the glistening steel and ornate handle with an etching of an angel on it. "Galen bought me that." Lo smiles as she watches me trace my finger carefully over it.

"I can't accept it," I say, closing the belt over. "It clearly means a lot to you."

"The dagger, yes, the belt not so much. I can order another one."

Lo slides a different dagger out from the side of her boot while I watch with my mouth hanging open. My friend is a serious badass, and I need to take a page out of her book. I have never had to think about leaving the house with a weapon before, but it's shortsighted. Things are scarily dangerous right now, and I should always have weapons on me. I make a silent vow to place my handgun in my purse and to wear this belt at all times.

Lo swaps the daggers around, placing the generic one in the belt and the angel one into her boot. She sets her hands over mine. "This belt saved my life during the showdown with The Sainthood. It will pass unnoticed through metal detectors, and no one would ever suspect it conceals a deadly weapon. I want you to wear it all the time. Promise me, Ash." Her troubled eyes probe mine. "I know you're deep in shit." She holds up one palm. "I know you'd tell me if you could, and it's cool. I understand. I truly do. Just promise me you'll wear this permanently. I know you've been training, and you're proficient with guns, but that's not always enough. This will give you peace of mind. Me too."

I throw my arms around her. "I'll only take it off to fuck and shower, I swear."

When I pull back, she's grinning. "We are soul sisters, Ashley. I have never been surer of anything."

"Love you, babe." I hug her again.

"Love you too."

The guys leave, and the last of the stragglers leave too. Baz returns to Chez Stewart with his father to check on progress, promising to call later with an update. We're all on tenterhooks waiting to find out if someone has cracked the password to Jasper Baldwin's flash drive and to discover what information it contains. My sixth sense tells me it's the break we are looking for. We desperately need some good news.

Together, we clean up the place and then change into more comfortable clothes and meet back in the living room. The mood is despondent, and Ares is sinking into a dark hole. I perch my butt on his lap and offer him what comfort I can.

"I'm going to call Baz," Jase says. "See if there's any news about the flash drive."

"I can talk to my mom," Chad offers. "Ask if she remembers anything that might help."

Warmth surges through me, filling me with hope we can make it as a foursome, because my guys are sincere. They hurt for Ares and what he's going through.

"I don't know how much more of this I can take." Ares's voice is strangled, his words laced with pain. "Lili is out there somewhere, surrounded by monsters and wolves, and I can't do a damn thing about it." Moisture pools in his eyes, and I feel his pain as if it's my own. "It feels like I wasted the last two and a half years chasing false leads, and I'm no further along. It's killing me."

"We're going to get her back safely, Ares," Jase says. "I know my dad will come through for us."

A loud pounding on the front door claims our attention. Ares swipes the tablet from the coffee table and checks the cameras. "It's Baz."

Bree jumps up and rushes out into the hallway.

I share a hopeful look with Jase, silently praying Baz has some good news because we sorely need it. Ares is close to his breaking point, and we need to give him something. If Baz has come back here, rather than calling, it must be urgent.

"Sup, fuckers?" Baz saunters into the room like he doesn't have a care in the world.

"Please say you have news for us," Chad says.

"Well, if you consider Manford and Salinger being found hung in their cells an hour ago good news, then yep." He waggles his brows before his expression changes. "Apologies, Ash. James was your uncle. I'm sorry for being flippant."

"I don't really have feelings about it either way. We weren't close." My mom will flip. "How did this happen? Your dad had guys on the doors." We know who is responsible. Just not how. Carter wasn't at the funeral. He knew better than to show his face. But most everyone else was, meaning it was the perfect time to make a move when everyone was preoccupied and unlikely to interfere.

"They have all conveniently disappeared." Baz's eyes darken.

"Carter is onto us," Ares says, verbalizing what we're all thinking.

"Unfortunately, yes." Baz props his butt on the edge of the coffee table. "If he bought into Dad's act before, he knows now it was all for show."

"He can't surely expect Luminary society to believe both men committed suicide while in custody?" Bree says.

"One he might be able to pass off as legit, but two is not in any way believable," I say.

"I honestly think the prick doesn't care anymore," Jase says. "He's getting ready to make his power move."

"Fuck." Ares dumps me on the couch and stands, pacing the floor and tugging on his hair. "We need to find my sister now."

"I have more good news," Baz flashes him a grin. "We cracked the password on the flash drive." His eyes bounce over to Chad. "Your dad amassed a considerable amount of intel. It's no wonder he was taken out. They were never going to let him go to trial with the knowledge he had unveiled."

"Does the drive exonerate him?" Chad rises to his feet.

"It's too early to tell, but I'm hopeful." Baz walks over to Ares, clamping a hand down on his shoulder. "We know where she is, man. We have her location, and we're going to get her."

Chapter Forty-Eight

Ashley

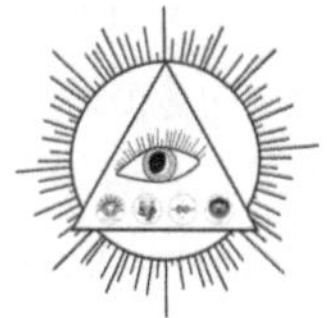

"You couldn't have led with that, asshole?" Jase grumbles, shooting daggers at his brother.

"You mean it?" Ares's choked tone brings tears to my eyes. "You really know where Lili is?"

Baz nods and lowers his arms to his sides. "I came straight here the second we found the intel."

"Where is she?"

"Colombia. Bogota."

"Does that mean?" Bree asks letting her sentence trail off on purpose.

Baz bobs his head. "Carter's hands are all over sex trafficking rings in South America. You stumbled upon him in the act, PC1."

"Fuck." I crawl over to Bree on the couch and hug her. "You were in so much danger. He could have killed you."

"Except he already had plans for you," Jase grits out, standing and stretching his arms over his head.

"We need to go." Ares snaps out of the shocked daze he's been in, striding toward the doorway. "I need to get Lili."

"Woah." Baz grabs a fistful of his shirt and hauls him back. "Hold your horses. We have a plan."

"We better be part of it," Ares growls, ready to throw down with his new friend.

"Of course, you are." Baz looks around at all of us. "We head out first thing in the morning."

"No." Ares shoves Baz. "We go now!"

"Ares." Jase steps up to him, standing alongside his brother. "These things take time to organize, and we can't go in fully blind. We are of no use to Lili if we all wind up dead."

I sidle up to Ares and take his hand. "I know how badly you want to go to her, but we have to be smart." His eyes are darting wildly around the place, and there are so many emotions flickering across his face. I squeeze his hand as I look at Baz. "What is the plan and how can we help?"

"Dad is mobilizing his contacts and troops on the ground. We know Carter has turned some of them, but the core is still loyal to Lust & Envy. He's getting eyes on the compound where Lili is right now. He has called in every available man he can spare here to come with us, and he's lining up a plane and gathering supplies."

Jase crosses over to my other side, taking my free hand in his as he eyeballs Ares. "This is what my father is good at. Remember I told you we've been taking down trafficking operations all over the world for years. We can mobilize fast. I know you're worried, but if anyone can get your sister out safely, it's my family."

"Jase is correct," Baz concurs. "You need to let our father do what he does best. I know it's hard not to participate in the planning, but us showing up will just distract them. It's a well-oiled machine, and they can ramp up fast. I suggest you all try to get some sleep. It's a seven-hour flight, and then it's going to be a shitshow. Wear full combat gear, and bring your Kevlar vests."

After Baz leaves, we talk for a bit and then head to bed. There is no point staying up all night worrying about things outside of our control, and Baz is right. We need sleep. We can't go into battle with the enemy if we are all exhausted and not on our A-game.

I offer to sleep in Ares's room with him, but he declines. I try not to take it to heart. He is not used to leaning on anyone. He is used to handling things himself. I still wish he would lean on me, but I know it's not personal, and it's going to take time to change the habits of a lifetime.

Jase and Chad are fast asleep behind me, the latter snoring intermittingly, when the door to my bedroom creaks open. A thin slice of light creeps in from the hallway as Ares slips into the room, wearing only boxers. Quietly, he closes the door and tiptoes across the room.

I peel back the covers and pat the empty space this side of me. I had gone to sleep in between Jase and Chad, but Chad must have gotten up to take a piss and climbed back in the wrong side of the bed.

Without uttering a word, Ares slides under the sheets and turns on his side. His intense brownish-green eyes drill into me as I turn on my side and move in closer. I'm wearing silk shorts and a camisole, but his body heat sears me through my light sleep clothes. Leaning down, I press a soft kiss just above the branding on his chest. Ares buries his head in my shoulder, nuzzling my neck as he pulls me in flush with his body. I wrap my arms around him and hold him close, and that is how we fall asleep.

"Get up!" Bree shrieks sometime later. "Oh my God! You need to get up." Ares wakes the same time I do, holding me against his chest as he sits upright in the bed. Beside us, Jase and Chad are rousing, the latter staring with wide eyes at Ares.

Bree yanks the covers off the bed, and all three of my guys instantly cover their morning wood with their hands. Thank fuck, they are all wearing boxers. I'd be having strong words with my bestie if they were naked.

Something she had no way of knowing when she pulled the covers off us without warning.

"What the hell, babe?" I stare at her through blurry eyes. "Can you give us some privacy, and what's with the early wake-up call? Did we oversleep or something?" We had all set alarms on our phones, so I don't see how that's possible.

"Shit." My words propel Ares into motion, and he scrambles out of the bed with his giant erection trying to poke a hole through his boxers.

"Ho. Lee. Mother of all—"

"Bree!" I snap my fingers in her face. "Focus and quit ogling my man."

"Sorry, sorry." She lifts her eyes to mine, fanning her face. "I didn't mean to. It was just *right there*." Her eyes lower to his crotch again.

"Bree." Ares growls, squinting at the time on my cell.

She jerks her head up, her lips twitching.

Cheeky little wench!

"What's going on? We don't have to leave for two hours," Ares says.

Which means it's sometime around five a.m.

"I have the best news ever." She gets up on the bed and starts bouncing around like a lunatic with the widest grin on her face.

"PC1. Stop." Jase lifts his sister off the bed. "Tell us."

"Baz just called me. He tried your cell, but you didn't pick up," she says, looking at Ares. "We have Lili!" Bree is fit to burst as she smiles at Ares. "Dad's team got her out, and she's on a plane on her way here. They are due to land at nine."

Did they lie to us last night? Had this been the plan all along? I don't like thinking we were deliberately kept out of the rescue operation. It's not exactly fair when Ares has given up his life these past couple of years to search for his little sister. He deserved to have been there. And I don't like being lied to. We're supposed to be working together, and it makes me uneasy.

But there's no point arguing the point. All that matters is Lili has been freed and she's on her way back to her brother.

Ares grips my cell tight in his hands, staring at Bree as if in a daze. "How?" he chokes out. "I thought there were plans and—"

Bree cuts him short. "There were, but somehow Carter got wind we were onto him, and we had to act fast or risk losing her."

Relief shuttles through me. This explains it, easing the anxiety I was feeling at the thought we'd been purposely misled.

"They tried to move Lili from the compound," Bree continues. "Dad's guys on the ground were keeping tabs on her, and the guy in charge made the decision to move in. And then there was a massive shootout—"

A strangled sound erupts from Ares's mouth.

"She's fine! Lili is safe, and she wasn't hurt during the rescue." Bree gently holds Ares's arm. "Sorry, I should have said that first. She's okay, Ares. She's even spoken to your mom." Bree pats his arm before removing her hand from his body. "My dad arranged it while she was on the plane, and he's arranging for Hera to come back. He's proposing to move Hera and Lili into the safe house where Carole and Tess are staying, if you agree."

Ares stares blankly into space, and I curl into him, wrapping my arms tight around his torso and squeezing him. His arms band around me, and he drops his head into my hair. His entire body is shaking, and then I hear it.

The sound of him crying.

The others quietly leave, and Ares sinks to the floor, taking me with him.

I wrap myself around him and hold him as he falls apart, clinging to me, crying and shaking, and releasing years of anguish he kept locked up inside.

"Is it really happening?" he asks when his tears have dried up. "Tell me I'm not dreaming. Lili is rescued. She's safe, and I'm going to see her soon?" He lifts his head, peering at me through bloodshot, red-rimmed eyes. His skin is blotchy, and his voice is hoarse from crying.

"Yes, babe. It's real."

"Thank fuck." He holds me tight, and then he starts to laugh. Fresh tears fill his eyes, but these are happy ones. "I'm so relieved, Ash. I'm so fucking relieved."

"I know, honey." I brush messy strands of dark hair out of his eyes. "I'm relieved too and so happy for you and Hera." I don't know how traumatized Lili will be, but I know her presence will be a huge comfort to Ares and his mom, and this will help Hera to overcome her grief over my father's loss. She will have a daughter to support and focus on.

Ares pulls my face to his and kisses me. It's intense and emotional, and I feel his powerful need for me in every stroke of his tongue and every sweep of his lips. I mount no protest when he removes my pajamas and his boxers, sets me down flat on the carpet, and drives inside me in one fluid move.

We don't speak, letting our bodies do all the talking.

We kiss and caress as Ares makes love to me in a way he never has before. His touch is still possessive and demanding but lacking his trademark roughness. He is worshiping me with his hands, his lips, and his cock, and I am awash in bliss, reveling in the riot of sensations he's coaxing from my pliable body.

Someone walks in, sees us moving against one another on the floor and walks back out. I am guessing it was Chad or Jase because there's no way Bree would have been able to walk off without watching for a bit or making some sound or comment.

After we take a quick shower, we get dressed and head downstairs to hear the latest from the others.

Chad pulls me into a hug and pecks my lips when I enter the kitchen with Ares at my side. "Bree made pancakes if you're hungry."

"I'm ravenous," I say, pecking his lips again before I move toward the coffee pot.

"I'll bet." Jase grins, his gaze bouncing between me and Ares as he hands me a mug of coffee, just how I like it. At least I know who walked in on us now.

"Is there any update?" Ares asks as Jase fixes him a coffee.

"They are still in the air, and all is good."

"Carter is AWOL," Baz says, striding into the kitchen dressed all in black. We gave him a key last night, and I see he's already putting it to good use. "We all need to be on high alert. He's making his move, and we need to be ready to act at a second's notice."

"I want to go to the airport," Ares says, nodding thanks at Jase when he hands him a coffee.

"Out of the question." Baz snatches a pancake from the plate and stuffs it in his mouth.

"Lili is my sister, and I should be there to greet her. She is probably terrified."

"We need to keep a low profile until someone gets eyes on Carter," Jase says, handing his brother a coffee. "We don't know what Carter has planned, only that it involves us. We can't give him an opening to get to us, so we need to stay out of public places. He must know we have Lili, and he'd be expecting us to show at the airport. We can't make it easy for him."

"What if he tries to retake Lili when she lands?" I ask, articulating what I'm sure Ares is thinking.

"He won't get to Lili. Dad has a cavalcade of armored vehicles and highly trained men escorting her to our house," Baz explains.

"It was never about Lili anyway," Chad says, leaning back against the counter and sipping from his mug. "She was bait to hold over Ares. Now that game is up, he's moved on to the next level. Lili isn't the one at risk now. We are."

His words hang heavy in the air.

"Get ready to ship out," Baz says. "I brought a crew to take you all to our place. Dad has the best of security, and it's safer for all of us if we hole up there. I suggest you pack a bag for a few days."

Chapter Forty-Nine

Ares

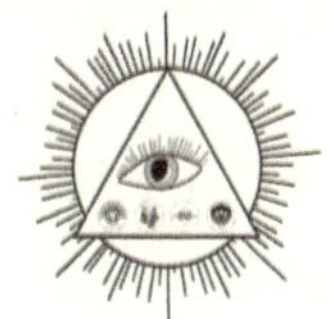

Ash has a firm hold of my hand as we stand outside the Stewart castle watching the cavalcade of blacked-out SUVs advance up the sweeping driveway toward us. Jase, Chad, Bree, and Baz are here too along with Jase's mom, Anna-Lynn, and their sixteen-year-old sister, Jocelyn. Eric Stewart hasn't emerged from his office during the time we've been here. His team is searching Lowell and farther afield, looking for any sign of Rhett Carter.

The past few hours have been agonizing. I have worn a path in the Stewarts' living room and bitten my nails to the quick, waiting for news of my sister. I breathed a sigh of relief when Baz confirmed the plane had landed safely, but I can't relax, won't relax, until I see my sister in the flesh.

The first SUV comes to a standstill in front of us, and I hold my breath as the back door opens. I'm conscious of Ash's eyes on the side of my face as she squeezes my hand in a silent show of support. I can scarcely breathe over the massive lump in my throat. My heart is jackhammering in my chest, and my legs feel wobbly.

"Ares!" Lili's tear-filled eyes lock on mine as my little sister hops down out of the SUV and runs toward me.

My legs give out, and I fall to my knees, not even feeling the gravel digging into my jeans. All I register is my sister is here. Safe and looking well and so grown-up compared to the last time I saw her. Tears stream down my face as I open my arms, and Lili hurls herself against me. She slides into my lap, circles her arms around my neck, and sobs as she clings to me.

My arms band around her back, and I hold her tight, openly crying as I drink her all in. My hand glides down her long blonde hair before I clasp the back of her head and pull her brow flush against mine. "Lili," I croak as tears continue spilling down my cheeks. "I love you so much. I've missed you so much."

"I never thought I'd see you or Mum again. I was so scared." She sobs, burying her face in my neck, and I run my hand up and down her back in what I hope is a soothing gesture.

"It's okay. You're safe now, and Mum is on her way to see you."

"We should move this inside," Vincent Fox says, his face showcasing alarm as he scans the grounds.

I lock eyes with him and nod. Although the Fox family is aligned to the Salinger Luminary family, Vincent and his older brother are close with Eric Stewart. No doubt Walter Salinger's betrayal helped to sway their loyalties in a different direction. Eric trusts and respects them as friends and work colleagues, and they have come through for us a lot recently.

"Thank you," I say, repositioning myself so I can stand. "Thank you for bringing my sister to me." I know he couldn't have been a part of the group on the ground in Colombia, but he was at the airport to greet their plane and ensure they got here safely. Carter is lurking somewhere, and he was always a concern, so I'm grateful Vincent got Lili home without issue.

Vincent smiles. "That is not necessary. I am glad I could play a part. Seeing you with your sister is all the repayment I need."

Jase helps me to stand as I carry my sister in my arms, neither of us able to let go. The difference in my Lili is noticeable. Her long gangly arms are almost choking my neck, and her elongated legs wrap awkwardly around my waist. She is heavier than I remember, not that I'm complaining. I worried about the state she'd be returned to us in, but she appears healthy and cared for. Appearances could be deceiving, but it seems like she was looked after, and I'm hopeful it means she was kept as a pawn and not as a sex slave.

The thought lands sourly in my mind, and I push it away to discuss later. Now isn't the time.

Lili stops crying when we enter the house, lifting her head and staring curiously all around her. "Where are we?" she asks.

"This is a friend's house," I explain as we walk down the long hallway toward the living room. Everyone has gone ahead except for Ash. She walks silently by my side.

"Who are you?" Lili asks, glancing at Ash while wriggling in my arms. "You can put me down. I'll walk," Lili says, looking up at me briefly before turning her attention to Ashley. I set Lili's feet on the ground, grasping her hand in mine and keeping her close.

"I'm Ashley. I'm a...friend of your brother's."

I scowl at her, not liking that one little bit. "She's my girlfriend," I say in a clipped tone, leveling Ash with a dark look. It doesn't feel like enough, but only lovesick fools verbalize words like life partner or love of my life.

"I wasn't sure what you wanted to say," Ash quietly replies, looking up at me.

"We both know you're way more than that, but this explanation will do for now."

Lili looks confused as her gaze bounces between us. Then her brow smooths out, and she smiles. It does something funny to my insides and I have to fight a fresh bout of tears.

"I have a lot to catch up on," Lili says.

Ash has tears in her eyes as she stares at me, and I understand the sentiment. This is more than I could have hoped for.

"We do, little sis." I press a kiss to the top of her head, amazed she is almost up to my shoulder now. "You have grown so tall and so beautiful." She's stunning with her long natural golden-blonde hair, big blue eyes, and porcelain skin. Her body has altered too with soft curves that hint at the woman she's becoming. She is only thirteen, but she looks so much older. I hate I missed the transition from little girl, and I intend to make Carter pay. That sick prick claimed he had discovered Lili's location and he was watching over her to ensure she was safe when he was the one behind her kidnapping all along.

Baz has been updating us regularly as Eric's team makes their way through the considerable number of files on the flash drive, discovering lots of intel. Carter was in cahoots with Luke McKenzie to funnel additional kids to sex trafficking rings he was running in South America. It was Luke who took Lili and got her out of the US—acting on Carter's instructions. Eric Stewart believes the Greed & Gluttony Luminary was probably operating rings in other locations too.

Rhett Carter sure lived up to his responsibility. He is greed personified.

Carter had no right to involve himself in sex trafficking, which is a Lust & Envy responsibility, and it's against the rules to sell children. It seems Carter had moles in Eric's operation, and instead of rescuing children and setting them free, these moles were hijacking the operation and funneling the kids back into the system.

The woman in charge of rehabilitating victims within Lust & Envy was bought by Carter to hide his despicable behavior. She has already been taken care of. Skilled experts and grunts have been assigned to a special task force to uncover other illegal sex trafficking rings being run by Carter and a second team created to identify other corrupt elements within our society. It's work that will need to continue for years to weed out all of Carter's supporters, but at least we are on top of it now.

We don't know if Carter was just greedy for more cash, did it to thwart the Lust & Envy Luminary, or if he was offering these kids as sex slaves to high-profile individuals in return for their support. It's possible he was planning to blackmail Eric Stewart if he needed a Plan B to force him to play ball. It wouldn't have taken much to convince others it was Stewart who was scamming the system for personal gain.

We have a solid case now with irrefutable evidence, and it's enough to justify killing the bastard. As soon as Carter is found, we're moving on him.

I am keen to end this. To get justice for my little sister, for Doug, for Chad's dad, and all the innocents who have been abused or killed at Carter's hands.

"Ares?"

Lili's soft tone drags me out of my head. "Yes, munchkin."

She smiles at my familiar nickname for her. "You zoned out."

"Sorry. I've had a lot on my mind." I didn't even realize we had stopped walking.

"Lili was commenting on how different you look too. She loves your ink." Ash waggles her brows.

"I love Ash's hair too," Lili adds, smiling at my woman.

"And I can't wait to meet Bree and see her blue hair. Do you think Mum would let me dye my hair pink or maybe purple?"

"I don't see why not." Mom is pretty free-spirited, and I think Lili will have both of us wrapped around her little finger now. I can't see myself denying my little sister anything after her ordeal.

"I can take you to the salon if Hera okays it," Ashley says. "We can make a day of it and get manis and pedis too."

Lili shrieks, the sound penetrating my eardrums. "That would be so awesome." Emotion swells my chest as my sister hugs my girl.

"Thank you," I mouth over Lili's head as Ash hugs her.

"Are we all going to live here now?" Lili asks, shucking out of Ash's embrace.

I shake my head. "Things are a bit up in the air. We need to keep you and Mum protected, so you'll be going to live in a secure location until it's safe for us all to be together."

The smile drops off her face. "I don't want to be separated from you." She snuggles into my side as tears pool in her eyes. "I missed you so much, and I always feel safe when I'm with you."

Taking her hands in mine, I hunch over so we're face-to-face. "I promise we'll all be together soon. This is only temporary."

"You'll be living with friends of ours," Ash says. "Tessa is fourteen, and I think you'll both get along great."

"I don't want to ever go back there, Ares." A visible shudder sweeps over her body. "It was horrible."

Acid churns in my gut, and I work hard not to show too much emotion. "Did they?." I stop, fighting the bile climbing up my throat. Ash moves to my side, offering silent comfort. "Did they hurt you?" I rasp.

Chapter Fifty

Ares

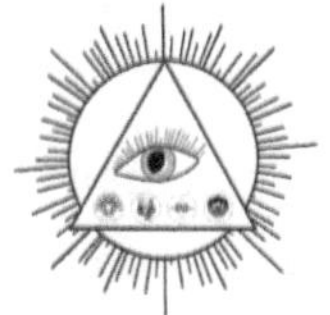

Slowly, Lili shakes her head. "No. Not like that," she whispers. "They didn't touch me, and I had my own room, and they fed me and gave me clothes. I wasn't allowed the internet or a phone, but they gave me books and art supplies and games. They let me swim every day, and if I was sick, they gave me medicine. Not like the other girls and boys." Her voice wobbles, and she looks down at her feet.

Relief comingles with horror at her words. Ash squeezes my arm in support. I bundle my sister into my arms, holding her against my chest. "I'm sorry for whatever you had to go through, Lili, and I promise, I swear to you on my life, that nothing like that will ever happen to you again. I would die before I let anyone take you away."

"They were so mean to the other kids," she says, her words muffled slightly against my chest. "They made me watch sometimes. If I was ever bratty or at times when I cried for you and Mum, they would force me to watch men doing...horrible things to them." A strangled sound rips from her throat, and I hold her closer, squeezing my eyes shut, hating my sister had to see anything like that. Hating how her innocence is now gone and fearing what all of this might do to her attitude and response to sex.

I'm grateful it wasn't her. Which sounds awful, because those other poor kids endured hell, but I'm so glad she wasn't subjected to that. It's more than I dared to hope.

"It was sick," she whispers, clinging more tightly to me. "And they beat them and starved them and...and killed them sometimes."

Ash wraps her arm around me from behind, and I lean into her as I hold my sister. Ash sniffles, and I press a kiss to her head.

"You should never have had to see anything like that, Lili. I'm sorry."

"It's not your fault." Lili sniffles, wiping her nose along the back of her sleeve as she eases out of my arms. "And I don't want to talk about it." She looks up at me with red-rimmed eyes and a weary expression way beyond her years.

It hurts me for her, but it could have been a lot worse.

"Could I have a shower and get into different clothes? I want to scrub that place from my skin."

"Of course. I'll organize that for you," Ash says as footsteps approach.

"I didn't mean to eavesdrop," Jase's mom says, materializing at our side. "But I couldn't help overhearing. My daughter Jocelyn has some clothes that should fit you, and she can show you one of the guest bedrooms upstairs if you want to get cleaned up."

Jocelyn appears behind her mom, smiling and waving shyly at Lili. "Hi, I'm Jocelyn. You can pick what you want from my closet."

"Can you come too?" Lili links her fingers in mine and looks up at me.

"Sure thing."

"I'll fix us some lunch," Anna-Lynn says. "Is there anything in particular you would like to eat, Lilianna?"

"You can call me Lili, and I would die for some pizza. I haven't had it in years."

"Pizza it is." Anna-Lynn smiles warmly at us as I steer Lili toward Jocelyn and let her lead the way.

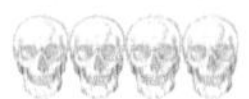

Ashley

"Is she okay?" I ask Ares when he reappears forty minutes later with his sister in tow. Lili is wearing skinny jeans, a Taylor Swift T-shirt, a hoodie, and sneakers, looking like a normal teenager.

Ares rests his butt on the corner of the couch as Jocelyn and Lili sit cross-legged on the floor, huddled together, deep in conversation. "I think so." He scrubs his hands down his face.

"She is so resilient and strong. I'm in awe of her."

"Me too." Ares's smile is proud. Watching them together has only made me love him even more. "I'm so relieved she wasn't abused and she seems okay," he says.

"Me too, but I hate she had to see others abused. That will still be traumatic for her. When we get through everything, we'll need to organize some therapy for her."

I'll be signing myself up too. I've been pushing stuff aside to deal with later, and I know I'll fall apart unless I allow myself the time to process everything that has happened to me in these past few months.

"For sure."

"They seem to be getting on well," Jase says, looming over us and nodding toward the girls.

Ares bobs his head. "They are like lifelong friends already," he admits as Anna-Lynn pops her head in the room and calls everyone to lunch. Ares slides his arm around my shoulders and draws me in close as Lili looks over at him. "Lili was so excited when she saw her closet. When things have died down, maybe you can take her shopping, get her whatever she needs?"

"I would love that."

Chad appears in the doorway, slipping his cell back in his pocket. He was talking to his mom and Tess on a secure line Baz organized for him.

Ares pulls me to my feet, threading his fingers through mine as we walk to where Lili is waiting with Jocelyn. She seems unwilling to let her brother out of her sight, and I don't blame her. After her ordeal, I think she'll be clinging to his side any chance she gets. I'm not looking forward to her leaving for the safe house. It won't be pleasant watching them be separated again.

Lunch is a lively affair, and it's remarkable we can all feel such normalcy with the threat hovering over our heads. Lili fits right in, and I don't see any of the shy girl Ares alluded to previously in the girl chatting with everyone around the table.

Eric returns wearing a somber expression, and the good mood dissipates. He pulls his wife into his arms. "Love, I think it's best you and Jocelyn move to the safe house for now. Just until we track Carter down and deal with him."

Anna-Lynn looks up at her husband with nothing but trust in her eyes. "We'll pack our bags."

A half hour later, Vincent shows up, with a bunch of armed guards, to collect Lili, Anna-Lynn, and Jocelyn.

"Is there any update on Hera?" Eric asks, and Ares's spine stiffens.

"She should be at the safe house by the morning," Vincent replies, looking over Eric's head. "We need to head out now before it's dark."

"I don't want to go." Lili suctions herself to Ares's side with tears clinging to her lashes.

"I know, munchkin." Ares hugs her tight, and my ovaries swoon. Ares loves his little sister so much. I was never in any doubt, but seeing them together makes it more real. I love the way he loves her. It's a thing of beauty. "But it's only for a little while, and you'll get to see Mom tomorrow."

Her lips kick up at the corner. "*Mom*," she teases. "Look at you, all Americanized."

Lili grew up in Europe, and I have noticed she sounds and speaks very much like a European, which is a little odd because Ares and Hera have a lot of US mannerisms and speech patterns, which I thought would have rubbed off on her. Plus, she lived here for a couple years before she was kidnapped.

"You will be too." Ares tweaks her nose. "Just wait and see." He lifts her up and her legs go around his waist. He holds her close. "I love you, Lili."

"Love you too, big brother." She sobs into his neck, before lifting her chin. "Promise I'll see you soon?"

"I promise." Ares sets her feet down on the ground and hands her the phone Bree set up for her. It's the same as the new ones she gave us with all the newfangled high-tech Stewart tools. "Use this to keep in touch. Text me or call me anytime. It doesn't matter how late or early it is. If you need anything, you call me."

"I added all our digits," Bree says, smiling at Lili. "If you can't reach Ares or you have any girly stuff you want to ask, call me or Ash."

Jocelyn links her arm in Lili's and rolls her eyes at her big sister. "If Lili wants to talk girly stuff, she has me and Tess. We'll look after her."

Ares smiles warmly at Jocelyn. "Thanks for taking care of my sister, Jocelyn. I owe you one."

Jocelyn pins him with a dreamy smile and googly eyes, and her cheeks stain red. I noticed her casting sly looks at him during Christmas dinner, and I think someone has a little crush. It's cute, but I doubt her brothers would agree.

Oh, boy. I hope Jase doesn't notice how she's currently looking at Ares.

"Get in the car, Lyn," Baz snaps, lacking his usual affable manner and flirty persona. "And quit that shit." He points between her and Ares.

"Baz." Bree thumps him in the arm. "Quit embarrassing her."

Ares chuckles, and poor Jocelyn's face turns an even darker shade of red.

"Be safe." Ares hugs Lili one last time before pressing his lips to her brow. "And call me when you get there."

"I will. I promise." She flings her arms around his neck before reluctantly letting him go.

I hold on to Ares as we watch them leave until they're merely a speck in the distance. Eric leaves with a few bodyguards to meet a contact who says he has a lead on Carter's whereabouts and we all head back inside.

We make coffee and shoot the shit as we wait for news. It's agony hanging around waiting, and we're all going stir crazy doing nothing. I'm casually making out with Chad on the couch when the squealing of tires outside claims all our attention. We watch through the living room window as Victor Fox jumps out of his SUV, leaves the car door open, and races toward the Stewarts' front door.

We are up on our feet in an instant, all rushing out to meet him.

Baz gets there first, yanking the door open as Victor pounds on it.

Butterflies go crazy in my chest, and blood thrums painfully in my ears at the look of sheer panic on Victor Fox's face.

"What's wrong?" Jase asks.

"I need to speak to your father. Now!" Victor charges past us into the hallway.

"He's not here!" Baz calls out. "He left to meet with Saunders."

"Fuck, fuck, fuck!" Victor grabs handfuls of his hair and paces the hallway.

"What the hell is going on?" Ares grabs him by the shoulders. "Is my mother safe?" he asks, assuming this must be something to do with her because Victor flew overseas to personally escort Hera to the safe house.

Air huffs out of Victor's mouth. "Hera is safe, but only Carole and Tessa were at the safe house when I arrived. Lili, Anna-Lynn, and Jocelyn weren't there."

Oh no. No, no, no!

"What do you mean?" All the blood drains from Ares's face. "Lili messaged me thirty minutes ago to say she was there and she was safe."

"Our mother and sister were with Lili, and we've had similar messages." Jase grabs Victor away from Ares and shoves him into the wall.

"I am guessing they were forced to send those," Victor replies. "Or someone took their phones and sent the messages. While I don't have proof, my gut says Carter has them."

Terror engulfs me. How is this happening? We thought we were being careful, but we've been stupid. We should not have let them leave without one of us. Hiding out here was the wrong decision. All it has done is place our loved ones in harm's way. If he can't get to us, Carter will use them to draw us out.

We all thought they were safe to go with men Eric trusted, but maybe the moles in his empire aren't just on the South American side. It's possible Carter has spies working for him within the US operation too. Or else the car was ambushed on the way to the safe house.

Not that it matters any longer. If Carter has them, we need to bring the fight to him.

Jase presses a gun to Victor's temple, and tension bleeds into the air. "What the fuck is going on?"

"I'm not your enemy, Jason." Victor visibly composes himself. His gaze swings around all of us. "I'm on your side. I swear, but we have been compromised."

"Dad isn't picking up," Baz says with his ear pressed to his cell.

"He won't. If he went to meet with Saunders, Carter has him."

"Saunders works for Carter?" Baz asks, incredulity oozing from his tone and his expression.

I have no clue who this Saunders person is, but obviously Eric Stewart considered him an ally, and he walked straight into a trap.

Ares is pacing the floor, repeatedly calling his sister, and growing increasingly agitated. Bree is also on the phone, attempting to reach her mother and sister.

"It would seem so."

Jase presses the muzzle into Victor's temple. "How would you know that?"

Victor squeezes his eyes closed for a second before opening them. Pain floods his face. "I had my suspicions, but I couldn't be sure until I had more proof. It's Vincent." His voice cracks.

"What is Vincent?" Baz takes out his gun and presses the muzzle into Victor's other temple. "I swear to God, Victor, if you don't spit it out, I'm going to riddle you full of bullets."

"Vincent has betrayed us. He's working with Carter, and I think he's taken your families directly to him to use as bait."

Chapter Fifty-One

Ashley

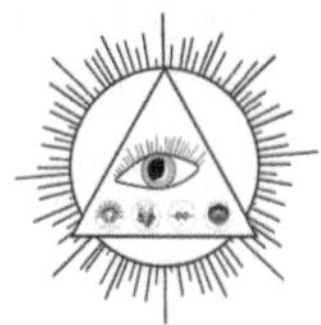

"You should have come to us when you first had suspicions." Baz is berating Victor as we head out in an armored van toward the crypt. We have four trusted Stewart guards with us, but we couldn't risk calling in anyone else because Baz is nervous about trusting anyone now. He had explained Saunders was a long-term contact of his father's and an old college buddy. If he could turn on him, anyone could.

It's a shit show.

But at least we know where they are, thanks to Victor. He suspected his brother was working for the other side in recent months, so he put a tracker in all of his boots while he investigated to see if his hunch was correct.

"I didn't want to raise the alarm unless I was sure," Victor explains. He rubs a hand along the back of his neck. "He's my brother, Baz. What if you suspected Jase of treachery? Would you be so quick to turn him over without proof?"

Strained silence filters into the air.

"Are you sure my mother is safe?" Ares asks.

His knee is bouncing up and down, and he's close to full-blown nuclear detonation. He only just got Lili back. If anything happens to her, he will never get over it. I try to take his hand, to comfort him, but he shoves me away.

It's typical Ares behavior in a crisis. I'm trying not to take it personally, but it's hard.

"I kept her whereabouts hidden from Vincent because of my suspicion. I wanted to keep Hera safe. Ultimately, I think that's what tipped him off."

"You should have fucking told us," Jase snaps. "We let him escort Mom, Lili, and Jocelyn thinking he was trustworthy."

"I didn't know that had happened. I was on my way back, and I've been trying to reach your father for hours."

"He's been in and out of meetings and fielding phone calls all day," Baz says. "I'm sure he meant to return your calls when he found the time."

"I'm sorry." Victor buries his head in his hands. "I'm so sorry." He lifts his head, piercing us with tortured eyes. "If anything happens to them, I will never forgive myself."

"Can we not point the finger of blame?" I ask. "I know we're all worried, but we need to keep our wits about us. If we don't, we are no good to anyone. We are their only hope now, and we need to maintain cool heads."

"Ash is right. We need to work out a plan." Jase sits on my other side, and he's equally worried. Baz and Bree too. Their parents and Jocelyn are unaccounted for, most likely in the crypt in Carter's clutches. Who knows what the fuck he has done or what he has planned? Unlike Ares, Jase's hand is firmly laced in mine as he leans on me for support.

"Does Carter know about the secret tunnels into the crypt?" I ask, my gaze dancing between Bree and Jase.

"What secret tunnels?" Victor and Baz ask at the same time.

"There are hidden tunnels accessible through a secret entrance in the woods at the eastern side of HQ," Bree says. "Jase and I discovered them by accident one time."

"We have a way onto the property that avoids the cameras at the gates and it's our best hope for getting into the crypt undetected," Jase says.

"He'll be well protected," Baz says, crossing his feet at the ankles. "We will most likely be outnumbered."

"At least we have the element of surprise," Bree says.

"Hopefully," Ares adds.

"So, what's the plan when we get inside?" I inquire.

"We need to take out the guards in the hallways as quietly and efficiently as possible and find out where Carter is holed up," Victor says.

"He'll be in the main room," Jase says. "There's no question about it."

"I agree," Baz says.

"Well, that's a problem," I say remembering the big wide space. "How can we creep up on him in there?"

"We can't." Victor balls his hands into fists. "All we can do is take out as much of his protective detail as possible and hope we can overpower the rest in the main room."

"That's a shit plan," Ares growls. "He has innocent children in there. They could get hit in the crossfire."

"If you come up with a better plan, I'm all ears," Victor replies.

"We need backup," I say, pulling out my cell.

"Knight?" Bree inquires, and I nod.

"Is that smart?" Victor replies.

"He's my brother, and I trust him."

Ares grabs my cell, ending the call. "He didn't call to warn us. He hasn't given us any leads, and he helped us to rescue Chad, which we now know was orchestrated."

"I trust him, but I think Rhett is on to him too, "I say." He let him help us to rescue Chad, and he has ensured nothing was leaked in Knight's presence because he didn't trust him not to tell us."

"I agree with Ash," Bree says. "Knight is trustworthy."

"Of course, you'd say that after a night spent bouncing on his dick," Baz unhelpfully supplies.

"That's got nothing to do with it, asshole." Bree flips him the bird. "Knight is a decent guy."

"I don't think we can make assumptions," Chad says. "Unless we know for sure he is definitely on our side, we can't involve him."

"I think Knight is legit," Jase says. "But Chad is right. It's too risky."

"So, we're going in there alone? With no backup and no one who will know if we all get slaughtered today?"

"The only one getting slaughtered is Rhett fucking Carter," Ares snarls, gripping the rifle slung over one shoulder. "And that's a fucking promise."

"Theo has eyes on us," Bree whispers an hour later as we are entering the tunnel from the woods. The only plan we could come up with was for Theo Westbrook to tap into our cells so he can listen and watch what is going down. "He's recording from now," she adds. Theo is back in Rhode Island with Lo and the other guys, so he's not close enough to help in person. I hated involving him, but we need someone to know where we are and what's going down in case we don't make it out of here alive.

Rhett Carter must be stopped.

The fate of the entire world depends on it.

I spoke briefly to Lo and the guys, filling them in as much as I could with the short amount of time we had, and Theo readily agreed to help.

We don't speak as we enter the tunnel, closing the door behind us. Frigid air wraps around us as we run, and I'm glad I wore pants and a long-sleeved top underneath the Kevlar vest my three guys insisted I wear. My pants are held up by Lo's belt with the dagger, and I have a knife strapped to one thigh, a gun in my hand, and a backup tucked into the waistband of my pants. The others are similarly attired, and Victor has a few smoke grenades.

Jase slows down when we reach the door that is the entry point to the crypt. My heart is pounding in my chest as he opens it gradually, peeking out for evidence of any welcoming party. He gives us a thumbs-up, and we emerge into the empty hallway. Adrenaline courses through my veins as I run alongside Chad. Jase is up front with Baz and Victor, just behind the four Stewart guards, Bree is directly in front of me, and Ares takes up the rear.

We slow down at every corner, so the others can check the way ahead is clear, before picking up our pace and moving forward. We are on high alert, carefully scanning our surroundings as we run. We make it to the stairs with no issue. The tricky part is directly ahead.

In order to get to the main ceremonial room, we have to go up these stairs, then cross the upper-level space to reach the other set of stairs that lead to that side of the basement area of the crypt. We expect to encounter opposition in the main room and possibly along the second stairs.

Dealing with them without making noise and alerting Carter to our presence will be challenging.

Victor goes up the stairs first, followed by the guards, and we trail them in single file because the steps are steep and narrow and not easy to navigate. This building has been around for centuries, and though it has been well maintained by The Luminaries, it shows.

Ares's breathing is heavy at my back as we ascend the stairs. My heart is in my throat the closer we get to the top. Victor stops around the last bend, lifting a finger to his lips to urge us to be extra quiet. He listens for a few minutes before gesturing for us to put our gas masks on. Everyone obliges, and I wipe my sweaty palms down the front of my pants while I try to calm my racing heart.

Behind me, Ares squeezes my waist, and Chad reaches back to briefly hook his pinkie in mine.

It's now or never.

What we do from this point on will determine our fates and those of the world.

I silently offer up a prayer to my dad, asking him to look over us if he's there and watching.

The quiet hum of conversation tickles my eardrums as Victor unpins a smoke grenade and throws it around the bend. Startled shouts ring out as we charge up the stairs, heading straight into the smoke. It's hard to see how many guards are here, but we split up and move into action. Victor instructed us only to use our hand weapons with the silencers so we don't alert the others of our arrival.

I swing my leg around, sideswiping the guy who appears in front of me. He goes down hard, his gun dropping from his hand. I kick it aside and lean over him, pressing my gun to his head and pulling the trigger. We discussed this on the way here too. Baz and Jase argued for direct kills instead of using tranquilizer darts to put these guys to sleep. Leaving them alive, even sleeping, is too risky, they said.

All around me, the unmistakable sounds of fighting and shooting ring out. I don't know how far the noise will travel, but it's possible it has carried to the ceremonial chamber below and we've lost the element of surprise. The guards are firing wildly in the smoke, at a disadvantage as they sway and cough and struggle to maintain their balance.

I take out another couple more, and then the smoke finally clears, leaving us standing amid a bunch of dead bodies. We take off our masks, doing a quick check to ensure everyone is okay.

Loud clapping rings out in the eerie space the same time the clicking of multiple weapons does. A gun presses into the back of my head as men surround us from behind. The vein in my neck pulses as blood rushes to my head, and acid churns in my gut.

Vincent Fox emerges from the stairs we just ascended, wearing a wide grin as his smug applause taunts us. "You all made this far too easy. So predictable." He shakes his head as he walks toward Victor, aiming a rifle at his head. "You should be ashamed of yourself, big brother, and you have no one to blame for your demise but yourself."

Guess Carter was aware of the tunnels after all.

We have walked straight into a trap, and all hope seems lost.

Chapter Fifty-Two

Ashley

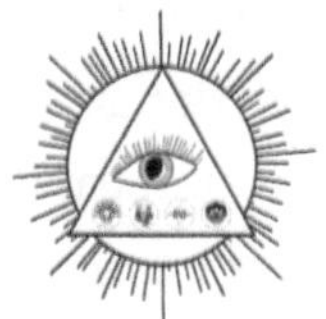

"Welcome, welcome," Rhett says as we are dragged into the main ceremonial room on the basement level of the crypt by Vincent and his guards. They bound our hands behind our backs upstairs before removing our weapons. Our cells were collected and thrown into a large bag. I'm not sure who has it now, but Theo will still be able to hear as long as they are powered on. Jase warned him not to call the authorities if something like this should happen because we suspect Carter has the authorities in his pockets, and all it will do is alert them to Theo's involvement. I hope he sticks to the promise he made us. I don't want anything to happen to Lo or my friends.

"Now that everyone is here, we can get this party started." Rhett grins as he welcomes us with a flourish of his hands, adding drama because he just can't help himself.

Not everyone is here though, I notice, taking in the people sitting on the floor against the wall with their hands and feet tied and tape over their mouths. My eyes skim over them quickly. Lili, Jocelyn, Anna-Lynn, Knight, Richard, and Eric Stewart.

Bree cries out at the sight of her father lying facedown on the cold stone floor with blood seeping out from a nasty-looking wound on his side. Anna-Lynn and Jocelyn have silent tears streaming down their faces. Lili locks panicked eyes on Ares as he shouts and wrestles with the men holding him hostage. I glance over my head and caution him with a look.

My mother's husband, Richard, is here, but there is no Pamela or Emilie. I hope it means she got away with her daughter and not that Carter has something special planned for them. Bile travels up my throat at the thought. Rhett hates my mother for what she did, and he's not going to let her get away with it. If Mom is on the run with my baby sister, it's only a matter of time before he finds her and drags her back.

"Why is your son and heir tied up?" I ask, not fighting when the two men holding my arms pull me toward my bio dad. Rhett is wearing a gold cloak with the hood down so I can see every expression on his evil face.

"Because he's a treacherous cunt." Rhett kicks Knight in the stomach, and I regret asking the question. "He's weak and soft, and he was never going to be my heir."

"He's worth a million of you, you sadistic prick." Despite how I just cautioned Ares, I can't hold the words back.

Pain rattles through my skull and radiates across my cheek as Carter slaps me.

Ares, Jase, and Chad roar and yell obscenities, and the sounds of flesh hitting flesh reminds me why I need to control my errant mouth.

"Oh, how you have disappointed me." Rhett grips my chin painfully, digging his nails into my flesh. The pretense is long gone, and there is no trace of that softer look he usually uses with me. All of it was a sham. "But most women do. We had plans for you, but you're too mouthy, too uncontrollable, too reckless. I blame Doug's influence. He ruined you."

I bite the inside of my cheek to trap my retort inside.

Carter flings me back at the guards. "Line them up beside the others."

We are shoved to the ground beside the others with Ares lined up alongside Lili, then me, Jase, Bree, and an unconscious Baz and Victor. Baz fought with his guards upstairs, and they drugged him to shut him up. Vincent knocked his brother out cold and carried him over his shoulder down here. They killed the four Stewart guards without hesitation.

"You may leave." Carter dismisses his guards with a cursory look.

One of Carter's men dumps the bag with the phones on the window ledge before leaving. Vincent stands in one corner, leaning against the wall and smirking as he crosses his feet at the ankles.

"You're a fool," Jase says, glaring at him. "Whatever he has promised you, he won't deliver."

"On the contrary, punk," Rhett says, landing a punch to Jase's ribs. "Vincent has proven his loyalty over the past twenty-plus years, and he will get everything I have promised him." Rhett nods at his coconspirator. "You are looking at the new Despond Luminary."

Rhett said he was going to elevate a master's family to Luminary status. We had been looking at Carter's master's families, trying to identify who it could be. But we were way off track. Their identity was under our noses all along. So, Vincent sold out his brother and his family and his Luminary for a seat at the new table. If he thinks he will have any power, he can think again. The role will be a figurehead in name only. Carter will be the only one calling the shots. How stupid do you have to be to do that man's bidding for twenty years with the promise of an empty crown?

"You said you needed us, but that was just a lie," I surmise, working hard to keep my voice calm as I attempt to loosen the rope binding my hands. I know the others will be doing the same, so keeping this narcissistic sociopath talking is our best angle. "What is it you are really planning?"

"It wasn't entirely a lie," he says, seating himself on a stone throne that wasn't in the room the last time. "I did need you. I needed you to complete the final steps in my plan so I could get to this point. Everything I have done, and everything I have allowed you to believe you have achieved, was all planned. Rescuing Chad. Rescuing Lili. Daphne escaping from HQ and letting her leave for overseas. The latter was done to make you trust the Foxes, the former so you'd get cocky and think you could take me down."

His arrogant chuckle bounces off the walls while I continue discreetly working at the rope, a little thrill going through me when it starts to loosen. Beside me, Ares flinches a little, not enough to be noticed by anyone but me. His arm moves imperceptibly, and I know he's already free.

"I needed you to help me to get rid of Manford and Salinger," Rhett adds. "I needed you to expose my son for the traitor I always suspected he was. You were supposed to murder my wife during Chad's rescue operation, but I wasn't too upset. I got to murder the whiny bitch myself after all."

Knight shouts behind his gag, and Rhett gets up off his throne and coldcocks him. My brother's head lolls forward, and he slumps sideways with his head resting against Anna-Lynn. Eric still hasn't stirred, and I'm not even sure if he's alive.

The psycho drones on. "Vincent helped Victor to hide Daphne and Blade after I ordered Clinton's murder, all those years ago, so I could keep tabs on you until I was ready to reveal your identity," Rhett says, reveling in the sound of his own voice as he stares at Ares. "Your sister never had cancer. I bribed the doctor to give you false reports so we could lure Daphne home. You were supposed to come too, but she let you disappear without telling Victor, and we lost track of you."

Oh my God. I know what he's going to say next.

Anger rolls off Ares in waves, and I hope he holds still until an opportune moment presents itself.

If Ares attacks now, he'll end up dead.

I turn my head, my eyes probing his and pleading with him to be smart.

"So, I took your sister, knowing you'd return to the US to look for her." Rhett leans back in his throne, and his eyes gleam with dark intent. "I had to keep her untainted in case things didn't go my way. She was bait and my Plan B if I needed it to reel you in. I knew if she was sold or abused I would lose her as insurance. If I'd known I wouldn't need it, I'd have let all those sick pricks defile her from the start."

"Ares," I hiss in warning, wishing I could sit on him to keep him in place.

He's fuming. I feel it exuding from his pores like a tangible thing. He breathes in and out, nostrils flaring, and all the veins stand out in his neck as I silently beg him to hold still.

Someone up there must be helping because he doesn't react. He holds his composure, offering words Carter expects to hear. "You're fucking dead," Ares seethes. "I am going to kill you with my bare hands and then piss on your grave."

Rhett chuckles. "It's a shame I must kill you. Such arrogance is worthy of the Pride & Wrath title."

"Why must we die if we've helped you to achieve your goals?" I ask, wanting to divert the conversation before Ares does something reckless and ends up dead.

"Because you're not trustworthy. None of you are, and you

three are all far too immature and inexperienced. You were always only placeholders, and you must die so you aren't a threat to the new Luminaries. I already have four successors lined up. People who will gladly do my bidding in exchange for such a powerful title and role. They have already agreed to my appointment as Lord of The Luminaries, and they are fully in support of my plan. We will rid the world of all sinners, starting with you." My bio dad eyeballs me. "You shall go first, my dear. I'd make it quick, only I like the idea of your lovers watching you suffering and bleeding out as I torture them by slowly killing each of their loved ones."

Rhett calls Vincent forward with a flick of his hand just as I pull my hands fully free of the rope. Jase and Chad exchange looks with Ares, and that's how I know they are free too. As Vincent draws nearer, I hold my head up high, waiting for the guys to give the signal or make a move.

The second Vincent withdraws his gun, Ares, Chad, and Jase swing into action. Ares throws himself at Vincent as Chad and Jase lunge for Rhett. I'm frozen for a few seconds, watching my guys wrestle with the enemy as fear charges through my veins. Ares has overpowered Vincent, lying on top of him on the ground with his hand wrapped around Vincent's wrist as they battle for control of the gun.

Rhett is on his feet, swinging punches at Chad and Jase now they have disarmed him. They seem to have it under control, so I snap out of it and move over to Bree, helping to untie her wrists.

"No!" she roars, and I whip my head around in time to see Vincent lift a knife and raise it over Ares, ready to plunge it into his back. My heart stops beating, and I scream at the same time Victor Fox moves, grabbing his brother's elbow. Ares rolls off Vincent as the knife clangs to the floor. I can only watch in horror as Vincent turns over on his side and shoots his brother in the stomach at close range. Ares grabs the knife and brings it down on Vincent's back, driving it into his spine and dragging it down, instantly severing his spinal cord.

Vincent slumps to the ground as Chad and Jase get the better of Rhett, overpowering him and pulling him into a headlock.

A creaking sound from behind has me spinning around in fear. Confusion is my initial reaction when my mother emerges from the ancestor's room, running toward me, sobbing, and shaking with her arms outstretched.

I walk slowly toward her in a bit of a daze.

"Ashley, no!" Jase yells, but it's too late.

Mom grabs me, spinning me around so my back is to her chest and I'm facing the horror-struck expressions on my lovers' faces as she presses a gun to my temple and says, "Release Rhett, or I'll kill her."

Chapter Fifty-Three

Ashley

"Don't do it," I yell. "Don't you dare let him go." I'm in a kind of dazed numbed state at this latest development, but there is no uncertainty when it comes to that man. A messy ball of emotion clogs my throat as I contemplate the situation. My mother is holding me hostage and threatening to kill me to protect a man she says raped and abused her as a young woman. Did that happen? Has he continued abusing her? Is this some type of Stockholm syndrome behavior, or has everything been a lie?

Chad has his arm under Rhett's chin, and Jase is jabbing Rhett's own gun into the side of his skull.

Mom digs the muzzle of her gun into my temple, and I bite the inside of my cheek to stop from crying out. One false move, and my guys will let Rhett go. That cannot happen.

"What the fuck is going on?" Ares points Victor's gun at Mom's head. "Why the fuck are you holding a gun to your daughter's head?"

I bark out a harsh laugh. "Because she doesn't care about me. She has clearly been working with him all along." Whatever the reason behind how it happened, there is no denying that truth.

I'm such an idiot. We're such idiots. It was staring us in the face all this time.

Mom scoffs as she digs the muzzle in again. "Pot. Kettle. Black. Darling. Rhett told you my life was at stake if you didn't cooperate, yet you still took risks knowing what it could mean. Let's not pretend you care about me either."

I'm not sure I can refute that except I would never want her to die. "If you had tried, I would have met you halfway. It's hard to care about someone when they give you nothing."

"You were always such a needy, whiny little bitch. I told Rhett he was lucky he didn't have to suffer through you growing up."

"You've been working with him from the very start?" Jase asks. Shock splays across his face.

"My love is everything I ever wanted in a partner. Pamela is my soul mate. She understands the concept of personal sacrifice for the greater good."

"The rape never happened," I say. "You lied to us."

"You are all so gullible." Pamela scoffs. "It has been far too easy to manipulate everyone over the years. Of course, Rhett never raped me. You were conceived out of love."

"So why didn't you just get married? Why overcomplicate things?"

"Because we needed to line up all the chess pieces to get us to this point where we can replace the board with loyal followers and appoint my love as Lord of The Luminaries."

"My god divined it to be like this, and our patience in putting this plan together, over so many years, consolidated our loyalty to his greatness," Rhett says, sounding like a bona fide nutjob. "We have spent more than twenty years building a loyal network of global supporters and infiltrating other Luminary families. We needed time to do it while keeping an eye on the key players. It would have been a lot harder to do this as a married couple. We needed Pamela in Europe to establish our network there, and she would not have been permitted to do that had she been my wife."

"I was put on this planet to love and serve Rhett," Mom says, sounding like a brainwashed fool. "You are everything, darling. My lover. My best friend. The father of my children. My lord and my king."

"Pass the puke bucket," Bree says from her position on the ground. Her hands remain behind her back, and she's pretending she's still tied up. Baz is out cold from whatever shit they injected into his veins, and I'm worried about him. I don't know if Knight has come to as I can't see him from this angle.

"Children? As in plural?" I ask, wanting to keep her talking. It shouldn't take much to distract them. They both have giant egos and love talking about themselves.

"Emilie isn't yours," Mom says, and I presume she's looking at Richard when she says this. "I never loved you. Not when I was a teenager and not now. At least it was bearable living with Doug. He never questioned me. You are always complaining, Richard, and it's tiresome. Asking where I am. Who I'm with. And you're so boring. My God, I have almost died of boredom living with you. I am glad this charade ends now."

Rhett chuckles, like he doesn't have a gun pressed to his head. "Your sacrifices have been noted by our god, and you shall be rewarded in this life and the next, my love. We have already been rewarded with our new daughter." He levels me with a scornful look. "This time, we will have gotten it right. Emilie is our second chance."

"Screw you, jerkface. You're going to rot in hell along with this bitch you love so much."

"Ashley!" Jase roars at me. "Stop goading him."

A clicking sound at my ear has me regretting my rash words. Adrenaline courses through my veins as knots twist and turn in my belly.

"Whatever happens," I say calmly to Jase as my fingers slowly creep up my side toward my belt, "do not let him go. He must die even if I must die for it to happen. He cannot live. His ambition must die with him."

Ares nods, watching my subtle fingers on the move. The guys know about the belt. I showed it to them after Lo gave it to me. If we time it right, we can get out of this. Locking down my emotions, I remind myself my mother has a gun to my temple and she's prepared to kill me. She has known Rhett planned to kill me all along, and she has no remorse.

They have both given Oscar-worthy performances these past few months and their entire lives. He even beat her up in front of us! Everything was a lie. All of it was part of their sick plan. They were the puppet masters pulling our strings.

They can't win.

Too much is at stake for that to happen.

Fuck her. I don't care if she must die at my hands.

Rhett chuckles again, and his lack of concern is pissing me off. Unless he has other backup hiding in the ancestor's room or the beauty room and that's why he's showing no fear.

Fuck.

"You should check the rooms back there," I suggest, looking at Ares. "We don't want any more surprises."

Ares walks forward, leveling the gun at Mom's head.

"Stop or I'll shoot," Mom says, dragging me back. "I mean it, Ares. Stop right there. You're not going anywhere." She digs the gun into my skull, and I wince as pain shuttles across my brow and pulses in my temple. "Nice try, bitch. Do you think I was born yesterday? Like he wouldn't try to shoot me when he gets behind me."

"You're holding the woman I love at gunpoint," Ares hisses. "I would hardly shoot you in the back when it could get Ashley killed."

"What happens to her doesn't concern me. My only concern is my love. No harm can come to us. My love has promised me, and what he says is the whole truth and nothing but the truth."

"Shoot her, and it'll be the last thing you do," Ares says. "I will kill you, and then your precious Rhett will die anyway. No fucking God can save you from this truth."

"This is wildly entertaining," Rhett offers.

"Shut your face, asshole," Chad says, tightening the arm under Rhett's chin.

"Do not be worried, my love." Rhett stares at my mother with lovestruck eyes. Those two psychos deserve one another. "Our god will save us. We have been chosen to do his work, and he will not fail us now." He stares at Jase. "Try it, son. You will be struck down instantly if you try to harm me."

He is completely delusional. Certifiably mad.

"Why did you ask me to marry Ashley, Pamela?" Chad asks, out of the blue, and I guess it's a tactic to stall them. "I was thinking about it lately. I thought it was so I could save her the same way your marriage and pregnancy saved you, but that can't be it now."

Mom laughs. "I just needed to distract you while my lover's men took Ashley from the car. She had left Doug's house far earlier than expected, and she was too close to the townhome. You were getting ready to go for a run. Of course, I didn't care if you discovered it and we had to kill you, but my daughter would have cared. We had a plan, and it couldn't be thwarted."

"You killed your own brother," I say. "James's blood is on your hands. Julia's too," I add, remembering her snide comments about my cousin.

"That little slut had it coming!" Mom's voice elevates to near hysteria, and I've clearly struck a nerve.

"Pamela. You know Julia was my sacrifice and burden to bear."

"Yes, my love. I know, but her filthy hands should never have been anywhere near you."

"She's burning in the fiery pits of hell," Rhett says.

"You two are fucking nuts," Bree says. "If anyone will be burning in hell, it'll be you."

"PC1!" Jase yells. "Shut your mouth and sit still. We have this covered."

I'm not sure we do, but I appreciate him telling his sister to stop whatever she's planning.

"Your tears at the graveside. They were for James, right?" I ask, wanting to distract Pamela as my fingers slowly creep toward my belt. If I can get to my knife and the guys can cause some kind of distraction, I can get Pamela away from me, stab her to distract her, and get the gun. "You already knew he was going to die, and you were mourning him, not my father."

"James was one sick puppy, but I used his obsessive love for me to play him for years. It was so easy." She laughs. "He was delighted when I killed Lucille, believing it proof that I loved him as much as he loved me. I only did it because that nosy bitch caught Rhett and I together. She was going to tell James and ruin everything we had been working toward."

"James was an idiot," Rhett agrees. "And we killed two birds with one stone. It was genius, my love, and further proof of how perfect you are for me. We even got control of Manford Media without any effort. James played right into our hands."

"You're a match made in hell," I say as my fingers touch the edge of my belt.

Shouting trickles down the stairs from the main room, and it's the perfect distraction. Ares nods, and it's on. Jamming my elbow back violently into Pamela's stomach, I duck down as Ares fires over my head at her. Rhett roars, and sounds of scuffling emerge from behind me as my fingers fumble with my belt. A hand grabs Ares's ankle, and I scream as a barely alive Vincent tugs Ares to the ground. The gun flies out of Ares's hand, and it all happens in slow motion as I watch Pamela straighten up, with fire in her eyes, and point the gun at my lover.

I don't think. I just react, lunging at Mom and plunging the dagger into her neck before she can fire at Ares. My aim is true, hitting her carotid artery. Her eyes pop wide for a split second as her fingers loosen, and the gun slips from her hand. Blood drips down her neck and bubbles in her mouth as she crumples to the floor, the light leaving her eyes, and she's dead the instant she hits the ground.

Bree screams as gunshots pepper the air, and I instinctively drop to the floor, my eyes meeting Knight's. He keeps eye contact with me, silently conveying all is okay as he nods slowly.

Deadly silence swirls through the air for a couple of beats until my sperm donor shatters it.

"It doesn't matter if you take me out," he rasps in a weak voice as arms lift me up from behind.

Chad pulls me into his arms, dotting kisses all over my face as I stare at Rhett Carter bleeding out in a pool of blood, his chest riddled with bullet holes. For as long as I live, I will never forget the manic evil look in his eyes as he stares at Jase, crouched over him.

"My supporters will continue my work, and they will come for you when you least expect it." He coughs out blood, his body jerking and spasming. "Sinners must be eliminated, and you are all going to die."

Chapter Fifty-Four

Ashley

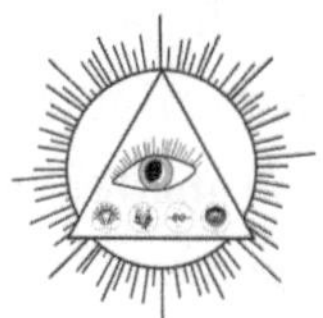

"Thanks so much for your help," Jase says, shaking Diesel's hand. "We appreciate it a lot." Turns out, Lo's friend D is Diesel Calloway, the man in charge of VERO. We were recently informed Theo works with him, and Theo called Diesel when shit went down. The commotion we heard from upstairs was Diesel and his team arriving. Like he alluded to previously that day he ambushed Chad and me in Chad's truck, there are Luminary ties with VERO, and with three Luminary leaders in the room, he didn't hesitate to clean up this mess and help us to present it as a murder-suicide.

Already, the major news channels are running with the story we concocted: Rhett Carter, CEO of Carter Construction & Development is dead by suicide after murdering his married lover, Pamela Stewart, and her other lover, Vincent Fox, after discovering them in bed together.

Suicide is considered a grievous sin within the Luminary world, and we are hopeful this will confuse Carter's supporters into inaction. We don't know what plans, if any, he made in the event of his demise. Given how nonchalant he was about his death, we are hoping he didn't have anything concrete in place. But we know he has supporters, and his final words were more than just a threat.

We hope our actions today have bought us time so we can clean house and weed out his followers before they put his plans into place. We expect a small percentage will become disillusioned and return fully to the fold. A further group will be torn, waiting to see what happens next. We expect we'll be able to win most of those back. But the majority will not believe any evidence presented no matter how compelling it is. We guesstimate about twenty percent of Luminaries worldwide are fanatics who will remain loyal to Carter and his ideals. Not enough for us to worry they will take over, but it's a sizable enough group to worry about retaliation and further planning in the future.

Which is why specialist task forces will work to identify these people, on an ongoing basis, and deal with them.

"You should go. You all look beat," Diesel says. "We'll finish up here."

We sent the others away hours ago. Ares went with a subdued Lili in a chopper Jase organized to take them back to the Stewart castle. Victor and Baz were both awake when the HQ ambulances took them to the hospital for a thorough screening. At least they didn't have too far to travel. Jocelyn went with Bree and their mother to the hospital. Eric was still unconscious when he was stretchered into an ambulance. The paramedics confirmed he has a pulse but it's weak, and his condition is precarious.

VERO has imprisoned all the guards at HQ and VERO teams oversee security there, in a temporary capacity, until we replace them with trusted Luminary guards.

The three of us stayed to sort out the mess, but it looks like our work here is done.

"What would you like me to do with the bodies?" Diesel asks.

"Burn them," I say, folding my arms around my chest. "We want no graves for fanatics to worship."

Jase and Chad nod, and Diesel walks off to make the arrangements.

"I have a chopper waiting to take you home," Jase says as we walk out of the crypt. "I'm going to head to the hospital."

"I'll stay with you." I wrap my hand in his.

"*We'll* stay with you," Chad says.

"You're tired," Jase argues.

"We're all tired, and this is nonnegotiable. We're coming with you."

After several hours spent at the hospital checking on everyone, we take a chopper straight to the Stewart residence with Baz and Jocelyn when hospital staff confirms Eric is stable and out of the woods. There is some concern he may be paralyzed, but they won't know his prognosis for a few days. Bree stayed with her mother, and they're going to crash at HQ.

We're all beat as we head upstairs, but I doubt I can switch my mind off. Everything that has gone down tonight is pressing down on my brain, and I want to shut it up.

I have the perfect remedy if the guys are up for it. "Are you guys tired or..." I say, licking my lips and eyeing their mouths. "Up for a little fun?"

"I'm not tired." Chad's eyes instantly darken with lust.

"I'm down for a little fun." Jase scoops me up into his arms and carries me toward his bedroom. I think he needs the distraction as much as I do. His father is gravely injured in the hospital, his brother was drugged and is still battling the side effects, and his two sisters and his mom were in the crypt watching all that shit go down.

It's a lot of the heavy.

I want to check on Ares, to see if Lili is okay and if he managed to speak to his mom, but it's three a.m., and I'm sure they're sleeping.

Jase pushes the door to his large bedroom open, and we head inside. It's like a rush to see who can shed their clothes the quickest. We grab a quick shared shower, kissing and groping as much as washing the events of today off our bodies, but we don't fuck because I want to do it in a bed with both my guys. After toweling dry, I run back into the bedroom, laughing when Chad whips the towel off me, and I dash naked into the room. I slam to a halt at the sight of Ares lounging in his boxers on top of the bed.

"Ooof." Chad slams into my back, and Jase narrowly avoids the same fate, swinging to the left in time to avoid a pileup.

"What's going on?" I ask. "Is Lili okay? Hera?"

"They're both fine." Ares stands. "Lili is sleeping. I was waiting up for you." He stares at our three naked forms, and his Adam's apple bobs in his throat as he slides his boxers down his legs and kicks them away.

My throat goes dry, and butterflies skid into my chest, doing jumps and loops and somersaults. I'm scared to hope this is what it looks like. "What are you doing?" I ask in a breathy tone, unsure if I'm misreading the situation.

"What does it look like?"

The other two stay quiet, understanding the magnitude of the moment.

"I'm asking you to spell it out for a reason, Ares. Don't get my hopes up if you can't do this." My voice cracks a little. "I don't think I could handle that tonight."

He strides confidently toward me, pulling me into his arms. "I love you," he says before kissing me deeply. He peers deep into my eyes when our kiss ends. "I'm in. I'm all in. I know I was fearful before, but I'm not afraid anymore. I know I can do this. I'm okay with sharing you because contemplating not having you in my life isn't an option." He cups my face and swivels his hips, digging his hard-on into my stomach. "I'm okay with sharing you in every possible way."

"Pinch me so I know I'm not dreaming."

Ares chuckles. "You're not dreaming yet, babe, but you will be soon." He waggles his brows as Chad makes a gagging sound from behind us.

Ares looks over my shoulders at the guys. "Can we be serious for a minute? I need to know if this is okay with you guys."

"Like we said before, it's all about Ash. Whatever she needs," Jase says.

"We have no beef with you, man," Chad adds. "It's in the past. If you can let it go, so can we."

Ares clears his throat, looking more than a little emotional. "We were a team today."

"We were," Chad agrees.

"We *are*," Jase says.

"I liked it." Ares's cheeks pink, and my mouth trails the ground. "It felt good."

"Oh my God. Are you blushing?" I probably shouldn't tease him, but this is too good not to.

"Careful, dollface. Just because I've agreed doesn't mean I've turned into a pussy. I can still put you over my knee and slap the shit out of your ass."

Warmth floods to my core, and I squeeze my thighs together.

Jase laughs as he picks me up and throws me down in the middle of the bed. "I think you know by now that's not a threat as much as an invitation."

Ares smirks that arrogant smirk of his as he crawls up onto the bed. "Why do you think I said it?"

I turn over, propping myself up on all fours, and offer my ass up to be spanked.

Then we spend the next few hours fucking like our lives depend on it. I ride Chad as Ares takes my ass and Jase fucks my mouth. Then we switch around, and Jase pounds my ass while Ares fucks my pussy as we lie on our sides, and Chad films it with his phone while sitting in a chair by the bed, jerking off to me being railed on both sides. Later, I kneel on the floor while they surround me with their erections in their hands, and I take turns sucking them off while fingering my cunt.

I lose count of my orgasms after five, and at some point, as the sun is rising in the sky, we fall asleep in a tangled heap of sweaty limbs, united, satiated, and suitably distracted.

Epilogue

Ashley – one year later

"Take your panties off, and wait for me upstairs," Ares says, groping my tits through my white dress. "I want you on your knees on the bed with your wedding dress bunched at your waist and your legs spread so I can see your glistening pussy."

Said pussy gushes liquid lust at his words, and I'll have no problem meeting his demands. Except the timing is off. "It's too early to ditch our own wedding. We can't be rude."

"I don't give a fuck, dollface." Ares slaps my ass hard and pulls me into him, pressing his erection against me. "Feel how hard I am for you?" I whimper against his lips as his hand lands on my lower back, and he holds me in place. "I've been that way since I saw you walking down that aisle. I can't wait another fucking second to chain you to my bed and ram my dick into your greedy cunt, your tight hole, and your fuckable mouth."

"Wow. That's some Shakespearian shit right there," Bree says, popping her head over Ares's shoulder. "You should give wooing advice to every newly married man. You'd earn a fortune."

"Fuck off. I'm having a private conversation with my wife." His face lights up at the words, and I swoon against him.

Bree and Ares got their marriage annulled a few days after the showdown in the crypt. From that first night when Ares joined us in the bedroom and claimed he was all in, he has more than proved it, and I've been living my dream this past year.

The four of us have found a structure and a rhythm that works for us. We still have one-on-one time, and there are regular occasions when it's me and two of the guys, and we have group sex at least twice a month. Ares has introduced Chad and Jase to his kinky fuckery, and we built a sex room in our new house with mirrors on the ceilings and some on the walls, a myriad of sex machines and toys, and an array of bondage equipment.

I didn't think Ares would want to get married, but I should have known his competitive nature would win out. He got down on one knee, totally surprising me, three months ago. The guys helped him to plan it, and I cried tears of joy when I heard that.

I never thought all three of my men would get along, but they are the best of friends now.

Of course, Ares is still an arrogant dick at times. Chad and Ares bicker like an old married couple, and Jase loves to wind the two of them up.

But mostly, they all get along.

And they are united in their devotion to me.

I'm such a lucky bitch.

"I think you're blushing again," Bree says, pinching his cheeks.

Ares glares at her before turning it on me. "You never

should've told her that. She's going to be teasing me about it when she's old and gray."

"You better believe it!" She thumps him in the arm.

"Oi! Carter." Ares hollers over our heads. "Come and claim your woman before I throw her out the nearest window."

"Fuck off, Ares," Bree hisses, shoving his chest before storming off.

Knight glowers at Ares before disappearing onto the dance floor with his date. I don't know who she is. Some unlucky substitute he chose to make Bree jealous, most likely. Since Bree broke things off with my brother, he has shown up all over town with different girls on his arm.

"You're such a dick." I shake my head at my new husband.

"How is it Bree cruelly dumps your brother, breaking his heart, and I'm a dick for calling her out on her shit?"

"Because it's not that cut-and-dried, and you know it." I have my own assumptions as to what went down. I don't know for sure because, when Bree and Knight first started dating, we made a rule we wouldn't discuss him or her relationship with him so it wouldn't impact our friendship if it didn't work out. I made the same pact with Knight, so I'm largely in the dark as to why they broke up when they seemed so good together.

I think Bree is running scared from the first real connection she's ever felt. And I believe Knight's pride is hurt so he's refusing to fight for her.

I'm not getting involved.

That shit never ends well.

But I'm rooting for them to get their act together.

I'm super close now with Knight and Paisley, but Daria and Kylo have consistently refused to have anything to do with me. It hurt at the start, but after months of therapy, I no longer care. It's their loss.

I think I'll be attending monthly therapy sessions for some

time to come. Dealing with the loss of my dad and the manner in which my bio parents died hasn't been easy. I wish I didn't care about Pamela. She never cared about me, and she was going to kill me or let her lover do it, so why do I have nightmares about killing her? She would not have lost any sleep if it was the other way around.

Hera has been great, helping me to deal with the fallout, and we are closer than ever. Lili too. I love Ares's sister as if she's my own.

And speaking of little sisters, Emilie's adoption paperwork went through yesterday. Richard Stewart is now her official dad. It hurt him to discover Pamela's betrayal was true, but he begged me to approve his adoption plans. He genuinely loved Pamela, and Emilie is a piece of her. Plus, he loves Emilie like a daughter, in the same way Doug loved me. I would never stand in the way of their bond, and I readily gave my permission as did Knight.

"Bree should be grateful our marriage was annulled and no one is forcing anyone into arranged marriages anymore," Ares says, thrusting his hips at me and reminding me he's still horny. "Otherwise, she could've ended up with that snake Toby."

"Do you regret freeing him?" I ask.

Toby *is* a snake, and it's no secret he resents Ares and all of us for the part he considers we played in his father's death. Pity he didn't cast that lens on himself. We are pretty sure he was aware his father conspired with Carter to kill Clinton Salinger. Toby knows he has no rightful claim to the Pride & Wrath Luminary, and he should be grateful Ares pardoned him with no punishment.

But he's a fucking jerk. Stomping around the place with a giant chip on his shoulder. He'll probably try something at some point and end up dead. Ares has people watching him and his family, and if they make a move, we'll know about it.

"It was the right thing to do. What kind of Luminary would I be if my first official act was to kill my uncle's wife and kids? I would be no better than him, and we're trying to prove we're different."

"Trying being the operative word," Jase says, coming up behind me and pressing his hot body into mine.

"Rome wasn't built in a day," I remind them. "And look at everything we've achieved so far."

Jase dropped out of college to give the Sloth Luminary role his full focus. Knight did the same with his Greed & Gluttony responsibility. He has his hands full with that and his siblings. Daria and Kylo have too much of Rhett's DNA in them, and they love causing problems for the sake of it. Knight loves them, but he's no idiot. He has them on a tight leash, and he is watching them in case they try anything. It seems unlikely they were privy to their father's plans, but we can't rule it out.

Ares is also very committed to Pride & Wrath in a way I wasn't expecting. He has stepped up and given it his focus. When he got access to the considerable inheritance his father, Clinton, left for him, he opened his own garage, and he loves nothing more than tinkering under the engine of a car or bike a few hours a week. I think it helps to keep him sane and remind him he's still the same person.

Eric survived Carter's attempt to kill him, but he ended up in a wheelchair. He is gradually handing over the wheel to Baz, who will be anointed as the Lust & Envy Luminary next year. Eric has been a huge help to all of us as we have transitioned into our roles.

Bree and I were able to stay in college—we are sophomores now—though we are both heavily committed to our Luminary responsibilities in our free time. It no longer involves the demeaning tasks we were charged with before. Victor is now the CEO of Manford Media, and when I graduate, I will take a more active role, working alongside him until he retires or I'm ready to take over, whichever happens first.

This is the youngest Luminary board in our history, and though we have made some progressive changes, there are a lot more to make. We must be careful not to change too much and make more enemies. The one change we were adamant about from the beginning was raising the age of initiation to sixteen and abolishing the sexual part of the ritual.

Surprisingly, we met minimal opposition. Most families welcomed the changes and the opportunity it now affords their children to remain children for longer.

While we have dedicated teams solely focused on weeding out Rhett Carter's supporters and putting an end to the separatist movement he set up, we know there is a big group of people who don't support us.

Carter's dying words still linger in all our minds.

The die-hard fanatics will come for us one day, but we'll be ready.

Until then, we are doing what we can to ensure no one else defects to Team Evil. Seasoned advisers have been appointed to the four Luminaries; all men handpicked by us with Eric's support. He knows most of these people in a way we don't, and he helped us recruit the best people within each family to lead us into the future. He also helped us to hire an interim CEO for Carter Construction.

We all sit on the boards of our respective family corporations, so we are apprised of what is going on, but we don't actively run them. In the future, that will most likely change.

Hera is now CEO of Salinger Finance, and she is going by the name Daphne Salinger again. Ares chose to retain the name Ares but change his surname to Salinger. Lili is now Lili Salinger, wanting to have the same name as her family. She is doing really well, attending regular therapy sessions and going to school with Tessa at Lowell Academy. Lili is a freshman, Tess is a sophomore, and Jocelyn is a junior this year.

Chad was able to clear his father's name, and the authorities wrote a big check to reimburse them for the house and assets they lost as well as compensation for the wrongful accusation. A public statement and apology were issued to Jasper and his family. Carole bought a new house near the private school, and she has set up her own florist business. Daphne and Carole hit it off, and as Ares's mom lives close to Carole, they spend a lot of their downtime together with the two girls who are more akin to sisters than friends.

"We have done good work," Jase says, dragging me out of my head and back into the moment. "But we have a lot more to do, and we still have enemies biting at our heels."

"Speaking of," Chad says, approaching with a glass of champagne for me. "What is Toby Salinger doing here?"

"Keep your friends close and your enemies closer," Ares grumbles, pouting, and I know why.

I can't keep the smirk off my face. "I think you can forget about your little plan." I waggle my brows. "Sharing is caring, remember."

"Fuck that. It's my wedding night," Ares stupidly says.

Chad punches him in the arm, and Jase glares at him. "You didn't give a shit about that last year when it was *our* wedding night," Jase says, jabbing him in the chest. "Asshole. I still haven't forgiven you for that."

"And it's our one-year anniversary," Chad reminds him.

Ares's jealous possessive streak means we married on the day that is the anniversary of my other wedding, and we are back at The Christmas House Inn too. At first, I said no, when he proposed the same date and venue, until he explained it. He wants us all to share the same wedding anniversary and have the same memories as if we had all gotten married together the first time.

I couldn't say no after that, especially when the guys were on board with it because Ares had asked them first before presenting it to me.

"We are entitled to spend time with our wife too. You can't monopolize her," Jase says.

"Want a bet?" Ares scoops me up and throws me over his shoulder. "If you want in, you better catch me, or else I'll be doing something neither of you thought to do last year." Ares takes off running as I scream and pummel his back to the backdrop of our guests amused laughter.

I swear he has a death wish when he hollers over my shoulder, "Locking the fucking door!" He chuckles as he races out of the room and up the stairs with Chad and Jase hot on his heels.

"Try it, dickface," Jase hollers.

"We know where the screwdriver is," Chad adds, bounding up the stairs behind us.

"Yay, me," I say, lifting my head and grinning at my two husbands chasing us up the stairs. "Let the sexy times begin."

And it officially is the best wedding night any woman ever had, at any time, anywhere on the planet. My three guys worship, fuck, lick, suck, and love me all night long until I pass out from pure exhaustion and sheer bliss, my body well and truly adored.

This is my life now, and I am one hell of a lucky bitch.

THE END

Everything changed the night my dad died.

The night I met Saint, Galen, Caz, and Theo.

Those manipulative a-holes set out to ruin me after our hot night together, but they didn't realize you can't destroy something that's already broken. And it only works if the victim cares.

Which I don't.

Because I've been in hell for years, and nothing penetrates the steel walls I've erected.

Until The Sainthood decides I belong to them and cracks appear in my veneer. Their cruel games, harsh words, and rough touch awakens something inside me, and now, I'm in trouble.

They draw me deeper into their dangerous world, until I'm in the middle of all the violence and gang warfare, tangled up in all the secrets and lies, and there's no turning back.

Because they own me.

And nothing has ever felt so right.

I'm exactly where I should be.

But with enemies on all sides, survival becomes a deadly game with no guarantees.

And, sometimes, saints become sinners.

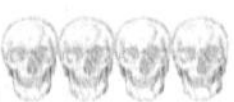

AVAILABLE NOW IN EBOOK, PAPERBACK, AND AUDIOBOOK. COMING SOON IN HARDCOVER.

About the Author

Siobhan Davis *is a USA Today, Wall Street Journal*, and Amazon Top 5 bestselling romance author. **Siobhan** writes emotionally intense stories with swoon-worthy romance, complex characters, and tons of unexpected plot twists and turns that will have you flipping the pages beyond bedtime! She has sold over 1.8 million books, and her titles are translated into several languages.

Prior to becoming a full-time writer, Siobhan forged a successful corporate career in human resource management.

She lives in the Garden County of Ireland with her husband and two sons.

You can connect with Siobhan in the following ways:

Website: www.siobhandavis.com
Facebook: AuthorSiobhanDavis
Instagram: @siobhandavisauthor
Tiktok: @siobhandavisauthor
Email: siobhan@siobhandavis.com

Books by Siobhan Davis

KENNEDY BOYS SERIES

Upper Young Adult/New Adult Contemporary Romance

Finding Kyler

Losing Kyler

Keeping Kyler

The Irish Getaway

Loving Kalvin

Saving Brad

Seducing Kaden

Forgiving Keven

Summer in Nantucket

Releasing Keanu

Adoring Keaton

Reforming Kent

Moonlight in Massachusetts

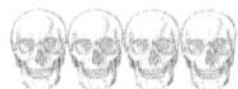

STAND-ALONES

New Adult Contemporary Romance

Inseparable

Incognito

When Forever Changes

No Feelings Involved

Still Falling for You

Second Chances Box Set

Holding on to Forever

Always Meant to Be

Tell It to My Heart

The One I Want

Reverse Harem Romance

Surviving Amber Springs

Dark Mafia Romance

Vengeance of a Mafia Queen

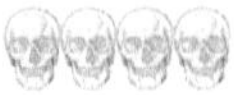

RYDEVILLE ELITE SERIES

Dark High School Romance

Cruel Intentions

Twisted Betrayal

Sweet Retribution

Charlie

Jackson

Sawyer

*The Hate I Feel^*

*Drew^*

MAZZONE MAFIA SERIES

Dark Mafia Romance

Condemned to Love

Forbidden to Love

Scared to Love

Mazzone Mafia: The Complete Series

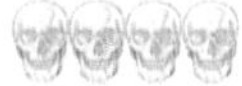

THE ACCARDI TWINS

Dark Mafia Romance

*CKONY #1^*

*CKONY #2^*

THE SAINTHOOD (BOYS OF LOWELL HIGH)

Dark HS Reverse Harem Romance

Resurrection

Rebellion

Reign

Revere

The Sainthood: The Complete Series

DIRTY CRAZY BAD DUET

Dark College Reverse Harem Romance

Dirty Crazy Bad - A Prequel Short Story

Dirty Crazy Bad # 1

Dirty Crazy Bad #2

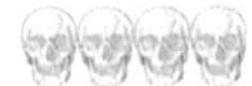

ALL OF ME DUET

Angsty New Adult Romance

Say I'm The One

Let Me Love You

Hold Me Close

*Reeve**

All of Me: The Complete Series

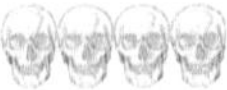

ALINTHIA SERIES

Upper YA/NA Paranormal Romance/Reverse Harem

The Lost Savior

The Secret Heir

The Warrior Princess

The Chosen One

*The Rightful Queen^*

SAVEN SERIES

Young Adult Science Fiction/Paranormal Romance

Saven Deception

Logan

Saven Disclosure

Saven Denial

Saven Defiance

Axton

Saven Deliverance

Saven: The Complete Series

^Release date to be confirmed

* Coming 2023

www.ingramcontent.com/pod-product-compliance
Lightning Source LLC
Chambersburg PA
CBHW030341310726
48979CB00001B/137

9781959194293